THE TIME MIGRATION
CIXIN LIU

TRANSLATED BY KEN LIU ET AL.

北京联合出版公司
Beijing United Publishing Co.,Ltd.

CONTENTS

时间移民

THE TIME MIGRATION

TRANSLATED BY JOEL MARTINSEN

周华 译

Where, before me, are the ages that have gone?
And where, behind me, are the coming generations?
I think of heaven and earth, without limit, without end,
And I am all alone and my tears fall down.

Migration

An Open Letter to All People

Due to insupportable environmental and population pressures, the government has been forced to undertake a time migration. A first group of 80 million time-migrants will migrate 120 years.

The ambassador was the last to leave. He[1] stood on empty ground before an enormous cold-storage warehouse that held four hundred thousand frozen people, as did another two hundred like it throughout the world. They resembled, the ambassador thought with a shudder, nothing so much as tombs.

Hua was not going with him. Although she met all of the conditions for migration and possessed a coveted migration card, she felt an attachment to the present world, unlike those headed toward a new life in the future. She would stay behind and leave the ambassador to travel 120 years on his own.

The ambassador set off an hour later, drowned by liquid helium that froze his life at near absolute zero, leading eighty million people on a flight along

---

1 英文通篇转换了大使的性别，已核对原文修订。——编者注

the road of time.

The Trek

Outside of perception time slipped past, the sun swept through the sky like a shooting star, and birth, love, death, joy, sorrow, loss, pursuit, struggle, failure, and everything else from the outside world screamed past like a freight train . . .

. . .10 years . . . 20 years . . . 40 years . . . 60 years . . . 80 years . . . 100 years . . . 120 years.

Stop 1: The Dark Age

Consciousness froze along with the body during zero-degree supersleep, leaving time's very existence imperceptible until the ambassador awoke with the impression that the cooling system had malfunctioned and he had thawed out shortly after departure. But the atomic clock's giant plasma display informed him that 120 years had passed, a lifetime and a half, rendering them time's exiles.

An advance team of one hundred had awakened the previous week to establish contact. Its captain now stood next to the ambassador, whose body had not yet recovered enough for speech. His inquiring gaze, however, drew only a head shake and forced smile from the captain.

The head of state had come to the freezer hall to welcome them. He looked weatherworn, as did his entourage, which came as a bit of a surprise 120 years into the future. The ambassador handed over the letter from the government of his time and passed on his people's greetings. The head said little, but clasped the ambassador's hand tightly. It was as rough as his face, and gave the ambassador the sense that things had not changed as much as he had imagined. It warmed him.

But the feeling vanished the moment he left the freezer. Outside was all black: black land, black trees, a black river, black clouds. The hovercar they rode in swirled up black dust. A column of oncoming tanks formed a line of black patches moving along the road, and low-flying clusters of helicopters passing overhead were groups of black ghosts, all the more so since they flew silently. The earth seemed scorched by fire from heaven. They passed a huge hole as large as an open-pit mine from the ambassador's time.

'A crater,' the head of state explained.

'From a . . . bomb?' the ambassador said, unable to say the word.

'Yes. Around fifteen kilotons,' the head of state said lightly, as if the misery was unremarkable for him.

The atmosphere of the cross-time meeting grew weighty.

'When did the war start?'

'This one? Two years ago.'

'This one?'

'There've been a few since you left.'

Then he changed the subject. He seemed less like a younger man from the future than an elder of the ambassador's own time, someone to show up at work sites or farms and gather up every hardship in his embrace, letting none slip by. 'We will accept all immigrants, and will ensure they live in peace.'

'Is that even possible, given the present circumstances?' The question was put by someone accompanying the ambassador, who himself remained silent.

'The current administration and the entire public will do all they can to accomplish it. That's our duty,' he said. 'Of course, the immigrants must do their best to adapt. That might be hard, given the substantial changes over one hundred and twenty years.'

'What kind of changes?' the ambassador asked. 'Human being are still irrational. There's still war, there's still slaughter . . .'

'You're only seeing the surface,' a general in fatigues said. 'Take war for example. Here's how two countries fight these days. First, they declare the type and quantity of all of their tactical and strategic weapons. Then a computer can determine the outcome of the war according to their mutual rates of destruction. Weapons are purely for deterrence and are never used. Warfare is a computer execution of a mathematical model, the results of which decide the victor and loser.'

'And the mutual destruction rates are obtained how?'

'From the World Weapons Test Organization. Like in your time there was a . . . World Trade Organization.'

'War is as regular and ordered as economics?'

'War is economics.'

The ambassador looked through the car window at the black world. 'But the world doesn't look like war is only a calculation.'

The head of state looked at the ambassador with heavy eyes. 'We did the calculations but didn't believe the results.'

'So we started one of your wars. With bloodshed. A "real" war,' the general said.

The head changed the subject again. 'We're going to the capital now to study the issues involved with immigrant unfreezing.'

'Take us back,' the ambassador said.

'What?'

'Go back. You can't take on any additional burdens, and this isn't a suitable age for immigrants. We'll go on a little further.'

The hovercar returned to Freezer No. 1. Before leaving, the head handed the ambassador a hardbound book. 'A chronicle of the past hundred and twenty years,' he said.

Then an official led over a 123-year-old man, the only known individual who had lived alongside the immigrants, and who had insisted on seeing the ambassador. 'So many things happened after you left. So many things!' The old man brought out two bowls from the ambassador's time and filled them to the brim with alcohol. 'My parents were migrants. They left me this when I was three to drink with them when they were thawed out. But now I won't see them. And I'm the last person from your time you'll see.'

After they had drunk, the ambassador looked into the man's dry eyes, and just as he was wondering why the people of this era seemed not to cry, the old man began to shed tears. He knelt down and clasped the ambassador's hands. 'Take care, Sir. "West of Yang Pass, there are no more old friends! "'[1]

Before the ambassador felt the supercooled freezing of the liquid helium, his wife suddenly appeared in his fragmented consciousness. Hua stood on a fallen leaf in autumn, and then the leaf turned black, and then a tombstone appeared. Was it hers?

The Trek

Outside of perception, the sun swept through the sky like a shooting star, and time slipped past in the outside world.

. . .120 years . . . 130 years . . . 150 years . . . 180 years . . . 200 years . . . 250 years . . . 300 years . . . 350 years . . . 400 years . . . 500 years . . . 600 years.

Stop 2: The Lobby Age

'Why did you wait so long to wake me up?' the ambassador asked, looking in surprise at the atomic clock.

'The advance team has mobilized five times at century intervals and even spent a decade awake in one age, but we didn't wake you because immigration was never possible. You yourself set that rule,' the advance-team captain said. He was noticeably older than at their last meeting, the ambassador realized.

'More war?'

'No. War is over forever. And although the environment continued to deteriorate over the first three centuries, it began to rebound two hundred years ago. The last two ages refused immigrants, but this one has agreed to accept them. The ultimate decision is up to you and the commission.'

---

1   A quotation from 'Seeing Off Yuan Er on a Mission to Anxi' by Tang Dynasty poet Wang Wei (701 ? – 761).

There was no one in the freezer lobby. When the giant door rumbled open, the captain whispered to the ambassador, 'The changes are far greater than you imagine. Prepare yourself.'

When the ambassador took his first step into the new age, a note sounded, haunting, like some ancient wind chime. Deep within the crystalline ground beneath his feet he saw the play of light and shadows. The crystal looked rigid, but it was as soft as carpet underfoot, and every step produced that wind-chime tone and sent concentric halos of color expanding from the point of contact, like ripples on still water. The ground was a crystalline plane as far as the eye could see.

'All the land on Earth is covered in this material. The whole world looks artificial,' the captain said, and laughed at the ambassador's flabbergasted expression, as if to say, *This surprise is only the beginning!* The ambassador also saw his own shadow in the crystal—or rather, shadows—spreading out from him in all directions. He looked up . . .

Six suns.

'It's the middle of the night, but night was gotten rid of two hundred years ago. What you see are six mirrors, each several hundred square kilometers in area, in synchronous orbit to reflect sunlight onto the dark side of the Earth.'

'And the mountains?' The ambassador realized that the line of mountains on the horizon was nowhere to be seen. The separation between ground and sky was ruler-straight.

'There aren't any. They've been leveled. All the continents are flat plains now.'

'Why?'

'I don't know.'

To the ambassador, the six suns were like six welcoming lamps in a bright hotel lobby. *A lobby!* The idea glimmered in his mind. This was, he realized, a peculiarly clean age. No dust anywhere, not even a speck. It beggared belief. The ground was as bare as an enormous table. And the sky was similarly clean, shining with a pure blue, although the presence of the six suns detracted from its former breadth and depth, so that it more resembled the dome of a lobby. *A lobby!* His vague idea crystallized: The entire world had been turned into a lobby. One carpeted in tinkling crystal and lit by six hanging lamps. This was an immaculate, exquisite age, contrasting starkly with the previous darkness. In the time immigrants' chronicles, it would be known as the Lobby Age.

'They didn't come to greet us?' the ambassador asked, gazing upon the broad plain.

'We have to visit them in person in the capital. Despite its refined appearance, this is an inconsiderate age, lacking even in basic curiosity.'

'What's their stance on immigration?'

'They agree to accept migrants, but we can only live in reservations separated from society. Whether these reservations are to be located on Earth or on other planets, or if we should build a space city, is up to us.'

'This is absolutely unacceptable!' the ambassador said angrily. 'All migrants must be integrated into society and into modern life. Migrants cannot be second-class citizens. This is the fundamental tenet of time migration!'

'Impossible,' the captain said.

'That's their position?'

'Mine as well. But let me finish. You've just been thawed out, but I've been living in this age for more than half a year. Please believe me, life is far stranger than you think. Even in your wildest imagination you'd never dream up even a tenth of life in this age. Primitive Stone Age humans would have an easier time understanding the era we are from!'

'This issue was taken into consideration before immigration began, which is why migrants were capped at age twenty-five. We'll do our best to study and to adapt to everything!'

'Study?' The captain shook his head with a smile. 'Got a book?' He pointed at the ambassador's luggage. 'Any will do.' Baffled, the ambassador took out a copy of Ivan Aleksandrovich Goncharov's *Frigate Pallada,* which he had gotten halfway through before migration. The captain glanced at the title and said, 'Open at random and tell me the page number.' The ambassador complied, and opened to page 239. Without looking, the captain rattled off what the navigator saw in Africa, accurate to the letter.

'Do you see? There's no need for learning whatsoever. They import knowledge directly into the brain, like how we used to copy data onto hard drives. Human memory has been brought to its apex. And if that's not enough, take a look at this—' He took an object the size of a hearing aid from behind his ear. 'This quantum memory unit can store all of the books in human history—down to every last scrap of notepaper, if you'd like. The brain can retrieve information like a computer, and it's far faster than the brain's own memory. Don't you see? I'm a vessel for all human knowledge. If you so desire, in under an hour you can have it too. To them, learning is a mysterious, incomprehensible ancient ritual.'

'So their children gain all knowledge the moment they're born?'

'Children?' The captain laughed again. 'They don't have any children.'

'So where are the kids?'

'No children at all. Did I mention that families vanished long ago?'

'You mean, they're the last generation?'

'"Generation" doesn't exist as a concept anymore.'

The ambassador's amazement turned to befuddlement, but he strove to understand. And he did, a little. 'You mean they live forever?'

'When a bodily organ fails, it's replaced with a new one. When the brain fails, its information is copied out and into a transplant. After several centuries of these replacements, memory is all that's left of an individual. Who's to say whether they're young or elderly? Maybe they think of themselves as old, and that's why they haven't come to meet us. Of course, they can have children if they desire, by cloning or in the old-fashioned way. But few do. This generation's survived for more than three hundred years and will continue to do so. Can you imagine how this determines the form of their society? The knowledge, beauty, and longevity we dreamed of is easily attainable in this age.'

'It sounds like the ideal society. What else do they desire but can't attain?'

'Nothing. But precisely because they have it all they have lost everything. It's hard for us to understand, but to them it's a real concern. This is far from an ideal society.'

The ambassador's confusion turned to contemplation. The six suns were heading west and soon dipped below the horizon. When only two remained, Venus rose, and then rays of the true sun's dawn spread from the east. Its gentle light gave the ambassador a smidgen of comfort; some things, at least, were unchanging in the universe.

'Five hundred years isn't all that long. Why have things changed so much?' he asked, as much to the whole world as to the captain.

'The acceleration of human progress. Compare our fifty years of progress to the previous five centuries. It's been another five centuries, which might as well be fifty millennia. Do you still think migrants can adapt?'

'And what's the end point of this acceleration?' the ambassador asked, eyes narrowed.

'I don't know.'

'There's no answer to that question in the sum total of human knowledge you possess?'

'The strongest feeling I've gotten from my time in this age is that we're beyond the time when knowledge can explain everything.'

'We'll continue onward!' the ambassador decided. 'Take that chip with you, as well as their device for importing knowledge into the brain.'

The ambassador saw Hua again before entering the haze of supersleep, only a glance after 620 years, a captivating, heartbreaking glance, but it anchored him to home within the lonely flow of time. He dreamed of a cloud of dust drifting over the crystal ground—was this the form her bones now took?

The Trek

Outside of perception, the sun swept through the sky like a shooting star, and time slipped past in the outside world.

. . .600 years. . .620 years . . . 650 years . . . 700 years . . . 750 years . . .

800 years . . . 850 years . . . 900 years . . . 950 years . . . 1,000 years.

Stop 3: The Invisible Age

The sealed door to the freezer rumbled open and for a third time the ambassador approached the threshold of an unknown age. This time he had mentally prepared himself for a brand-new era, but he discovered that the changes weren't as great as he had imagined.

The crystal carpet that blanketed the ground was still present and six suns still shone in the sky. But the impression given by this world was entirely different from the Lobby Age. First of all, the crystal carpet seemed dead; although there was still light in the depths, it was far dimmer, and footsteps no longer tinkled on its surface, nor did gorgeous patterns appear. Four of the six suns had gone dim, the dull red they emitted serving only to mark their position but doing nothing to light the world below. The most conspicuous change was the dust. A thin layer covered all the crystal. The sky wasn't spotless, but held gray clouds, and the horizon was no longer a ruled line. It all contributed to a feeling that the previous age's lobby had gone vacant, and the natural world outside had begun to invade.

'Both worlds refuse to take migrants,' the advance-team captain said.

'Both worlds?'

'The visible and invisible worlds. The visible world is the one we know, different though it may be. People like us, even if most of them are no longer primarily formed of organic material.'

'There's no one to be seen on the plain, just like last time,' the ambassador said, straining to look.

'People haven't needed to walk on the ground for several hundred years. See—' The captain pointed at a place in the air, where, through the dust and clouds, the ambassador saw indistinct flying objects, little more than a cluster of black dots at this distance. '—those could be planes or people. Any machine might be someone's body. A ship in the ocean, for instance, could be a body, and the computer memory directing it might be a copy of a human brain. People generally have several bodies, one of which is like ours. And that one, although it's the most fragile, is the most important, perhaps due to a sort of nostalgia.'

'Are we dreaming?' the ambassador murmured.

'Compared to this visible world, the invisible world is the real dream.'

'I've got an idea of what that might be. People don't even use machines for bodies.'

'Right. The invisible world is stored in a supercomputer, and each individual is a program.'

The captain pointed ahead to a peak, glittering metallic blue in the sunlight, that stood alone on the horizon. 'That's a continent in the invisible world. Do you remember those little quantum memory chips from last time? It's an entire mountain of them. You can imagine, or maybe you can't, the capacity of that computer.'

'What sort of life is it on the inside, when people are nothing more than a collection of quantum impulses?'

'That's why you can do whatever you please, and create whatever you desire. You can build an empire of a hundred billion people and reign as king, or you could experience a thousand different romances, or fight in ten thousand wars and die a hundred thousand times. Everyone is master of their personal world, and more powerful than a god. You could even create your own universe with billions of galaxies containing billions of planets, each that can be whatever different world you desire, or that you dare not desire. Don't worry about not having the time to experience it all. At the computer's speed, centuries pass every second. On the inside, the only limit is your imagination. In the invisible world, imagination and reality are the same thing. When something appears in your imagination, it becomes reality. Of course, as you said, reality in quantum memory is a collection of impulses. The people of this age are gradually transitioning to the invisible world, and more of them now live there than in the visible world. Even though a copy of the brain can be in both worlds, the invisible world is like a drug. No one wants to come back once they've experienced life there. Our world with its cares is like hell for them. The invisible world has the upper hand and is gradually assuming control of the whole world.'

As if sleepwalking across a millennium, they stared at the quantum memory mountain and forgot about time, and only when the true sun lit up the east as it had for billions of years did they return to reality.

'What's going to come next?' the ambassador asked.

'As a program in the invisible world, it's simple to make lots of copies of yourself, and whatever parts of your personality you dislike—being too tormented by emotions and responsibility, for example—you can get rid of, or off-load for use the next time you need them. And you can split yourself into multiple parts representing various aspects of your personality. And then you can join with someone else to form a new self out of two minds and memories. And then you can join with several or dozens or hundreds of people. . . . I'll stop before I drive you mad. Anything can happen at any time in the invisible world.'

'And then?'

'Only conjecture. The clearest signs point to the disappearance of the individual; everyone in the invisible world will combine into a single program.'

'And then?'

'I don't know. This is a philosophical question, but after so many times thawing out I'm afraid of philosophy.'

'I'm the opposite. I've become a philosopher now. You're right that it's a philosophical question and needs to be studied from that standpoint. We really should have done that thinking long ago, but it's not yet too late. Philosophy is a layer of gauze, but at least for me, it's been punctured, and in an instant, or practically an instant, I know what lies on the road ahead.'

'We need to terminate our migration in this age,' the captain said. 'If we continue onward, migrants will have an even harder time adapting to the target environment. We can rise up and fight for our own rights.'

'That's impossible. And unnecessary.'

'Do we have any other choice?'

'Of course we do. And it's a choice as clear and bright as the sun rising in front of us. Call out the engineer.'

The engineer had been thawed out together with the ambassador and was now inspecting and repairing the equipment. His frequent thaws had turned him from a young man to an old one. When the confused captain called him out, the ambassador asked, 'How long can the freezer last?'

'The insulation is in excellent condition, and the fusion reactor is operating normally. In the Lobby Age, we replaced the entire refrigeration equipment with their technology and topped up the fusion fuel. Without any equipment replacement or other maintenance, all two hundred freezer rooms will last twelve thousand years.'

'Excellent. Then set a final destination on the atomic clock and put everyone into supersleep. No one is to wake up until that destination is reached.'

'And that destination is . . .'

'Eleven thousand years.'

Again, Hua entered the ambassador's fragmented consciousness, more real than ever: her dark long hair floated about in the chill wind, her eyes wet with tears, and she called out to him. Before he entered the void of unconsciousness, he said to her, 'Hua, we're coming home! We're coming home!'

The Trek

Outside of perception, the sun swept through the sky like a shooting star, and time slipped past in the outside world.

. . .1,000 years . . . 2,000 years . . . 3,500 years . . . 5,500 years . . . 7,000 years . . . 9,000 years . . . 10,000 years . . . 11,000 years.

Stop 4: Back Home

This time, even in supersleep time felt endless. Over the long ten-thousand-year night, the hundred-century wait, even the computer steadfastly controlling the world's two hundred superfreezers went to sleep.

During the final millennium, parts began to fail, and one by one its myriad sensor-eyes closed, its integrated circuit nerves paralyzed, its fusion reactor energy petered out, leaving the freezers holding at zero through the final decades only by virtue of their insulation. Then the temperature began to rise, quickly reaching dangerous levels, and the liquid helium began to evaporate. Pressure rose dramatically inside the supersleep chambers, and it seemed as if the eleven-thousand-year trek would terminate unconsciously in an explosion.

But then, the computer's last remaining set of open eyes noticed the time on the atomic clock, and the tick of the final second called its ancient memory to send out a weak signal to boot up the wake-up system. A nuclear magnetic resonance pulse melted the cellular liquid within the bodies of the advance-team captain and a hundred squad members from near absolute zero in a fraction of a second, and then elevated it to normal body temperature. A day later they emerged from the freezer. A week later, the ambassador and the entire migration commission were awakened.

When the huge freezer door was open just a crack, a breath of wind came in from the outside. The ambassador inhaled the outside air; unlike that of the previous three ages, it carried the scent of flowers. It was the smell of springtime, of home. He was practically certain that the decision he made ten thousand years ago was the correct one.

The ambassador and the commissioners crossed into the age of their final destination.

The ground, made of soil, beneath their feet was covered in green grass as far as the eye could see. Just outside the freezer door was a brook of clear water in which beautiful, colored stones were visible on the riverbed and fish swam leisurely. A few young advance-team members washed their faces in the brook, where mud covered their bare feet and a light breeze carried off their laughter. A blue sky held snow-white clouds and just one sun. An eagle circled languidly and smaller birds called. In the distance, the mountain range that had vanished ten thousand years ago during the Lobby Age was back again against the sky, topped with a thick forest. . . .

To the ambassador, the world before them seemed rather bland after the previous three ages, but he wept hot tears for its blandness. Adrift for eleven thousand years, he—and all of them—needed this, a world soft and warm as goose down into which they could lay their fractured, exhausted minds.

The plain held no signs of human life.

The advance-team captain came over to face the focused attention of the ambassador and the commissioners, the stare of the day of judgment for humanity.

'It's all over,' he said.

Everyone knew the significance of his words. They stood silent between the sacred blue sky and green grass as they accepted this reality.

'Do you know why?' the ambassador asked.

The captain shook his head.

'Because of the environment?'

'No, not the environment. It wasn't war, either. Nor any other reason we can think of.'

'Are there any remains?'

'No. They left nothing behind.'

The commissioners gathered round and launched into an urgent interrogation:

'Any signs of an off-world migration?'

'No. All nearby planets have returned to an undeveloped state, and there are no signs of interstellar migration.'

'There's really nothing left behind? No ruins or records of any kind?'

'That's right. There's nothing. The mountains were restored using stone and dirt extracted from the ocean. Vegetation and the ecology have returned nicely, but there's no sign of any work by human hands. Ancient sites are present up to one century before the Common Era, but there's nothing more recent. The ecosystem has been running on its own for around five thousand years, and the natural environment now resembles the Neolithic period, although with far fewer species.'

'How could there be nothing left?'

'There's nothing they wanted to say.'

At this, they all fell silent.

Then the captain said to the ambassador, 'You anticipated this, didn't you? You must have thought of the reason.'

'We can know the reason, but we'll never understand it. It's a reason rooted deeply in philosophy. When their contemplation of existence reached its highest point, they concluded that nonexistence was the most rational choice.'

'I told you that philosophy scares me.'

'Fine. Let's drop philosophy for the moment.' The ambassador took a few steps forward and turned to face the commission.

'The migrants have arrived. Thaw them all out!'

A last burst of powerful energy from the two hundred fusion reactors produced an NMR pulse to thaw out eighty million people. The next day, humanity emerged from the freezers and spread out onto continents that had been unpeopled for thousands of years. Tens of thousands gathered on the plain outside Freezer No. 1 as the ambassador stood facing them on a huge platform before the entrance. Few of them were listening, but they spread her words to the rest like ripples through water.

'Citizens, we had planned to travel one hundred and twenty years but have arrived here at last after eleven thousand. You have now seen everything. They're gone, and we're the only surviving humans. They left nothing behind, but they left everything behind. We've been searching for even a few words from them since awaking, but we've found nothing. There's nothing at all. Did they really have nothing to say? No! They did, and they said it. The blue sky, the green earth, the mountains and forests, all of this re-creation of nature is what they wanted to say. Look at the green of the land: This is our mother. The source of our strength! The foundation of our existence and our eternal resting place! Humanity will still make mistakes in the future, and will still trek through the desert of misery and despair, but so long as we remain rooted in mother earth we won't disappear like they did. No matter the difficulty, life and humanity will endure. Citizens, this is our world now, and we embark on a new round for humanity. We begin with nothing except all that humanity has to offer.'

The ambassador took out the quantum chip from the Lobby Age, and held that sum total of human knowledge up for everyone to see. Then, he froze as his eyes were drawn to a tiny black dot flying swiftly over the crowd. As it drew near, he saw the black hair he'd glimpsed countless times in his dreams, and the eyes that had turned to dust a hundred centuries ago. Hua had not remained eleven thousand years in the past, but had come after him in the end, crossing the ceaseless desert of time in his wake. When they embraced, sky, earth, and human became one.

'Long live the new life!' someone shouted.

'Long live the new life!' resounded the plain. A flock of birds flew overhead, singing joyously.

At the close of everything, everything began.

MIRROR

镜子

TRANSLATED BY CARMEN YILING YAN

二〇一零 译

As research delves deeper, humanity is discovering that quantum effects are nothing more than surface ripples in the ocean of existence, shadows of the disturbances arising from the deeper laws governing the workings of matter. With these laws beginning to reveal themselves, quantum mechanics' ever-shifting picture of reality is once again stabilizing, deterministic variables once again replacing probabilities. In this new model of the universe, the chains of causality that were thought eliminated have surfaced once more, and clearer than before.

Pursuit

In the office were the flags of China and the CPC. There were also two men, one on either side of the broad desk.

'I know you're very busy, sir, but I must report this. I've honestly never seen anything like it,' said the man in front of the desk. He wore the uniform of a police superintendent second class. He was near fifty, but he stood ramrod-straight, and the lines of his face were hard and vigorous.

'I know the weight of that last sentence coming from you, Jifeng[1], veteran investigator of thirty years.' The Senior Official looked at the red and blue pencil slowly twirling between his fingers as he spoke, as if all his attention were focused on assessing the merit of its sharpening. He tucked away his gaze like this much of the time. In the years Chen Jifeng had known him, the Senior Official had looked him in the eyes no more than three times. Each

---

time had come at a turning point in Chen's life.

'Every time we take action, the target escapes one step ahead of us. They know what we're going to do.'

'Surely you've seen similar things before,' the Senior Official said.

'If it were simply that, it wouldn't be a big deal, of course. We considered the possibility of an inside job right off.'

'Knowing your subordinates, I find that rather improbable.'

'We found that out for ourselves,' Chen said. 'Like you instructed, we've reduced the participants in this case as much as possible. There are only four people in the task force, and only two know the full story. But just in case, I planned to call a meeting of all the members and question them one by one. I told Chenbing to handle it—you know him, the one from the Eleventh Department, very reliable, took care of the business with Song Cheng—and that's when it happened.

'Don't take this for a joke, sir. What I'm going to say next is the honest truth.' Chen Jifeng laughed a little, as if embarrassed by his own defensiveness. 'Right then, they called. Our target called me on the phone! I heard him say on my cell phone, *You don't need this meeting, there's no traitor among you.* Less than thirty seconds after I told Chenbing I wanted to call a meeting!'

The Senior Official's pencil stilled between his fingers.

'You might be thinking that we were bugged, but that's impossible. I chose the location for the conversation at random to be the middle of a government agency auditorium while it was being used for chorus rehearsals for National Day. We had to talk right into each other's ears to hear.

'And similar funny business kept happening after that. He called us eight times in total, each time about things we had just said or done. The scariest part is, not only does he hear everything, he sees everything. One time, Chenbing decided to search the target's parents' home. He and the other task force member were just standing up, not even out of the department office, when they got the target's call. *You guys have the wrong search warrant,* they told them. *My parents are careful people. They might think you guys are frauds.*

Chenbing took out the warrant to check, and sir, he really had taken the wrong one.'

The Senior Official set the pencil lightly on his desk, waiting in silence for Chen Jifeng to continue, but the latter seemed to have run out of steam. The Senior Official took out a cigarette. Chen Jifeng hurriedly patted at his coat pockets for a lighter, but couldn't find one.

One of the two phones on the desk began to ring.

Chen Jifeng swept his gaze over the caller ID. 'It's him,' he said quietly.

Unperturbed, the Senior Official motioned at him. Chen pressed the speaker button. A voice immediately sounded, worn and very young. 'Your lighter is in the briefcase.'

Chen Jifeng glanced at the Senior Official, then began to rummage through the briefcase on the desk. He couldn't find anything at first.

'It's wedged in a document, the one on urban household registration reform.'

Chen Jifeng took out the document. The lighter fell onto the desk with a clatter.

'That's one fine lighter there. French-made S. T. Dupont brand, solid palladium-gold alloy, thirty diamonds set in each side, worth . . . let me look it up . . . 39,960 yuan.'

The Senior Official didn't move, but Chen Jifeng raised his head to study the office. This wasn't the Senior Official's personal office; rather, it had been selected at random from the rooms in this office building.

The target continued the demonstration of his powers. 'Senior Official, there are five cigarettes left in your box of Chunghwas. There's only one Mevacor cholesterol tablet left in your coat pocket—better have your secretary get some more.'

Chen Jifeng picked up the box of cigarettes on the desk; the Senior Official took out the blister pack of pills from his pocket. The target was correct on both counts.

'Stop coming after me. I'm in a tricky situation just like you. I'm not sure what to do now,' the target continued.

'Can we discuss this in person?' asked the Senior Official.

'Believe me, it would be a disaster for both sides.' With that, the phone went dead.

Chen Jifeng exhaled. Now he had the proof to back up his story—the thought of disbelief from the Senior Official unsettled him more than his opponent's antics. 'It's like seeing a ghost,' he said, shaking his head.

'I don't believe in ghosts, but I do see danger,' said the Senior Official. For the fourth time in his life, Chen Jifeng saw that pair of eyes bore into his.

The Inmate and the Pursued

In the No. 2 Detention Center at the city outskirts, Song Cheng walked under escort into the cell. There were already six other prisoners inside, mostly other inmates with long pre-trial detention.

Cold looks greeted Song Cheng from all directions. Once the guard left, shutting the door behind him, a small, thin man came up.

'Hey, you, Pig Grease!' he yelled. Seeing Song Cheng's confusion, he continued, 'The law of the land here ranks us Big Grease, Second Grease, Third Grease . . . Pig Grease at the bottom, that's you. Hey, don't think we're taking advantage of the latecomer.' He pointed his thumb at a heavily bearded man leaning in the corner. 'Brother Bao's only been here three days, and he's already Big Grease. Trash like you may have held a pretty government rank before, but here you're lowest of the low!' He turned toward the other man and asked respectfully, 'How will you receive him, Brother Bao?'

'Stereo sound,' came the careless reply.

Two other inmates sprang up from the bunks and grabbed Song Cheng by the ankles, dangling him upside down. They held him over the toilet and slowly lowered him until his head was largely inside.

'Sing a song,' Skinny Guy commanded. 'That's what stereo sound means. Give us a comrade song like "Left Hand, Right Hand"!'

Song Cheng didn't sing. The inmates let go, and his head pitched all the way into the toilet.

Struggling, Song Cheng pulled his head out. He immediately began to vomit. Now he realized that the story designed by those who had framed him would make him the target of all his fellow inmates' contempt.

The delighted prisoners around him suddenly scattered and dashed back to their bunks. The door opened; the police guard from earlier came in. He looked with disgust at Song Cheng, still crouched in front of the toilet. 'Wash off your head at the tap. You have a visitor.'

Once Song Cheng rinsed off, he followed the guard into a spacious office where his visitor awaited. He was very young, thin-faced with messy hair and thick glasses. He carried an enormous briefcase.

Song Cheng sat down coldly without looking at the visitor. He had been permitted a visit at this time, and here, not in a visitation room with a glass partition; from that, Song Cheng had a good guess as to who sent him. But the first words out of his visitor's mouth made Song lift his head in surprise.

'My name's Bai Bing. I'm an engineer at the Center for Meteorological Modeling. They're coming after me for the same reason they came after you.'

Song Cheng looked at the visitor. His tone of voice seemed odd: this was a subject that should have been discussed in whispers, but Bai Bing spoke at a normal volume, as if he wasn't talking about anything that needed hiding.

Bai Bing seemed to have noticed his confusion. 'I called the Senior Official two hours ago. He wanted to talk face-to-face with me, but I turned him down. After that, they got on my trail, followed me all the way to the detention center doors. They haven't seized me because they're curious about our meeting. They want to know what I'll tell you. They're listening in to our conversation right now.'

Song Cheng shifted his gaze from Bai Bing to the ceiling. He found it hard to trust this person, and regardless, he wasn't interested in the matter. The law might have spared him the death penalty, but it had sentenced and executed his spirit all the same. His heart was dead. He could no longer muster interest in anything.

'I know the truth, all of it,' Bai Bing said.

A smirk flickered at the corner of Song Cheng's mouth. *No one knows the truth but them,* but he didn't bother to say that out loud.

'You began working for the provincial-level Commission for Discipline Inspection seven years ago. You were promoted to this rank just last year.'

Song Cheng remained silent. He was angry now. Bai Bing's words had dragged him back into the memories he'd worked so hard to escape.

The Big Case

At the beginning of the century, the Zhengzhou Municipal Government began a policy of setting aside a number of deputy-level positions for holders of Ph.D.s. Many other cities followed its example, and later, provincial governments began to adopt the same practice, even removing graduation-year requirements and offering higher starting positions. It was an excellent way to demonstrate the recruiters' magnanimity and vision to the world, but in reality, the attractive concept amounted to little more than political record engineering. The recruiters were farsighted indeed—they knew perfectly well that these book-smart, well-educated young people lacked any sort of political experience. When they entered the unfamiliar and vicious political sphere, they found themselves swallowed whole in labyrinthine bureaucracy, unable to gain any foothold. The whole business was no big loss in job vacancies, while substantially padding the recruiters' political résumés.

An opportunity like this led Song Cheng, already a law professor at the time, to leave his peaceful campus study for the world of politics. His peers who chose the same road didn't last a year before they left in utter despair, beaten men and women, their only achievement being the destruction of their dreams. But Song Cheng was an exception. He not only stayed in politics, but did exceptionally well.

The credit belonged to two people. One was his college classmate Lv Wenming. In their last year as undergraduates, he'd placed in the civil service even as Song Cheng tested into grad school. With his advantageous family background and his own dedicated effort, ten years later he'd become the youngest provincial secretary of discipline inspection in the nation, head of the organization in charge of maintaining discipline within the provincial-level Party. He was the one who'd advised Song Cheng to give up his books for governance.

When the simple scholar first began, Lv didn't lead him by the hand so much as he toddled him along by the feet, hand-placing Song's every step as he taught him how to walk. He'd steered Song Cheng around traps and treachery that the latter could never have spotted himself, allowing him to progress up the road that had led to today. The other person he should thank was the Senior Official . . . on that thought, Song Cheng's heart gave a spasm.

'You have to admit, you chose this for yourself. You can't say they didn't give you a way out.'

Song Cheng nodded. Yes, they'd given him a way out, a boulevard with his name in lights at that.

Bai Bing continued, 'The Senior Official met with you a few months ago. I'm sure you remember it well. It was in a villa out in the exurbs, by the Yang River. The Senior Official doesn't normally see outsiders there.

'Once you were out of the car, you found him waiting for you at the gate, a very high honor. He clasped your hand warmly and led you into the drawing room.

'The décor would've given off a first impression of unassuming simplicity, but you'd be wrong there. That aged-looking mahogany furniture is worth millions. The one plain scroll painting hanging on the wall looks even older, and there's insect damage if you look closely, but that's *Dangheqizi* by the Ming Dynasty painter Wu Bin, bought at a Christie's auction in Hong Kong for eight million HKD. And the cup of tea the Senior Official personally steeped for you? The leaves were ranked five stars at the International Tea Competition. It goes for nine hundred thousand yuan per half kilo.'

Song Cheng really could recall the tea Bai Bing spoke of. The liquid had sparkled the green of a jewel, a few delicate leaves drifting in its clarity like the languid notes from a mountain saint's zither. . . . He even recalled how he'd felt: *If only the outside world could be this lovely and pure.* The tarp of apathy was torn from Song Cheng's stifled thoughts, his blurred mind snapping back into focus. He stared at Bai Bing, eyes wide with shock.

How could he know all this? The whole affair had been dispatched to the deepest oubliettes, a secret among secrets. No more than four people in all the world knew, and that was counting himself.

'Who are you?!' He opened his mouth for the first time.

Bai Bing smiled. 'I introduced myself earlier. I'm an ordinary person. But I'll tell you straight off, not only do I know a lot, I know everything, or at least have the means to know everything. That's why they want to get rid of me like they got rid of you.'

Bai Bing continued his account. 'The Senior Official sat close, one hand on your knee. That benevolent gaze he turned on you would have moved anyone from the junior ranks. From what I know (and remember, I know everything), he'd never shown anyone else the same intimacy. He told you, *Don't worry, young man, we're all comrades here. Whatever the matter, just speak honestly and trust that you'll get honesty in return. We can always come to a solution . . . you have ideas, you're capable, you have a sense of duty and a sense of mission. Those last two in particular are as precious as an oasis in a desert among young cadres nowadays. This is why I think so highly of you. In you, I see the reflection of what I was once like.*

'I should mention that the Senior Official may have been telling the truth. Your official work didn't give you many chances to interact with him, but quite a few times, you'd run into him in the hallways of the government building or coming out of a meeting, and he'd always be the one to come up to you to chat. He very rarely did that with lower-ranking officials, especially the younger ones. People took notice. He might not have said anything to help you at organizational meetings, but those gestures did a lot for your career.'

Song Cheng nodded again. He'd known all this, and had been immensely grateful. All that time, Song had wanted the opportunity to repay him.

'Then the Senior Official raised his hand and gestured behind him. Immediately, someone entered and quietly set a big stack of documents and materials on the table. You must have noticed that he wasn't the Senior Official's normal secretary.

'The Senior Official passed a hand over the documents and said, *The project you just completed fully demonstrates those priceless assets of yours. It required such an immense and difficult investigation to collect evidence, but these documents are ample, detailed, and reliable, the conclusions drawn profound. It's hard to believe you did it all in half a year. It would be the Party's great fortune to have more outstanding Discipline Inspection officials like you. . . . .* I don't need to tell you how you felt at that moment, I think.'

Of course he didn't. Song Cheng had never been so horrified in his life. That stack of documents first sent him shaking as if electrocuted, then froze him into stone.

Bai Bing continued: 'It all started with the investigation into the illegal apportionment of state-owned land you undertook on behalf of the Central Commission, yes. . . .

'I recall that when you were a child, you and two of your friends went exploring in a cave, called Old Man Cavern by the locals. The entrance was only half a meter high, and you had to crouch down to enter. But inside was an enormous, dark vault, its ceiling too high for your flashlights to reach. All you could see were endless bats swishing past the beams of light. Every little sound provoked a rumbling echo from the distance. The dank cold seeped into your bones. . . . It's a lively metaphor for the investigation: walking along, following that seemingly run-of-the-mill trail of clues, only to find yourself led toward places that made you afraid to believe your own eyes. As you deepened your investigation, a grand network of corruption spanning the entire province unfolded before you, and every strand of the web led in one direction, to one person. And now, the top-secret Discipline Inspection report you'd prepared for the Central Commission was in his hands! In this investigation, you'd considered all sorts of worst-case scenarios, but you never dreamed of the one that you faced now. You were thrown into total panic. You stammered, *H-how did this end up in your hands, sir?* The Senior Official smiled indulgently and lifted his hand to gesture lightly again. You immediately got your answer: The secretary of discipline inspection, Lv Wenming, walked into the room.

'You stood and glared at Lv Wenming. *How—how could you do this? How could you go against our organization's rules and principles like this?* Lv Wenming cut you off with a wave of his hand and asked in the same furious tone of voice as you, *How could you go ahead with something like this without telling me?*

'*I've taken over your duties as secretary for the year you're undergoing training at the Central Party School,* you shot back. *Of course I couldn't tell you, it was against the rules of the organization!*

'Lv Wenming shook his head sorrowfully, looking as if he wanted to weep in despair. *If I hadn't caught this report in time . . . can you even imagine the consequences? Song Cheng, your fatal flaw is that insistence on dividing the world into black and white, when reality is nothing more than gray!*'

Song Cheng exhaled long and slow. He remembered how he'd stared dumbly at his classmate, unable to believe that he could say something like that. He'd never revealed thoughts in that vein before. Was the hatred of internal corruption he'd shown in their many late-night conversations, the steadfast courage he displayed as they tackled sensitive cases that drew pressure from all directions, the deeply personal concern for the Party and the nation he'd expressed at so many dawns, after grueling all-nighters at work— was all that nothing but pretense?

'It's not that Lv Wenming was lying before. It's more that he never delved *that* deeply into his soul in front of you. He's like that famous dessert, Baked Alaska, flash-cooked ice cream. The hot parts and the cold parts are both real. But the Senior Official didn't look at Lv Wenming. Instead, he slammed a hand into the table. *What gray? Wenming, I really can't stand this side of you! What Song Cheng did was outstanding, faultless. In that respect he's better than you!* He turned to you and said, *Young man, you did exactly as you should have done. A person, especially a young person, is gone forever if they lose that faith and sense of mission. I look down on people like that.'*

The part that had struck Song Cheng the deepest was that, although he and Lv Wenming were the same age, the Senior Official only called him 'young,' and emphasized it repeatedly at that. The unspoken implication was clear: *With me as an opponent, you're still nothing but a child.* In the present, Song Cheng could only concede that he was right.

'The Senior Official continued on. *Nonetheless, young man, we still need to mature a little. Let's take an example from your report. There really are problems with the Hengyu Aluminum Electrolysis Base, and they're even worse than you discovered in your investigations. Not only are domestic officials implicated, foreign investors have collaborated with them in serious legal trespasses. Once the matter is dealt with, the foreigners will withdraw their investments. The largest aluminum-electrolysis enterprise in the country will be put out of business. Tongshan Bauxite Mines, which provides the aluminum ore for Hengyu, will be in deep trouble too. Next comes the Chenglin nuclear power plant. It was built too big due to the energy crisis the last few years, and with the severe domestic overproduction of electricity now, most of this brand-new power plant's output goes to the aluminum-electrolysis base. Once Hengyu collapses, Chenglin Nuclear Facility will face bankruptcy as well. And then Zhaoxikou Chemical Plant, which provides the enriched uranium for Chenglin, will be in trouble. . . . With that, nearly seventy billion yuan in government investment will be gone without a trace, and thirty to forty thousand people will lose their jobs. These corporations are all located within the provincial capital's outskirts—this vital city will be instantly thrown into turmoil. . . . And the Hengyu issue I went into is only a small part of this investigation. The case implicates one provincial-level official, three sub-provincial-level officials, two hundred and fifteen prefectural-level officials, six hundred and fourteen county-level officials, and countless more in lower ranks. Nearly half of the most successful large-scale enterprises and the most promising investment projects in the province will be impacted in some way. Once the secrets are out, the province's entire economy and political structure will be dead in the water! And we don't know, and have no way of predicting, what even worse consequences might arise from so large-scale and severe a disturbance.*

The political stability and economic growth our province has worked so hard to attain will be gone without a trace. Is that really to the benefit of the Party and the country? Young man, you can't think like a legal scholar anymore, demanding justice by the law come hell or high water. It's irresponsible. We've progressed along the road of history to today because of balance, arising from the happy medium between various elements. To abandon balance and seek an extreme is a sign of immaturity in politics.

'When the Senior Official finished, Lv Wenming began. I'll take care of things with the Central Commission. You just make sure you take over properly from the cadres in that project group. I'll break off training at the Central Party School next week and come back to help you—

'Scoundrel! The Senior Official once again slammed the table. Lv Wenming jumped in fright. Is that how you took my words? You thought I was trying to get this young man to abandon his principles and duty?! Wenming, you've known me for years. From the depths of your heart, do you really think I have so little sense of Party and principle? When did you become so oily? It saddens me. Then he turned to you. Young man, you've done a truly exceptional job so far on your work. You must stand fast in the face of interference and pressure, and hand the corrupt elements their comeuppance! This case hurts the eyes and heart to look upon. You must not spare them, in the name of the people, in the name of justice! Don't let what I just said burden you. I was just reminding you as an old Party member to be careful, to avoid serious consequences beyond your prediction. But there's one thing I know—you must get to the bottom of this terrible corruption case. The Senior Official took out a piece of paper as he spoke, handing it to you solemnly. Is this wide enough in scope for you?'

Song Cheng had known right then that they'd set up a sacrificial altar and were ready to lay out the offerings. He looked at the list of names. It was wide enough in scope, truly enough, enough in both rank and quantity. It would be a corruption case to astound the entire nation, and with the case's triumphant conclusion, Song Cheng would become known throughout the country as an anti-corruption hero, revered by the people as a paragon of justice and virtue.

But he was clear in his heart that this was nothing more than a lizard severing its own tail in a crisis. The lizard would escape; the tail would grow back in no time. He saw the Senior Official watching him, and in that moment he really did think of a lizard, and he shivered. But Song Cheng knew, too, that the Senior Official was afraid, that he'd made him afraid, and it made Song Cheng proud. The pride made him vastly overestimate his own capabilities at that moment, but more vitally, there was that ineffable thing running in the blood of every scholar-idealist. He made the fatal choice.

'You stood and took up the pile of documents with both hands. You said to the Senior Official, *By the Internal Supervision Regulations of the CPC, the secretary of discipline inspection has the authority to conduct inspections upon Party officials of the same rank. According to the rules, sir, these documents can't stay with you. I'll take them.*

'Lv Wenming went to stop you, but the Senior Official gently tugged him back. At the door, you heard your classmate say in a low voice behind you, *You've gone too far, Song Cheng.*

'The Senior Official walked you to your car. As you were about to leave, he took your hand and said slowly, *Come again soon, young man.*'

Only later did Song Cheng fully realize the deeper meaning to his words: *Come again soon. You don't have much time left.*

The Big Bang

'Who the hell are you?' Song Cheng stared at Bai Bing fearfully. How could he know this much? No one could know this much!

'Okay, we'll end the reminiscing here.' Bai Bing cut off his narrative with a wave of his hand. 'Let me go into the whys and wherefores, to clear up the questions you have. Hmm . . . do you know what the big bang is?'

Song Cheng stared blankly at Bai Bing, his brain unable to immediately process Bai's words. At last he managed the response of a normal human and laughed.

'Okay, okay,' Bai Bing said. 'I know that was sudden. But please trust that I'm all there in the head. To go through everything clearly, we really do need to start with the big bang. This . . . Damn, how do I even explain it to you? Let's return to the big bang. You probably know at least a little.'

'Our universe was created in a massive explosion twenty billion years ago. Most people picture the big bang like some ball of fire bursting forth in the darkness of space, but that's incorrect. Before the big bang, there was nothing, not even time and space. There was only a singularity, a single point of undefined size that rapidly expanded to form our universe today. Anything and everything, including us, originated from the singularity's expansion. It is the seed from which all living things grew! The theory behind it all is really deep, and I don't fully understand it myself, but the relevant part is this: With the advancement of physics and the appearance of "theories of everything" like string theory, physicists are starting to figure out the structure of that singularity and create a mathematical model for it. This is different from the quantum-theory models they had before. If we can determine the fundamental parameters of the singularity before the big bang, we can determine everything in the universe it forms too. An uninterrupted chain of cause and effect running through the entire history of the universe . . .' He sighed. 'Seriously, how am I supposed to explain it all?'

Bai Bing saw Song Cheng shake his head, as if he didn't understand, or as if he didn't even want to keep listening.

Bai Bing said, 'Take my advice and stop thinking about the suffering you've gone through. Honestly, I haven't been much luckier. Like I said, I'm just an ordinary person, but now they're hunting me, and I may end up even worse than you, all because I know everything. You can hold on to the fact that you were martyred for your sense of duty and faith, but I'm . . . I just have really shitty luck. Enough shit luck for eight reincarnations. I've been screwed over even worse than you.'

Song Cheng only continued to look at him, silently, as if to say: *No one can be screwed over worse than me.*

Framed

A week after he met with the Senior Official, Song Cheng was arrested for murder.

To be fair, Song Cheng had already known they'd take extraordinary measures against him. The usual administrative and political methods were too risky to use on someone who knew so much and was already in the process of taking action. But he hadn't imagined his opponent would move so quickly, or strike so viciously.

The victim was a nightclub dancer called Luo Luo, and he'd died in Song Cheng's car. The doors were locked from the outside. Two canisters of propane, the type used to refill cigarette lighters, had been tossed into the car, both slit open. The liquid inside had completely evaporated, and the high concentration of propane vapor in the car had fatally poisoned the victim. When the body was discovered, it was clutching a battered, broken cell phone in one hand, clearly used in an attempt to smash the car windows.

The police produced ample evidence. They had two hours of recordings to prove that Song Cheng had been in most irregular association with Luo Luo for the last three months. The most incriminating piece of evidence was the 110 call Luo Luo had made to the police shortly before his death.

COMPUTER-A

Luo Luo

. . .Hurry. Hurry! I can't open the car doors! I can't breathe, my head hurts . . .

110

Where are you? Can you clarify your situation?!

Luo Luo

. . .Song . . . Song Cheng wants to kill me . . .
[End of transmission]

END

Afterward, the police found a short phone-call recording on the victim's cell, preserving an exchange between Song Cheng and the victim.

COMPUTER-A

Song Cheng

Now that we've gone this far, how about you break things off with Xu Xueping?

Luo Luo

Why the need, Brother Song? Me and Sister Xu just have the usual man-woman relations. It won't affect our thing. Hell, it might help.

Song Cheng

It makes me uncomfortable. Don't make me take action.

Luo Luo

Brother Song, let me live my life.

[End of transmission]

END

This was a highly professional frame-up. Its brilliance lay in that the evidence the police held was just about 100 percent real.

Song Cheng really had been associating with Luo Luo for a while, in secret, and it could indeed be called irregular. The two recordings weren't faked, although the second had been distorted.

Song Cheng met Luo Luo because of Xu Xueping, director general of Changtong Group, who held intimate financial ties to many nodes of the network of corruption and no doubt considerable knowledge of its background and inner workings. Of course, Song Cheng couldn't get any information directly from her, but with Luo Luo he had an in.

Luo Luo didn't provide Song Cheng information out of any inner sense of righteousness. In his eyes, the world was already good for nothing but wiping his ass on. He was in it for revenge.

This hinterland city shrouded in industrial smog and dust might have been ranked at the bottom of the list of similar-sized Chinese cities for average income, but it had some of the most opulent nightclubs in the nation. The young scions of Beijing's political families had to watch their image in the capital city, unable to indulge their desires like the rich without Party affiliations. Instead, they got in their cars every weekend and zipped four or five hours along the highway to this city, spent two days and one night in hedonistic extravagance, and zipped back to Beijing on Sunday night.

Luo Luo's blue Wave was the highest-end of all the nightclubs. Requesting a song cost at least three thousand yuan, and bottles of Martell and Hennessy priced at thousands each sold multiple cases every night. But blue Wave's real claim to fame was that it catered exclusively to female guests.

Unlike his fellow dancers, Luo Luo didn't care about how much his clients paid, but how much that money meant to them. A white-collar worker from foreign companies making just two or three hundred thousand yuan a year (rare paupers in blue Wave) could give him a few hundred and he'd accept. But Sister Xu wasn't one. Her fortune of billions had made waves south of the Yangtze the last few years, and likewise she was smashing the opposition in her expansion northward. But after several months spent together, she'd sent Luo Luo off with a mere four hundred thousand.

It had taken a lot to catch Sister Xu's eye; after she had broken it off, any other dancer would have, in Luo Luo's words, swigged enough champagne to make his liver hurt. But not Luo Luo, who was now filled with hatred for Xu Xueping. The arrival of a high-ranking Discipline Inspection official gave him hope of revenge, and he used his talents to entangle himself with Sister Xu once more. Normally, Xu Xueping was closemouthed even with Luo Luo, but once they had too many drinks or snorted too many lines, it was a different story. Luo Luo knew how to take the initiative, too; in the darkest hours before dawn, while Sister Xu slept soundly beside him, he'd silently climb out of bed and search her briefcase and drawers, snapping pictures of documents that he and Song Cheng needed.

Most of the video recordings the police used to prove Song Cheng's association with Luo Luo had been taken in the main dance hall in blue Wave. The camera liked to start with the pretty young boys dancing enthusiastically on the stage, before shifting to the expensively dressed female guests gathered in the dim areas, pointing at the stage, now and then smiling confidentially. The final shot always captured Song Cheng and Luo Luo, often sitting in some corner in the back, seeming very intimate as they conversed quietly with heads bent close. As the only male guest in the club, Song Cheng was instantly recognizable. . . .

Song Cheng didn't have anything to say to that. Most of the time, he could only find Luo Luo at blue Wave. The lighting in the dance hall was always dim, but these recordings were high resolution and clear. They could only have been taken with a high-end low-light camera, not the sort of equipment normal people would have. That meant they'd noticed him from the very beginning, showing Song Cheng how very amateur he had been compared to his opponent.

That day, Luo Luo wanted to report his latest findings. When Song Cheng met him at the nightclub, Luo Luo uncharacteristically asked to talk in the car. Once they were done, he'd told Song that he felt unwell. If he went back to the club now, his boss would make him get on stage for sure. He wanted to rest for a while in Song Cheng's car.

Song Cheng had thought that Luo Luo's addiction might have been acting up again, but he didn't have a choice. He could only drive back to his office to take care of the work he hadn't finished during the day, parking in front of the department building with Luo Luo waiting in the car. Forty minutes later, when he came back out, someone had already found Luo Luo dead in a car full of propane fumes. And Song Cheng was the only one who can open the car door from the outside.

Later, a close friend in the police force who'd participated in the investigation told Song that the lock on his car door didn't show any signs of sabotage, and the evidence elsewhere really was enough to rule out the possibility of another killer. Logically enough, everyone assumed that Song Cheng had killed Luo Luo. But Song Cheng knew the only possible explanation: Luo Luo had brought the two propane canisters into the car himself.

This was too much for Song Cheng to fight against. He gave up his attempts to clear his name: if someone had used his own life and death as a weapon to frame him, he didn't have a chance of escape.

Really, Luo Luo committing suicide didn't surprise Song Cheng; his HIV test had returned positive. But someone else must have prompted him to use his death to frame Song Cheng. What would have been in it for him? What would money be worth to him now? Was the money for someone else? Or maybe his recompense wasn't money. But what was it, then? Was there some temptation or fear even stronger than his hatred of Xu Xueping? Song Cheng would never know now, but here he could see even more clearly his opponent's capabilities, and his own naïveté.

This was his life as the world knew it: a high-ranked Discipline Inspection cadre living a secret life of corruption and affairs, arrested for murdering his paramour in a lover's spat. The temperance he'd previously displayed in his heterosexual relationship only became further proof in the public mind. Like a trampled stinkbug, everything he had possessed disappeared without a trace. Even if someone remembered him, they would remember his misdeed.

Now Song Cheng realized that he'd been so prepared to sacrifice everything for faith and duty only because he hadn't even understood what sacrificing everything entailed. He'd of course imagined that death would be the bottom line. Only later did he realize that sacrifice could be far, far crueler. The police took him home one time when they searched his house. His wife and daughter were both there. He reached toward his daughter, but the child shrieked in disgust and buried her face in her mother's arms, shrinking into a corner. He'd seen the look they gave him only once before, one morning when he'd found a mouse in the trap under the wardrobe, and showed it to them. . . .

'Okay, let's set aside the big bang and the singularity and all the abstract stuff for now.' Bai Bing broke off Song Cheng's painful reminiscences and hauled the large briefcase onto the table. 'Take a look at this.'

Superstring Computer, Ultimate Capacity, Digital Mirror

'This is a superstring computer,' Bai Bing said, patting the briefcase. 'I brought it over, or, if you prefer, stole it from the Center for Meteorological Modeling. I'll depend on it to escape pursuit.'

Song Cheng shifted his gaze to the briefcase, clearly confused.

'These are expensive. There are only two in the province as of now. According to superstring theory, the fundamental particles of matter aren't point-like objects, but an infinitely thin one-dimensional string vibrating in eleven dimensions. Nowadays, we can manipulate this string to store and process information along the dimension of its length. That's the theory behind a superstring computer.

'A CPU or piece of internal storage in a traditional electronic computer is just an atom in a superstring computer! The circuits are formed by the particles' eleven-dimensional microscale structure. This higher-dimensional subatomic array has given humanity practically infinite storage and operational capacity. Comparing the supercomputers of the past to superstring computers is like comparing our ten fingers to those supercomputers. A superstring computer has ultimate capacity, that is to say, it has the capacity to store the current status of every fundamental particle existing in the known universe and perform operations with them. In other words, if we only look at three dimensions of space and one of time, a superstring computer can model the entire universe on the atomic level. . . .'

Song Cheng alternately looked at the briefcase and Bai Bing. Unlike before, he seemed to be listening to Bai Bing's words with full attention. In truth, he was desperately seeking any kind of relief, letting this mysterious visitor's rambling extricate him from his painful memories.

'Sorry for going on and on like this—big bang this and superstring that. It must seem completely unrelated to the reality we're facing, but to give a proper explanation I can't sidestep it. Let's talk about my career next. I'm a software engineer specializing in simulation software. That is, you create a mathematical model and run it in a computer to simulate some object or process in the real world. I studied mathematics, so I do both the model-creating and the programming. In the past I've simulated sandstorms, soil erosion on the Loess Plateau, energy generation and economic development trends in the Northeast, so on. Now I'm working on large-scale weather models. I love my work. Watching a piece of the real world running and evolving inside a computer is honestly fascinating.'

Bai Bing looked at Song Cheng, who was staring at him unblinkingly. He seemed to be listening attentively, so Bai Bing continued.

'You know, the field of physics has had huge breakthroughs one after another in recent years, a lot like at the beginning of the last century. Now, if you give us the boundary conditions, we can lift the fog of quantum effects to accurately predict the behavior of fundamental particles, either singly or in a group.

'Notice I mentioned groups. A group of enough particles means a macroscopic body. In other words, we can now create a mathematical model of a macroscopic object on the atomic level. This sort of simulation is called a digital mirror. We gave the name digital mirror to it, because it can simulate the macroscopic objects or their development process precisely, just like a mirror. I'll give an example. If we used digital mirror to create a mathematical model of an egg—as in, we input the status of every atom in the egg into the model's database—and run it in the computer, given suitable boundary conditions, the virtual egg in memory will hatch into a chick. And the virtual chick in memory would be perfectly identical to the chick hatched from the egg in real life, down to the tips of every feather! And think further, what if the object being modeled were bigger than an egg? As big as a tree, a person, many people. As big as a city, a country, or even all of Earth?' Bai Bing was getting worked up, gesturing wildly as he spoke.

'I like to think this way, pushing every idea to its limit. This led me to wonder, what if the object being digitally mirrored were the entire universe?' Bai Bing could no longer control his passion. 'Imagine, the entire universe! My god, an entire universe running in RAM! From creation to destruction—'

Bai Bing broke off his enthusiastic account and stood up, suddenly on guard. The door swung open soundlessly. Two grim-faced men entered. The slightly older one turned to Bai Bing and raised his hands to show that he should do the same. Bai Bing and Song Cheng saw the leather handgun holster under his open jacket; Bai Bing obediently put his hands up. The younger man patted Bai Bing down carefully, then shook his head at the older man. He picked up the large briefcase as well, setting it down farther from Bai Bing.

The older man walked to the door and made a welcoming gesture outward. Three more people entered. The first was the city's chief of police, Chen Jifeng. The second was the province's secretary of discipline inspection, his old classmate, Lv Wenming. Last came the Senior Official.

The younger cop took out a pair of handcuffs, but Lv Wenming shook his head at him. Chen Jifeng turned his head minutely toward the door, and the two plainclothes police left. One of them removed a small object from the table leg as he left, clearly a listening device.

Initial State

Bai Bing's face didn't show any sign of surprise. He smiled placidly. 'You've finally caught me.'

'More accurately, you flew into our net on purpose. I have to admit, if you really wanted to escape, we would've had a hard time catching you,' said Chen Jifeng.

Lv Wenming glanced at Song Cheng, his expression complicated. He seemed to want to say something, but stopped himself.

The Senior Official slowly shook his head. He intoned solemnly, 'Oh,

Song Cheng, how did you fall so low . . .' He stood silent for a long time, hands resting on the table's edge, his eyes a little damp. No onlooker could have doubted that his grief was real.

'Senior Official, I don't think you need to playact here,' Bai Bing said, coldly watching the proceedings.

The Senior Official didn't move.

'You were the one who arranged to frame him.'

'Proof?' the Senior Official asked indulgently, still unmoving.

'After that meeting, you only said one thing about Song Cheng, to him.' Bai Bing pointed at Chen Jifeng. 'Jifeng, you know what that whole business with Song Cheng means, of course. Let's put a little effort into it.'

'What does that prove?'

'It won't count for anything in court, of course. With your cleverness and experience, you didn't let anything slip, even in a secret conversation. But he,' Bai Bing pointed again at Chen Jifeng, 'got the message loud and clear. He's always understood you perfectly. He ordered one of the two people earlier to carry out the framing. His name is Chenbing, and he's his most competent subordinate. The whole process was one formidable engineering project. I don't think I need to go into detail here.'

The Senior Official slowly turned around and sat down in a chair by the office table. He looked at the ground as he said, 'Young man, I have to admit, your sudden appearance has been astonishing in many ways. To use Chief Chen's words, it's like seeing a ghost.' He was silent for a while, and then his voice rang out with sincerity. 'How about you tell us your real identity? If you really were sent by the central officials, please trust that we'll assist you however we can.'

'I wasn't. I've said again and again that I'm an ordinary guy. My identity is nothing more than what you've already looked up.'

The Senior Official nodded. It was impossible to tell whether Bai Bing's words had reassured him, or added to his concern.

'Sit, let's all sit.' The Senior Official waved a hand at Lv and Chen, both still standing, and drew closer to Bai Bing. 'Young man,' he said solemnly.

'Let's get to the bottom of all this today, okay?'

Bai Bing nodded. 'That's my plan too. I'll start from the beginning.'

'No, that won't be necessary. We heard everything you said to Song Cheng earlier. Just continue where you left off.'

Bai Bing was momentarily at a loss for words, unable to remember where he'd stopped.

'Atomic-level model of the entire universe,' the Senior Official reminded him, but seeing that Bai Bing still couldn't figure out how to start talking again, he added his own input. 'Young man, I don't think your idea is feasible. Superstring computers have ultimate capacity, yes, providing the hardware basis for running this sort of simulation. But have you considered the problem of the initial state? To make a digital mirror of the universe, you must start the simulation from some initial state—in other words, to construct a model that represents the universe on an atomic level, for the instant the model starts at, you'll have to input the status at that instant of every atom in the universe into the computer, one by one. Is this possible? It wouldn't be possible with the egg you mentioned, let alone the universe. The number of atoms in that egg outnumber the number of eggs ever laid since the beginning of time by orders of magnitude. It wouldn't even be possible with a bacterium, which still contains an astonishing number of atoms. Taking a step back, even if we put forth the near unimaginable manpower and computing power needed to find the initial state of a small object like the bacterium or the egg on an atomic level, what about the boundary conditions for when the model runs? For example, the outside temperature, humidity, and so on needed for a chicken egg to hatch. Taken on the atomic level, these boundary conditions will require unimaginable quantities of data too, perhaps even more than the modeled object itself.'

'You've laid out the technical problems beautifully. I admire that,' Bai Bing said sincerely.

'The Senior Official was once a star student in the field of high-energy physics. After Deng Xiaoping's reforms restored university degrees, his was one of the first classes to receive master's degrees in physics in China,' said Lv

Wenming.

Bai Bing nodded in Lv Wenming's direction, then turned toward the Senior Official. 'But you forget, there's a moment in time in which the universe was extremely simple, even simpler than eggs and bacteria, simpler than anything in existence today. The number of atoms in it at the time was zero, see. It had no size and no composition.'

'The big bang singularity?' the Senior Official said immediately, almost no delay between Bai Bing's words and his. It was a glimpse at the quick, agile mind beneath his slow and steady exterior.

'Yes, the big bang singularity. Superstring theory has already established a perfect model of the singularity. We just need to represent the model digitally and run it on the computer.'

'That's right, young man. That really is the case.' The Senior Official stood and walked to Bai Bing's side to pat his shoulder, revealing rare excitement. Chen Jifeng and Lv Wenming, who hadn't understood the exchange that had just taken place, looked at them with puzzled expressions.

'Is this the superstring computer you brought out of the research center?' the Senior Official asked, pointing at the briefcase.

'Stole,' said Bai Bing.

'Ha, no matter. The software for the digital mirror of the big bang is on it, I expect?'

'Yes.'

'Run it for us.'

Creation Game

Bai Bing nodded, hauled the briefcase onto the desk, and opened it. Beside the display equipment, the briefcase also contained a cylindrical vessel. The superstring computer's processor was in fact only the size of a pack of cigarettes, but the atomic circuitry required ultralow temperatures to operate, so the processor had to be kept submerged in the insulated vessel of liquid nitrogen. Bai Bing set the LCD screen upright and moved the mouse, and the superstring computer awoke from sleep mode. The screen brightened, like a dozing eye blinking open, displaying a simple interface composed of just a drop-down text box and a header reading:

Please Select Parameters to Initiate Creation of the Universe

Bai Bing clicked the arrow beside the drop-down text box. Row upon row of data sets, each composed of a sizable number of elements, appeared below. Each row seemed to differ considerably from the others. 'The properties of the singularity are determined by eighteen parameters. Technically, there's an infinite number of possible parameter combinations, but we can determine from superstring theory that the number of parameter combinations that could have resulted in the big bang is finite, although their exact number is still a mystery. Here we have a small selection of them. Let's select one at random.'

Bai Bing selected a group of parameters, and the screen immediately went white. Two big buttons appeared in striking contrast at the center of the screen.

Initiate Cancel

Bai Bing clicked Initiate. Now only the white background was left. 'The white represents nothingness. Space doesn't exist at this time, and time itself hasn't begun. There really is nothing.'

A red number '0' appeared in the lower left corner of the screen.

'This number indicates how long the universe has been evolving. The zero appearing means that the singularity has been generated. Its size is undefined, so we can't see it.'

The red number began to increment rapidly.

'Notice, the big bang has begun.'

A small blue dot appeared in the middle of the screen, quickly growing into a sphere emitting brilliant blue light. The sphere rapidly expanded, filling the entire screen. The software zoomed out, and the sphere once again shrank into a distant dot, but the ballooning universe quickly filled the screen once more. The cycle repeated again and again in rapid frequency, as if marking the beats to some swelling symphony.

'The universe is currently in the inflationary epoch. It's expanding at a rate far exceeding the speed of light.'

As the sphere slowed in its growth, the field of view began to zoom out less frequently, too. With the decrease in energy density, the sphere turned from blue to yellow, then red, before the color of the universe stabilized at red and began to darken. The field of view no longer zoomed out, and the now-black sphere expanded very slowly now on the screen.

'Okay, it's ten billion years after the big bang. At this point, this universe is in a stable stage of evolution. Let's take a closer look.' Bai Bing moved the mouse, and the sphere rushed forward, filling the whole screen with black. 'Right, we're in this universe's outer space.'

'There's nothing here?' said Lv Wenming.

'Let's see. . . .' As Bai Bing spoke, he right-clicked and pulled up a complicated window. A script began to calculate the total matter present in the universe. 'Ha, there are only eleven fundamental particles in this universe.' He pulled up another massive data report and read it carefully. 'Ten of the particles are arranged in five mutually orbiting pairs. However, in each pair, the two particles are tens of millions of light-years apart. They take millions of years to move one millimeter with respect to each other. The last particle is free.'

'Eleven fundamental particles? But after all that talk, there's still nothing here,' said Lv Wenming.

'There's space, nearly a hundred billion light-years in diameter! And time, ten billion years of it! Time and space are the true measures of existence! This particular universe is actually one of the more successful ones. In a lot of the universes I created before, even the dimensions of space quickly disappeared, leaving only time.'

'Dull,' harrumphed Chen Jifeng, turning away from the screen.

'No, this is very interesting,' said the Senior Official delightedly. 'Do it again.'

Bai Bing returned to the starting interface, selected a new set of parameters, and initiated another big bang. The formation process of the new universe looked to be about the same as the earlier one, an expanding and dimming sphere. Fifteen billion years after creation, the sphere became fully black: the evolution of the universe had stabilized. Bai Bing moved the viewpoint into the universe. Even Chen Jifeng, least interested out of all of them, exclaimed. Beneath the vast darkness of space, a silvery surface extended endlessly in all directions. Small, colorful spheres decorated the membrane like multicolored dewdrops tumbling on the broad surface of a mirror.

Bai Bing brought up the analysis window again. He looked at it for a while and said, 'We were lucky. This is a universe rich in variety, about forty billion light-years in radius. Half of its volume is liquid, while the other half is empty space. In other words, this universe is a massive ocean, forty billion light-years in depth and radius, with the solid celestial bodies floating on its surface!' Bai Bing pushed the field of view closer to the ocean's surface, allowing them to see that the silvery ocean surface was gently rippling. A celestial body appeared in their close-up view. 'This floating object is . . . let me see, about the size of Jupiter. Whoa, it's rotating by itself! The mountain ranges look amazing when they're coming in and out of—let's just call this liquid water! See the water being flung up by the mountain ranges, along its orbit. It forms a rainbow arc above the surface!'

'It's beautiful, indeed, but this universe goes against the basic laws of physics,' the Senior Official said, looking at the screen. 'Never mind an ocean forty billion light-years deep, a body of liquid four light-years deep would have collapsed into a black hole due to gravity long ago.'

Bai Bing shook his head. 'You've forgotten a fundamental point: This isn't our universe. This universe has its own set of laws of physics, completely different from ours. In this universe, the gravitational constant, Planck's constant, the speed of light, and other basic physical constants are all different. In this universe, one plus one might not even equal two.'

Encouraged by the Senior Official, Bai Bing continued the demonstration, creating a third universe. When they entered for a closer look, a chaotic jumble of colors and shapes appeared on the screen. Bai Bing immediately exited. 'This is a six-dimensional universe, so we have no way of observing it. In fact, this is the most common case, and we were lucky to get two three-dimensional universes on our first two tries. Once the universe cools down from its high-energy state, the odds of having three available dimensions on the macroscopic scale is only three out of eleven.'

A fourth universe manifested. To the bafflement of everyone: the universe appeared as an endless black plane, with countless bright, silvery lines intersecting it perpendicularly. After reading the analysis profile, Bai Bing said, 'This universe is the opposite of the previous one—it has fewer dimensions than our own. This is a two-and-a-half-dimensional universe.'

'Two and a half dimensions?' The Senior Official was astonished.

'See, the black two-dimensional plane with no thickness is this universe's outer space. Its diameter is around five hundred billion light-years. The bright lines perpendicular to the plane are the stars in space. They're hundreds of millions of light-years long, but infinitely thin, because they're one-dimensional. Universes with fractional dimensions are rare. I'm going to make note of the parameters that produced this one.'

'A question,' said the Senior Official. 'If you use these parameters to initialize a second big bang, would it produce a universe exactly the same as this one?'

'Yes, and the evolution process would be identical too. Everything was predetermined at the time of the big bang. See, after physics got past the obfuscation of quantum effects, the universe once again displayed an inherently causal and deterministic nature.' Bai Bing looked at the others one by one. He said seriously, 'Please keep this point in mind. This will be key to understanding the terrifying things we'll be seeing later.'

'This really is fascinating,' the Senior Official sighed. 'Playing God, aloof and ethereal. It's been a long time since I've felt this way.'

'I felt the same,' Bai Bing said as he stood up from the computer to pace back and forth, 'so I played the creation game again and again. By now, I've initiated more than a thousand big bangs. The awe-inspiring wonder of those thousand-plus universes is impossible to describe with words. I felt like an addict . . . I could have kept going like that, never coming into contact with you, never getting involved. Our lives would have continued along our orbits. But . . . ah, hell . . . It was a snowy night at the beginning of the year, nearly two in the morning, really quiet. I ran the last big bang of the day. The superstring computer gave birth to the one thousand two hundred and seventh universe—this one. . . .'

Bai Bing returned to the computer, scrolled to the bottom of the drop-down list, and selected the last set of parameters. He initiated the big bang. The new universe rapidly expanded in a glow of blue light before extinguishing to black. Bai Bing moved the mouse and entered his Universe No. 1207 at nineteen billion years after creation.

This time, the screen displayed a radiant sea of stars.

'1207 has a radius of twenty billion light-years and three dimensions. In this universe, the gravitational constant is 6.67 times 10^{-11} N·m^2 /kg^2, and the speed of light in a vacuum is three hundred thousand kilometers per second. In this universe, an electron has a charge of 1.602 times 10^{-19} coulombs. In this universe, Planck's constant is 6.62 . . .' Bai Bing leaned in toward the Senior Official, watching him with a chilling gaze. 'In this universe, one plus one equals two.'

'This is our own universe.' The Senior Official nodded, still steady, but his forehead was now damp.

Searching History

'Once I found Universe No. 1207, I spent more than a month building a search engine based on shape and pattern recognition. Then I looked through astronomy resources to find diagrams of the geometrical placement of the Milky Way with respect to the nearby Andromeda Galaxy, Large and Small Magellanic Clouds, and so on. Searching for the arrangement within the entire universe gave me more than eighty thousand matches. Next I searched those results for matches for the internal arrangement of the galaxies themselves. It didn't take long to locate the Milky Way in the universe.' Onscreen, a silver spiral appeared against a backdrop of pitch-black space.

'Locating the sun was even easier. We already know its approximate location in the Milky Way—' Bai Bing used his mouse to click and drag a small rectangle over the tip of one arm of the spiral.

'Using the same pattern-recognition method, it didn't take long to locate the sun in this area.' A brilliant sphere of light appeared onscreen, surrounded by a large disk of haze.

'Oh, the planets in the solar system haven't formed yet right now. This disk of interstellar debris is the raw material they're made up of.' Bai Bing pulled up a slider bar at the bottom of the window. 'See, this lets you move through time.' He slowly dragged the slider forward. Two hundred million years passed before them; the disk of dust around the sun disappeared. 'Now the eight planets have formed. The video window shows real distances and proportions, unlike your planetarium displays, so finding Earth is going to take more work. I'll use the coordinates I saved earlier instead.' With that, the nascent planet Earth appeared on the screen as a hazy gray sphere.

Bai Bing scrolled the mouse wheel. 'Let's go down . . . good. We're about ten kilometers above the surface now.' The land below was still shrouded in haze, but crisscrossing glowing red lines had appeared in it, a network like the blood vessels in an embryo.

'These are rivers of lava,' Bai Bing said, pointing. He kept scrolling down, past the thick acidic fog. The brown surface of the ocean appeared, and the point of view plunged lower, into the ocean. In the murky water were a few specks. Most were round, but a few were more complicated in shape, most obviously different from the other suspended particles in that they were moving on their own, not just floating with the current.

'Life, brand-new,' Bai Bing said, pointing out the tiny things with the mouse.

He rapidly scrolled the mouse wheel in the other direction, raising their point of view back into space to once again show the young Earth in full. Then he moved the time slider. Countless years flew past; the thick haze covering Earth's surface disappeared, the ocean began to turn blue, and the land began to turn green. Then the enormous supercontinent Pangaea split and broke apart like ice in spring. 'If you want, we can watch the entire evolution of life, all the major extinctions and the explosions of life that followed them. But let's skip them and save some time. We're about to see what this all has to do with our lives.'

The fragmented ancient continents continued to drift until, at last, a familiar map of the world appeared. Bai Bing changed the slider-bar settings, advancing in smaller increments through time before coming to a stop. 'Right, humans appear here.' He carefully shifted the slider a little further forward. 'Now civilization appears.

'You can only see most of distant history on a macro scale. Finding specific events isn't easy, and finding specific people is even harder. Searching history mainly relies on two parameters: location and time. It's rare that historical records give them accurately this far back. But let's try it out. We're going down now!' Bai Bing double-clicked a location near the Mediterranean Sea as he spoke. The point of view hurtled downward with dizzying speed. At last, a deserted beach appeared. At the far side of the yellow sand was an unbroken grove of olive trees.

'The coast of Troy in the time of the ancient Greeks,' said Bai Bing.

'Then . . . can you move the time to the Trojan Horse and the Sack of Troy?' Lv Wenming asked excitedly.

'The Trojan Horse never existed,' Bai Bing said coolly.

Chen Jifeng nodded. 'That sort of thing belongs in children's stories. It would be impossible in a real war.'

'The Trojan War never happened,' said Bai Bing.

'If that's the case, did Troy fall due to other reasons?' The Senior Official sounded surprised.

'The city of Troy never existed.'

The other three exchanged looks of astonishment.

Bai Bing pointed at the screen. 'The video window is now displaying the real coast of Troy at the time the war supposedly happened. We can look five hundred years forward and back. . . .' Bai Bing carefully shifted the mouse. The beach onscreen flashed rapidly as night and day alternated, and the shape of the trees changed quickly, too. A few shacks appeared at the far end of the beach, human silhouettes occasionally flickering past them. The shacks grew and fell in number, but even at their greatest they formed no more than a village. 'See, the magnificent city of Troy only ever existed in the imaginations of the poet-storytellers.'

'How is that possible?' Lv Wenming cried. 'We have archaeological evidence from the beginning of the last century! They even dug up Agamemnon's gold mask.'

'Agamemnon's gold mask? Fuck that!' Bai Bing laughed harshly. 'Well, as the historical records improve in quality and quantity, later searches get increasingly easy. Let's do it again.'

Bai Bing returned their point of view to Earth's orbit. This time, he didn't use the mouse, but entered the time and geographical coordinates by hand. The view descended toward western Asia. Soon, the screen displayed a stretch of desert, and a few people lying under the shade of a cluster of red willows. They wore ragged robes of rough cloth, their skin baked dark, their hair long and matted into strands by sweat and dust. From a distance, they looked like heaps of discarded rubbish.

'They aren't far from a village, but the bubonic plague has been going around and they're afraid to go there,' Bai Bing said.

A tall, thin man sat up and looked around. After checking that the others were soundly asleep, he picked up a neighbor's sheepskin canteen and took a swig. Then he reached into another neighbor's battered pack and took out a piece of traveler's bread, broke off a third, and put it in his own bag. Satisfied, he lay back down.

'I've run this at normal speed for two days and seen him steal other people's water five times and other people's food three times,' Bai Bing said, gesturing with his mouse at the man who'd just lain down.

'Who is he?'

'Marco Polo. It wasn't easy to search him up. The Genoan prison where he was imprisoned gave me fairly precise times and coordinates. I located him there, then backtraced to that naval battle he was in to extract some identifying traits. Then I jumped much earlier and followed him here. This is in what used to be Persia, near the city of Bam in modern Iran, but I could have saved myself the effort.'

'That means he's on his way to China. You should be able to follow him into Kublai Khan's palace,' said Lv Wenming.

'He never entered any palace.'

'You mean, he spent his time in China as just a regular commoner?'

'Marco Polo never went to China. The long and even more dangerous road ahead scared him off. He wandered around West Asia for a few years, and later told the rumors he heard along the way to his friend in prison, who wrote the famous travelogue.'

His three listeners once again exchanged looks of astonishment.

'It's even easier to look up specific people and events later on. Let's do it one more time with modern history.'

The room was large and very dim. A map—a naval map?—had been spread out on the broad wooden table, surrounded by several men in Qing Dynasty military uniforms. The room was too dark to see their faces.

'We're in the headquarters of the Beiyang Fleet, quite a ways to go before the First Sino-Japanese War. We're in the middle of a meeting.'

Someone was talking, but the heavy southlands accent and the poor sound quality made the words unintelligible. Bai Bing explained, 'They're saying that for coastal defense purposes, given their limited funds, purchasing heavy-tonnage ironclads from the West is less worthwhile than buying a large number of fast, steam-powered torpedo boats. Each vessel could hold four to six gas torpedoes, forming a large, fast attack force, maneuverable enough to evade Japanese cannon fire and strike at close range. I asked a number of naval experts and military historians about this. They unanimously believe that if this idea had been implemented, the Beiyang Fleet would have won their battles in the First Sino-Japanese War. He's brilliantly ahead of his time, the first in naval history to discover the weaknesses of the traditional big-cannons-and-big-ships policy with the new innovations in armaments.'

'Who is it?' Chen Jifeng asked. 'Deng Shichang?'

Bai Bing shook his head. 'Fang Boqian.'

'What, that coward who ran away halfway through the Battle of the Yellow Sea?'

'The very one.'

'Instinct tells me that all this is what history was really like,' the Senior Official mused.

Bai Bing nodded. 'That's right. I didn't feel so aloof and ethereal after this stage. I started to despair. I had discovered that practically all the history we know is a lie. Of all the noble, vaunted heroes we hear about, at least half were contemptible liars and schemers who used their influence to claim achievements and write the histories, and managed to succeed. Of those who really did give everything for truth and justice, two-thirds choked to death horribly and quietly in the dust of history, forgotten by everyone, and the remaining one-third had their reputations smeared into eternal infamy, just like Song Cheng. Only a tiny percentage were remembered as they were by history, less than the exposed corner of the iceberg.'

Only then did everyone notice Song Cheng, who'd remained silent throughout. They saw him quietly stir, his eyes alight. He looked like a felled warrior rising to stand once more, taking up his weapon astride a fresh warhorse.

Searching the Present

'Then you came to Universe No. 1207's present day, am I correct?' asked the Senior Official.

'That's right, I set the digital mirror to our time.' As he spoke, Bai Bing moved the time slider to the far end. The point of view once again returned to space. The blue Earth below didn't look particularly different from how it had appeared in ancient times.

'This is our present day shown through the mirror of Universe No. 1207: after decades of continuous exporting of natural resources and energy, our hinterland province still doesn't have a presentable industry to its name aside from mining and power generation. All we have is pollution, most of the rural areas still below the poverty line, severe unemployment in the cities, deteriorating law and order . . . naturally, I wanted to see how our leaders and planners did their jobs. What I saw, well, I don't need to tell you that.'

'What were you after?' asked the Senior Official.

Bai Bing smiled bitterly, shaking his head. 'Don't think I had some lofty goal like him,' he said, pointing at Song Cheng. 'I was just an ordinary person, happy to mind my own business and live out my days in peace. What do your antics have to do with me? I wasn't planning to mess with you, but . . . I put so much work into this supersimulation software, and naturally I wanted to get some material benefits out of it. So I called a couple of your people, hoping they'd give me a bit of cash for keeping quiet. . . .' He abruptly swelled with indignation.

'Why did you have to overreact? Why did I have to be eliminated? If you'd just given me the money, we'd all be done here! . . . Anyway, I've finished explaining everything.'

The five people sank into a long silence, all of them watching the image of Earth on the screen. This was the digital mirror of the current Earth. They were in there, too.

'Can you really use this computer to observe everything in the world that's ever happened?' Chen Jifeng said, breaking the silence.

'Yes, every detail of history and the present day is data in the computer, and that data can be freely analyzed. Anything, no matter how secret, can be observed by extracting the corresponding information from the database and processing it. The database holds an atomic-level digital replica of the entire world, and any part of it can be extracted at will.'

'Can you prove it?'

'That's easy. You leave the room, go anywhere you want, do anything you want, and come back.'

Chen Jifeng looked at the Senior Official and Lv Wenming in turn, then left the room. He returned two minutes later and looked at Bai Bing wordlessly.

Bai Bing moved the mouse so that the point of view rapidly descended from space to hover above the city, which seamlessly filled the screen. He panned around, searching carefully, and quickly found the No. 2 Detention Center at the city outskirts, then the three-story building they were in. The point of view entered the building, gliding along the empty hallway on the second floor. The two plainclothes detectives sitting on the bench outside appeared onscreen, Chenbing lighting a cigarette. At last, the screen displayed the door of the office they were in.

'Right now, the simulation only lags behind reality as it happens by 0.1 seconds. Let's go back a few minutes.' Bai Bing nudged the time slider left.

Onscreen, the door swung open and Chen Jifeng walked out. The two police on the bench immediately stood; Chen waved them an all's-well and walked in the opposite direction. The point of view followed closely, as if someone were filming from right behind him with a camera. In the digital mirror, Chen Jifeng entered the restroom, took a handgun from his trouser pocket, pulled the trigger, and returned it to his pocket. Bai Bing paused the simulation here and rotated the view around to different angles as if it were a 3-D cartoon. Chen Jifeng walked out of the restroom, and the point of view followed him back to the office, revealing the four people waiting for him.

The Senior Official watched the screen expressionlessly. Lv Wenming raised his head warily and eyed Chen Jifeng. 'That thing really is impressive,' Lv Wenming said with a dark expression.

'Next I'll demonstrate an even more impressive feature,' said Bai Bing, pausing the simulation. 'Since the universe is stored in the digital mirror on the atomic level, we can search up any and every detail in the universe. Next, let's see what's in Chief Chen's coat pocket.'

On the paused screen, Bai Bing clicked and dragged a rectangle over the area of Chen Jifeng's coat pocket, then opened an interface to process it. With a series of actions, he removed the cloth on the outside of the pocket, revealing a small piece of folded-up paper inside. Bai Bing pressed Ctrl+C to copy the piece of paper, then started up a 3-D model-processing program and pasted in the copied data. A few more actions unfolded the piece of paper. It was a foreign exchange check for 250,000 USD.

'Next, we'll track this check to its origin.' Bai Bing closed the model-processing software and returned to the paused video window. Bai Bing right-clicked the already-selected check in Chen Jifeng's coat pocket, then chose Trace from the list of options. The check flashed, and the still screen jumped to life. Time was flowing backward, showing the Senior Official and his retinue backing out of the office, then out of the building, then onto a car. Chen Jifeng and Lv Wenming put on earphones, clearly listening in on Bai Bing and Song Cheng's conversation. The trace search continued, the surroundings continuing to change, but the flashing check remained at the center of the screen as the subject of the search, seeming to tug Chen Jifeng with it through scene after scene. Finally, the check jumped out of Chen's coat pocket and slipped into a small basket, which then jumped from Chen's hand into another person's. At that moment, Bai Bing paused the simulation.

'I'll resume playing here,' said Bai Bing, selecting normal playback speed. They seemed to be looking at Chen Jifeng's living room. Onscreen, a middle-aged woman in a black suit stood with the fruit basket in her hand, as if she'd just entered. Chen Jifeng was sitting on the sofa.

'Chief Chen, Director Wen sent me to visit you, and to express his gratitude for last time. He wanted to come in person, but thought it was best not to show up here too often to prevent idle gossip.'

Chen Jifeng said, 'When you go back, tell Wen Xiong that he'd better stay on the straight and narrow, now that he's in good shape. Going too far all the time doesn't do anyone good. He'd better not blame me for losing patience!'

'Yes, of course, how could Brother Wen forget your advice? Nowadays, he's been actively contributing to society—he's built four elementary schools in impoverished districts. He's also dedicated to making progress in politics. The city has already elected him as its delegate to the National People's Congress!' As she spoke, the visitor set the fruit basket onto the coffee table.

'Take that with you,' Chen Jifeng said, waving a hand.

'We would never bring anything too fancy, Chief Chen. We know how you'd hate it. This is just some fruit as a token of our gratitude. I suppose you haven't seen the way Chief Wen tears up whenever he mentions you. He calls you our loving parents reborn, you know.'

Once the visitor left, Chen Jifeng shut the door and returned to the coffee table. He tipped all the fruit out of the basket, picked up the check at the bottom, and slid it in his pocket.

The Senior Official and Lv Wenming eyed Chen Jifeng coldly. Clearly they hadn't known any of this. Wen Xiong was the director general of Licheng Group, an enormous corporation spanning dining, long-distance travel, and many other services. Its start-up money had come from drug profits from Wen Xiong's crime syndicate, which had made this city into a crucial hub in the Yunnan-Russia drug-trafficking route. With Wen Xiong's successful expansion into aboveboard commerce, his underground business, drawing nourishment from the former, grew even more rapidly. The result in the hinterland city was the proliferation of drugs and the decline of public safety. And Chen Jifeng, the backstage supporter, was a powerful safeguard for its continued survival.

'You took payment in dollars? It must have gone to your son,' Bai Bing said cheerfully. 'The money that's paying for his American college education all came from Wen Xiong, after all. . . . Speaking of which, don't you want to see what he's doing right now, on the other side of the planet? That's easy enough. It's midnight in Boston right now, but the last two times I saw him, he wasn't sleeping yet.' Bai Bing sent the point of view up into space, twirled the Earth 180 degrees, then zoomed in on North America. He found the city splendid with lights on the Atlantic coast, then located the apartment building so quickly it was clear he must have searched it before. The point of view entered an apartment bedroom, exposing an awkward scene: the boy in his room with two prostitutes, one white and one black.

'See how your son's spending your money, Chief Chen?'

Furious, Chen Jifeng tipped the monitor screen-side down onto the briefcase.

The deeply stunned group once again sank into a long silence. At last Lv Wenming asked, 'Why did you spend all this time just running away? Didn't you consider using more . . . conventional means to free yourself from this predicament?'

'You mean, report to Discipline Inspection? Excellent idea, yes. I had the same idea at first, so I used the digital mirror to run a search on the Discipline Inspection leadership.' Bai Bing raised his head to look at Lv Wenming. 'You can guess what I saw. I didn't want to end up like your old college buddy here. In that case, could I go to the public prosecutors or the Anti-Corruption Bureau? I'm sure Director Guo and Chief Chang process the vast majority of serious accusations strictly by the law, and very carefully tiptoe around a small portion. For what I'd report, they'd join you in hunting me down the moment I told them. Where else could I go? Could I get the press to run an exposé? I think you're all familiar with those certain key figures in the provincial news media groups. After all, weren't they the ones who came up with the Senior Official's shining résumé? The only difference between those reporters and prostitutes is that they sell a different body part. It's all tied together in one big web, not a strand safe to touch. I didn't have anywhere to go.'

'You could go to the Central Commission,' the Senior Official said neutrally, closely observing Bai Bing for a reaction.

Bai Bing nodded. 'It's the only choice left. But I'm a nobody. I don't know anyone. I came to see Song Cheng first to find reliable connections, pursuit or no.' Bai Bing paused, then continued, 'But this decision wasn't an easy one. You're all smart people. You know the ultimate consequences of doing this.'

'It means that this technology will be revealed to the world.'

'That's right. Every bit of the fog that covers history and reality will be swept away. Anything and everything, in light and darkness, past and present, will be stripped naked and paraded before the light of day. At that time, light and dark will be forced into a deciding battle for supremacy unlike anything in history. The world's going to descend into chaos—'

'But the end result will be the victory of the light,' said Song Cheng, who'd been silent until then. He walked in front of Bai Bing and looked straight at him. 'Do you know how shadows derive their power? It comes from their very nature of secrecy. Once they're exposed to the light, their power is gone. You see that with most cases of corruption. And your digital mirror is the burning brand that will tear the darkness open.'

The Senior Official exchanged looks with Chen and Lv.

Silence fell. On the superstring computer screen, the atomic-level digital mirror of Earth hovered placidly in space.

'There is an opportunity.' The Senior Official stood up suddenly, said to Lv and Chen, 'There is probably an opportunity.'

The Senior Official put a hand on Bai Bing's shoulder. 'Why don't you move the time slider in the simulation farther forward?'

Bai Bing, Chen Jifeng, and Lv Wenming looked uncomprehendingly at the Senior Official.

'If we can accurately predict the future, we can change the present and control the course the future will take. We'd control everything—young man, don't you think this is possible? Perhaps, together, we can shoulder the great duty of shaping the history to come.'

Bai Bing realized what he was saying and gave a pained smile, shaking his head. He stood and walked over to the computer. He clicked and dragged the time slider bar, extending its length beyond Now into the future. Then he said to the Senior Official, 'Try it for yourself.'

Infinite Recursion

The Senior Official leapt toward the computer, quicker than anyone had ever seen him move, bringing to mind the dark image of a hungry eagle spotting a baby chick on the ground. He moved the mouse with practiced motions, sliding the time past the Now. In the instant that the slider entered the future, an error window popped up.

Stack Overflow

Bai Bing took the mouse from the Senior Official's hand. 'Let's run a debugging program and trace that step by step.'

The simulation software returned to the state it had been in before the error and began to run line by line. When the real Bai Bing moved the slider past the present, the simulation Bai Bing in the digital mirror did the same. The debugging program immediately zoomed in on the digital mirror's superstring computer display, allowing them to see that, on the simulated screen, the simulated simulated Bai Bing two layers down was also moving the slider past the present. Then the debugging program zoomed in on the superstring computer display in the third layer. . . . In this way the debugger progressed layer after layer deeper, each layer's Bai Bing in the process of moving the slider past the present time, an infinite Droste image.

'This is recursion, a programming approach where a piece of code calls itself. Under normal circumstances, it finds its answer a finite number of layers down, after which the answer follows the chain of calls back to the surface. But here we see a function calling itself without end, forever unable to find an answer, in infinite recursion. Because it needs to store resources used by the previous layer on the stack at every call, it created the stack overflow we saw earlier. With infinite recursion, even a superstring computer's ultimate capacity can be used up.'

'Ah.' The Senior Official nodded.

'As a result, even though the course of the universe was decided at the big bang, we still can't know the future. For people who hate the determinist idea that everything comes from a chain of cause and effect, this probably provides some consolation.'

'Ah . . .' The Senior Official nodded again. He dragged out the sound for a long, long time.

The Age of the Mirror

Bai Bing discovered that a strange change had overcome the Senior Official, as if something had been sucked out of him. His whole body seemed to be withering, swaying as if it had lost the strength to keep itself upright. His face was pale, his breathing rapid. He put both hands on the chair's arms and lowered himself into the seat, the movement difficult and painstaking, as if he were afraid his bones would snap.

'Young man, you have destroyed my life's work,' the Senior Official said eventually. 'You win.'

Bai Bing looked at Chen Jifeng and Lv Wenming, finding that they were at a loss like himself. But Song Cheng stood straight-backed and unafraid among them, his face alight with victory.

Chen Jifeng slowly stood, drawing his gun from his trouser pocket.

'Stop,' said the Senior Official, not loudly, but with unsurpassed authority in his voice. The gun in Chen Jifeng's hand stilled in midair. 'Put the gun down,' the Senior Official commanded, but Chen didn't move.

'Sir, at this stage, we have to act decisively. We can explain away their deaths, shot and killed while resisting arrest and attempting escape—'

'Put the gun down, you mad dog!' the Senior Official roared.

The hand holding the gun fell to Chen Jifeng's side. He slowly turned toward the Senior Official. 'I'm no mad dog. I'm a loyal dog, a dog who understands gratitude! A dog who will never betray you, sir! You can trust someone like me, who's crawled step by step up from the bottom, to know right and wrong like a good dog toward the superior who made him into who he is today. I don't think the slick thoughts of intelligentsia.'

'What are you trying to say?' Lv Wenming, who had long been silent, got to his feet.

'Everyone knows what I mean. I'm not like some people, taking a step only after making sure there's two or three steps of retreat open. Where's my road out? At a time like this, if I don't protect myself, who will do it for me?!'

Bai Bing said calmly, 'It's useless to kill me. That's the fastest way to expose the digital mirror technology to the public.'

'Even an idiot would have realized he'd take precautionary measures. You've really lost all reason,' Lv Wenming said quietly to Chen Jifeng.

Chen Jifeng said, 'Of course I know the bastard wouldn't be that stupid, but we have our own technological resources. If we put in everything we have, we might be able to completely wipe out the digital mirror technology.'

Bai Bing shook his head. 'That's impossible. Chief Chen, this is the era of the internet. Concealing and distributing information is easy, and I have the defender's advantage. You can't beat me at my game, not even if you put in your best tech experts. I could tell you where I've hidden the digital mirror software backups and how I plan to release them after my death, and you wouldn't be able to do a thing. The initialization parameters are even easier to hide and distribute. Forget about that idea.'

Chen Jifeng slowly put the gun back into his pocket and sat down.

'You think you're already standing on the summit of history, yes?' the Senior Official said tiredly to Song Cheng.

'Justice stands on the summit of history,' Song Cheng said solemnly.

'Indeed, the digital mirror has destroyed us all. But its power to destroy far exceeds this.'

'Yes, it will destroy all evil.'

The Senior Official nodded slowly.

'Then it will destroy all the corruption and immorality that comes short of evil.'

The Senior Official nodded again. 'In the end, it will destroy all of human civilization.'

His words made the others take pause. Song Cheng said, 'Human civilization has never beheld such a bright future. This battle between good and evil will wash away all its grime.'

'And then?' the Senior Official asked softly.

'And then, the great age of the mirror will arrive. All of humanity will face a mirror in which every action can be perfectly seen and no crime can be hidden. Every sinner will inevitably meet their judgment. It will be an era without darkness, where the sun shines into every crevice. Human society will become as pure as crystal.'

'In other words, society will be dead,' the Senior Official said. He raised his head to look Song Cheng in the eyes.

'Care to explain?' Song Cheng said, with the mocking note of a victor looking at a loser.

'Imagine if DNA never made mistakes, always replicating and inheriting with perfect fidelity. What would life on Earth become?'

While Song Cheng considered this, Bai Bing answered for him. 'In that case, life would no longer exist on Earth. The basis of the evolution of life is mutation, caused by mistakes in DNA.'

The Senior Official nodded at Bai Bing. 'Society is the same way. Its evolution and vitality is rooted in the myriad urges and desires departing from the morality laid out by the majority. A fish can't live in perfectly clear water. A society where no one ever makes mistakes in ethics is, in reality, dead.'

'Your attempt to defend your crimes is laughable,' Song Cheng said contemptuously.

'Not completely,' Bai Bing said immediately, surprising the others. He hesitated for a few seconds, as if to steel his resolve. 'To be honest, there was another reason I didn't want to make the mirror simulation software public. I . . . I don't much like the idea of a world armed with the digital mirror either.'

'Are you afraid of the light like them?' Song Cheng demanded.

'I'm an ordinary guy. I'm not involved in any shady business, but there are different kinds of the light you're talking about. If someone beams a searchlight through your bedroom window in the middle of the night, that's called light pollution. . . . I'll give an example. I've only been married two years, but I've already experienced that . . . wearying of the aesthetics, so to speak. So I got . . . uh, *involved* with a coworker. My wife doesn't know, of course. Everyone's lives are good—better this way even I suspect. I wouldn't be able to live this kind of life in the age of the mirror.'

'It's an immoral and irresponsible life to begin with!' Song Cheng said, anger entering his voice.

'But doesn't everyone live like that? Who doesn't have some sort of secret? If you want to be happy these days, sometimes, you have to bend a little. How many people can be shining spotless saints like you? If the digital mirror makes everyone into perfect people who can't take a step out of line, then— then what's even fucking left?'

The Senior Official laughed, and even Lv and Chen, who'd been grim-faced all this time, cracked a smile. The Senior Official patted Bai Bing on the shoulder. 'Young man, your argument might not be particularly high-minded, but you've thought far deeper than our scholar over here.' He turned toward Song Cheng as he spoke. 'There's no way we can extricate ourselves now, so you can put aside your hatred and thirst for vengeance toward us. As one so well-learned on the subject of social philosophy, surely you're not so shallow-minded as to think that history is made from virtue and justice?'

The Senior Official's words were a potent tranquilizer for Song Cheng. He recovered from the fever of victory. 'My duty is to punish the evil, protect the virtuous, and uphold justice,' he said after a moment of hesitation, his tone much calmer.

The Senior Official nodded, satisfied. 'You didn't give a straight answer. Very good, it shows that you're not quite that narrow-minded yet.'

Here, the Senior Official suddenly shuddered all over, as if someone had dumped cold water over him. He broke out of his daze. The weakness was gone; whatever vitality had deserted him earlier seemed to have returned. He stood, gravely buttoned his collar, and meticulously smoothed the wrinkles from his clothes. Then he said with utmost solemnity to Lv Wenming and Chen Jifeng, 'Comrades, from now on, everything can be seen in the digital mirror. Please take care with your behavior and image.'

Lv Wenming stood, his expression heavy. He attended to his appearance as the Senior Official had, then gave a long sigh. 'Yes, from now on, Heaven watches from above.'

Chen Jifeng stood unmoving with his head hanging.

The Senior Official looked at everyone in turn. 'Very well, I'll be leaving now. I have a busy day at work tomorrow.' He turned toward Bai Bing. 'Young man, come to my office tomorrow at six in the evening. Bring the superstring computer.' Then he turned toward Chen and Lv. 'As for you two, do your best. Jifeng, keep your chin up. We may have committed sins beyond pardon, but we don't need to feel so ashamed. Compared to them,' he pointed to Song Cheng and Bai Bing, 'what we've done really doesn't amount to much.'

He opened the door and left with his head held high.

Birthday

The next day really was a busy day for the Senior Official.

As soon as he entered the office, he summoned key officials in charge of industry, agriculture, finance, environmental protection, and more, one by one, to debrief them on their next orders of business. Though each meeting was short, the Senior Official drew on his ample experience to zero in on important aspects of the work and problems requiring attention. With his well-honed conversational skills, too, each official left thinking that this was only another typical work debriefing. They noticed nothing unusual.

At ten thirty in the morning, after sending away the last official, the Senior Official settled down to document his views on the province's economic development, and problems he foresaw with large-and medium-scale province-owned enterprises. The compilation wasn't long, less than two thousand characters, but it distilled decades of reflection and work experience.

Anyone familiar with the Senior Official's philosophies would be astonished reading this document—it differed considerably from his previous views. In his long years at the apex of power, this was the first time he expressed views unadulterated by personal considerations, solely coming from concern for the Party and the country's best interests.

It was past noon by the time the Senior Official finished writing. He didn't eat, only drank a cup of tea, and continued work.

The first indication of the age of the mirror occurred then. The Senior Official was informed that Chen Jifeng had shot himself in his office; meanwhile, Lv Wenming seemed to be in a trance, compulsively reaching for his collar button and straightening his clothes, as if someone could be snapping a picture of him at any instant. The Senior Official met the two pieces of news with only a smile.

The age of the mirror had not yet arrived, but the darkness was already breaking.

The Senior Official ordered the Anti-Corruption Bureau to immediately assemble a task force; with the cooperation of the police and the related Departments of Finance and Commerce, they were to immediately seize all records and accounts belonging to his son's Daxi Trade and Commerce Group and his daughter-in-law's Beiyuan Corporation, and contain the legal entities according to the law. He took care of his other relatives' and cronies' various financial bodies in the same manner.

At four thirty, the Senior Official began to draft a list of names. He knew that, upon the arrival of the age of the mirror, thousands of officials at or above the county rank throughout the province would be sacked. The immediate concern was to seek suitable successors for key roles within each organization, and the list, meant for the provincial and central leadership, presented his suggestions. In reality, this list had existed in his mind long before the appearance of the digital mirror. These were the people he'd planned to eliminate, supplant, and retaliate against.

It was already five thirty, time to leave work. He felt a gratification he had never experienced before: he had spent at least today as a human being.

Song Cheng entered the office, and the Senior Official handed him a thick stack of documents. 'This is the evidence you obtained on me. You should report to the Central Commission as soon as possible. I wrote a confession last night complete with supporting evidence and added them here. Aside from looking through and checking the results of your investigations, I also supplemented some material to fill in the gaps.'

Song Cheng accepted the documents, nodding solemnly. He didn't say anything.

'In a moment, Bai Bing will arrive with the superstring computer. You should tell him that you're about to inform your superiors of the digital mirror software. The central officials, after considering the matter from all directions, will use it conservatively to begin with. He should therefore make sure the software doesn't leak to the public beforehand. That would pose serious dangers and adverse effects. Therefore, you will have him delete all the backup copies, whether online or elsewhere, that he made to protect himself. As for the initialization parameters, if he told them to anyone else, have him make a list of names. He trusts you. He'll do as you say. You must make sure all the backups are gone.'

'We already plan to,' said Song Cheng.

'Then,' the Senior Official looked Song Cheng in the eye, 'kill him, and destroy his superstring computer. At this point, you can hardly think I'm plotting for my own sake.'

Once Song Cheng recovered from his surprise, he shook his head, smiling.

The Senior Official smiled, too. 'Very well, I've said everything I have to say. Whatever happens next has nothing to do with me. The mirror has recorded these words of mine; perhaps one day, in the distant future, someone will listen.'

The Senior Official waved away Song Cheng, then leaned against the back of the chair. He exhaled, slowly, subsumed in a sense of relief and release.

After Song Cheng left, the clock struck six. Bai Bing entered the office on the dot, carrying the briefcase that contained the digital mirror of history and reality.

The Senior Official invited him to sit. Looking at the superstring computer resting on the table, he said, 'Young man, I have something to ask of you: May I see my own life in the digital mirror?'

'Of course you can, no problem!' Bai Bing said, opening the briefcase and booting up the computer. He opened the digital mirror software, then set the time to the present and the location to the office. The two occupants appeared in real time on the screen. Bai Bing selected the Senior Official, right-clicked, and activated the tracking capability.

The image onscreen began to change rapidly, so rapidly that the whole image window filled with a blur. But the Senior Official, as the subject of the search, remained in the middle of the screen the entire time, steady like the center of the world. He was flickering rapidly, too, but the figure was discernibly becoming younger. 'This is a reverse chronology tracking search. The image recognition software can't use your current form to identify younger versions of you, so it has to track you step by step through your age-related changes to find the beginning.'

Several minutes later, the screen stopped flashing through time, now displaying a newborn baby's slick, wet face. The maternity ward nurse had just removed him from the scale. The little creature didn't laugh or scream; his eyes were open and charming, taking stock of the new world around him.

The Senior Official chuckled. 'That's me, all right. My mother always told me that I opened my eyes as soon as I was born,' the Senior Official said, smiling. He was clearly feigning lightheartedness to conceal the breach in his calm; this time, unlike many other times, he wasn't particularly successful.

'Look here, sir,' Bai Bing said, pointing to a menu bar below the image. 'These buttons let you zoom and change angles. This is the time slider bar. The digital mirror program will continue to move forward in time following you as the search object. If you want to find a particular time or event, it's not that different from how you'd use the scrollbar to look up things in a large document in a word processor. First find the approximate location with large steps through time, then make smaller adjustments, moving the slider left or right based on scenes you recognize. You should be able to find it. It's also similar to the fast-forward and rewind functions on a DVD player, although, of course, this disk playing at normal speed would take—'

'I believe nearly five hundred thousand hours,' said the Senior Official, doing the mental math for Bai Bing. He accepted the mouse and zoomed out, revealing the young mother on the maternity bed, and the rest of the hospital room. There were a bedside table and lamp in the plain style of that era, and a window with a wooden frame. What caught his attention was a spot of red-orange light on the wall. 'I was born in the evening, about the same time as now. Perhaps this is the last ray of the setting sun.'

The Senior Official shifted the time slider, and the image again began to jump rapidly. Time flew past. When he stopped, the screen showed a small circular table lit by a bare bulb hanging from the ceiling. At the table, his plainly dressed, bespectacled mother was tutoring four children. An even younger child of three or four, clearly the Senior Official himself, was clumsily feeding himself from a small wooden bowl. 'My mother was an elementary school teacher. She liked to bring the students having trouble with schoolwork back home for tutoring. That way, she could pick me up from nursery school on time.' The Senior Official watched for a while. His child self accidentally spilled the bowl of porridge all over himself. His mother hurriedly got up, reaching for a towel. Only then did the Senior Official move the time slider.

Time skipped forward a few years. The screen suddenly lit up in a blaze of red, apparently the mouth of a blast furnace. Several workers in dirty asbestos work suits were moving, their silhouettes flickering in and out of the furnace flames. The Senior Official pointed to one of the figures. 'That's my father, a furnace worker.'

'You can change the angle to the front,' said Bai Bing. He tried to take the mouse from the Senior Official, who refused him politely.

'Oh, no. This year, the factory worked everyone overtime to increase production. The workers had to be brought meals by family members, and I went. This was the first time I saw my father at work, from this exact angle. His silhouette against the furnace fire impressed itself into my mind very deeply.'

Once more, years passed in the wake of the time slider, stopping on a clear, sunny day. The bright red flag of the Young Pioneers of China waved against the azure sky. A boy in a white shirt and blue trousers gazed up at it as other hands fastened a red scarf around his neck. The boy's right hand flew above his head in a salute, passionately announcing to the world that he would always be prepared to struggle for the cause of Communism. His eyes were as clear as the cloudless blue sky.

'I joined the Young Pioneers in second grade of elementary school.'

Time jumped forward, and a different flag appeared: that of the Communist Youth League, against the backdrop of a memorial to the fallen. A small group of older children were swearing their oaths to the flag. He stood in the back row, his eyes as bright as before, but tinged with new fervor and longing.

'I joined the Youth League first year of secondary school.'

The slider moved. The third red flag of his life appeared, the flag of the Communist Party this time, in what appeared to be an enormous lecture hall. The Senior Official zoomed in on one of the six teenagers taking their oaths, letting his face fill the screen.

'I joined the Party sophomore year of college.' The Senior Official pointed at the screen. 'Look at my eyes. What do you see in them?'

In that pair of young eyes could still be seen the spark of childhood, the fervor and longing of youth, but there was a new and yet immature wisdom, too.

'I feel you were . . . sincere,' Bai Bing said, looking at those eyes.

'You'd be right. Until then, I still meant every word of the oath.' The Senior Official wiped at his eye, the motion minute enough that Bai Bing didn't notice it.

The slider moved forward another few years. This time it sped too far, but after a few small adjustments, a tree-shaded path appeared on the screen. He stood there, looking at a young woman turning to leave. She turned her head to look at him one last time, her eyes bright with tears. She gave a powerful impression, solemn but resolute. Then she left, disappearing into the distance between the two rows of tall poplars. Tactfully, Bai Bing got up and prepared to leave some space, but the Senior Official stopped him.

'Don't worry, this is the last time I saw her.' He put down the mouse, his gaze leaving the screen. 'Very well, thank you. You may turn off the computer.'

'Don't you want to keep watching?'

'That's all I have worth reminiscing.'

'We can find where she is right now, no problem!'

'That won't be necessary. It's getting late; you should leave. Thank you, truly.'

Once Bai Bing left, the Senior Official telephoned the security station, requesting that the building guard come up to his office for a moment. Soon after, the armed police guard entered and saluted.

'You're . . . Yang, yes?'

'You have an excellent memory, sir.'

'I didn't call you up here for anything important. I just wanted to tell you that today is my birthday.'

Taken by surprise, the guard was momentarily lost for words.

The Senior Official smiled indulgently. 'Send my regards to the ranks. You may go.' The guard saluted, but just as he turned to leave, the Senior Official seemed to think of something. 'Oh, leave the gun behind.'

The guard hesitated, but pulled out his handgun. He walked over and carefully set it on one end of the broad office desk, before saluting again and leaving.

The Senior Official picked up the gun, detached the magazine, and took out the bullets, one by one, until there was only the last. Then he pushed the magazine back in. The next person to handle this gun could be his secretary, or the janitor who came in at night. An empty gun was always safer.

He put down the gun, then stood the removed bullets on the table in a circle, like the candles on a birthday cake. After that he strode to the window, looking across the city to the sun on the verge of setting. Behind the outer city's industrial air pollution, it appeared as a deep red disk. He thought it looked like a mirror.

The last thing he did was to take the small 'Serve the People' pin from his lapel and set it on the flag stand on the desk, beneath the miniature flags of China and the CPC.

Then he sat at his desk, calmly awaiting the last ray of the setting sun.

The Future

That night, Song Cheng entered the main computer room of the Center for Meteorological Modeling. He found Bai Bing alone, looking quietly at the screen of the booting superstring computer.

Song Cheng came over and patted his shoulder. 'Hey, Bai, I've already notified your manager. A special car will arrive shortly to take you to Beijing. You'll give the superstring computer to a central official. Some other experts in the field might listen to your report too. With such an extraordinary technology, it won't be easy to get people to understand and believe it all. You'll have to be patient when you explain and give the demonstrations . . . Bai Bing, what's wrong?'

Bai Bing remained quiet, not turning from his seat. In the mirrored universe on the screen, the Earth floated suspended in space. The ice caps had altered in shape, and the ocean was a grayer shade of blue, but the changes weren't obvious. Song Cheng didn't notice them.

'He was right,' Bai Bing said.

'What?'

'The Senior Official was right.' Bai Bing turned slowly toward Song Cheng. His eyes were bloodshot.

'Did you spend an entire day and night coming up with that conclusion?'

'No, I got the future-time recursion to work.'

'You mean . . . the digital mirror can simulate the future now?'

Bai Bing nodded listlessly. 'Just the very distant future. I thought of a completely new algorithm last night. It avoids the relatively near future, which allows it to sidestep the disruption in the causal chain resulting from knowledge of the future changing the present. I jumped the mirror directly into the far future.'

'How far?'

'Thirty-five thousand years later.'

'What's society like, then?' Song Cheng asked cautiously. 'Is the mirror having its effect?'

Bai Bing shook his head. 'The digital mirror won't exist by that time. Society won't either. Human civilization already disappeared.'

Song Cheng was speechless.

On the screen, the viewing angle descended rapidly, coming to a stop above a city surrounded by desert.

'This is our city. It's empty, already dead for two thousand years.'

The first impression the dead city gave was of a world of squares. All the buildings were perfect cubes, arrayed in neat columns and rows to form a perfectly square city. Only the clouds of sandy dust that rose at times in the square grid streets prevented one from mistaking the city for an abstract geometrical figure in a textbook.

Bai Bing maneuvered the viewing angle to enter a room in one of the cube-shaped edifices. Everything in it had been buried by countless years of sand and dust. On the side with the window, the accumulated sand rose in a slope, already high enough to touch the windowsill. The surface of the sand bulged in places, perhaps indicating buried appliances and furniture. A few structures like dead branches extended from one corner; that was a metal coatrack, now mostly rust. Bai Bing copied part of the view and pasted it into another program, where he processed away the thick layer of sand on top, revealing a television and refrigerator rusted down to the bare frames, as well as a writing desk. A picture frame, long fallen over, lay on the desk. Bai

Bing adjusted the viewing angle and zoomed in so that the small photo in the frame filled the screen.

It was a family portrait of three, but the three people in the photo were practically identical in appearance and dress. One could guess their gender only by the length of hair, and age only by height. They wore matching outfits similar to Mao suits, orderly and stiff, buttoned to the collar. When Song Cheng looked closer, he found that their features still displayed some variation. The effect of indistinguishability had come from their identical expressions, a sort of wooden serenity, a sort of dead graveness.

'Everyone in the photos and video fragments I could find had the same expression on their face. I haven't seen any other emotion, certainly not tears or laughter.'

'How did it end up like this?' Song Cheng asked, horrified. 'Can you look through the historical records they left?'

'I did. The course of history after us goes something like this: The age of the mirror will start in five years. During the first twenty years, digital mirrors will only be used by law enforcement, but they'll already be substantially affecting human society and causing structural changes. After that, digital mirrors will seep into every corner of life and society. History calls it the beginning of the Mirror Era. For the first five centuries of the new era, human society still gradually develops. The signs of total stagnation first appear in the mid-sixth century ME. Culture stagnates first, because human nature is now as pure as water, and there is nothing left to depict and express. Literature disappears, then all of the humanities. Science and technology will grind to a standstill after them. The stagnation of progress lasts thirty thousand years. History calls that protracted period the Middle Age of Light.'

'What happens after?'

'The rest is straightforward. Earth runs out of resources, and all the arable land is lost to desertification. Meanwhile, humanity still doesn't have the technology to colonize space, or the power to excavate new resources. In those five thousand years, everything slowly winds down. . . . In the era I showed you, there are still people living on all the continents, but there's really not much to see.'

'Ah . . .' The sound Song Cheng made resembled the Senior Official's slow sigh. A long time passed before his shaking voice could ask, 'Then . . . what do we do? Do we destroy the digital mirror right now?'

Bai Bing took out two cigarettes, handing one to Song Cheng. He lit his own and drew deeply, blowing the smoke at the three dead faces on the screen. 'I'm definitely destroying the digital mirror. I only kept it around until now so you can see. But nothing we do now matters. That's one bit of consolation: everything that happens afterward has nothing to do with us.'

'Someone else created a digital mirror too?'

'The theory and technology for it are both out there, and according to superstring theory, the number of viable initialization parameter sets is enormous, but still finite. If you keep going down the list, you'll eventually run into that one set. . . . More than thirty thousand years from now, till the last days of civilization, humanity will still be thanking and worshiping a guy named Nick Kristoff.'

'Who is he?'

'According to the historical records: a devout Christian, physicist, and inventor of the digital mirror software.'

Five months later, at the Princeton University Center of Experimental Cosmology.

When the radiant sea of stars appeared on one of the fifty display screens, all of the scientists and engineers present erupted into cheers. Five superstring computers stood here, each simulating ten virtual machines, for a total of fifty sets of big bang simulations running day and night. This newly created virtual universe was the 32,961st.

Only one middle-aged man remained unmoved. He was heavy-browed and alert-eyed, imposing in appearance, the silver cross at his breast all the more striking against his black sweater. He made the sign of the cross, and asked:

'Gravitational constant?'

'6.67 times 10^{-11}N·m² /kg²!'

'Speed of light in a vacuum?'

'2.998 times 10^5 kilometers per second!'

'Planck's constant?'

'6.626!'

'Charge of electron?'

'1.602 times 10^{-19} coulombs!'

'One plus one?' He gravely kissed the cross at his chest.

'Equals two! This is our universe, Professor Kristoff!'

2018-04-01

2018 年 4 月 1 日

TRANSLATED BY JOHN CHU

朱中宜－译

It's yet another day where I can't make up my mind. I've been dragging my feet for a couple of months already, as though I were walking through a pool of thick, heavy sludge. I feel my life being used up dozens of times faster than before—where 'before' is before the Gene Extension program was commercialized. And before I came up with my plan.

I gaze into the distance from a window on the top floor of an office building. The city spreads below me like an exposed silicon die, and me no more than an electron running along its dense nanometer-thick routes. In the scheme of things, that's how small I am. The decisions I make are no big deal. If I could only make a decision . . . But as so many times before, I can't decide. The waffling continues.

Hadron shows up late, again, bringing a gust of wind with him into the office. He has a bruise on his face. A bandage is stuck on his forehead, but he seems very self-possessed. He holds his head high, as though a medal were stuck there. His desk is opposite mine. He sits down, turns on his computer, then stares at me, clearly waiting for me to ask a question. However, I'm not interested.

'Did you see it on TV last night?' Hadron finally asks.

He's talking about the 'Fair Life' attack on a hospital downtown, also the biggest Gene Extension Center in the country. Two long, black burn scars mar the hospital's snow-white exterior as though dirty hands had fondled the face of a jade-like beauty. Frightening. 'Fair Life' is the largest and also most extreme of the many groups opposed to Gene Extension. Hadron is a member, but I didn't see him on TV. The crowd outside the hospital had roiled like the tide.

'We just had an all-hands,' I say in response. 'You know the company policy. Keep this up and you won't have a way to feed yourself.'

Gene Extension is short for Gene Reforming Life-Extension Technology. By removing those gene segments that produce the aging clock, humanity's typical life span can be extended to as long as three hundred years. This technology was first commercialized five years ago, and it quickly became a disaster that's spread to every society and government in the world. Though it's widely coveted, almost no one can afford it. Gene Extension for one person costs as much as a mansion, and the already widening gap between the rich and the poor suddenly feels even more insurmountable.

'I don't care,' Hadron says. 'I'm not going to live even a hundred years. What do I have to care about?'

Smoking is strictly prohibited in the office, but Hadron lights a cigarette now. Like he's trying to show just how little he cares.

'Envy. Envy is hazardous to your health.' I wave away the smoke from my eyes. 'The past also had lots of people who died too early because they couldn't afford to pay the medical bills.'

'That's not the same thing. Practically everyone could afford health care at that time. Now, though, the ninety-nine percent look helplessly at the one percent who have all the money and will live to be three hundred. I'm not afraid to admit I'm envious. It's envy that's keeping society fair.' He leans in toward me from the table. 'Are you so sure you're not envious? Join us.'

Hadron's gaze makes me shiver. For a moment, I wonder if he's looking through me. Yes, I want to become who he envies. I want to become a Gene Extended person.

But the fact is, I don't have much money. I'm in my thirties and still have an entry-level job. It's in the finance department, though. Plenty of opportunities to embezzle funds. After years of planning, it's all done. Now, I only have to click my mouse, and the five million I need for Gene Extension will go into my secret bank account. From there, it'll be transferred to the Gene Extension Center's account. I've installed layers upon layers of camouflage into the labyrinthian financial system. It'll be at least half a year before they discover the money is missing. When they do, I'll lose my job, I'll be sentenced, I'll lose everything I own, I'll suffer the disapproving gazes of countless people . . .

But, by then, I'll be someone who can live for three hundred years.

And yet I'm still hesitating.

I've researched the statutes carefully. The penalties for corruption are five million yuan and at most twenty years. After twenty years, I'll still have over two hundred years of useful life ahead of me. The question now is, given that the math is so simple, can I really be the only one planning something like that? In fact, besides crimes that get the death penalty, once you've become one of Gene Extended, they're all worth committing. So, how many people are there like me, who've planned it but are hesitating? This thought makes me to want to act right now and, at the same time, makes me flinch.

What makes me waver the most, though, is Jian Jian. Before I met her, I didn't believe there was any love in the world. After I met her, I didn't believe that there was anything but love in the world. If I leave her, what would be the point in living even two thousand years? On the scales of life, two and a half centuries sits on one side and the pain of leaving Jian Jian sits on the other. The scales are practically balanced.

The head of our department calls a meeting, and I can guess from the look on his face that it isn't to discuss work. Rather, it's directed at a specific person. Sure enough, the chief says, today, he wants to talk about the 'intolerable' conduct of some of the staff. I don't look at Hadron, but I know he's in trouble. The chief, however, says someone else's name.

'Liu Wei, according to reliable sources, you joined the IT Republic?'

Liu Wei nods, as self-assured as Louis XVI walking to the guillotine. 'This has nothing to do with work. I don't want work interfering with my personal freedoms.'

The chief sternly shakes his head. He thrusts a finger at Liu Wei. 'Very few things have nothing to do with work. Don't bring your cherished university ideals into the workplace. If a country can condemn its president on Main Street, that's called democracy. However, if everyone disobeys their boss, then this country will collapse.'

'The virtual nation is about to be recognized.'

'Recognized by whom? The United Nations? Or a world power? Stop dreaming.'

The chief doesn't seem to have much faith in his last utterance. The territory human society owns is divided into two parts. One part is every continent and island on Earth. The other part is cyberspace.

The latter recapitulated human history at a hundred times the speed. In cyberspace, after tens of years of a disorganized Stone Age, nations emerged as a matter of course. Virtual nations chiefly stem from two sources. The first is every sort of bulletin-board system aggregated together. The second is massively multiplayer online games. Virtual nations have heads of state and legislatures similar to those of physical nations. They even have online armed forces. Their borders and citizenships are not like those of physical nations. Virtual nations chiefly take belief, virtue, and occupation as their organizing principles. Citizens of every virtual nation are spread all over the world. Virtual nations, with a combined population of over two billion, established a virtual United Nations comparable to the physical one. It's a huge political entity that overlaps the traditional nations.

The IT Republic is a superpower in the virtual world. Its population is eighty million and still rapidly growing. The country is composed mostly of IT professionals, and makes aggressive political demands. It also has formidable power against the physical world. I don't know what Liu Wei's citizenship is. They say that the head of the IT Republic is an ordinary employee of some IT company. Conversely, more than one head of a physical nation has been exposed as an ordinary citizen of a virtual nation.

The chief gives everyone on our team a stern warning. No one can have a second nationality. He allows Liu Wei to go the president's office, then he ends the meeting. We haven't even risen from our seats when Zheng Lili, who had stayed at her desk during the meeting, lets out a head-splitting scream. Something horrible has happened. We rush to turn on the news.

Back at my desk I pull up a news site. A broadcast is streaming on the homepage; the newsreader is in a daze. He announces that the United

Nations has voted down Resolution 3617. That was the IT Republic's request for diplomatic recognition. It had passed the Security Council. In response, the IT Republic has declared war against the physical world. It began attacking the world's financial systems half an hour ago.

I look at Liu Wei. This seems to have surprised him, too.

The picture changes to that of a large city, a bird's-eye view of a street of tall buildings, and a traffic jam. People stream out of cars and buildings. It's like the aftermath of an earthquake. The shot cuts to a large supermarket. A crowd pushes in like the tide. Madly, they scramble for cans and packages of food. Row after row of shelves shake and crash into each other, like sandbars broken up by a tidal wave. . . .

'What's happening?' I ask, terrified.

'You still don't understand?' Zheng Lili asks. 'There's no rich or poor anymore. Everyone is penniless. Steal or you won't eat!'

Of course, I understand, but I don't dare to believe this nightmare is real. Coins and paper money stopped circulating three years ago. Even buying a pack of cigarettes from a kiosk on the side of the street requires a card reader. In this total information age, what is wealth? Ultimately, it's no more than strands of pulses and magnetic marks inside computer storage. As far as this grand office building is concerned, if the electronic records in relevant departments are deleted, even though a company holds title deeds, no one will recognize its property rights. What is money? Money isn't worth shit. Money is just a strand of electromagnetic marks even smaller than bacteria and pulses that disappear in a flash. As far as the IT Republic is concerned, close to half the IT workers in the physical world are its citizens. Erasing those marks is extremely easy.

Programmers, network engineers, and database managers form the main body of the IT Republic. They are a twenty-first-century revival of the nineteenth-century industrial army, except physical labor is now mental labor, and gets more and more difficult. They work with code as indistinct as thick fog and labyrinthine network hardware and software. Like dockworkers from two hundred years ago, they bear a heavy load on their backs.

Information technology advances in great strides. Except for those lucky enough to climb into management, everyone's knowledge and skills grow obsolete quickly. New IT graduates pour in like hungry termites. The old workers (not actually old, most are just over thirty) are forced to the side, replaced and abandoned. The newcomers, though, don't last long either. The vast majority of them don't have long-term prospects. . . . This class is known as the technology proletariat.

Do not say that we own not a thing. We're about to reformat the world! This is a corrupt version of 'The Internationale'.

A thought strikes me like lightning. Oh, no. My money, which doesn't belong to me but will buy me over two hundred years of life, will it be deleted? But if everything will be reformatted, won't the result be the same? My money, my Gene Extension, my dreams . . . It grows dark before my eyes. My chest grows tight and I stumble away from my desk.

Zheng Lili laughs then, and I stop. She stands near me.

'Happy April Fool's Day,' a sober Liu Wei says, glancing at the network switch at a corner of the office.

I look at the corner where he just glanced at. The office network isn't connected to the outside world. Zheng Lili's laptop is sitting on the switch, acting as a server. That bitch! She must have gone to a lot of trouble to pull off this April Fool's joke, most of it to produce that news footage. An in-house designer, though, could have used 3-D software to produce that footage. It wouldn't have been that hard.

Others obviously don't think Zheng Lili's joke went too far. 'Oh, come on,' Hadron says to me. 'Practical jokes are supposed to raise the hair on your neck if they're being done right. What's there to be afraid of?' He points at the executives upstairs.

I break into a cold sweat, wondering whether he suspects anything because of my reaction to Zheng Lili's prank. Can he see through me? But even that's not my biggest worry.

Reformatting the world, is that really just the mad ravings of IT Republic extremists? Is this really just an April Fool's joke? How long can the hair that suspends the sword last?

In an instant, like a bright light driving away the dark, my doubt is gone. I have decided.

I ask Jian Jian to meet me this evening. When I see her against the backdrop of a sea of the city's streetlamps, my hard heart softens again. She seems so delicate, like a candle flame that can be snuffed out by the slightest breeze. How can I hurt her? As she comes closer and I can see her eyes, the scales in my heart have already tilted completely to the other side. Without her, what do I even want those two-hundred-plus years for? Will time truly heal all wounds? It could simply be two centuries of nonstop punishment. Love elevates me, an extremely selfish man, to lofty heights.

Jian Jian speaks first, though. Unexpectedly, she says what I prepared to say to her, word for word: 'I've been turning this over in my head for a long time now. I think we should break up.'

Lost, I ask her why.

'Many years from now, I'll still be young. You'll already be old.'

It takes a long moment for me to understand what she's saying. Then I realize what the look on her face as she was walking toward me meant. I mistook her solemn expression as her having guessed what I was about to do. Laughter bubbles through me. It grows until it is loud and pitched at the sky. I am such an idiot. I never considered what era this is, what temptations appear before us. When I stop laughing, I feel relieved. My body is so light, I might float away. At the same time, though, I'm genuinely happy for Jian Jian.

'Where did you get so much money?' I ask her.

'It's just enough for me.' Her voice is low. She avoids my gaze.

'I know. It doesn't matter. I mean, it takes a lot of money for just you, too.'

'My dad gave me some. One hundred years is enough. I saved some money. By then, the interest ought to be sizable.'

I guessed wrong. She doesn't want Gene Extension. She wants hibernation, another achievement of life science that's been commercialized.

At about fifty degrees below zero, drugs and an extracorporeal circulation system reduce the metabolism down to 1 percent of normal. Someone hibernating for one hundred years will only age one.

'Life is tiring, and tedious. I just want to escape,' Jian Jian says.

'Can you escape after a century? By then, no one will recognize your academic credentials. You won't be used to what society will have become. Will you be able to cope?'

'The times always get better, don't they? In the future, maybe I can do Gene Extension. By then, it will surely be more affordable.'

Jian Jian and I leave without saying anything else. Perhaps, one century later, we can meet again, but I didn't promise her anything. Then, she will still be her, but I'll be someone who has experienced another hundred years of change.

Once she is gone, I don't hesitate. I take out my cell phone, log into the online banking system, and transfer five million into the Gene Extension Center's bank account. Although it's close to midnight, I still receive a call from the center's director right away. He says that the manipulations to improve my genes can start tomorrow. If all goes smoothly, it will be over in a week. He earnestly repeats the center's promise of secrecy. Out of the Gene Extended whose identities have been revealed, three have already been murdered.

'You'll be happy with your decision,' the director says. 'Because you will receive not just over two centuries but possibly eternal life.'

I understand what he's getting at. Who knows what technologies may arise over the next two centuries? Perhaps, by then, it'll be possible to copy consciousness and memory, create permanent backups that can be poured into a new body whenever we want. Perhaps we won't even need bodies. Our consciousnesses will drift on the network like gods, passing through countless sensors to experience the world and the universe. This truly is eternal life.

The director continues: 'In fact, if you have time, you have everything. Given enough time, a monkey randomly hitting keys on a typewriter can type out the complete works of Shakespeare. And what you have is time.'

'Me? Not us?'

'I didn't go under Gene Extension.'

'Why?'

After a long silence, he says, 'This world changes too quickly. Too many opportunities, too many temptations, too many desires, too many dangers. I get dizzy thinking about it. When all is said and done, you're still old. But don't worry.' He then says the same thing Jian Jian says. 'The times always get better.'

Now, I'm sitting in my cramped apartment writing in this diary. This is the first diary I've ever kept. I'll keep diaries from now on because I should leave something behind. Time also allows someone to lose everything. I know. I'm not just a long lifetime. The me of two centuries from now will surely be a stranger. In fact, considering it carefully, what I thought at first is very dubious. The union of my body, memory, and consciousness is always changing. The me before I broke up with Jian Jian, the me before I paid the embezzled money, the me before I spoke with the director, even up to the me before I typed out 'even,' they are all already different people. Having realized this, I'm relieved.

But I should leave something behind.

In the dark sky outside the window, predawn stars send out their last, pallid light. Compared to the brilliant sea of streetlamps in the city, the stars are dim. I can just make them out. They are, however, symbols of the eternal. Just tonight, I don't know how many are like me, a new generation setting off on a journey. No matter good or bad, we will be the first generation to truly touch eternity.

太原之恋

CURSE 5.0

TRANSLATED BY ELIZABETH HANLON

韩恩立 —译

Curse 1.0 was born on December 8, 2009.

It was the second year of the financial crisis. The crisis was supposed to end quickly; no one expected it was only just beginning. Society was mired in anxiety. Everyone needed to let off steam, and they poured their energies into creating new ways to do so. Perhaps the birth of the Curse was related to this prevailing mood.

The author of the Curse was a young woman between the ages of 18 and 28. That was all the information that later IT archaeologists could uncover about her.

The target of the Curse was a young man, twenty years old. His personal details were well-documented. His name was Sa Bi[1], and he was a fourth-year student at Taiyuan University of Technology. Nothing extraordinary had occurred between him and the young woman, just the usual, everyday, garden-variety drama that afflicts young men and women. Later there were thousands of versions of the story, and perhaps one of them was true, but no one had any way of knowing what had actually transpired between them. In any case, after things ended between them, the young woman felt only bitter hatred toward the young man, and so she wrote the Curse 1.0.

The young woman was an expert programmer, although it isn't known where and how she learned her craft. In that day and age, despite the ballooning ranks of IT practitioners, the number of people who had truly mastered low-level systems programming had not increased. There were too many tools available, programming was too convenient. It was unnecessary

---

1   The young man was unfortunately named. Sa Bi sounds very similar to the Chinese word for 'stupid asshole'.

to toil through line after line of code like a coolie, when most of it could be generated directly by existing tools. It was even the same for viruses like the one the young woman was about to write. Many hacker tools made creating a virus as easy as assembling a few ready-made modules, or, even simpler still, slightly modifying a single module. The last big virus before the Curse, the so-called 'Panda Burning Incense' worm, was created in this way. The young woman, however, elected to start from scratch, without the assistance of any tools whatsoever. She wrote her code line by line, like a hardworking peasant weaving cotton threads into cloth on a rudimentary loom. Imagining her hunched in front of a monitor, grinding her teeth and hammering away at the keyboard, lines from Heinrich Heine's *The Silesian Weavers* spring to mind: *Old Germany, we weave your funeral shroud; And into it we weave a threefold curse – we weave; we weave.*

The Curse 1.0 was the most widely disseminated computer virus in history. Its success can be attributed to two principal factors. First, the Curse did not inflict any damage on infected host computers. In fact, most viruses lacked destructive intent. The damage they caused was largely the result of shoddy propagation and execution mechanisms. The Curse was perfectly designed to avoid such side-effects. Its behavior was quite restrained, and most infected host computers exhibited no symptoms whatsoever. It was only a certain combination of system conditions – present in approximately one out of every ten infected computers – that triggered the virus, and then it only ever manifested on a given computer once. The virus displayed a notification on the screen of an infected computer that read:

Go die Sa Bi!!!

If you clicked the window, the virus would display further information about Sa Bi, informing you that the accursed was a student at Taiyuan University of Technology in Taiyuan, Shanxi Province, China. He was enrolled in the xx Department, was majoring in xx, belonged in Class xx, and lived in Dormitory xx Room xx. If you didn't click it, the information would disappear in three minutes and would never appear again. The virus was recorded on the computer's firmware, so even if you reinstalled the operating system, the result was the same.

The second factor underlying the success of Curse 1.0 was its ability to mimic operating systems. It was not the young woman's own invention, but she made expert use of it. System mimicry involved editing many parts of the virus' own code to match that of the host system, and then adopting behaviors that were similar to normal system processes. When anti-malware programs attempted to eliminate the virus, they risked damaging the system itself. In the end, they simply gave up, like a housewife unwilling to throw a slipper at a mouse sitting next to the good china.

In fact, Rising, Norton, and other anti-malware developers had put Curse 1.0 in their sights, but they quickly discovered that pursuing it was getting them into trouble, with even worse consequences than in 2007 when Norton AntiVirus mistakenly deleted Windows XP operating system files. This, coupled with the fact that Curse 1.0 caused no real harm and placed a negligible strain on system resources, lead one after another developer to delete it from their virus signature databases.

On the same day the Curse was born, science fiction author Liu Cixin visited Taiyuan on business for the 264th time. Although it was the city he hated most in the world, he always paid a visit to a small shop in the red light district to buy a bottle of lighter fluid for his archaic Zippo lighter. It was one of the very few things he could not buy on Taobao or EBay. Snow had fallen two days ago, and like always, it was quickly packed down into a blackened crust of ice. Liu slipped and fell painfully on his backside. When he arrived at the train station, the pain in his ass caused him to forget to move the little bottle of lighter fluid from his travelling bag to his pocket. As a result, it was discovered during the security check, and after it was confiscated, he was also fined 200 yuan.

He loathed this city.

*

The Curse 1.0 lived on. Five years passed, ten years passed, and still it quietly multiplied in an ever-expanding virtual world.

Meanwhile, the financial crisis passed, and prosperity returned.

As the world's petroleum reserves gradually dried up, coal's share of the world energy balance rapidly increased. All that buried black gold brought the money rolling into Shanxi, transforming the formerly impoverished province into the Arabia of East Asia. Taiyuan, the provincial capital, naturally became a new Dubai. The city had the character of a coal boss who was terrified of being poor again. In those down-and-out days at the beginning of the century, it wore designer suit jackets over tattered pants. Even as unemployed laborers jammed the city streets day in and day out, the construction of China's most luxurious concert hall and bathhouse continued apace.

Now, Taiyuan had joined the ranks of the nouveau riche, and the city howled with hysterical laughter at its own wanton extravagance. The skyline of Shanghai's Pudong district paled in comparison to the colossal high-rises that lined Yingze Avenue, and the thoroughfare, second only to Chang'an Avenue[1] in terms of width, became a deep, sunless canyon. Rich and poor alike flocked to the city with their dreams and desires, only to instantly forget who they were and what they wanted as they tumbled into a vortex of affluence and commotion that churned three-hundred and sixty-five every year.

That day, on his 397th trip to Taiyuan, Liu Cixin had gone to the red light district to buy yet another bottle of lighter fluid. Walking along the city's streets, he suddenly saw an elegant and handsome young man with a striking white blaze in his long dark hair. The man was Pan Dajiao, who had started out writing science fiction, switched to fantasy, and then finally settled somewhere in between. Attracted by the city's newfound prosperity, Pan Dajiao had abandoned Shanghai and moved to Taiyuan. At the time, Liu and

---

1   The thoroughfare that runs east–to–west through Beijing just north of Tian'anmen Gate.

Pan stood on opposite sides of the soft-hard divide in science fiction. This chance meeting was a delightful coincidence.

Tucked away in a *Tounao*[1] restaurant and flushed with liquor, Liu chattered excitedly about his next grand endeavor. He planned to write a ten-volume, three million-character sci-fi epic describing the two thousand deaths of two hundred civilizations in a universe repeatedly wiped clean by vacuum collapses. The tale would conclude with the entire known universe falling into a black hole, like water draining from a toilet bowl. Pan was captivated, and he raised the possibility of collaboration: working from the same concept, Liu would write the hardest possible science fiction edition for male readers, while Pan would write the softest possible fantasy edition for female readers.

Liu and Pan got on like a house on fire, and immediately abandoned all worldly affairs in favour of feverish creation.

*

As Curse 1.0 turned ten years old, its final day drew near.

After VISTA, Microsoft was hard-pressed to justify frequent upgrades to its operating system, which prolonged the life of Curse 1.0 for a time. But operating systems were like the wives of new-made billionaires: upgrades were inevitable. The Curse's code grew less and less compatible, and it began to sink toward the bottom of the Internet. But just as it lay poised to disappear, a new field of study was born: IT archaeology. Although common sense suggested that the Internet, with less than a half-century of history, lacked any artifacts ancient enough to study, there were quite a few nostalgic individuals who devoted themselves to the field. IT archaeology was largely concerned with uncovering various relics that still lived in the nooks and crannies of cyberspace, like a ten-year-old webpage that had never felt the click of a mouse, or a BBS that had not seen a visitor in twenty years but still permitted new posts. Of these virtual artifacts, the viruses of 'antiquity' were

---

1   A traditional local lamb soup.

the most highly sought-after by IT archaeologists. Finding a living specimen of a virus written over a decade ago was like discovering a dinosaur at Lake Tianchi.

It was in this way that Curse 1.0 was discovered. Its finder upgraded the entire code of the virus to a new operating system, thus ensuring its continued survival. The finder didn't announce its existence, probably in order to let his or her precious antique survived in better environment.

This was Curse 2.0. The woman who had created Curse 1.0 was dubbed the Primogenitor, and the IT archaeologist who rescued it became known as the Upgrader.

*

The moment Curse 2.0 appeared online found Liu and Pan next to a trash can in the vicinity of the Taiyuan train station. They were fighting over half a pack of ramen that had been fished from the garbage only moments before. They had slept on floorboards and tasted gall for six years, until at last they had turned out one three million-character, ten-volume work of science fiction and one three million-character, ten-volume work of fantasy. They had titled their works *The Three Thousand-Body Problem* and *Novantamilalands*. The two men had full confidence in their masterpieces, but were unable to find a publisher. So together they sold off every last possession, including their houses, borrowed against their pensions and self-published. In the end, *The Three Thousand-Body Problem* and *Novantamilalands* respectively sold fifteen and twenty-seven copies. This made forty-two copies in total, which sci-fi fans knew was a lucky number. After a grand signing session in Taiyuan (also at personal expense), the two men began their careers as drifters.

There was no city friendlier to vagrants than Taiyuan. The trash cans of the profligate metropolis were an inexhaustible source of food. At worst, it was always possible to find a few discarded nine-to-five pills. Finding a place to live was not much of a problem, either. Taiyuan modeled itself after Dubai, and each of its bus stops was equipped with heating and air conditioning.

If one grew tired of the streets, it was simple enough to spend a few days in a shelter. There they would not only receive food and lodging. Taiyuan's thriving sex industry had answered the government's call and designated every Sunday as a Day for Sexual Aid to Vulnerable Groups. The shelters were popular locations at which volunteers from the red light district conducted their charitable activities. In the city's official Social Happiness Index, migrant beggars ranked first. Liu and Pan rather regretted that they had not adopted this lifestyle earlier.

The weekly invitations of the *King of Science Fiction* editorial department were by far the most pleasant occasions in their new lives. They usually went somewhere fancy, like Tang City Restaurant. *King of Science Fiction* had grasped the essence of what it meant to be a sci-fi magazine. The soul of this literary vehicle was wonder and alienation, but high-tech fantasies had lost the ability to evoke those feelings. Technological miracles were trite: they happened every day. It was low-tech fantasies that awed and unsettled modern readers. So the editors developed a subgenre known as counter-wave science fiction that imagined an unsophisticated future era. Its enormous success ushered in a second golden age of science fiction. In an effort to embrace the spirit of counter-wave science fiction, the *King of Science Fiction* editorial department rejected computers and the Internet wholesale. They accepted only handwritten manuscripts, and adopted letterpress printing. They bought dozens of Mongolian steeds at the price of a BMW per horse, and built a luxurious stable next to the editorial office. The magazine's staff exclusively rode steeds that had never surfed the web. The clip-clop of horseshoes around the city signaled the imminent approach of an SFK company man.

The editors often invited Liu and Pan to dinner. In addition to the stories they had written in the past, it was also in acknowledgement of the fact that, while the science fiction they wrote now could hardly be called science fiction, their adherence to counter-wave science fiction principles was very science fiction. They lived completely offline, was low-tech indeed.

Neither Liu, Pan, nor the SFK staff could ever have guessed that this mutual quirk would save their lives.

The Curse 2.0 thrived for another seven years. Then, one day, the woman who became known as the Weaponizer found it. She carefully studied the code of Curse 2.0. Even seventeen years later in its upgraded form, she could sense the hatred and bile the Progenitor had woven into its code. She and the Progenitor had had the same experience, and she, too, hated a man so much it made her teeth ache. But she thought the other young woman was pathetic and laughable: what was the point? Had it touched a hair on the head of that jerk Sa Bi? She was like the scorned maidens of the last century, sticking pins into little cloth effigies. Silly little games could solve nothing, and would only make her sink deeper into depression. But Big Sister was here to help (in fact, the Primogenitor was almost certainly still alive, but given their age difference the Weaponizer should have called her Auntie).

*

Seventeen years had passed since the birth of the Curse and a new era had arrived – the entire world was caught in the web. Once, only computers had been connected to the Internet. But the Internet of the present was like a spectacular Christmas tree, festooned and blinking with almost every object on Earth. In the home, for example, every electric appliance was connected and controlled by the web. Even nail clippers and bottle openers were no exception. The former could detect calcium deficiencies in nail trimmings and send an alert via text or email. The latter could determine whether the alcohol about to be consumed was genuine, or send notifications to sweepstakes winners. The bottle openers could also prevent users from drinking to excess by refusing to open bottles until enough time had passed. Under these circumstances, it became possible for the Curse to directly manipulate hardware.

The Weaponizer added a new function to Curse 2.0:

>*if Sa Bi rides in a cab, kill him in a car crash!*

In fact, this was hardly a difficult task for the AI programmers of this age. All modern vehicles were already driverless, piloted by the web. When a passenger swiped his credit card to hire a cab, the Curse could identify him via the name on their card. Once Sa Bi was identified as the passenger of a taxi, the ways in which he could be killed defied counting. The simplest method was to crash the cab into a building or drive it off a bridge. But the Weaponizer decided a simple collision would not do. Instead, she chose a far more romantic death for Sa Bi, one more fitting for the man who had wronged Little Sister seventeen years ago (in truth, the Weaponizer knew no better than anyone else what Sa Bi had done to the Primogenitor, and it was possible the fault did not lie with him).

Once the upgraded Curse learned its target was in the cab, it would ignore his selected destination and burn up the road from Taiyuan to Zhangjiakou, which had become a vast wasteland. The cab would park itself deep in the desert and cut off all communication with the outside world (by then the Curse would have taken up residence in the onboard computer and would not need the Internet). The risk of detection was very small. Even if people or other vehicles occasionally drew near, the cab would just hide in another corner of the desert, no matter how much time had passed. The car doors would remain sealed from the inside. That way, in winter, Sa Bi would freeze to death; in summer, he would bake to death; in the spring or fall, he would die of thirst or starvation.

Thus, Curse 3.0 was born, and it was a real curse.

The Weaponizer was a member of a new breed of AI artists. They manipulated networks to produce performance art of no practical significance but great beauty (naturally, the aesthetics of the present era were markedly different from the aesthetics of just a decade ago). They might, for instance, strike up a tune by causing every vehicle in the city to honk simultaneously, or arrange brightly-lit hotel windows to form an image on the building's exterior. The Curse 3.0 was one such creation. Whether or not it could truly realize its function, it was a remarkable work of art in and of itself. As a result, it received high critical praise at Shanghai Biennale 2026. Even though the police declared it illegal due to its intent to cause bodily harm, it continued to percolate through the web. A multitude of other AI artists joined in the collective creation. The Curse 3.0 evolved rapidly as more and more functions were added to its code:

>*If Sa Bi is at home, suffocate him with gas fumes!*

This was relatively easy, as the kitchen in every household was controlled via the web, which allowed homeowners to prepare meals remotely. Naturally, this included the ability to turn on the gas, and Curse 3.0 could disable the hazardous gas detectors in the room.

>*If Sa Bi is at home, kill him with fire!*

This, too, was straightforward. In addition to the gas, there were many things in every household that could be set alight. For example, even mousse and hairspray were connected to the web (which allowed a professional stylist to do one's hair at home). Fire alarms and extinguishers, of course, could also be made to fail.

>*If Sa Bi takes a shower, kill him with scalding water!*

Like the above methods, this was another piece of cake.

>*If Sa Bi goes to the hospital, kill him with a toxic prescription!*

This was slightly more complicated. It was simple enough to prescribe a specific medicine to a target. Pharmacies in modern hospitals dispensed prescriptions automatically, and their systems were connected to the web. The key issue was the packaging of the medication. Sa Bi, despite his name, was no fool, and the plan fell apart if he was unwilling to take the medicine. To achieve this end, Curse 3.0 had to trace medicine back to the factory where it was produced and packaged and then follow it down the sales chain. Ensuring that the fatal drug was sold to the target was complicated, but feasible. And for the AI artists, the more complicated it was, the more beautiful the finished product would be.

>*If Sa Bi gets on plane, kill him!*

This was not easy. It was significantly more difficult than taking control of a cab, because only Sa Bi had been cursed, and Curse 3.0 could not kill others. Since it was unlikely Sa Bi had a personal jet, crashing the plane was not an option. But there was an alternative solution: any plane that Sa Bi boarded would suffer a sudden loss of cabin pressure (by opening a cabin door or some other method). Then, when all of the passengers put on their oxygen masks, only Sa Bi's mask would fail.

>*If Sa Bi eats, choke him to death!*

This sounded absurd, but was actually quite simple. The superfast pace of modern society had given rise to superfast food: a small pill known as a nine-to-five pill. Nine-to-five pills were incredibly dense, and weighed like a bullet in the hand. Once ingested, the pills would expand in the stomach, like hardtack. The key was to tamper with the manufacturing process to produce a rapidly-expanding pill. Then the Curse could control the sales process to ensure Sa Bi was the one who bought it. As soon as he popped the pill on his lunch break and washed it down with water, the pill would balloon out in his throat.

But Curse 3.0 never found its target and never killed anyone. After the birth of Curse 1.0, Sa Bi had been harassed by strangers and hounded by reporters. He had no choice but to change his name, even his surname. There were few people surnamed Sa to begin with, and thanks to the name's indecent homophone, there were exactly zero other people in the city named Sa Bi. At the same time, it was not as if Sa Bi had updated his address and place of employment with the Curse. The virus still thought he attended Taiyuan University of Technology, which made it impossible to locate him. The Curse had been outfitted with the function to search for records of its target's name change in the Public Security Department, but its search was fruitless. So in the four years that followed, Curse 3.0 remained nothing but a piece of AI art.

Then, the Wildcards appeared: Liu and Pan.

A wildcard character was an ancient concept, originating from the Age of Mentors (the ancient era of DOS computing). The two most commonly used wildcard characters were '*' and '?'. These two characters could represent one or more characters in a string. '?' referred to a single character, while '*' referred to any number of characters and was the most frequently used wildcard.

For instance, 'Liu*' referred to every person with the surname Liu; 'Shanxi*' referred to every string of characters starting with 'Shanxi'. A single '*' referred to any and all possible strings of characters. Therefore, in the Age of Mentors, 'del*.*' was a most wicked command ('del' was a delete command, and all file names consisted of a name and an extension separated with a dot). As operating systems evolved, wildcards survived, but as graphical user interfaces began to replace command-line interfaces in popular usage, they gradually faded from the memories of most computer users. But in some software programs, including Curse 3.0, they could still be used.

The Mid-Autumn Festival had arrived. Next to the glittering lights of Taiyuan, the full moon looked like a greasy sesame seed cake. Liu and Pan were sitting on a bench in Wuyi Square. They had laid out the goodies they had scavenged that afternoon: five half-empty bottles of liquor, two half-full bags of Pingyao beef strips, one almost untouched bag of Jinci donkey meat, and three nine-to-five pills. It was a good haul, and the two were ready to celebrate. Just after nightfall, Liu had fished a broken laptop computer from a trashcan. He swore he would fix it up, or else a lifetime of working with computers had been for naught. He squatted next to the bench and set to fiddling with the computer's innards. Meanwhile, Pan continued to air his thoughts about the sexual aid they had received at the shelter that afternoon. Liu enthusiastically invited Pan to help himself to the three nine-to-five pills in the hopes of scoring a large share of the liquor and meat for himself. But Pan was not fooled, and he skipped the pills altogether.

The computer was soon running again, and its screen emitted a faint blue glow as it booted up. When Pan saw that the laptop had a functioning wireless internet connection, he snatched it from Liu's hands. He checked QQ first, but his account had long since been deactivated. Next he checked the *Novolands* website, the Castle in the Sky, Douban, the NewSMTH Tsinghua BBS, Jiangdong – but those links were now broken. He threw the laptop aside and heaved a sigh: 'Long ago, a man flew away on the back of a yellow crane.[1]'

Liu, who had been consolidating the bottles of liquor, glanced at the screen and responded: 'And even Yellow Crane Tower hasn't been left.' He picked up the laptop and began to carefully examine its contents. He discovered many hacker tools and virus specimens installed on it. Perhaps the laptop had belonged to a hacker, and had been ditched in a trashcan as its owner fled from the AI police.

He opened a file on the desktop and found a decompiled C-language program. Liu recognized it: it was Curse 3.0. Casually skimming through the code, he recalled his own days as a digital poet. As the liquor set to work upon his brain, he browsed over the target identification section of the code. At his side, Pan was prattling on about the towering science fiction of bygone years, and Liu was soon infected with nostalgia. He pushed the laptop away and joined Pan in reminiscing. Those were the days! His omniscient, virile epics of destruction had struck chords with so many young men, had made their hearts overflow with martial and dogmatic fervor! But now, fifteen copies… he had sold only fifteen copies! Fuck! He took a big swig from his bottle. The flavor was no longer recognizable but its alcohol content was unmistakable. He was overcome with a hatred for male readers, and then

---

1　引自崔灏的诗歌《黄鹤楼》。——编者注

all men. He fixed a loathsome stare on the target parameters of Curse 3.0. 'Nowerdays there snotta single deshent man alive,' he slurred, as he changed the target name from 'Sa Bi' to '*'.Then, he changed the occupation and address parameters from 'Taiyuan University of Technology, enrolled in xx Department, majoring in xx, living in Dormitory xx Room xx' to '*, *, *, *, *'. Only the gender parameter remained unchanged: 'male'.

By now, Pan, too, was sniveling. He thought of the colorful, profound works of his early years, like poems, like dreams. It was not so long ago that his prose had bewitched hordes of teenage girls. He had been their idol. But now, those young women passed him by without a single glance! What an indignity! Hurling away an empty bottle, he muttered, 'If men are all rotten, shen whad are wimmen?' He changed the gender parameter from 'male' to 'female'.

Liu would not have it. He had nothing against women; his vulgar novels never stood a chance with female readers anyway. He changed the gender parameter back to 'male', but Pan immediately changed to 'female' again. The two men began to argue over how to punish their ungrateful, treacherous readers, and Taiyuan's future vacillated between widowhood and bachelorhood. Liu and Pan began to take wild swings at each other with empty bottles until a patrolman intervened. Rubbing the bumps on their heads, the two men came to a compromise: they changed the gender parameter to '*', thereby completing the wildcarding of Curse 3.0. Perhaps it was the officer's intervention, or perhaps it was their utter inebriation, but three parameters escaped their alterations: 'Taiyuan, Shanxi Province, China.'

Thus, Curse 4.0 was born.

Taiyuan had been cursed.

*

At the instant of its creation, the new version immediately understood the grand mission with which it had been entrusted. Because of the immensity of the task before it, Curse 4.0 did not immediately spring to action. Instead, it gave itself time to penetrate, propagate. Once it was thoroughly entrenched throughout the web, it considered its plan of attack: it would start by eliminating soft targets, and then transition to hard targets and escalate things from there.

Ten hours later, as the first rays of dawn appeared on the horizon, Curse 4.0 went live.

The Curse's soft targets were the sensitive, the neurotic, and the impulsive, in particular those men and women who suffered from depression or bipolar disorder. In an era of rampant mental illness and ubiquitous psychological counseling, it was easy for Curse 4.0 to find this sort of target. In the first round of operations, thirty thousand individuals who had just undergone hospital examinations were notified that they had been diagnosed with a liver, gastric, lung, brain, colon, or thyroid cancer, or leukemia. The most common diagnosis was esophageal cancer (which had the highest incidence rate in the region). Another twenty thousand individuals who had recently drawn blood were informed they tested positive for HIV. This was not a matter of simply falsifying diagnostic results. Instead, Curse 4.0 took direct control of ultrasounds, CT-scans, MRIs, and blood testing instruments to produce 'genuine' results. Even if patients sought a second opinion at a different hospital, the results would remain the same. Of the initial fifty thousand, most elected to begin treatment. But about four hundred individuals, already weary of life, immediately ended it all. In the days that followed, a steady trickle of people made the same choice.

Soon afterward, fifty thousand sensitive, depressed, or bipolar men and women received phone calls from their spouses or significant others. The men heard their wives and girlfriends say: 'Look at you, shit brick. Are you even a man? Well, I'm with [*] now and we are very happy together, so you can go to hell.' For their part, the women heard their husbands and boyfriends say: 'You're really looking your age and, to be honest, you were fugly from the get-go. I have no idea what I ever saw in you. Well, I'm with [*] now, and we are very happy together, so you can go to hell.'

By and large, these fabricated rivals were people the targets already loathed. Of these fifty thousand, most of them sought out their loved one and directly resolved the misunderstanding. But about one percent elected to kill their partner or themselves, and some did both. The Curse picked out a few other soft targets. For instance, it provoked bloody fights between irreconcilably opposed gangs. It changed the sentences of criminals serving long terms or life in prison, and slated them for immediate execution. But overall, the efficacy of these operations was low, and it eliminated only a few thousand targets in total. However, Curse 4.0 had the right attitude. It knew that great things came from small beginnings. It would shy away from no evil, no matter how small, and it would leave no method untried.

In the initial phase of its plan, Curse 4.0 eliminated its own creator. In the years after she created the Curse, the Primogenitor had maintained a rigorous mistrust of men. She had essentially become a surveillance expert, using the most up-to-date methods to monitor her (unwaveringly faithful) husband for twenty years. So when she received one of those phone calls, she suffered a heart attack. Once admitted to the hospital, she was given drugs that further exacerbated her myocardial infarction, and she died at the hand of her own Curse.

*

Five days later, hard target operations commenced. The abnormally high suicide and homicide rates caused by the preceding soft operations had thrown the city into a panic. But Curse 4.0 was still flying beneath the government's radar, so the first few hard operations were conducted with great secrecy. First, the number of patients receiving the wrong drugs skyrocketed. The medicines were packaged normally, but ingesting a single dose usually proved fatal. At the same time, there was a surge in the number of people choking to death at the dinner table. The compression density of nine-to-five pills began to vastly exceed industry standards. Diners, weighing the heavy pills in their hands, thought they were getting great value for their money.

The first large-scale elimination attempt targeted the water supply. Even in a city completely controlled by artificial intelligence, it was impossible to add cyanide or mustard gas directly to the tap water. The Curse 4.0 chose to introduce two species of genetically modified bacteria. While typically harmless, they would produce a deadly toxin when combined. The Curse did not add the two cultures simultaneously. Instead, it added one species first, and when that culture had mostly cleared from the system, the second culture was added. The actual mixing of the two species of bacteria took place inside the human body. As the bacteria met in the stomach or the blood, they would produce the deadly toxin. If the toxin did not prove fatal, when the target was admitted to hospital, he or she would receive medicine that would react with the two bacterial cultures, striking the final blow.

By now, the Public Security Department and the Ministry of Artificial Intelligence Safety had pinpointed the source of the disaster, and were frantically developing specialized tools to combat Curse 4.0. In response, the Curse rapidly accelerated and escalated its operations. Its covert machinations became an earth-shaking nightmare.

That day, during the early morning rush hour, a series of muffled explosions echoed beneath the city. It was the sound of trains colliding. Taiyuan had only recently built its subway. The design process had coincided with the city's explosive growth, so it was a highly advanced system. The maglev trains that zipped through vacuum tunnels became known for their incredible speeds. They were nicknamed 'Punctual Portals' – almost as soon as they stepped into the carriage, passengers arrived at their terminal destinations. The trains' speed made for exceptionally violent collisions. The ground swelled and bulged with the force of the explosions, heaving smoke-belching hummocks skyward, like angry pustules erupting on the face of the city.

Now, almost all of the vehicles in the city were under the control of the Curse (in this day and age, all vehicles could be piloted by AI). These were the most powerful tools in the virus' arsenal. All at once, like particles set in Brownian motion, millions of vehicles began to zigzag recklessly all over the city. Though the whole scene looked chaotic, the collisions actually conformed to rigorously optimized patterns and sequences. Each vehicle was instructed to first run down as many pedestrians as possible. With precise coordination, cars herded people through the city streets and closed together in enormous rings in plazas and other open spaces. The largest such formation was in Wuyi Square. Several thousand cars surrounded the square and then rushed towards the center in unison, swiftly eliminating tens of thousands of targets.

When most of the pedestrians had been eliminated or had taken shelter, the cars began to slam themselves against the nearest buildings, killing all passengers still trapped inside. These collisions, too, were precisely organized. Cars would assemble in groups and concentrate their attacks against high-occupancy buildings. Those in the rear would barrel across the pulverized remains of their compatriots, stacking themselves one by one. At the foot of the tallest building in the city, the three hundred-story Coal Exchange Tower, the cars formed a pile-up that reached ten stories high. The twisted wrecks blazed fiercely, like an immense funeral pyre. The night before the Great Crash, Taiyuan's citizens beheld a peculiar spectacle: the city's taxis had all gathered in long lines to refuel. The virus had guaranteed that their tanks would be full when the moment of disaster came. At the same time, there are hundreds of airplanes which were all out of control taking off from two airports in this city. And then they landed in the urban districts, like an endless rain of firebombs, fanning the flames ever higher.

The government issued an emergency bulletin, declaring a state of emergency and instructing all citizens to remain in their homes. At first, this seemed like the correct response. Compared to the skyscrapers, the Great Crash's assault on residential buildings was not so serious. The streets of the residential districts were much narrower than the city's main thoroughfares, and soon after the Great Crash began, they were completely grid-locked. Instead, Curse 4.0 set about turning each house into a deathtrap. It opened up gas valves and when the air / gas mixture reached an explosive threshold, it lit a spark. Row upon row of apartment buildings were engulfed in flames. Entire buildings were blown sky-high.

The government's next step was to cut all power to the city. But it was too late. Curse 4.0 may have been knocked out of action, but it had accomplished its mission. The whole city was in flames. As the inferno strengthened, its ferocity replicated the effect of the firebombing of Dresden during World War II: as the oxygen was sucked from the air, even those who escaped the fire could not escape death.

*

Because of their minimal contact with the web, Liu and Pan, together with their vagrant brothers, had managed to escape the early operations of the Curse. As the later operations began, they relied on the skills they had honed from years of roving the city streets to keep them alive. With agility that belied their old age, they dodged every car that hurtled towards them. Armed with a deep familiarity with every avenue and alley, they managed to survive the Great Crash. But circumstances soon grew more perilous. As the entire city became a sea of fire, they stood at the center of the four-way intersection near Dayingpan. Suffocating waves of heat billowed down upon them, and flames lashed out from the surrounding skyscrapers like the tongues of giant lizards.

Liu, who had described the destruction of the universe on innumerable occasions, was scared witless. On the other hand, Pan, whose works brimmed with humanist warmth, was calm and collected.

Stroking his beard, Pan looked at the inferno all around them. In drawn-out tones, he mused: 'Who knew . . . that destruction . . . could be so spectacular . . . why did I never . . . write about it?'

Liu's legs caved beneath him. 'If I had known that destruction was so terrifying, I would not have written so much of it!' He moaned. 'Damn me and my big mouth. This is just perfect.'

Eventually, they came to a consensus: the most gripping destruction was one's own destruction.

Just then, they heard a silvery voice, like the touch of an ice crystal in the sea of flames: 'Liu, Pan, come quick!!' Following the voice, they saw a pair of stallions pierce the flames like spirits. Two beautiful young women from the SFK editorial department rode atop the horses, their long hair trailing behind them. The riders pulled Liu and Pan up onto the backs of the horses. Then, like lightning, they took off through the gaps in the blistering sea, vaulting the burning wreckage of cars.

Not a moment later, the smoke cleared from their vision. The horses had galloped onto the bridge that spanned the Fen River. Liu and Pan took deep breaths of the clean, cool air. Holding the slender waists of the young women and enjoying the tickle of hair against their faces, the men lamented that their flight was not longer.

They crossed the bridge into safety. They were shortly reunited with the rest of the SFK editorial department, all mounted on powerful steeds. The magnificent cavalry set off in the direction of Jin Ci Temple, drawing surprised and jealous looks from the survivors fleeing on foot as they passed. Liu, Pan, and the SFK staff spotted a single cyclist among the ranks of the survivors. His presence was noteworthy for a single reason: in this day and age bicycles were connected to and controlled by the web, and the Curse had locked their wheels as soon as it began its assault.

The cyclist was an old man, the man once known as Sa Bi.

Thanks to the Curse's early campaign of harassment, Sa Bi had developed an instinctive fear and abhorrence toward the web. He had minimized his exposure to it in his daily life – by riding a twenty-year-old antique bicycle, for instance. He lived on the bank of the Fen River, near the outskirts of the city. When the Great Crash began, he made a break for safety on his absolutely offline bicycle. In fact, Sa Bi was one of the few people these days who was truly content. He had found satisfaction in a series of romantic affairs, and he was prepared to face death with no complaints or regrets.

Sa Bi and the cavalry crested a mountain on the edge of the city. Standing on the summit, they gazed down at the burning city below. A fierce gale howled through the hills, sweeping in from every direction and down into the Taiyuan basin, replenishing the air lost to the rising heat.

Not far from them, the prominent officials from the provincial and municipal governments were disembarking from the helicopter that had plucked them from the inferno. A draft of a speech still lay tucked inside the mayor's pocket. He had prepared it in advance of the city's anniversary celebrations. It was easy to confirm the birth date of Taiyuan city. According to historical experts, founded in 497 B.C.E. as the capital of the state of Jin, the city had survived the turbulence of the Spring and Autumn period and the Warring States period. During the Tang Dynasty, Taiyuan waxed in importance as a strategic military stronghold in Northern China. The city was razed by Song troops in 979 C.E., but it rose again, flourishing throughout the Song, Jin, Yuan, Ming, and Qing dynasties. It was not just a city of great military significance, but also a renowned hub of culture and trade. The suggested slogan for the city's anniversary festivities was 'Celebrating 2,500 years of Taiyuan!' But now, the city that had survived twenty-five centuries had been reduced to ashes by a sea of flames.

A military radio communications link was briefly established with the central government. The officials were informed that aid was rushing toward Taiyuan from every corner of the country. But communications were soon lost again, and they heard only static. One hour later, they received a report that the rescuers had halted their advance, that and the rescue planes had turned back to base.

Back at the Shanxi Bureau of Artificial Intelligence Safety, a senior director opened his laptop computer. The screen displayed the most recently compiled version of the virus, Curse 5.0. The target parameters for 'Taiyuan, Shanxi Province, China' now read '*, *, *'.

CONTRACTION

坍缩

TRANSLATED BY JOHN CHU

朱中宜 译

The contraction will start at 01:24:17 AM.

It will be observed in the auditorium of the country's largest astronomical observatory. The auditorium will receive images sent back from a space telescope in geosynchronous orbit, then project them onto a gigantic screen about the size of a basketball court. Right now, the screen is still blank. There aren't many people here, but they are all authorities in theoretical physics, astrophysics, and cosmology, the few people in the world who can truly understand the implications of the moment to come. Waiting for that moment, they sit still, like Adam and Eve, having just been created from mud, waiting for the breath of life from God. The exception is the observatory head, impatiently pacing back and forth.

The gigantic screen isn't working and the engineer responsible for maintaining it hasn't shown up yet. If she doesn't show up in time, the image coming from the space telescope can be projected only on the small screen. The historic sense of the moment will be ruined.

Professor Ding Yi walks into the hall.

The scientists all come to life. They stand in unison. Aside from the universe itself, only he can hold them all in awe.

As usual, Ding Yi holds everyone beneath his notice. He doesn't greet anyone and he doesn't sit in the large, comfortable chair prepared for him. Instead, he strolls aimlessly until he reaches a corner of the auditorium, where there's a large glass cabinet. He admires the large clay plate, one of the observatory head's local treasures, propped up inside. It's a priceless relic of the Western Zhou era. Carved onto its surface is a star atlas as seen by the naked eye on a summer night several thousand years ago. Having suffered the ravages of time, the star atlas is now faint and blurred. The starry sky outside the hall, though, is still bright and clear.

Ding Yi digs out a pipe and tobacco from his jacket pocket. Self-assured, he lights the pipe, then takes a puff. This surprises everyone, because he has severe tracheitis. He's never smoked before and no one has ever dared to smoke around him. Furthermore, smoking is strictly prohibited in the auditorium, and that pipe produces more smoke than ten cigarettes.

However, Professor Ding is entitled to do anything he wants. He founded the unified field theory, realizing Albert Einstein's dream. The series of predictions his theory has made about space over a vast scale have all been confirmed by actual observations. For three years, as many as a hundred supercomputers ran a mathematical model of the unified field theory nonstop and obtained a result that was hard to believe: The universe that had been expanding for about twenty billion[1] years would, in two years, start collapsing. Now, out of those two years, there's only one hour left.

White smoke lingers around his head. It forms a dreamlike pattern, as if his incredible ideas are floating out of his mind. . . .

Cautiously, the observatory head approaches Ding Yi. 'Professor Ding, the governor will be here. Persuading him to accept the invitation wasn't easy. Please, I beg you, use the influence you have so that he'll increase our funding. Originally, we weren't going to bother you with this, but the observatory is out of funds. The national government can't give us any more money this year. We can only ask the province. We are the main observatory for the country. You can see what we've been reduced to. We can't even afford the electric bill for our radio telescope. We're already trying now to figure out what to do about this.' The observatory head points to the ancient star atlas plate Ding Yi has been admiring. 'If selling antiquities weren't illegal, we would have sold it long ago.'

At that moment, the governor and his entourage of two enter the auditorium. The exhaustion on their faces drags a thread of the mundane into this otherworldly place.

1　译文为 140 亿年，此处已参照原文修订。——编者注

'My apologies. Oh. Hello, Professor Ding. Everyone. So sorry for being late. This is the first time it hasn't been pouring outside in days. We're still worried about flooding. The Yangtze River is close to its 1998 record high.'

Excitedly, the observatory head welcomes the governor and brings him to Ding Yi. 'Why don't we have Professor Ding introduce you to the idea of universal contraction...' He winks at Ding Yi.

'Why don't I first explain what I understand, then Professor Ding and everyone else can correct me. First, Hubble discovered redshifts. I don't remember when. The electromagnetic radiation that we measure from a galaxy is shifted toward the red end of the spectrum. This means, according the Doppler effect, galaxies are receding from us. From that, we can draw this conclusion: The universe is expanding. We can also draw another conclusion: About twenty billion years ago, the big bang brought the universe into being. If the total mass of the universe is less than some value, the universe will continue to expand forever; if it is greater than that value, then gravity will gradually slow the expansion until it stops and, eventually, gravity will cause it to contract. Previous measurements of the amount of mass in the universe suggested the first alternative. Then we discovered that neutrinos have mass. Moreover, we discovered a vast amount of previously undetected dark matter in the universe. This greatly increased the amount of mass in the universe and people changed their minds in favor of the other alternative, that the universe will expand ever more slowly until it finally starts to contract. All the galaxies in the universe will begin to gather at the gravitational center. At the same time, due to the same Doppler effect, we will see a shift in stars' electromagnetic radiation toward the blue end of the spectrum, namely a blueshift. Now, Professor Ding's unified field theory has calculated the exact moment the universe will switch from expansion to contraction.'

'Brilliant!' The observatory head claps his hands a few times flatteringly. 'So few leaders have such an understanding of fundamental theory. I bet even Professor Ding thinks so.' He winks again at Ding Yi.

'What he said is basically correct.' Ding Yi slowly knocks the ash from his pipe onto the carpet.

'Right, right. If Professor Ding thinks so—' The observatory head beams with happiness.

'Just enough to show his superficiality.' Ding Yi digs more tobacco out of his coat pocket.

The observatory head freezes. The scientists around him titter.

The governor smiles tolerantly. 'I also majored in physics, but the last thirty years, I've forgotten practically all of it. Compared to you all here, my knowledge of physics and cosmology, I'm afraid, isn't even superficial. Hell, I only remember Newton's three laws.'

'But that's a long way from understanding it.' Ding Yi lights his newly filled pipe.

The observatory head shakes his head, not knowing whether to laugh or cry.

'Professor Ding, we live in two completely different worlds.' The governor sighs. 'My world is a practical one. No poetry. Bogged down with details. We spend our days bustling around like ants, and like ants, our view is just as limited. Sometimes, when I leave my office at night, I stop to look up at the stars. A luxury that's hard to come by. Your world is brimming with wonder and mystery. Your thoughts stretch across hundreds of light-years of space and billions of years of time. To you, the Earth is just a speck of dust in the universe. To you, this era is just an instant in time too short to measure. The entire universe seems to exist to satisfy your curiosity and fulfill your existence. To be frank, Professor Ding, I truly envy you. I dreamed of this when I was young, but to enter your world was too difficult.'

'But it's not too difficult tonight. You can at least stay in Professor Ding's world for a while. See the world's greatest moment together,' the observatory head says.

'I'm not so lucky. Everyone, I'm extremely sorry. The Yangtze dykes are ready to burst. I must go right away to make sure that doesn't happen. Before I go, though, I still have some questions I'd like to ask Professor Ding. You'll probably find these questions childish, but I've thought hard about them and I still don't understand. First question: The sign of contraction is the universe changing from redshift to blueshift. We will see light from all the galaxies shift toward blue at the same time. However, right now, the farthest galaxies we can observe are about twenty billion light-years away. According to your calculations, the entire universe will contract at the same moment. If that's the case, it should be about twenty billion years before we can see the blueshift from them. Even the closest star system, Alpha Centauri, should still need four years.'

Ding Yi slowly lets out a puff of smoke. It floats in the air like a minimal spiral galaxy.

'Very good. You can understand a little. It makes you seem like a physics student, albeit still a superficial one. Yes, we will see all the stars in the universe blueshift at the same time, not one at a time from four years to twenty billion years from now. This is due to quantum effects over a cosmic scale. Its mathematical model is extremely complex. It's the most difficult idea in physics and cosmology to explain. I have no hope of making you understand it. From this, though, you've already received the first revelation. It warns you that the effects produced from the universe contracting will be more complex than what people imagine. Do you still have questions? Oh, you don't have to go right away. What you have to take care of is not as urgent as you think.'

'Compared to your entire universe, the flooding of the Yangtze River is obviously not worth mentioning. But while the mysterious universe admittedly has its appeal, the real world still takes priority. I really must go. Thank you, Professor Ding, for the physics lesson. I hope everyone sees what they want to see tonight.'

'You don't understand what I mean,' Ding Yi says. 'There must be many workers battling the flood right now.'

'I have my responsibilities, Professor Ding. I must go.'

'You still don't understand what I mean. I'm saying those workers must be extremely tired. You can let them go.'

Everyone is dumbstruck.

'What . . . let them go? To do what? Watch the universe contract?'

'If they aren't interested, they can go home and sleep.'

'Professor Ding, surely you're joking!'

'I'm serious. There's no point to what they're doing.'

'Why?'

'Because of the contraction.'

After a long silence, the governor points at the ancient star atlas plate displayed in the corner of the auditorium: 'Professor Ding, the universe has been expanding all along, but from ancient times until today, the universe that we can see hasn't changed much. Contracting is the same. The extent of humanity in space-time, compared to that of the universe, is negligible. Besides the importance to pure theory, I don't believe the contraction will have any effect on human life. In fact, after one hundred million years, we still won't observe even a tiny shift caused by contraction, assuming we're still around.'

'One and a half billion years,' Ding Yi says. 'Even with our most accurate instruments, it will be one and a half billion years before we can observe the shift. By then, the sun will already have gone out. We probably won't be around.'

'And the complete contraction of the universe needs about twenty billion years. Humanity is a dewdrop on the great tree of the universe. During its brief life span, it absolutely cannot perceive the maturing of the great tree. You surely don't believe the ridiculous rumors from the internet that the contraction will squash the Earth flat!'

A young woman enters, her face pale and her gaze gloomy. She's the engineer responsible for the gigantic screen.

'Miss Zhang, this is inexcusable! Do you know what time it is?' The flustered observatory head rushes to her as he shouts.

'My father just died at the hospital.'

The observatory head's anger dissipates instantly. 'I'm so sorry. I didn't know. But considering . . .'

The engineer doesn't say any more. She just walks silently over to the computer that controls the screen and sinks herself into diagnosing the problem. Ding Yi, biting his pipe, walks over to her slowly.

'If you truly understood the meaning of the universe contracting, your father's death wouldn't grieve you so much.'

Ding Yi's words infuriate everyone there. The engineer stands suddenly. Her face grows red with fury. Tears fill her eyes.

'You're not from this world! Perhaps compared to your universe, fathers aren't much, but mine's important to me. They're important to us ordinary people! And your contraction, that's just the frequency of light that can't possibly be weaker in the night sky changing a little. Without precise instruments to amplify it over ten thousand times, no one can see even the change, not to mention the light in the first place. What is the contraction? As far as ordinary people are concerned, it's nothing! The universe expanding or contracting, what's the difference? But fathers are important to us. Do you understand?'

When the engineer realizes who she lost her temper to, she masters herself, then turns back to her work.

Ding Yi sighs, shaking his head. He says to the governor, 'Yes, like you said, two worlds. Our world.' He waves his hand, drawing a circle around the physicists and cosmologists in the room, then points at the physicists. 'Small scale is ten-quadrillionths of a millimeter.' He points at the cosmologists. 'Large scale is ten billion light-years. This is a world that you can grasp only through imagination. Your world has the floods of Yangtze River, tight budgets, dead and living fathers . . . a practical world. But what's lamentable is people always want to separate the two worlds.'

'But you can see that they're separate,' the governor says.

'No! Although elementary particles are tiny, we are made of them. Although the universe is vast, we are inside it. Every change in the microscopic and macroscopic world affects everything.'

'But what is the coming contraction going to affect?'

Ding Yi starts to laugh loudly. It's not just a nervous laugh, but also seems to embody something mystical. It scares the hell out of everyone.

'Okay, physics student. Please recite what you remember about the relationship between space-time and matter.'

The governor, like a pupil, recites: 'As proved by the theories of relativity and quantum physics that form modern physics, time and space cannot be separated from matter. They have no independent existence. There is no absolute space-time. Time, space, and the material world are all inextricably linked together.'

'Very good. But who truly understands this? You?' Ding Yi first asks the governor, then turns to the observatory head. 'You?' Then to the engineer buried in her work. 'You?' Then to the technicians in the auditorium. 'You?' Then, finally, to the scientists. 'Not even you? No, none of you understand. You still think of the universe in terms of absolute space-time as naturally as you stamp your feet on the ground. Absolute space-time is your ground. You have no way to leave it. Speaking of expansion and contraction, you believe that's just the stars in space scattering and gathering in absolute space-time.'

As he speaks, he strolls to the glass display case, opens its door, then takes out the irreplaceable star atlas plate. He runs a hand lightly over its surface, admiring it. The observatory head nervously holds his hands beneath the plate to protect it. This treasure has been here for over twenty years and no hand has dared to touch it until now. The observatory head waits anxiously for Ding Yi to put the star atlas plate back, but he doesn't. Instead, he flings the plate away.

The priceless ancient treasure lies on the carpet, smashed into too many pieces to count.

The air freezes. Everyone stares dumbstruck. Ding Yi continues his leisurely stroll, the only moving element in this deadlocked world. He continues to speak.

'Space-time and matter are not separable. The expansion and contraction of the universe comprises the whole of space-time. Yes, my friends, they comprise all of time and space!'

Another cracking sound rings through the room. It's a glass cup that fell out of a physicist's grasp. What shocks the physicists isn't what shocks everyone else. It isn't the star atlas plate. It's what Ding Yi's words imply.

'What you're saying . . .' A cosmologist fixes his gaze on Ding Yi. His words catch in his throat.

'Yes.' Ding Yi nods, then says to the governor, 'They understand now.'

'So, this is the meaning of the negative time parameter in the calculated result of the unified mathematical model?' a physicist blurts. Ding Yi nods.

'Why didn't you announce this to the world earlier? You have no sense of responsibility!' another physicist shouts.

'What would be the point? It could have only caused global chaos. What can we do about space-time?'

'What are you all talking about?' the governor asks, bewildered.

'The contraction . . .' the observatory head, also an astrophysicist, mumbles as if he were dreaming. 'The contraction of the universe will influence humanity?'

'Influence? No, it will change it completely.'

'What can it change?'

The scientists are scrambling to recalibrate their thoughts. No one answers him.

'Tell me, all of you, when the universe contracts or when the blueshift starts, what will happen?' the governor, now worried, asks.

'Time will play back,' Ding Yi answers.

'. . .Play back?' The governor looks at the observatory head, puzzled, then at Ding Yi.

'Time will flow backward,' the observatory head says.

The gigantic screen has been repaired. The magnificent universe appears on it. To better observe the contraction, computers process the image the space telescope returns to exaggerate the effect of the frequency shift in the visual range. Right now, the light all the stars and galaxies emit appears red on the screen to represent the redshift of the still-expanding universe. Once the contraction starts, they will all turn blue at once. A countdown appears on a corner of the screen: 150 seconds.

'Time has followed the expansion of the universe for about twenty billion years, but now, there isn't even three minutes of expansion left. Afterward, time will follow the contraction of the universe. Time will flow backward.' Ding Yi walks over to the stupefied observatory head, pointing at the smashed star atlas plate. 'Don't worry about this relic. Not long after the blueshift, its shattered pieces will fuse back together like new. It will return to the display case. After many years, it will return to the ground where it was buried. After thousands of years, it will return to a burning kiln, then become a ball of moist clay in the hands of an ancient astronomer. . . .'

He walks to the young engineer. 'And you don't need to grieve your father. He will come back to life and you two will reunite soon. If your father is so important to you, then you should take comfort from this because, in the contracting universe, he will live longer than you. He will see you, his daughter, leave the world as an infant. Yes, we old folk will have all just started life's journey and you young folk will have already entered your declining years. Or maybe your childhood.'

He returns to the governor. 'The Yangtze River will never overflow its dykes during your term of office if it hasn't done so, because there's only one hundred seconds left to this universe. The contracting universe's future is the expanding universe's past. The greatest danger won't occur until 1998. By then, though, you will be a child. It won't be your responsibility. There's still a minute. It doesn't matter what you do now. There won't be any consequences in the future. Everyone can do what they like and not worry about the future. There is no future now. As for me, I now just do what I wanted to do but couldn't because of my tracheitis.' He digs out a bowl of tobacco from a pocket with his pipe. He lights the pipe, then smokes contentedly.

The blueshift countdown: fifty seconds.

'This can't be!' the governor shouts. 'It's illogical. Time playing back? If everything will go in reverse, are you saying that we'll speak backward? That's inconceivable!'

'You'll get used to it.'

The blueshift countdown: forty seconds.

'In other words, afterward, everything will be repeated. History and life will become boring and predictable.'

'No, it won't. You will be in another time. The current past will become your future. We are now in the future of that time. You can't remember the future. Once the blueshift starts, your future will become blank. You won't remember any of it. You won't know any of it.'

The blueshift countdown: twenty seconds.

'This can't be!'

'As you will discover, going from old age to youth, from maturity to naïveté, is quite rational, quite natural. If anyone speaks about time going in another direction, you will think he's a fool. There's about ten seconds left. Soon, in about ten seconds, the universe will pass through a singularity. Time won't exist in that moment. After that, we will enter the contracting universe.'

The blueshift countdown: eight seconds.

'This can't be! This really can't be!!'

'No matter. You'll know soon.'

The blueshift countdown: five, four, three, two, one, zero.

The starlight in the universe changes from a troublesome red to an empty white . . .

. . .time reaches a singularity. . .

. . .starlight changes from white to a beautiful, tranquil blue. The blueshift has begun. The contraction has begun.

. . .

. . .

.nugeb sah noitcartnoc ehT .nugeb sah tfihseulb ehT .eulb liuqnart ,lufituaeb a ot etihw morf segnahc thgilrats . . .

. . .ytiralugnis a sehcaer emit . . .

. . .etihw ytpme na ot der emoselbuort a morf segnahc esrevinu eht ni thgilrats ehT

.orez ,eno ,owt ,eerht ,ruof ,evif :nwodtnuoc tfihseulb ehT

'.noos wonk ll'uoY .rettam oN'

'!!eb t'nac yllaer sihT !eb t'nac sihT'

.sdnoces thgie :nwodtnuoc tfihseulb ehT

'.esrevinu gnitcartnoc eht retne lliw ew ,taht retfA .tnemom taht ni tsixe t'now emiT . ytiralugnis a hguorht ssap lliw esrevinu eht ,sdnoces net tuoba ni ,nooS .tfel sdnoces net tuoba s'erehT .loof a s'eh kniht lliw uoy ,noitcerid rehtona ni gniog emit tuoba skaeps enoyna fI .larutan etiuq...'

赡养上帝

TAKING CARE OF GOD

TRANSLATED BY KEN LIU

刘宇昆 — 译

Chapter 1

Once again, God had upset Qiusheng's family.

This had begun as a very good morning. A thin layer of white fog floated at the height of a man over the fields around Xicen village like a sheet of rice paper that had just become blank: the quiet countryside being the painting that had fallen out of the paper. The first rays of morning fell on the scene, and the year's earliest dewdrops entered the most glorious period of their brief life . . . but God had ruined this beautiful morning.

God had gotten up extra early and gone into the kitchen to warm some milk for himself. Ever since the start of the Era of Support, the milk market had prospered. Qiusheng's family had bought a milk cow for a bit more than ten thousand yuan, and then, imitating others, mixed the milk with water to sell. The unadulterated milk had also become one of the staples for the family's God.

After the milk was warm, God took the bowl into the living room to watch TV without turning off the liquefied petroleum gas stove.

When Qiusheng's wife, Yulian, returned from cleaning the cowshed and the pigsty, she could smell gas all over the house. Covering her nose with a towel, she rushed into the kitchen to turn off the stove, opened the window, and turned on the fan.

'You old fool! You're going to get the whole family killed!' Yulian shouted into the living room. The family had switched to using liquefied petroleum gas for cooking only after they began supporting God. Qiusheng's father had always been opposed to it, saying that gas was not as good as honeycomb coal briquettes. Now he had even more ammunition for his argument.

As was his wont, God stood with his head lowered contritely, his broom-like white beard hanging past his knees, smiling like a kid who knew he had done something wrong. 'I . . . I took down the pot for heating the milk. Why didn't it turn off by itself?'

'You think you're still on your spaceship?' Qiusheng said, coming down the stairs. 'Everything here is dumb. We aren't like you, being waited on hand and foot by smart machines. We have to work hard with dumb tools. That's how we put rice in our bowls!'

'We also worked hard. Otherwise how did you come to be?' God said carefully.

'Enough with the "how did you come to be?"Enough! I'm sick of hearing it. If you're so powerful, go and make other obedient children to support you!' Yulian threw her towel on the ground.

'Forget it. Just forget it,' Qiusheng said. He was always the one who made peace. 'Let's eat.'

Bingbing got up. As he came down the stairs, he yawned. 'Ma, Pa, God was coughing all night. I couldn't sleep.'

'You don't know how good you have it,' Yulian said. 'Your dad and I were in the room next to his. You don't hear us complaining, do you?'

As though triggered, God began to cough again. He coughed like he was playing his favorite sport with great concentration.

Yulian stared at God for a few seconds before sighing. 'I must have the worst luck in eight generations.'Still angry, she left for the kitchen to cook breakfast.

God sat silently through breakfast with the rest of the family. He ate one bowl of porridge with pickled vegetables and half a *mantou* bun. During the entire time he had to endure Yulian's disdainful looks – maybe she was still mad about the liquefied petroleum gas, or maybe she thought he ate too much.

After breakfast, as usual, God got up quickly to clean the table and wash the dishes in the kitchen. Standing just outside the kitchen, Yulian shouted, 'Don't use detergent if there's no grease on the bowl! Everything costs money.

The pittance they pay for your support? Ha!'

God grunted nonstop to show that he understood.

Qiusheng and Yulian left for the fields. Bingbing left for school. Only now did Qiusheng's father get up. Still not fully awake, he came downstairs, ate two bowls of porridge, and filled his pipe with tobacco. At last he remembered God's existence.

'Hey, old geezer, stop the washing. Come out and play a game with me!' he shouted into the kitchen.

God came out of the kitchen, wiping his hands on his apron. He nodded ingratiatingly at Qiusheng's father. Playing Chinese Chess with the old man was a tough chore for God; winning and losing both had unpleasant consequences. If God won, Qiusheng's father would get mad: *You old idiot! You trying to show me up? Shit! You're God! Beating me is no great accomplishment at all. Why can't you learn some manners? You've lived under this roof long enough!* But if God lost, Qiusheng's father would still get mad: *You old idiot! I'm the best chess player for fifty kilometers. Beating you is easier than squishing a bedbug. You think I need you to let me win? You . . . to put it politely, you are* insulting *me!*

In any case, the final result was the same: the old man flipped the board, and the pieces flew everywhere. Qiusheng's father was infamous for his bad temper, and now he'd finally found a punching bag in God.

But the old man didn't hold a grudge. Every time after God picked up the board and put the pieces back quietly, he sat down and played with God again – and the whole process was repeated. After a few cycles of this, both of them were tired, and it was almost noon.

God then got up to wash the vegetables. Yulian didn't allow him to cook because she said God was a terrible cook. But he still had to wash the vegetables. Later, when Qiusheng and Yulian returned from the fields, if the vegetables hadn't been washed, she would be on him again with another round of bitter, sarcastic scolding.

While God washed the vegetables, Qiusheng's father left to visit the neighbors. This was the most peaceful part of God's day. The noon sun filled every crack in the brick-lined yard and illuminated the deep crevasses in his memory. During such periods God often forgot his work and stood quietly, lost in thought. Only when the noise of the villagers returning from the fields filled the air would he be startled awake and hurry to finish his washing.

He sighed. *How could life have turned out like this?*

This wasn't only God's sigh. It was also the sigh of Qiusheng, Yulian, and Qiusheng's father. It was the sigh of more than five billion people and two billion Gods on Earth.

Chapter 2

It all began with an autumn evening three years ago.

'Come quickly! There are toys in the sky!' Bingbing shouted in the yard. Qiusheng and Yulian raced out of the house, looked up, and saw that the sky really was filled with toys, or at least objects whose shapes could only belong to toys.

The objects spread out evenly across the dome of the sky. In the dusk, each reflected the light of the setting sun – already below the horizon – and each shone as bright as the full moon. The light turned Earth's surface as bright as it is at noon. But the light came from every direction and left no shadow, as though the whole world was illuminated by a giant surgical lamp.

At first, everyone thought the objects were within our atmosphere because they were so clear. But eventually, humans learned that these objects were just enormous. They were hovering about thirty thousand kilometers away in geostationary orbits.

There were a total of 21,513 spaceships. Spread out evenly across the sky, they formed a thin shell around Earth. This was the result of a complex set of maneuvers that brought all the ships to their final locations simultaneously. In this manner, the alien ships avoided causing life-threatening tides in the oceans due to their imbalanced mass. The gesture assured humans somewhat, as it was at least some evidence that the aliens did not bear ill will toward

Earth.

During the next few days, all attempts at communicating with the aliens failed. The aliens maintained absolute silence in the face of repeated queries. At the same time, Earth became a nightless planet. Tens of thousands of spaceships reflected so much sunlight onto the night side of Earth that it was as bright as day, while on the day side, the ships cast giant shadows onto the ground periodically. The horrible sight pushed the psychological endurance of the human race to the limit, so that most ignored yet another strange occurrence on the surface of the planet and did not connect it with the fleet of spaceships in the sky.

Across the great cities of the world, wandering old people had begun to appear. All of them had the same features: extreme old age, long white hair and beards, long white robes. At first, before the white robe, white beard, and white hair got dirty, they looked like a bunch of snowmen. The wanderers did not appear to belong to any particular race, as though all ethnicities were mixed in them. They had no documents to prove their citizenship or identity and could not explain their own history.

All they could do was to gently repeat, in heavily accented versions of various local languages, the same words to all passersby:

'We are God. Please, considering that we created this world, would you give us a bit of food?'

If only one or two old wanderers had said this, then they would have been sent to a shelter or nursing home, like the homeless with dementia. But millions of old men and women all saying the same thing – that was an entirely different thing.

Within half a month, the number of old wanderers had increased to more than thirty million. All over the streets of New York, Beijing, London, Moscow . . . these old people could be seen everywhere, shuffling around in traffic-stopping crowds. Sometimes it seemed as if there were more of them than the original inhabitants of the cities.

The most horrible part of their presence was that they all repeated the same thing: 'We are God. Please, considering that we created this world, would you give us a bit of food?'

Only now did humans turn their attention from the spaceships to the uninvited guests. Recently, large-scale meteor showers had been occurring over every continent. After every impressive display of streaking meteors, the number of old wanderers in the corresponding region greatly increased. After careful observation, the following incredible fact was discovered: the old wanderers came out of the sky, from those alien spaceships.

One by one, they leaped into the atmosphere as though diving into a swimming pool, each wearing a suit made from a special film. As the friction from the atmosphere burned away the surface of the suits, the film kept the heat away from the wearer and slowed their descent. Careful design ensured that the deceleration never exceeded 4G, well within the physical tolerance of the bodies of the old wanderers. Finally, at the moment of their arrival at the surface, their velocity was close to zero, as though they had just jumped down from a bench. Even so, many of them still managed to sprain their ankles. Simultaneously, the film around them had been completely burned away, leaving no trace.

The meteor showers continued without stopping. More wanderers fell to Earth. Their number rose to almost one hundred million.

The government of every country attempted to find one or more representatives among the wanderers. But the wanderers claimed that the 'Gods' were absolutely equal, and any one of them could represent all of them. Thus, at the emergency session of the United Nations General Assembly, one random old wanderer, who was found in Times Square and who now spoke passable English, entered the General Assembly Hall.

He was clearly among the earliest to land: his robe was dirty and full of holes, and his white beard was covered with dirt, like a mop. There was no halo over his head, but a few loyal flies did hover there. With the help of a ratty bamboo walking stick, he shuffled his way to the round meeting table and lowered himself under the gaze of the leaders. He looked up at the Secretary-General, and his face displayed the childlike smile particular to all the old wanderers.

'I . . . ha— . . . I haven't had breakfast yet.'

So breakfast was brought. All across the world, people stared as he ate like a starved man, choking a few times. Toast, sausages, and a salad were quickly gone, followed by a large glass of milk. Then he showed his innocent smile to the Secretary-General again.

'Haha . . . uh . . . is there any wine? Just a tiny cup will do.'

So a glass of wine was brought. He sipped at it, nodding with satisfaction. 'Last night, a bunch of new arrivals took over my favorite subway grille, one that blew out warm air. I had to find a new place to sleep in the Square. But now with a bit of wine, my joints are coming back to life. . . . You, can you massage my back a little? Just a little.'

The Secretary-General began to massage his back. The old wanderer shook his head, sighed, and said, 'Sorry to be so much trouble to you.'

'Where are you from?' asked the President of the United States.

The old wanderer shook his head. 'A civilization only has a fixed location in her infancy. Planets and stars are unstable and changing. The civilization must then move. By the time she becomes a young woman, she has already moved multiple times. Then they will make this discovery: no planetary environment is as stable as a sealed spaceship. So they'll make spaceships their home, and planets will just be places where they sojourn. Thus, any civilization that has reached adulthood will be a starfaring civilization, permanently wandering through the cosmos. The spaceship is her home. Where are we from? We come from the ships.' He pointed up with a finger caked in dirt.

'How many of you are there?'

'Two billion.'

'Who are you really?' The Secretary-General had cause to ask this. The old wanderers looked just like humans.

'We've told you many times.' The old wanderer impatiently waved his hand. 'We are God.'

'Could you explain?'

'Our civilization – let's just call her the God Civilization – had existed long before Earth was born. When the God Civilization entered her senescence, we seeded the newly formed Earth with the beginnings of life. Then the God Civilization skipped across time by traveling close to the speed of light. When life on Earth had evolved to the appropriate stage, we introduced a new species based on our ancestral genes, eliminated its enemies, and carefully guided its evolution until Earth was home to a new civilized species just like us.'

'How do you expect us to believe you?'

'That's easy.'

Thus began the half-year-long effort to verify these claims. Humans watched in astonishment as spaceships sent the original plans for life on Earth and images of the primitive Earth. Following the old wanderer's direction, humans dug up incredible machines from deep below Earth's crust, equipment that had through the long eons monitored and manipulated the biosphere on this planet.

Humans finally had to believe. At least with respect to life on Earth, the Gods really were God.

Chapter 3

At the third emergency session of the United Nations General Assembly, the Secretary-General, on behalf of the human race, finally asked God the key question: why did they come to Earth?

'Before I answer this question, you must have a correct understanding of the concept of civilization.' God stroked his long beard. This was the same God who had been at the first emergency session half a year ago. 'How do you think civilizations evolve over time?'

'Civilization on Earth is currently in a stage of rapid development. If we're not hit by natural disasters beyond our ability to resist, I think we will continue our development indefinitely,' said the Secretary-General.

'Wrong. Think about it. Every person experiences childhood, youth, middle age, and old age, finally arriving at death. The stars are the same way. Indeed, everything in the universe goes through the same process. Even the universe itself will have to terminate one day. Why would civilization be an exception? No, a civilization will also grow old and die.'

'How exactly does that happen?'

'Different civilizations grow old and die in different ways, just like different people die of different diseases or just plain old age. For the God Civilization, the first sign of her senescence was the extreme lengthening of each individual member's life span. By then, each individual in the God Civilization could expect a life as long as four thousand Earth years. By age two thousand, their thoughts had completely ossified, losing all creativity. Because individuals like these held the reins of power, new life had a hard time emerging and growing. That was when our civilization became old.'

'And then?'

'The second sign of the civilization's senescence was the Age of the Machine Cradle.'

'What?'

'By then our machines no longer relied on their creators. They operated independently, maintained themselves, and developed on their own. The smart machines gave us everything we needed: not just material needs, but also psychological ones. We didn't need to put any effort into survival. Taken care of by machines, we lived as though we were lying in comfortable cradles.

'Think about it; if the jungles of primitive Earth had been filled with inexhaustible supplies of fruits and tame creatures that desired to become food, how could apes evolve into humans? The Machine Cradle was just such a comfort-filled jungle. Gradually we forgot about our technology and science. Our civilization became lazy and empty, devoid of creativity and ambition, and that only sped up the aging process. What you see now is the God Civilization in her final dying gasps.'

'Then . . . can you now tell us the goal for the God Civilization in coming to Earth?'

'We have no home now.'

'But . . .' The Secretary-General pointed upward.

'The spaceships are old. It's true that the artificial environment on the ships is more stable than any natural environment, including Earth's. But the ships are so old, old beyond your imagination. Old components have broken down. Accumulated quantum effects over the eons have led to more and more software errors. The system's self-repair and self-maintenance functions have encountered more and more insurmountable obstacles. The living environment on the ships is deteriorating. The amount of life necessities that can be distributed to individuals is decreasing by the day. We can just about survive. In the twenty thousand cities on the various ships, the air is filled with pollution and despair.'

'Are there no solutions? Perhaps new components for the ships? A software upgrade?'

God shook his head. 'The God Civilization is in her final years. We are two billion dying men and women each more than three thousand years old. But before us, hundreds of generations had already lived in the comfort of the Machine Cradle. Long ago, we forgot all our technology. Now we have no way to repair these ships that have been operating for tens of millions of years on their own. Indeed, in terms of the ability to study and understand technology, we are even worse than you. We can't even connect a circuit for a lightbulb or solve a quadratic equation . . .

'One day, the ships told us that they were close to complete breakdown. The propulsion systems could no longer push the ships near the speed of light. The God Civilization could only drift along at a speed not even one-tenth the speed of light, and the ecological support systems were nearing collapse. The machines could no longer keep two billion of us alive. We had to find another way out.'

'Did you ever think that this would happen?'

'Of course. Two thousand years ago, the ships already warned us. That was when we began the process of seeding life on Earth so that in our old age we would have support.'

'Two thousand years ago?'

'Yes. Of course I'm talking about time on the ships. From your frame of reference, that was three-point-five billion years ago, when Earth first cooled down.'

'We have a question: you say that you've lost your technology. But doesn't seeding life require technology?'

'Oh. To start the process of evolving life on a planet is a minor operation. Just scatter some seeds, and life will multiply and evolve on its own. We had this kind of software even before the Age of the Machine Cradle. Just start the program, and the machines can finish everything. To create a planet full of life, capable of developing civilization, the most basic requirement is time, a few billion years of time.'

'By traveling close to the speed of light, we possess almost limitless time. But now, the God Civilization's ships can no longer approach the speed of light. Otherwise we'd still have the chance to create new civilizations and more life, and we would have more choices. We're trapped by slowness. Those dreams cannot be realized.'

'So you want to spend your golden years on Earth.'

'Yes, yes. We hope that you will feel a sense of filial duty toward your creators and take us in.' God leaned on his walking stick and trembled as he tried to bow to the leaders of all the nations, and he almost fell on his face.

'But how do you plan to live here?'

'If we just gathered in one place by ourselves, then we might as well stay in space and die there. We'd like to be absorbed into your societies, your families. When the God Civilization was still in her childhood, we also had families. You know that childhood is the most precious time. Since your civilization is still in her childhood, if we can return to this era and spend the rest of our lives in the warmth of families, then that would be our greatest happiness.'

'There are two billion of you. That means every family on Earth would have to take in one or two of you.' After the Secretary-General spoke, the meeting hall sank into silence.

'Yes, yes, sorry to give you so much trouble . . .' God continued to bow while stealing glances at the Secretary-General and the leaders of all the nations. 'Of course, we're willing to compensate you.'

He waved his cane, and two more white-bearded Gods walked into the meeting hall, struggling under the weight of a silvery, metallic trunk they carried between them. 'Look, these are high-density information storage devices. They systematically store the knowledge the God Civilization had acquired in every field of science and technology. With this, your civilization will advance by leaps and bounds. I think you will like this.'

The Secretary-General, like the leaders of all the nations, looked at the metal trunk and tried to hide his elation. 'Taking care of God is the responsibility of humankind. Of course this will require some consultation between the various nations, but I think in principle . . .'

'Sorry to be so much trouble. Sorry to be so much trouble . . .' God's eyes filled with tears, and he continued to bow.

After the Secretary-General and the leaders of all the nations left the meeting hall, they saw that tens of thousands of Gods had gathered outside the United Nations building. A white sea of bobbing heads filled the air with murmuring words. The Secretary-General listened carefully and realized that they were all speaking, in the various tongues of Earth, the same sentence:

'Sorry to be so much trouble. Sorry to be so much trouble . . .'

Chapter 4

Two billion Gods arrived on Earth. Enclosed in suits made of their special film, they fell through the atmosphere. During that time, one could see the bright, colorful streaks in the sky even during the day. After the Gods landed, they spread out into 1.5 billion families.

Having received the Gods' knowledge about science and technology, everyone was filled with hopes and dreams for the future, as though humankind was about to step into paradise overnight. Under the influence of such joy, every family welcomed the coming of God.

*

That morning, Qiusheng and his family and all the other villagers stood at the village entrance to receive the Gods allocated to Xicen.

'What a beautiful day,' Yulian said.

Her comment wasn't motivated solely by her feelings. The spaceships had disappeared overnight, restoring the sky's wide open and limitless appearance. Humans had never been allowed to step onto any of the ships. The Gods did not really object to that particular request from the humans, but the ships themselves refused to grant permission. They did not acknowledge the various primitive probes which Earth sent and sealed their doors tightly. After the final group of Gods leaped into the atmosphere, all the spaceships, numbering more than twenty thousand, departed their orbit simultaneously. But they didn't go far, only drifting in the asteroid belt.

Although these ships were ancient, the old routines continued to function. Their only mission was to serve the Gods. Thus, they would not move too far. When the Gods needed them again, they would come.

Two buses arrived from the county seat, bringing the one hundred and six Gods allocated to Xicen. Qiusheng and Yulian met the God assigned to their family. The couple stood on each side of God, affectionately supported him by the arms, and walked home in the bright afternoon sun. Bingbing and Qiusheng's father followed behind, smiling.

'Gramps, um, Gramps God.' Yulian leaned her face against God's shoulder, her smile as bright as the sun. 'I hear that the technology you gave us will soon allow us to experience true Communism! When that happens, we'll all have things according to our needs. Things won't cost any money. You just go to the store and pick them up.'

God smiled and nodded at her, his white hair bobbing. He spoke in heavily accented Chinese. 'Yes. Actually, "to each according to need" fulfills only the most basic needs of a civilization. The technology we gave you will bring you a life of prosperity and comfort surpassing your imagination.'

Yulian's laughed so much her face opened up like a flower. 'No, no! "To each according to need" is more than enough for me!'

'Uh-huh,' Qiusheng's father agreed emphatically.

'Can we live forever without aging like you?' Qiusheng asked.

'We can't live forever without aging. It's just that we can live longer than you. Look at how old I am! In my view, if a man lives longer than three thousand years, he might as well be dead. For a civilization, extreme longevity for the individual can be fatal.'

'Oh, I don't need three thousand years. Just three hundred.' Qiusheng's father was now laughing as much as Yulian. 'In that case, I'd still be considered a young man right now. Maybe I can . . . hahahaha.'

*

The village treated the day like it was Chinese New Year. Every family held a big banquet to welcome its God, and Qiusheng's family was no exception.

Qiusheng's father quickly became a little drunk with cups of vintage *huangjiu*. He gave God a thumbs-up. 'You're really something! To be able to create so many living things – you're truly supernatural.'

God drank a lot, too, but his head was still clear. He waved his hand. 'No, not supernatural. It was just science. When biology has developed to a certain level, creating life is akin to building machines.'

'You say that. But in our eyes, you're no different from immortals who have deigned to live among us.'

God shook his head. 'Supernatural beings would never make mistakes. But for us, we made mistake after mistake during your creation.'

'You made mistakes when you created us?' Yulian's eyes were wide open. In her imagination, creating all those lives was a process similar to her giving birth to Bingbing eight years ago. No mistake was possible.

'There were many. I'll give a relatively recent example. The world-creation software made errors in the analysis of the environment on Earth, which resulted in the appearance of creatures like dinosaurs: huge bodies and low adaptability. Eventually, in order to facilitate your evolution, they had to be eliminated.

'Speaking of events that are even more recent, after the disappearance of the ancient Aegean civilizations, the world-creation software believed that civilization on Earth was successfully established. It ceased to perform further monitoring and microadjustments, like leaving a wound-up clock to run on its own. This resulted in further errors. For example, it should have allowed the civilization of ancient Greece to develop on her own and stopped the Macedonian conquest and the subsequent Roman conquest. Although both of these ended up as the inheritors of Greek civilization, the direction of Greek development was altered . . .'

No one in Qiusheng's family could understand this lecture, but all respectfully listened.

'And then two great powers appeared on Earth: Han China and the Roman Empire. In contrast to the earlier situation with ancient Greece, the two shouldn't have been kept apart and left to develop in isolation. They ought to have been allowed to come into full contact . . .'

'This "Han China" you're talking about? Is that the Han Dynasty of Liu Bang and Xiang Yu?' Finally Qiusheng's father heard something he knew. 'And what is this "Roman Empire"?'

'I think that was a foreigners' country at the time,' Qiusheng said, trying to explain. 'It was pretty big.'

Qiusheng's father was confused. 'Why? When the foreigners finally showed up during the Qing Dynasty, look how badly they beat us up. You want them to show up even earlier? During the Han Dynasty?'

God laughed at this. 'No, no. Back then, Han China was just as powerful as the Roman Empire.'

'That's still bad. If those two great powers had met, it would have been a great war. Blood would have flowed like a river.'

God nodded. He reached out with his chopsticks for a piece of beef braised in soy sauce. 'Could have been. But if those two great civilizations, the Occident and the Orient, had met, the encounter would have generated glorious sparks and greatly advanced human progress. . . Eh, if those errors could have been avoided, Earth would now probably be colonizing Mars, and your interstellar probes would have flown past Sirius.'

Qiusheng's father raised his bowl of *huangjiu* and spoke admiringly. 'Everyone says that the Gods have forgotten science in their cradle, but you are still so learned.'

'To be comfortable in the cradle, it's important to know a bit about philosophy, art, history, etc – just some common facts, not real learning. Many scholars on Earth right now have much deeper thoughts than our own.'

*

For the Gods, the first few months after they entered human society were a golden age, when they lived very harmoniously with human families. It was as though they had returned to the childhood of the God Civilization, fully immersed in the long-forgotten warmth of family life. This seemed the best way to spend the final years of their extremely long lives.

Qiusheng's family's God enjoyed the peaceful life in this beautiful southern Chinese village. Every day he went to the pond surrounded by bamboo groves to fish, chatted with other old folks from the village, played chess, and generally enjoyed himself. But his greatest hobby was attending folk operas. Whenever a theatre troupe came to the village or the town, he made sure to go to every performance.

His favorite opera was *The Butterfly Lovers*. One performance was not enough. He followed one troupe around for more than fifty kilometers and attended several shows in a row. Finally Qiusheng went to town and bought him a VCD of the opera. God played it over and over until he could hum a few lines of *Huangmei* opera and sounded pretty good.

One day Yulian discovered a secret. She whispered to Qiusheng and her father-in-law, 'Did you know that every time Gramps God finishes his opera, he always takes a little card out from his pocket? And while looking at the card, he hums lines from the opera. Just now I stole a glance. The card is a photo. There's a really pretty young woman on it.'

That evening, God played *The Butterfly Lovers* again. He took out the photograph of the pretty young woman and started to hum. Qiusheng's father quietly moved in. 'Gramps God, is that your . . . girlfriend from a long time ago?'

God was startled. He hid the photograph quickly and smiled like a kid at Qiusheng's father. 'Haha. Yeah, yeah. I loved her two thousand years ago.'

Yulian, who was eavesdropping, grimaced. Two thousand years ago! Considering his advanced age, this was a bit gag inducing.

Qiusheng's father wanted to look at the photograph. But God was so protective of it that it would have been embarrassing to ask. So Qiusheng's father settled for listening to God reminisce.

'Back then we were all so young. She was one of the very few who wasn't completely absorbed by life in the Machine Cradle. She initiated a great voyage of exploration to sail to the end of the universe. Oh, you don't need to think too hard about that. It's very difficult to understand. Anyway, she hoped to use this voyage as an opportunity to awaken the God Civilization, sleeping so soundly in the Machine Cradle. Of course, that was nothing more than a beautiful dream. She wanted me to go with her, but I didn't have the courage. The endless desert of the universe frightened me. It would have been a journey of more than twenty billion light-years. So she went by herself. But in the two thousand years after that, I never stopped longing for her.'

'Twenty billion light-years? So like you explained to me before, that's the distance that light would travel in twenty billion years? Oh my! That's way too far. That's basically good-bye for life. Gramps God, you have to forget about her. You'll never see her again.'

God nodded and sighed.

'Well, isn't she now about your age, too?'

God was startled out of his reverie. He shook his head. 'Oh, no. For such a long voyage, her explorer ship would have to fly at close to the speed of light. That means she would still be very young. The only one that has grown old is me. You don't understand how large the universe is. What you think of as "eternity" is nothing but a grain of sand in space-time.

'Well, the fact that you can't understand and feel this is sometimes a blessing.'

Chapter 5

The honeymoon between the Gods and humans quickly ended.

People were initially ecstatic over the scientific material received from the Gods, thinking that it would allow mankind to realize its dreams overnight. Thanks to the interface equipment provided by the Gods, an enormous quantity of information was retrieved successfully from the storage devices. The information was translated into English, and in order to avoid disputes, a copy was distributed to every nation in the world.

But people soon discovered that realizing these God-given technologies was impossible, at least within the present century. Consider the situation of the ancient Egyptians if a time traveler had provided information on modern technology to them, and you will have some understanding of the awkward situation these humans faced.

As the exhaustion of petroleum supplies loomed over the human race, energy technology was at the top of everyone's minds. But scientists and engineers discovered that the God Civilization's energy technology was useless for humans at this time. The Gods' energy source was built upon the basis of matter-antimatter annihilation. Even if people could understand all the materials and finally create an annihilation engine and generator (a basically impossible task within this generation), it would still have been for naught. This was because the fuel for these engines, antimatter, had to be mined from deep space. According to the material provided by the Gods, the closest antimatter ore source was between the Milky Way and the Andromeda galaxy, about 550,000 light-years away.

The technology for interstellar travel at near the speed of light also involved every field of scientific knowledge, and the greater part of the theories and techniques revealed by the Gods were beyond human comprehension. Just to get a basic understanding of the foundations would require human scholars to work for perhaps half a century. Scientists, initially full of hope, had tried to search the material from the Gods for technical information concerning controlled nuclear fusion, but there was nothing. This was easy to understand: our current literature on energy science contained no information on how to make fire from sticks, either.

In other scientific fields, such as information science and life sciences (including the secret of human longevity), it was the same. Even the most advanced scholars could make no sense of the Gods' knowledge. Between the Gods' science and human science, there was still a great abyss of understanding that could not be bridged.

The Gods who arrived on Earth could not help the scientists in any way. Like the God at the United Nations had said, among the Gods now there were few who could even solve quadratic equations. The spaceships adrift among the asteroids also ignored all hails from the humans. The human race was like a group of new elementary school students who were suddenly required to master the material of Ph.D. candidates, and were given no instructor.

On the other hand, Earth's population suddenly grew by two billion. These were all extremely aged individuals who could no longer be productive. Most of them were plagued by various diseases and put unprecedented pressure on human society. As a result, every government had to pay each family living with a God a considerable support stipend. Health care and other public infrastructures were strained beyond the breaking point. The world economy was pushed near the edge of collapse.

The harmonious relationship between God and Qiusheng's family was gone. Gradually the family began to see him as a burden that fell from the sky. They began to despise him, but each had a different reason.

Yulian's reason was the most practical and closest to the underlying problem: God made her family poor. Among all the members of the family

God also worried the most about her; she had a tongue as sharp as a knife, and she scared him more than black holes and supernovas. After the death of her dream of true Communism, she unceasingly nagged God: *Before you came, our family had lived so prosperously and comfortably. Back then everything was good. Now everything is bad. All because of you. Being saddled with an old fool like you was such a great misfortune.* Every day, whenever she had the chance, she would prattle on like this in front of God.

God also suffered from chronic bronchitis. This was not a very expensive disease to treat, but it did require ongoing care and a constant outlay of money. Finally one day Yulian forbade Qiusheng from taking God to the town hospital to see doctors and stopped buying medicine for him. When the Secretary of the village branch of the Communist Party found out, he came to Qiusheng's house.

'You have to pay for the care of your family God,' the Secretary said to Yulian. 'The doctor at the town hospital already told me that if left untreated, the chronic bronchitis might develop into pulmonary emphysema.'

'If you want him treated, then the village or the government can pay for it,' Yulian shouted at the Secretary. 'We're not made of money!'

'Yulian, according to the God Support Law, the family has to bear these kinds of minor medical expenses. The government's support fee already includes this component.'

'That little bit of support fee is useless!'

'You can't talk like that. After you began getting the support fee, you bought a milk cow, switched to liquefied petroleum gas, and bought a big, new color TV! You're telling me now that you don't have money for God to see a doctor? Everyone knows that in your family, your word is law. I'm going to make it clear to you: right now I'm helping you save face, but don't push your luck. Next time, it won't be me standing here trying to persuade you. It will be the County God Support Committee. You'll be in real trouble then.'

Yulian had no choice but to resume paying for God's medical care. But after that she became even meaner to him.

One time, God said to Yulian, 'Don't be so anxious. Humans are very smart and learn fast. In only another century or so, the easiest aspects of the Gods' knowledge will become applicable to human society. Then your life will become better.'

'Damn. A whole century. And you say "only". Are you even listening to yourself?' Yulian was washing the dishes and didn't even bother looking back at God.

'That's a very short period of time.'

'For you! You think we can live as long as you? In another century, you won't even find my bones! But I want to ask you a question: how much longer do you think you'll be living?'

'Oh, I'm like a candle in the wind. If I can live another three or four hundred years, I'll be very satisfied.'

Yulian dropped a whole stack of bowls on the ground. 'This is not how "support" is supposed to work! Ah, so you think not only I should spend my entire life taking care of you, but you have to have my son, my grandson, for ten generations and more!? Why won't you die?'

*

As for Qiusheng's father, he thought God was a fraud, and in fact, this view was pretty common. Since scientists couldn't understand the Gods' scientific papers, there was no way to prove their authenticity. Maybe the Gods were playing a giant trick on the human race. For Qiusheng's father, there was ample support for this view.

'You old swindler, you're way too outrageous,' he said to God one day. 'I'm too lazy to expose you. Your tricks are not worth my trouble. Heck, they're not even worth my grandson's trouble.'

God asked him what he had discovered.

'I'll start with the simplest thing: our scientists know that humans evolved from monkeys, right?'

God nodded. 'More accurately, you evolved from primitive apes.'

'Then how can you say that you created us? If you were interested in creating humans, why not directly make us in our current form? Why bother first creating primitive apes and then go through the trouble of evolving? It makes no sense.'

'A human begins as a baby, and then grows into an adult. A civilization also has to grow from a primitive state. The long path of experience cannot be avoided. Actually, humans began with the introduction of a much more primitive species. Even apes were already very evolved.'

'I don't believe these made-up reasons. All right, here's something more obvious. This was actually first noticed by my grandson. Our scientists say that there was life on Earth even three billion years ago. Do you admit this?'

God nodded. 'That estimate is basically right.'

'So you're three billion years old?'

'In terms of your frame of reference, yes. But according to the frame of reference of our ships, I'm only thirty-five hundred years old. The ships flew close to the speed of light, and time passed much more slowly for us than for you. Of course, once in a while a few ships dropped out of their cruise and decelerated to come to Earth so that further adjustments to the evolution of life on Earth could be made. But this didn't require much time. Those ships would then return to cruise at close to the speed of light and continue skipping over the passage of time here.'

'Bullshit,' Qiusheng's father said contemptuously.

'Dad, this is the Theory of Relativity,' Qiusheng interrupted. 'Our scientists already proved it.'

'Relativity, my ass! You're bullshitting me, too. That's impossible! How can time be like sesame oil, flowing at different speeds? I'm not so old that I've lost my mind. But you – reading all those books has made you stupid!'

'I can prove to you that time does indeed flow at different rates,' God said, his face full of mystery. He took out that photograph of his beloved from two thousand years ago and handed it to Qiusheng. 'Look at her carefully and memorize every detail.'

The second Qiusheng looked at the photograph, he knew that he would be able to remember every detail. It would be impossible to forget. Like the other Gods, the woman in the picture had a blend of the features of all ethnicities. Her skin was like warm ivory, her two eyes were so alive that they seemed to sing, and she immediately captivated Qiusheng's soul. She was a woman among Gods, the God of women. The beauty of the Gods was like a second sun. Humans had never seen it and could not bear it.

'Look at you! You're practically drooling!' Yulian grabbed the photograph from the frozen Qiusheng. But before she could look at it, her father-in-law took it away from her.

'Let me see,' Qiusheng's father said. He brought the photograph to his ancient eyes, as close as possible. For a long time he did not move, as though the photograph provided sustenance.

'Why are you looking so close?' Yulian said, her tone contemptuous.

'Shut it. I don't have my glasses,' Qiusheng's father said, his face still practically on the photograph.

Yulian looked at her father-in-law disdainfully for a few seconds, curled her lips, and left for the kitchen.

God took the photograph out of the hands of Qiusheng's father, whose hands lingered on the photo for a long while, unwilling to let go. God said, 'Remember all the details. I'll let you look at it again this time tomorrow.'

The next day, father and son said little to each other. Both thought about the young woman, so there was nothing to say. Yulian's temper was far worse than usual.

Finally the time came. God had seemingly forgotten about it and had to be reminded by Qiusheng's father. He took out the photograph that the two men had been thinking about all day and handed it first to Qiusheng. 'Look carefully. Do you see any change in her?'

'Nothing really,' Qiusheng said, looking intently. After a while, he finally noticed something. 'Aha! The opening between her lips seems slightly narrower. Not much, just a little bit. Look at the corner of the mouth here . . .'

'Have you no shame? To look at some other woman that closely?' Yulian grabbed the photo again, and again, her father-in-law took it away from her.

'Let me see—' Qiusheng's father put on his glasses and carefully examined the picture. 'Yes, indeed the opening is narrower. But there's a much more obvious change that you didn't notice. Look at this wisp of hair. Compared to yesterday, it has drifted farther to the right.'

God took the picture from Qiusheng's father. 'This is not a photograph, but a television receiver.'

'A . . . TV?'

'Yes. Right now it's receiving a live feed from that explorer spaceship heading for the end of the universe.'

'Live? Like live broadcasts of football matches?'

'Yes.'

'So . . . the woman in the picture, she's alive!' Qiusheng was so shocked that his mouth hung open. Even Yulian's eyes were now as big as walnuts.

'Yes, she's alive. But unlike a live broadcast on Earth, this feed is subject to a delay. The explorer spaceship is now about eighty million light-years away, so the delay is about eighty million years. What we see now is how she was eighty million years ago.'

'This tiny thing can receive a signal from that far away?'

'This kind of super long-distance communication across space requires the use of neutrinos or gravitational waves. Our spaceships can receive the signal, magnify it, and then rebroadcast to this TV.'

'Treasure, a real treasure!' Qiusheng's father praised sincerely. But it was unclear whether he was talking about the tiny TV or the young woman on the TV. Anyway, after hearing that she was still 'alive,' Qiusheng and his father both felt a deeper attachment to her. Qiusheng tried to take the tiny TV again, but God refused.

'Why does she move so slowly in the picture?'

'That's the result of time flowing at different speeds. From our frame of reference, time flows extremely slowly on a spaceship flying close to the speed of light.'

'Then . . . can she still talk to you?' Yulian asked.

God nodded. He flipped a switch behind the TV. Immediately a sound came out of it. It was a woman's voice, but the sound didn't change, like a singer holding a note steady at the end of a song. God stared at the screen, his eyes full of love.

'She's talking right now. She's finishing three words: "I love you." Each word took more than a year. It's now been three and a half years, and right now she's just finishing "you." To completely finish the sentence will take another three months.' God lifted his eyes from the TV to the domed sky above the yard. 'She still has more to say. I'll spend the rest of my life listening to her.'

*

Bingbing actually managed to maintain a pretty good relationship with God for a while. The Gods all had some childishness to them, and they enjoyed talking and playing with children. But one day, Bingbing wanted God to give him the large watch he wore, and God steadfastly refused. He explained that the watch was a tool for communicating with the God Civilization. Without it, he would no longer be able to connect with his own people.

'Hmm, look at this. You're still thinking about your own civilization and race. You've never thought of us as your real family!' Yulian said angrily.

After that, Bingbing was no longer nice to God. Instead, he often played practical tricks on him.

*

The only one in the family who still had respect and feelings of filial piety toward God was Qiusheng. Qiusheng had graduated from high school and liked to read. Other than a few people who passed the college-entrance examination and went away for college, he was the most learned individual in the village. But at home, Qiusheng had no power. On practically everything he listened to the direction of his wife and followed the commands of his father. If somehow his wife and father had conflicting instructions, then all he could do was to sit in a corner and cry. Given that he was such a softy, he had no way to protect God at home.

Chapter 6

The relationship between the Gods and humans had finally deteriorated beyond repair.

The complete breakdown between God and Qiusheng's family occurred after the incident involving instant noodles. One day, before lunch, Yulian came out of the kitchen with a paper box and asked why half the box of instant noodles she had bought yesterday had already disappeared.

'I took them,' God said in a small voice. 'I gave them to those living by the river. They've almost run out of things to eat.'

He was talking about the place where the Gods who had left their families were gathering. Recently there had been frequent incidents of abuse of the Gods in the village. One particularly savage couple had been beating and cursing out their God, and even withheld food from him. Eventually that God tried to commit suicide in the river that ran in front of the village, but luckily others were able to stop him.

This incident caused a great deal of publicity. It went beyond the county, and the city's police eventually came, along with a bunch of reporters from CCTV and the provincial TV station, and took the couple away in handcuffs. According to the God Support Law, they had committed God abuse and would be sentenced to at least ten years in jail. This was the only law that was universal among all the nations of the world, with uniform prison terms.

After that, the families in the village became more careful and stopped treating the Gods too poorly in front of other people. But at the same time, the incident worsened the relationship between the Gods and the villagers. Eventually, some of the Gods left their families, and other Gods followed. By now almost one-third of the Gods in Xicen had already left their assigned families. These wandering Gods set up camp in the field across the river and lived a primitive, difficult life.

In other parts of the country and across the world, the situation was the same. Once again, the streets of big cities were filled with crowds of wandering, homeless Gods. The number quickly increased like a repeat of the nightmare three years ago. The world, full of Gods and people, faced a gigantic crisis.

'Ha, you're very generous, you old fool! How dare you eat our food while giving it away?' Yulian began to curse loudly.

Qiusheng's father slammed the table and got up. 'You idiot! Get out of here! You miss those Gods by the river? Why don't you go and join them?'

God sat silently for a while, thinking. Then he stood up, went to his tiny room, and packed up his few belongings. Leaning on his bamboo cane, he slowly made his way out the door, heading in the direction of the river.

Qiusheng didn't eat with the rest of his family. He squatted in a corner with his head lowered and not speaking.

'Hey, dummy! Come here and eat. We have to go into town to buy feed this afternoon,' Yulian shouted at him. Since he refused to budge, she went over to yank his ear.

'Let go,' Qiusheng said. His voice was not loud, but Yulian let him go as though she had been shocked. She had never seen her husband with such a gloomy expression on his face.

'Forget about him,' Qiusheng's father said carelessly. 'If he doesn't want to eat, then he's a fool.'

'Ha, you miss your God? Why don't you go join him and his friends in that field by the river, too?' Yulian poked a finger at Qiusheng's head.

Qiusheng stood up and went upstairs to his bedroom. Like God, he packed a few things into a bundle and put it in a duffel bag he had once used when he had gone to the city to work. With the bag on his back, he headed outside.

'Where are you going?' Yulian yelled. But Qiusheng ignored her. She yelled again, but now there was fear in her voice. 'How long are you going to be out?'

'I'm not coming back,' Qiusheng said without looking back.

'What? Come back here! Is your head filled with shit?' Qiusheng's father followed him out of the house. 'What's the matter with you? Even if you don't want your wife and kid, how dare you leave your father?'

Qiusheng stopped but still did not turn around. 'Why should I care about you?'

'How can you talk like that? I'm your father! I raised you! Your mother died early. You think it was easy to raise you and your sister? Have you lost your mind?'

Qiusheng finally turned back to look at his father. 'If you can kick the people who created our ancestors' ancestors' ancestors out of our house, then I don't think it's much of a sin for me not to support you in your old age.'

He left, and Yulian and his father stood there, dumbfounded.

*

Qiusheng went over the ancient arched stone bridge and walked toward the tents of the Gods. He saw a few of the Gods had set up a pot to cook something in the grassy clearing strewn with golden leaves. Their white beards and the white steam coming out of the pot reflected the noon sunlight like a scene out of an ancient myth.

Qiusheng found his God and said stubbornly, 'Gramps God, let's go.'

'I'm not going back to that house.' God waved his hand.

'I'm not, either. Let's go together into town and stay with my sister for a while. Then I'll go into the city and find a job, and we'll rent a place together. I'll support you for the rest of my life.'

'You're a good kid,' God said, patting his shoulder lightly. 'But it's time for us to go.' He pointed to the watch on his wrist. Qiusheng now noticed that all the watches of all the Gods were blinking with a red light.

'Go? Where to?'

'Back to the ships,' God said, pointing at the sky. Qiusheng lifted his head and saw that two spaceships were already hovering in the sky, standing out starkly against the blue. One of them was closer, and its shape and outline loomed huge. Behind it, another was much farther away and appeared smaller. But the most surprising sight was that the first spaceship had lowered a thread as thin as spider silk, extending from space down to Earth. As the spider silk slowly drifted, the bright sun glinted on different sections like lightning in the bright blue sky.

'A space elevator,' God explained. 'Already more than a hundred of these have been set up on every continent. We'll ride them back to the ships.' Later Qiusheng would learn that when a spaceship dropped down a space elevator from a geostationary orbit, it needed a large mass on its other side, deep in space, to act as a counterweight. That was the purpose of the other ship he saw.

When Qiusheng's eyes adjusted to the brightness of the sky, he saw that there were many more silvery stars deep in the distance. Those stars were spread out very evenly, forming a huge matrix. Qiusheng understood that the twenty thousand ships of the God Civilization were coming back to Earth from the asteroid belt.

Chapter 7

Twenty thousand spaceships once again filled the sky above Earth. In the two months that followed, space capsules ascended and descended the various space elevators, taking away the two billion Gods who had briefly lived on Earth. The space capsules were silver spheres. From a distance, they looked like dewdrops hanging on spider threads.

The day that Xicen's Gods left, all the villagers showed up for the farewell. Everyone was affectionate toward the Gods, and it reminded everyone of the day a year ago when the Gods first came to Xicen. It was as though all the abuse and disdain the Gods had received had nothing to do with the villagers.

Two big buses were parked at the entrance to the village, the same two buses that had brought the Gods here a year ago. More than a hundred

Gods would now be taken to the nearest space elevator and ride up in space capsules. The silver thread that could be seen in the distance was in reality hundreds of kilometers away.

Qiusheng's whole family went to send off their God. No one said anything along the way. As they neared the village entrance, God stopped, leaned against his cane, and bowed to the family. 'Please stop here. Thank you for taking care of me this year. Really, thank you. No matter where I will be in this universe, I will always remember your family.' Then he took off the large watch from his wrist and handed it to Bingbing. 'A gift.'

'But . . . how will you communicate with the other Gods in the future?' Bingbing asked.

'We'll all be on the spaceships. I have no more need for this,' God said, laughing.

'Gramps God,' Qiusheng's father said, his face sorrowful, 'your ships are all ancient. They won't last much longer. Where can you go then?'

God stroked his beard and said calmly, 'It doesn't matter. Space is limitless. Dying anywhere is the same.'

Yulian suddenly began to cry. 'Gramps God, I . . . I'm not a very nice person. I shouldn't have made you the target of all my complaints, which I'd saved up my whole life. It's just as Qiusheng said: I've behaved as if I don't have a conscience . . .' She pushed a bamboo basket into God's hands. 'I boiled some eggs this morning. Please take them for your trip.'

God picked up the basket. 'Thank you.' Then he took out an egg, peeled it, and began to eat, savoring the taste. Yellow flakes of egg yolk soon flaked his white beard. He continued to talk as he ate. 'Actually, we came to Earth not only because we wanted to survive. Having already lived for two, three thousand years, what did we have to fear from death? We just wanted to be with you. We like and cherish your passion for life, your creativity, your imagination. These things have long disappeared from the God Civilization. We saw in you the childhood of our civilization. But we didn't realize we'd bring you so much trouble. We're really sorry.'

'Please stay, Gramps,' Bingbing said, crying. 'I'll be better in the future.'

God shook his head slowly. 'We're leaving not because of how you treated us. The fact that you took us in and allowed us to stay was enough. But one thing made us unable to stay any longer: in your eyes, the Gods are pathetic. You pity us. Oh, you pity us.'

God threw away the pieces of eggshell. He lifted his face, trailing a full head of white hair, and stared at the sky, as though through the blue he could see the bright sea of stars. 'How can the God Civilization be pitied by man? You have no idea what a great civilization she was. You do not know what majestic epics she created, or how many imposing deeds she accomplished.

'It was 1857, during the Milky Way Era, when astronomers discovered a large number of stars was accelerating toward the center of the Milky Way. Once this flood of stars was consumed by the supermassive black hole found there, the resulting radiation would kill all life found in the galaxy.

'In response, our great ancestors built a nebula shield around the center of the galaxy with a diameter of ten thousand light-years so that life and civilization in the galaxy would continue. What a magnificent engineering project that was! It took us more than fourteen million years to complete . . .

'Immediately afterward, the Andromeda galaxy and the Large Magellanic Cloud united in an invasion of our galaxy. The interstellar fleet of the God Civilization leaped across hundreds of thousands of light-years and intercepted the invaders at the gravitational balance point between Andromeda and the Milky Way. When the battle entered into its climax, large numbers of ships from both sides mixed together, forming a spiraling nebula the size of the Solar System.

'During the final stages of the battle, the God Civilization made the bold decision to send all remaining warships and even the civilian fleet into the spiraling nebula. The great increase in mass caused gravity to exceed the centrifugal force, and this nebula, made of ships and people, collapsed under gravity and formed a star! Because the proportion of heavy elements in this star was so high, immediately after its birth, the star went supernova and illuminated the deep darkness between Andromeda and the Milky Way! Our ancestors thus destroyed the invaders with their courage and self-sacrifice, and left the Milky Way as a place where life could develop peacefully . . .

'Yes, now our civilization is old. But it is not our fault. No matter how hard one strives, a civilization must grow old one day. Everyone grows old, even you.

'We really do not need your pity.'

'Compared to you,' Qiusheng said, full of awe, 'the human race is really nothing.'

'Don't talk like that,' God said. 'Earth's civilization is still an infant. We hope you will grow up fast. We hope you will inherit and continue the glory of your creators.' God threw down his cane. He put his hands on the shoulders of Bingbing and Qiusheng. 'I have some final words for you.'

'We may not understand everything you have to say,' Qiusheng said, 'but please speak. We will listen.'

'First, you must get off this rock!' God spread out his arms toward space. His white robe danced in the autumn wind like a sail.

'Where will we go?' Qiusheng's father asked in confusion.

'Begin by flying to the other planets in the solar system, then to other stars. Don't ask why, but use all your energy toward the goal of flying away, the farther the better. In that process, you will spend a lot of money, and many people will die, but you must get away from here. Any civilization that stays on her birth world is committing suicide! You must go into the universe and find new worlds, new homes, and spread your descendants across the galaxy like drops of spring rain.'

'We'll remember,' Qiusheng said and nodded, even though neither he nor his wife nor father nor son really understood God's words.

'Good,' God sighed, satisfied. 'Next I will tell you a secret, a great secret.' He stared at everyone in the family with his blue eyes. His stare was like a cold wind and caused everyone's heart to shudder. 'You have brothers.'

Qiusheng's family looked at God, utterly confused. But Qiusheng finally figured out what God meant. 'You're saying that you created other Earths?'

God nodded slowly. 'Yes, other Earths, other human civilizations. Other than you, there were three others. All are close to you, within two hundred light-years. You are Earth Number Four, the youngest.'

'Have you been to the other Earths?' Bingbing asked.

God nodded again. 'Before we came to you, we went first to the other three Earths and asked them to take us in. Earth Number One was the best among the bunch. After they obtained our scientific materials, they simply chased us away.

'Earth Number Two, on the other hand, kept one million of us as hostages and forced us to give them spaceships as ransom. After we gave them one thousand ships, they realized that they could not operate the ships. They then forced the hostages to teach them how, but the hostages didn't know how, either, since the ships were autonomous. So they killed all the hostages.

'Earth Number Three took three million of us as hostages and demanded that we ram Earth Number One and Earth Number Two with several spaceships each because they were in a prolonged state of war with the other two Earths. Of course, even a single hit from one of our antimatter-powered ships would destroy all life on a planet. We refused, and so they killed all the hostages.'

'Unfilial children!' Qiusheng's father shouted in anger. 'You should punish them!'

God shook his head. 'We will never attack civilizations we created. You are the best of the four brothers. That's why I'm telling you all this. Your three brothers are drawn to invasion. They do not know what love is or what morality is. Their capacity for cruelty and bloodlust are impossible for you to imagine.

'Indeed, in the beginning we created six Earths. The other two were in the same solar systems as Earth Number One and Earth Number Three, respectively. Both were destroyed by their brothers. The fact that the other three Earths haven't yet destroyed one another is only due to the great distances separating their solar systems. By now, all three know of the existence of Earth Number Four and possess your precise coordinates. Thus, you must go and destroy them first before they destroy you.'

'This is too frightening!' Yulian said.

'For now, it's not yet too frightening. Your three brothers are indeed more advanced than you, but they still cannot travel faster than one-tenth the speed of light, and cannot cruise more than thirty light-years from home. This is a race of life and death to see which one among you can achieve near-light-speed space travel first. It is the only way to break through the prison of time and space. Whoever can achieve this technology first will survive. Anyone slower will die a sure death. This is the struggle for survival in the universe. Children, you don't have much time. Work hard!'

'Do the most learned and most powerful people in our world know these things?' Qiusheng's father asked, trembling.

'Yes. But don't rely on them. A civilization's survival depends on the effort of every individual. Even the common people like you have a role to play.'

'You hear that, Bingbing?' Qiusheng said to his son. 'You must study hard.'

'When you fly into the universe at close to the speed of light to resolve the threat of your brothers, you must perform another urgent task: find a few planets suitable for life and seed them with some simple, primitive life from here, like bacteria and algae. Let them evolve on their own.'

Qiusheng wanted to ask more questions, but God picked up his cane and began to walk. The family accompanied him toward the bus. The other Gods were already aboard.

'Oh, Qiusheng.' God stopped, remembering. 'I took a few of your books with me. I hope you don't mind.' He opened his bundle to show Qiusheng. 'These are your high school textbooks on math, physics, chemistry.'

'No problem. Take them. But why do you want these?'

God tied up the bundle again. 'To study. I'll start with quadratic equations. In the long years ahead, I'll need some way to occupy myself. Who knows? Maybe one day, I'll try to repair our ships' antimatter engines and allow us to fly close to the speed of light again!'

'Right,' Qiusheng said, excited. 'That way, you'll be able to skip across time again. You can find another planet, create another civilization to support you in your old age!'

God shook his head. 'No, no, no. We're no longer interested in being supported in our old age. If it's time for us to die, we die. I want to study because I have a final wish.' He took out the small TV from his pocket. On the screen, his beloved from two thousand years ago was still slowly speaking the final word of that three-word sentence. 'I want to see her again.'

'It's a good wish, but it's only a fantasy,' Qiusheng's father said. 'Think about it. She left two thousand years ago at the speed of light. Who knows where she is now? Even if you repair your ship, how will you ever catch her? You told us that nothing can go faster than light.'

God pointed at the sky with his cane. 'In this universe, as long as you're patient, you can make any wish come true. Even though the possibility is minuscule, it is not nonexistent. I told you once that the universe was born out of a great explosion. Now gravity has gradually slowed down its expansion. Eventually the expansion will stop and turn into contraction. If our spaceship can really fly again at close to the speed of light, then we will endlessly accelerate and endlessly approach the speed of light. This way, we will skip over endless time until we near the final moments of the universe.

'By then, the universe will have shrunk to a very small size, smaller even than Bingbing's toy ball, as small as a point. Then everything in the entire universe will come together, and she and I will also be together.'

A tear fell from God's eye and rolled onto his beard, glistening brightly in the morning sun. 'The universe will then be the tomb at the end of *The Butterfly Lovers*. She and I will be the two butterflies emerging from the tomb . . .'

Chapter 8

A week later, the last spaceship left Earth. God left.

Xicen village resumed its quiet life.

On this evening, Qiusheng's family sat in the yard, looking at a sky full of stars. It was deep autumn, and insects had stopped making noises in the fields. A light breeze stirred the fallen leaves at their feet. The air was slightly chilly.

'They're flying so high. The wind must be so severe, so cold—' Yulian murmured to herself.

'There isn't any wind up there,' Qiusheng said. 'They're in space, where there isn't even air. But it is really cold. So cold that in the books they call it *absolute zero*. It's so dark out there, with no end in sight. It's a place that you can't even dream of in your nightmares.'

Yulian began to cry again. But she tried to hide it with words. 'Remember those last two things God told us? I understand the part about our three brothers. But then he told us that we had to spread bacteria onto other planets and so on. I still can't make sense of that.'

'I figured it out,' Qiusheng's father said. Under the brilliant, starry sky, his head, full of a lifetime of foolishness, finally opened up to insight. He looked up at the stars. He had lived with them above his head all his life, but only today did he discover what they really looked like. A feeling he had never had before suffused his blood, making him feel as if he had been touched by something greater. Even though it did not become a part of him, the feeling shook him to his core. He sighed at the sea of stars, and said, 'The human race needs to start thinking about who is going to support us in our old age.'

赡养人类

FOR THE BENEFIT OF MANKIND

TRANSLATED BY ELIZABETH HANLON

韩恩立 译

Business was business, nothing more, nothing less. This was the principle by which Smoothbore operated, but this particular client had left him feeling bewildered.

First, the client had gone about the commission all wrong. He wanted to speak in person, which was extremely unusual in this line of business. Smoothbore remembered his instructor's repeated admonitions three years prior: their relationship with clients should be like that of the forehead to the back of the skull; the two should never meet. This, of course, was in the best interest of both parties.

Smoothbore was even more surprised by the client's choice of meeting place. The opulent Presidential Hall in the most luxurious five-star hotel in the city was a spectacularly unsuitable venue for this sort of transaction. According to the other party, this contract would involve processing three units. This was no trouble – he did not mind a little extra work.

An attendant held open the gilded doors of the Presidential Hall. Before he entered, Smoothbore inconspicuously reached a hand into his jacket and gently undid the snaps on the holster under his left armpit. In truth, it was unnecessary – no one would try to pull anything unexpected in a place like this.

The hall was resplendent in glittering greens and golds, a world apart from the reality outside. This world's sun was a massive crystal chandelier, shining down on an endless plain of scarlet carpet. At first glance the room seemed empty, but Smoothbore quickly spied its occupants clustered around two French windows in the corner of the hall, lifting the heavy curtains to look at sky outside. He glanced over at them and counted thirteen people. Smoothbore had anticipated a client, not clients. His instructor had also said that clients were like mistresses: you could have more than one, but you should never let them meet.

Smoothbore knew exactly what they were looking at: the Elder Brothers' spaceship. It had moved back over the Southern Hemisphere and was clearly visible in the sky. Three years had passed since the Creator[1] civilization had left Earth. Their grand cosmic visit had drastically increased humanity's ability to mentally cope with alien civilizations. Moreover, the Creators' fleet of 20,000 spaceships had blotted out the sky, but only one ship from the Elder Brothers' world had arrived on Earth. It was not as bizarrely shaped as the spaceships of the Creators. Cylindrical with rounded ends, it looked like an intergalactic cold relief capsule.

Seeing Smoothbore enter, the thirteen clients left the windows and returned to the large round table in the center of the hall. When he recognized some of the faces around the room, the magnificent hall suddenly felt shabby. The most conspicuous among them was SinoSys Group's Zhu Hanyang, whose 'Orient-3000' operating system was replacing the outdated Windows OS worldwide. The others all ranked in the top fifty on a list of the world's wealthiest people. Their annual earnings were probably equivalent to the GDP of a middle-income country. Smoothbore felt as if he were attending some global forum for the wealthy, except it was a small one.

These people were nothing like Brother Teeth, thought Smoothbore. Brother Teeth had made his fortune overnight, these were dynastic heirs, the polished products of generations of wealth. They were the aristocrats of this age, utterly habituated to the wealth and power they wielded. It was just like the delicate diamond ring that sat on Zhu Hanyang's slender finger: it was barely visible but for the occasional glint of warm light, but it was easily worth a dozen times more than the shiny, walnut-sized golden baubles that adorned Brother Teeth's fingers.

But now, these thirteen financial princelings had assembled to hire a professional hitman to kill three people, and according to his contact, this

---

1 本篇 "Creator" 译法与《赡养上帝》不同，本书保持原译文。——编者注

was only the first batch.

Smoothbore paid the diamond ring no attention. His eyes were fixed on the three photographs in Zhu's hand – clearly the units that required processing. Zhu leaned across the table and slid the photographs in front of him.

With a glance, Smoothbore felt faint frustration creep in again. His instructor had said, in the area in which he did business, it was wise to familiarize himself with units who might conceivably be processed in the future. At least in this city, Smoothbore had done just that. But Smoothbore was completely unable to identify the three faces in front of him. The photographs had been taken with a long-focus lens, and the disheveled and dirty subjects hardly seemed of the same species as the refined figures in front of him. Closer inspection revealed that one of the three faces belonged to a woman. She was still young, and her appearance was tidier than that of the others. Her hair, though coated with dust, was neatly combed. The look in her eyes was unusual. Smoothbore paid attention to people's expressions – people in this business always did. He usually saw one of two expressions: anxious desire or numbness. But her eyes were filled with rare serenity. Smoothbore's heart stirred faintly, but the feeling passed as quickly as it came, like a fine mist blown away by the wind.

'This is the task that the Council for Liquidation of Social Wealth entrusts to you. This is the standing committee of the Council, and I am its Chairman,' said Zhu.

The Council for Liquidation of Social Wealth? It was a strange name. Apart from being an organization composed of the world's wealthiest individuals, Smoothbore could not ponder the implications of its name. Without further particulars, it was probably impossible to unravel its true purpose.

'Their locations are written on the back. They have no fixed addresses, so those are approximations. You will have to search for them, but they should not prove difficult to find. The money has already been wired to your account. Please verify the transfer,' instructed Zhu.

Looking up, Smoothbore found the expression on Zhu's face to be anything but noble. His eyes were anxious. Somewhat to Smoothbore's surprise, they held not even a trace of desire.

Smoothbore pulled out his cellphone and checked his account. After counting the long string of zeroes after the number, he said coolly: 'First, not so much. My original quote stands. Second, pay half up front, and half on completion.'

'Fine,' Zhu sniffed dismissively.

Smoothbore punched several keys. 'The excess funds have been returned. Please verify the transfer, sir. We, too, have professional standards.'

'Indeed. These days your line of work is oversubscribed. But we value your professionalism and sense of honor,' said Xu Xueping with a charming smile. She was the chief executive of Far Source Group, Asia's largest energy development entity born out of the full liberalization of the electric power market.

'This is the first order, so please handle it cleanly,' said the offshore oil baron Xue Tong.

'Fast cooling or delayed cooling?' asked Smoothbore, quickly adding, 'I can explain if necessary.'

'We understand, and it doesn't matter. Do as you see fit,' answered Zhu.

'Verification method? Video or physical specimen?'

'No need for either. Just complete the task – we have our own methods of checking.'

'Will that be all?'

'Yes, you may go.'

*

As he left the hotel, Smoothbore could see the Elder Brothers' spaceship passing slowly overhead in the narrow strips of sky between the towering buildings. The ship seemed larger than before, and its speed had increased. Evidently it had reduced the altitude of its orbit. The ship's smooth sides bloomed with slowly shifting iridescent patterns, exercising a hypnotic effect on those who looked too long. In fact, the surface of the ship was a perfect mirror, and the patterns seen by observers on the ground were only the distorted reflections of Earth below. Smoothbore imagined the ship as purest silver, a thing of beauty in his eyes. He preferred silver to gold. Silver was quiet, cold.

Before their departure three years ago, the Creators told humanity that they had created six Earths in total; the four that now remained were within two hundred light years of each other. They urged the people of Earth to devote their full efforts to technological development – we needed to eliminate our brother planets, lest we be destroyed ourselves.

But this warning came too late.

Locking their ship into orbit around Earth, emissaries from one of those three planets, the first Earth, arrived in the solar system not long after the departure of the Creators. The First Earth civilization was twice as old as mankind, and so the people of this Earth came to call them 'Elder Brothers'.

Smoothbore took out his cellphone and checked his account balance again. *Brother Teeth, I'm as rich as you now, but it still feels like I'm missing something. And you always thought you already had it all, and everything you did was only a desperate attempt to keep it.* He shook his head, as if to clear the dark cloud from his mind. It was an ill omen to think of Brother Teeth now.

*

Brother Teeth took his name from the saw that never left his side. The blade was thin and flexible, its serrations razor-sharp. The handle was carved from solid coral and decorated with beautiful *ukiyo-e* patterns. He kept the saw wrapped around his waist like a belt, and in idle moments, he would unwind it and draw a violin bow across the back of the blade. By bending the blade and bowing across sections of different widths, he could produce haunting, melancholy music that hung in air like the mournful cries of spirits. Of course, Smoothbore had heard tales of the saw's other application, but he had only seen Brother Teeth use it in action once. It was during a high-stakes game of dice in an old warehouse. Brother Teeth's second-in-command, a man named Half-Brick, had gambled big and lost everything, even his parents' house. With bloodshot eyes, he offered to put both his arms on the table in a double-or-nothing bet.

Brother Teeth rattled the dice and smiled at him. Half-Brick's arms, he said, were an unacceptable bet. After all, the future was long – and without hands, how could they play dice together?

'Bet your legs,' he said.

So Half-Brick had bet both his legs – and when he lost again, Brother Teeth unwound his saw and removed both of his legs where the calf met the knee.

Smoothbore distinctly remembered the sound of the sawblade as it carved through tendon and bone. Brother Teeth had placed a foot on Half-Brick's throat to muffle his hideous shrieks, and only the snarl of the blade on flesh echoed through the dark, cavernous warehouse. As the saw sang merrily across Half-Brick's knee caps, it produced a rich, resonant timbre. Fragments of snow-white bone lay scattered in a pool of bright red blood, forming a beautiful, even seductive composition.

The strange beauty shook Smoothbore to his core. Every cell in his body was bewitched by the song of saw on flesh. This was living! It had been his eighteenth birthday, and this was the best possible rite of passage.

When he was finished, Brother Teeth wiped the blood off his beloved saw and wrapped it around his waist once more. Half-Brick and his legs had already been carried away. Pointing at the trail of blood, he said, 'Tell Brick that I will provide for him from now on.'

Although Smoothbore was young, he had been a trusted member of Brother Teeth's entourage. Having followed the man in his rise to power from a very young age, he was no stranger to bloodshed. When Brother Teeth finally scraped together a fortune from the bloody gutters of society and sought to shift his business empire into more respectable channels, his most loyal retainers were enfeoffed as Chairman of the Board, Vice President, and other such titles. Only Smoothbore was left to serve as Brother Teeth's bodyguard.

Those who knew Brother Teeth understood that the level of trust implied by this appointment was no small matter. The man was extraordinarily cautious, perhaps as a result of the fate that befell his godfather. Brother Teeth's godfather had also been extremely cautious; in Brother Teeth's words, the man would have wrapped himself in iron if given the opportunity. After many years without incident, he boarded a flight and took his assigned seat, flanked on either side by two of his most trusted bodyguards. When the plane landed in Zhuhai, the stewardess noticed the three men remained seated, as if lost in thought. A second look revealed that their blood had already trickled past more than ten rows. Long, micro-thin steel needles had been inserted through their seat backs, and the bodyguards had been impaled through the heart with three needles each. As for Brother Teeth's godfather, he had been pierced through with fourteen needles, like a butterfly carefully pinned and mounted in a specimen box. The number of needles was certainly some sort of message. Perhaps it hinted at fourteen million embezzled yuan, or the fourteen years his killer waited to take vengeance . . . Like his godfather before him, Brother Teeth's journey to the top had been eventful. Now, navigating society was like crossing a forest of hidden blades or a marsh cratered with pitfalls. He was truly placing his life into Smoothbore's hands.

But Smoothbore's new status soon came under threat with the arrival of Mr K. Mr K was Russian. At that time, it was the fashion among those who could afford it to employ ex-KGB officers as bodyguards. Having such a person in one's employ was something worth flaunting, like a movie star lover. Those who ran in Brother Teeth's circles struggled to pronounce his Russian name, and simply called the newcomer 'KGB'. Over time, they settled on Mr K. In reality, Mr K had no relation to the KGB. Most former KGB officers were cubicle-bound civil servants, and even those on the front lines of the secret conflict were untrained in the art of personal security. Instead, Mr K had worked in the Central Security Bureau of the Soviet Union. He was every bit the genuine article, a true expert in keeping his clients breathing. Brother

Teeth had hired him on a vice-chairman's salary not out of a desire to boast, but out of real concern for his own safety.

From the moment of Mr K's arrival, it was clear that he was utterly unlike other bodyguards. At the dinner table, other bodyguards would out-eat and out-drink their wealthy employers, and felt perfectly comfortable interrupting their shop talk. When real danger reared its head, they would either charge in with all the art of a street thug or leave their client in the dust of their panicked retreat. In stark contrast, at banquets or negotiations, Mr K would stand quietly behind Brother Teeth, his hulking figure like an immovable wall, ready to intercept any potential threat. While Mr K never had the opportunity to protect his client in a crisis situation, his professionalism and dedication left no doubt that should such a situation arise, he would fulfill his duties with consummate expertise. Smoothbore was more professional than the other bodyguards and did not share their obvious failings, but he was fully aware of the world of difference between himself and Mr K. For example, it was a long time before he realized that Mr K wore sunglasses at all hours of the day not to look cool, but to conceal his gaze.

Although Mr K picked up Chinese quickly, he kept aloof from the people in his employer's inner circles, including the employer himself. He maintained this distance carefully, until one day he asked Smoothbore to step into his Spartan room. After he poured two glasses of vodka, he told Smoothbore in stilted Chinese, 'I, want to teach you to speak.'

'To speak?'

'A foreign language.'

So Smoothbore began to learn a foreign language from Mr K. He did not realize he was being taught English and not Russian until a few days later. Smoothbore was a quick learner, and when they could communicate in both English and Chinese, Mr K told him, 'You are not like the others.'

'I know,' nodded Smoothbore.

'In my thirty years of experience, I have learned to accurately distinguish those people with potential from the rest. You are one such rare talent, and the first time I saw you it chilled me. It's easy to act in cold blood, but it's difficult to stay cold-blooded without ever thawing. You could become one of the best in this business, if you don't bury your talents.'

'What can I do?'

'First, study abroad.'

Brother Teeth agreed readily to Mr K's suggestion and promised to cover Smoothbore's expenses in full. He had hoped to rid himself of Smoothbore ever since Mr K's arrival, but there were no open positions in the company.

And so, one wintry night, this boy who had been orphaned at a young age and raised in the underbelly of society boarded a passenger jet bound for a strange and distant land.

*

Driving a rundown Santana, Smoothbore made his way across the city to inspect each of the locations written on the photographs. His first stop was Blossom Plaza. It did not take him long to find the man in the photo. He was rummaging through a garbage can when Smoothbore arrived, and after a few minutes, he hauled his bulging trash bag to a nearby bench. His search had born fruit in the form of a large, almost untouched takeout box; a pork sausage missing only a bite; several perfectly good slices of bread; and half a bottle of cola. Smoothbore had expected him to eat with his hands, but he watched with surprise as the tramp pulled out a small aluminum spoon from the pocket of the dirty overcoat he wore even in summer. He finished his dinner slowly and then threw what remained back into the garbage can. Looking around the plaza, Smoothbore saw the lights of the city begin to flicker on in all directions. He was very familiar with this area, but something felt off. In a flash, it occurred to him why the man had been able to leisurely eat his fill. The plaza was a common gathering place for the city's homeless population, but at the moment, no one could be seen but his mark. Where had they gone? Had they all been processed?

Smoothbore drove on to the address on the second photograph. Under an overpass on the outskirts of the city, faint yellow light spilled out from a shack cobbled together from corrugated cardboard. Smoothbore cautiously pushed the busted door of the shack open just a crack. As he poked his head in, he suddenly found himself in a fantastical world of color. The walls of the shack were hung with oil paintings of all sizes, creating a separate wall of art. Smoothbore's eyes traced a wisp of smoke back to the itinerant artist, who lay splayed out beneath a broken easel like a bear in hibernation. His hair was long, and his paint-splattered t-shirt was so baggy it looked like a robe. He was smoking a cheap pack of jade butterfly cigarettes. His eyes roved over his artwork, and his gaze was filled with wonder and loss, as if he was seeing it for the first time. Smoothbore guessed most of his time was spent fawning over his own works. This particular breed of starving artist had been common in the nineties of the previous century, but nowadays they were few and far between.

'It's all right, come in,' said the artist, his eyes never leaving his paintings to look at the door. His tone indicated this was an imperial palace. As soon as Smoothbore stepped inside, he asked, 'Do you like my paintings?'

Smoothbore glanced around and saw that most of the paintings were just chaotic splotches of color – paint splashed directly onto a canvas would have seemed rational by comparison. But there were a few pictures in a very realistic style, and Smoothbore's eyes were quickly drawn to one of these: a canvas dominated by a cracked yellow earth. A few dead plants protruded from the fissures in the ground, looking as if they had withered away centuries ago, if indeed water had ever existed in this world at all. A skull lay on the parched earth. Though it was bleach-white and permeated with cracks, two green, living plants sprouted from its mouth and one eye-socket. In sharp contrast with the drought and death surrounding them, these plants were green and luxuriant, and a tiny, delicate flower crowned the tip of one sprout. The skull's other eye-socket contained a human eyeball. Its limpid pupil stared at the sky, and its gaze was filled with the same wonder and loss as its painter.

'I like this one,' Smoothbore said, pointing to the painting.

'It's called *Barren No. 2*. Will you buy it?'

'How much?'

'How much you got?'

Smoothbore pulled out his wallet and removed all the hundred yuan notes it contained. He handed them to the artist, but the latter only took two bills.

'It's only worth this much. It's yours now.'

Smoothbore started the car and picked up the third photograph to study the last address. He cut the ignition a mere moment later, as his destination lay right alongside the overpass: the city's largest landfill. He took out his binoculars and peered through the windshield, searching for his mark amongst the scavengers clambering over the rubbish dump.

300,000 junkmen made a living off the garbage of the metropolis, forming their own class, complete with its own distinct castes. The highest ranking junkmen could enter the city's ritzy villa districts. There, it was possible to pick a daily haul of shirts, socks, and bed sheets, used only once, from the delicately sculpted waste bins – in these neighborhoods, these were considered single-use goods. All kinds of things found their way into the garbage: lightly scuffed premium leather shoes and belts, half-smoked Havana cigars, expensive chocolate nibbled only at the corners . . . But picking garbage there necessitated hefty bribes to the residential security guards that only a few could afford, and those who could afford it became aristocrats among scavengers.

The middle ranks of junkmen gathered around the city's many waste transfer stations, the first collection stops for municipal waste. There, the most valuable refuse – waste electronics, scrap metal, intact paper products, discarded medical devices and expired pharmaceuticals – was quickly snapped up. These sites were not open to just anyone, however. Each station was the domain of a junk boss. Any scavenger who entered without their permission was harshly punished: perpetrators of minor offenses were violently beaten and driven off, while serious offenders could lose their lives.

Little of value remained in the waste that passed through the transfer stations to the rubbish dumps and landfills on the outskirts of the city, and yet it was this waste that supported the largest number of people. These were the lowliest of junkmen, the kind of people right in front of Smoothbore. Worthless, unrecyclable broken plastic and shredded paper was all that was left for the scavengers on the bottom rungs of junkman society. There were also scraps of rotten food, which could be gleaned from the rubbish and sold as pig feed to neighboring farms at one fen per kilo. In the distance, the metropolis shone like a great brilliant jewel, its radiance casting a flickering halo over the fetid mountain of garbage. The junkmen experienced the luxury of the nearby city by sifting through its trash. Mingled in the rotten food, it was often possible to make out a roast suckling pig with only the legs eaten away, a barely touched grouper, whole chickens . . . Recently, it had become common to find whole Silkie hens, owing to the popularity of a new dish called White Jade Chicken. The dish was prepared by slitting open the stomach of the chicken, filling it with tofu, and letting it simmer. The slices of tofu were the real delicacy; the chicken, while delicious, was merely casing. Like the reed leaves around rice dumplings, any diner foolish enough to eat the chicken itself would become the laughingstock of more discerning patrons . . .

The last garbage truck of the day pulled into the lot. As it tipped its load on the ground, a group of junkmen scrambled to meet the avalanche of waste, quickly vanishing into the rising dust and debris. It was like they had passed into a new phase of evolution, unaffected by the stench of the garbage heap, the germs and the toxic filth. Of course, this was an illusion, maintained by people who only saw how they lived and not how they died. Just like people barely saw the corpses of insects and rats and didn't care how they died. In fact, the bodies of junkmen littered the landfill. They passed away quietly here, soon buried by new trash.

In the dim light emanating from the flood lamps at the edge of the lot, the junkmen appeared as dusty, indistinct shadows, but Smoothbore still swiftly located his mark among them. The speed with which he spotted her was due in part to his own keen vision, but there was also another reason: like the vagrants in Blossom Plaza, there were significantly fewer junkmen on the landfill today. What was going on?

Smoothbore observed his mark through his binoculars. At first glance, she seemed no different than any other scavenger. There was a rope tied around her waist, and she carried a large woven bag and a long-handled rake. She was perhaps a bit skinnier than the others. Unable to squeeze through the throng of junkmen, she could only scrounge along the periphery, sifting through the trash of trash.

Smoothbore lowered the binoculars and thought for a moment, shaking his head slightly. Something truly fantastical was unfolding before him: a homeless man, an itinerant starving artist, and a girl who lived off garbage – three of the poorest, weakest people in the world – somehow posed a threat to the world's wealthiest and most powerful plutocrats. The threat was so great, in fact, that they felt compelled to hire a hitman to deal with the problem.

Barren No. 2 lay on the back seat. In the dark, the skull's single eye bored into Smoothbore, like a thorn in his flesh.

There was a chorus of panicked cries from the landfill, and Smoothbore saw that the world outside his car was bathed in a blue light. The glow emanated from the east, where a blue sun was rapidly rising over the horizon. It was the Elder Brothers' spaceship, arriving in the southern hemisphere. The spaceship did not typically emit light; at night, the sunlight reflecting off its sides made it shine like a small moon. But every so often, it would suddenly illuminate the world in a bluish glow, thrusting humanity into nameless terror. This time, the spaceship's glow was brighter than ever before, perhaps because it was in a lower orbit than usual. The blue moon rose above the city, stretching the shadows of skyscrapers all the way to the landfill like the grasping arms of giants. As spaceship continued its ascent, the shadows gradually shrank away.

The scavenger girl on the landfill was illuminated by the glow of the Elder Brothers' spaceship. Smoothbore raised his binoculars again and confirmed his earlier observations. She indeed was his mark. She knelt with her bag in her lap, the slightest trace of alarm in her upturned gaze, but she mostly projected the same sort of serenity Smoothbore had seen in the photograph. Smoothbore's heart stirred again, but it was as fleeting as before. He knew it was a ripple of emotion from somewhere deep within his soul, and he regretted having lost it again.

The spaceship streaked across the sky and sank below the western horizon, leaving an eerie blue afterglow in the heavens. The landfill settled back into darkness, and the lights of the city sparkled once more.

Smoothbore's thoughts returned to the puzzle at hand: the thirteen wealthiest people on Earth desired to kill the three poorest people. It was beyond absurd, and any possible explanation escaped his imagination. But his mind had not strayed far before he slammed the brakes on his thoughts. He slapped the steering wheel in self-reproach as he suddenly realized he had violated the cardinal rule of his own profession. His tutor's words unfurled in his mind, laying out their profession's maxim: the gun does not care at whom it is aimed.

*

To this day, Smoothbore did not even know in which country he had studied abroad, much less the exact position of the academy. He knew only that first leg of the trip was to Moscow. Upon arrival, he was met by a man who spoke English without a trace of a Russian accent. He was made to put on opaque sunglasses, and disguised as a blind person, he passed the remainder of the journey in darkness. After another three-hour flight and a day's drive, he arrived at the academy, and Smoothbore could not say for certain that he was still in Russia at that point.

The academy was located deep in the mountains and ringed by high walls. Under no circumstances were students permitted to leave before graduation. After he was permitted to remove the sunglasses, Smoothbore discovered the buildings of the academy were divided into two distinct styles: the first type of building was gray and devoid of any distinguishing features, and the second type was very peculiar in both shape and form. He later found out buildings belonging to the latter style were actually assembled from giant building blocks, and could be reconfigured at will to simulate a myriad of combat environments. The entire institute was essentially one big state-of-the-art target range.

The convocation ceremony was the first and only time the student body would gather together, and their number just exceeded four hundred. The silver-haired principal, who had the commanding manner of a classical scholar, gave the following address:

'Students, over the next four years, you will learn the theoretical knowledge and the practical skills required by our line of work – a line of work whose name we shall never speak aloud. It is one of humanity's most ancient professions, and it is a profession assured of a bright future. On the small scale, our work, and only our work, can resolve difficult problems for desperate clients; but on the large scale, our work can change history.

'In the past, different government organizations have offered us great sums of money to train guerilla fighters. We refused them all, because we only train independent professionals. Yes, independent, from everything but money. After today, you must think of yourself as a gun. Your duty is to perform the function of a gun, and to demonstrate its beauty in the process. A gun does not care at whom it is aimed. A raises his gun and shoots B, B wrests the gun away and shoots A – the gun makes no distinction between the two, and completes both assignments with the same level of excellence. This is the most basic principle of our profession.'

During the ceremony, Smoothbore also learned a few of the most common terms in his new profession: their fundamental business was called 'processing', their targets were 'units' or 'work', and death was 'cooling'.

The academy was divided into L, M and S disciplines, or long-, mid-, and short-range. L discipline was the most mysterious and most expensive course of study. The few students who elected this specialty kept to themselves and rarely mixed with M and S students. Likewise, Smoothbore's instructors advised them to keep their distance from L students: 'They are the nobility of this profession, as they are the most likely to change the course of history.'

The knowledge taught to L students was broad and profound, and the sniper rifles reserved for their use cost hundreds of thousands of dollars and were nearly two meters long when fully assembled. L specialists processed work at an average distance of one thousand meters, although it was said that some could hit their marks from three thousand meters away. Processing at distances over fifteen hundred meters was a complicated operation, and part of the preparatory work included placing a series of 'wind chimes' at set distances along the firing range. The ingeniously crafted micro-anemometers could wirelessly transmit data to goggles worn by the shooter, sharpening his (or her) understanding of wind speed and direction along the entire range of the shot.

M specialists processed work at a distance of ten to three hundred meters. It was the most traditional discipline, and it boasted the largest number of students, who generally used standard-issue rifles. While there was rarely a shortage of work for M specialists, this discipline was considered pedestrian and rather lacking in mystique.

Smoothbore belonged to S discipline, learning to process work at a range of less than ten meters. This discipline lacked stringent weapons requirements, and S specialists typically used pistols or even blades and other melee weapons. Of the three specialties, S discipline was undoubtedly the most dangerous, but it was also the most romantic.

The principal was a master of this discipline, and he personally instructed S courses. But to everyone's surprise, the first course he taught was English literature.

'You must first understand the value of S discipline,' the principal said gravely, gazing at the baffled students before him. 'In the L and M disciplines, the unit and the processor never meet, and the unit is processed and cooled without ever realizing its plight. A blessing for the unit, perhaps, but not necessarily for the client. Some clients need their targets to know who has marked them for processing and why, and it falls to us to inform them. In that moment, we are not ourselves, but an incarnation of the client. We must solemnly and perfectly communicate his or her final message to the unit, and thus inflict the maximum psychic shock and torment possible prior to cooling. This is the romance and beauty of S discipline – the look of terror and despair in the unit's eyes just before cooling. We can find no greater pleasure than this in our work, but to this end, we must cultivate our verbal dexterity and literary acumen.'

So for one year, Smoothbore studied literature. He read Homer's epics, memorized Shakespeare, and studied works by many other classical and contemporary authors. Smoothbore felt this was the most rewarding year of his overseas education. He was more or less familiar with the subjects that followed, and if he did not master them at the institute, he could learn them elsewhere. But this was his only chance to deeply engage with literature. Through literature, he rediscovered humanity, and he marveled at the subtleties of human nature. Before, killing had simply felt like smashing a crudely-made pot filled with red liquid; now, he was amazed to find that he had smashed exquisite jadeware, which only heightened the thrill of the act.

His next course of study was human anatomy. Compared to the other two disciplines, S discipline's other major advantage was that it was possible to control the time needed to cool units during processing. The technical terms were 'fast cooling' and 'delayed cooling'. Many clients requested delayed cooling and a recording of the entire process – a treasured keepsake they could appreciate ever after. Of course, this required precise technical skills and extensive experience, and knowledge of human anatomy was indispensable.

Then, his real courses began.

*

The junkmen on the landfill gradually dispersed, until only his mark and a few others remained. Smoothbore decided then and there to process this unit by the end of the night. It went against standard practice to act during the initial observation period, but there were exceptions, should a suitable opportunity for processing present itself.

Smoothbore maneuvered his car out from under the overpass and jolted along the pot-holed road next to the landfill. He observed that any junkman leaving the landfill had to pass this way. The darkness revealed only the shadows of the wild grass swaying in the night breeze. It was an excellent location for processing, and he decided to wait here for the unit.

Smoothbore drew out his gun and placed it gently on the dashboard. It was an inelegant, 7.6mm revolver that was chambered for large Black Star cartridges. He called it Snubnose because of its shape. He had purchased the privately-fabricated, untraceable gun for three thousand yuan on the black market in Xishuangbanna. Although it looked crude, it was made well, and each component part had been machined with precision. Its biggest flaw was that the manufacturer had not bothered with rifling: the barrel walls were smooth metal. It was not as if Smoothbore was unable to procure better, name-brand firearms. Brother Teeth had equipped him with a 32-round Uzi when he had started his bodyguard career and had later gifted him a Type 77 as a birthday present. But Smoothbore had stuffed both guns in the bottom of his trunk, and never carried them on his person. He simply preferred Snubnose. Now, it glinted icily in the halo of the metropolis, drawing Smoothbore's thoughts back to his years at the academy.

On the first day of their real training, the principal made each student present his or her weapon. As he placed Snubnose in that line of finely-crafted pistols, he had felt deeply embarrassed. The principal, however, picked up Snubnose, hefted it in his hand, and said with sincere admiration: 'This is a fine gun.'

'It doesn't have rifling, and you can't even attach a silencer,' sneered another student.

'Precision and range are of little importance to S specialists, and rifling even less so. And silencers? A small pillow will do the trick. Boy, do not allow yourself to be limited by stale convention. In the hands of a master, this gun can yield artistry that all your expensive toys cannot.'

The principal was right. Without rifling, bullets fired by Snubnose would turn somersaults in flight, emitting a shrill, terror-inducing whistle that ordinary bullets lacked. They would continue to spin even after striking their targets, like a rotary blade shredding everything in its path.

'From now on, we will call you Smoothbore!' said the headmaster, handing the gun back to him. 'Hold on to this, boy. It looks like you will have to study knife-throwing.'

Smoothbore immediately grasped the principal's meaning: an expert knife thrower held his knife by the blade as he threw it in order to build momentum through rotation, but this required that the knife arrive point-first as it reached its target. The principal hoped Smoothbore would learn to wield Snubnose as a knife thrower mastered his blades! Such artistry would give Smoothbore unprecedented control over the wounds Snubnose's tumbling bullets inflicted. After two years of bitter practice and nearly thirty thousand bullets, Smoothbore acquired a level of skill that was beyond even the academy's best firearms instructors.

During his studies abroad, Smoothbore became completely inseparable from snubnose. In his fourth year, he became familiar with another student in his own discipline who went by the name of Fire, perhaps because of her mane of red hair. It was impossible to know her nationality, but Smoothbore guessed she came from Western Europe. There were few female students at the academy, and almost all of them were natural sharpshooters. Fire, however, had terrible aim, and her dagger skills were downright embarrassing. Smoothbore had no idea how she made a living before the academy. But in their first garroting class, she plucked a filament so fine as to be nearly invisible from the delicate ring on her finger. She wrapped the razor wire around the neck of the goat being used as a teaching aid, and with a deftness that spoke of practice, neatly sliced its head off. Fire had called it a nanowire, a super-strong material that might be used to build space elevators in the future.

Fire felt no real affection for Smoothbore – that sort of thing was impossible at the academy. She also hung around Frost Wolf, a Nordic student from another discipline. She hopped back and forth between them, stirring them up like stirring two fighting crickets, trying to instigate a bit of bloodshed to disrupt the monotony of student life. She soon succeeded, and the two men agreed to settle their feud with a game of Russian roulette. In the dead of night, their classmates reconfigured the enormous building blocks of the shooting range into the shape of the Coliseum. The duel was to commence in the center of the arena, and the weapon of choice was Snubnose.

Fire presided over the entire scene. With a graceful flourish, she inserted a single cartridge into Snubnose's empty cylinder. Then, holding the barrel, she rolled the cylinder across her pale, slender forearm a dozen times. After the two men politely declined their chance to go first, she smiled and handed the gun to Smoothbore. Smoothbore slowly raised the gun to his head. As the cool muzzle touched his temple, a wave of emptiness and isolation, stronger than anything he had ever felt, washed over him. He felt a formless, frigid wind sweep through the world, until his heart was the last speck of heat in a pitch-dark universe. He steeled his heart and pulled the trigger five times. The hammer fell five times. The cylinder turned five times. The gun did not fire.

Click click click click click – just like that, a crisp, metallic death knell sounded for Frost Wolf. A cheer rose from their classmates. Shedding tears of delight, Fire cried to Smoothbore that she was his. In the middle of all this, Frost Wolf stood with an easy smile on his face. He nodded towards Smoothbore and said with sincerity, 'You Oriental bastard, that was the most brilliant wager since the first Colt was made.' He turned to Fire, 'It's all right, my dear. Life was only ever a gamble anyway.'

He seized Snubnose and pointed it against his temple. With a muffled bang, blood and bone bloomed across the arena floor.

Smoothbore graduated not long after. Wearing the same dark glasses he wore when he arrived, he departed the nameless academy and returned to the place he grew up. He never heard another word about the academy, and it was as if it had never really existed at all.

*

It was not until he returned to the outside world that Smoothbore heard the news: the Creators had arrived to claim the support of the human civilization they themselves had once fostered, but, unable to live comfortably on Earth, left after only one year. Their fleet of 20,000 ships had already vanished into the endless cosmos.

Smoothbore had barely stepped off the plane when received his first processing order.

Brother Teeth warmly welcomed Smoothbore home with an extravagant banquet in his honor. Smoothbore asked to meet privately with him after dinner, saying he had many things he wanted to get off his chest. When everyone else had left, Smoothbore told Brother Teeth, 'I grew up at your side. In my heart, you have never been my brother, but rather my father. I ask you, should I practice the profession I have studied? Just say the word, and I will obey.'

Brother Teeth put his arm around Smoothbore's shoulder. 'If you like it, you should do it. I can tell you enjoy it. Don't worry about high roads and low roads – people with bright futures will do well whatever path they follow.'

'As you say.'

Smoothbore drew his pistol and fired into Brother Teeth's stomach. At just the right angle, the twisting bullets ripped a line across the man's abdomen and buried themselves into the floorboards. As the smoke cleared, Brother Teeth looked at Smoothbore. A flicker of shock registered in his eyes before it was replaced by the numbness that follows revelation. He laughed faintly and nodded.

'You've already made something of yourself, kid.' Brother Teeth spat blood as he spoke and sank gently to the ground.

Smoothbore's processing order had specified an hour of delayed cooling, but no recording. The client trusted him. He poured a glass of liquor and watched the blood pool around Brother Teeth with cold detachment. The dying man slowly rearranged his spilled intestines, as thoughtfully as if he were stacking mahjong tiles. As soon as he pushed them back into his abdomen, the slippery lengths slid right out again. Gingerly, Brother Teeth began to gather them up . . . As he repeated the process for the twelfth time, he gasped his last breath. Precisely one hour had passed since Snubnose rang out.

Smoothbore had spoken truthfully when he said Brother Teeth was like a father to him. On a rainy day when he was five, Smoothbore's biological father, livid after a huge gambling loss, demanded that his mother relinquish every savings deposit book in the house. When she refused, he simply beat her to death. And when Smoothbore tried to block his father, the man broke his son's nose and arm and then vanished into the rain. Later, Smoothbore had searched far and wide for him without success. If he ever did find his father, the man had earned himself the pleasure of a slow cooling.

Smoothbore heard afterwards that Mr K had returned every penny of his salary to Brother Teeth's family and flown back to Russia. Before leaving, the Russian said that the day he sent Smoothbore to study abroad, he knew Brother Teeth would die by his hand. Brother Teeth had lived his life on a knife's edge, but he never understood what made a true killer.

One after another, the junkmen left the landfill until only Smoothbore's mark remained. She rooted through the garbage, buried in her work. She was too weak to claim a good spot when the trucks arrived, and she could only make up for it by working longer hours. Her persistence meant there was no need for Smoothbore to wait for her outside. Thrusting Snubnose into his jacket pocket, he left the car and headed straight for his mark on the garbage heap.

There was a sponginess and tepid warmth to the garbage underfoot, like he was walking on the body of some enormous beast. When he was within four or five meters from his target, Smoothbore drew his revolver from his pocket.

At that moment, a bolt of blue light shot up from the east. The Elder

Brothers' spaceship had completed a full orbit around Earth and returned, still glowing, to the Southern Hemisphere. The abrupt appearance of the blue sun drew the gaze of the two figures on the landfill. They studied the strange star for a moment, and then glanced at each other. When their eyes met, Smoothbore did something no professional hitman should ever do: he nearly let his gun slip out of his hand. For an instant, the shock made him forget Snubnose even existed, and he almost cried out without thinking: Sweet Pea! – but Smoothbore knew it was not Sweet Pea. Fourteen years ago, he had watched Sweet Pea's agonizing death. But she had lived on in Smoothbore's heart, growing older and stronger. He often saw her in his dreams, and he imagined she would look just like the young woman in front of him now.

In his upstart years, Brother Teeth had dealt in an unspeakable trade: he purchased handicapped children from the hands of human traffickers and put them to work in the city as beggars. In those years, the public had not yet exhausted its compassion, and the children proved quite profitable, playing no small part in Brother Teeth's accumulation of seed capital.

Once, Smoothbore accompanied Brother Teeth to receive a new group of children from a trafficker. When they arrived at the old warehouse, they found five children waiting there. Four of them suffered from congenital deformities, but one little girl was whole and healthy. Sweet Pea was six years old and adorable. In stark contrast to the children around her, her big, wide eyes were still full of life. Smoothbore's heart broke as he recalled those eyes and the curiosity with which the little girl examined everything around her, totally unaware of the fate that awaited her.

'That's them,' said the trafficker, pointing at the four deformed children.

'I thought we agreed on five?' asked Brother Teeth.

'The carriage was packed. One of them didn't make it.'

'What about this one?' Brother Teeth pointed at Sweet Pea.

'She's not for you.'

'I want her. Same price as the others.' The tone in his voice brooked no argument.

'But . . . she's perfectly fine. How will you make money with her?'

'You dumb. A few finishing touches will do it.'

As Brother Teeth spoke, he unwound his saw from his waist and drew it across one of Sweet Pea's delicate calves, opening a gaping wound on the girl's leg. Blood gushed out and Sweet Pea shrieked and shrieked.

'Bind it up and stop the bleeding, but don't give her antibiotics. It needs to fester,' Brother Teeth instructed Smoothbore.

So Smoothbore bandaged the Sweet Pea's wound, but the blood continued to seep through the layers of gauze, and the little girl's face grew deathly pale. He snuck her a few doses of Erythromycin and Sulfamethoxazole behind Brother Teeth's back, but it was no use. Sweet Pea's wound grew infected.

Two days later, Brother Teeth sent Sweet Pea to beg on the streets. The effect produced by her pathetic expression and crippled leg immediately exceeded Brother Teeth's expectations. On the very first day she earned three thousand yuan, and over the week that followed, she never brought in less than two thousand per day. On her most fruitful day on the street, a foreign couple took one glance at her and handed her four hundred US dollars. Despite this, Sweet Pea was rewarded with a single box of spoiled food per day. This was not just miserliness on the part of Brother Teeth, but a deliberate way to preserve the child's starved appearance. Smoothbore could only give her scraps stealthily.

One evening, as Smoothbore went to retrieve Sweet Pea from the curbside on which she begged, the little girl leaned close to his ear and whispered, 'Brother, my leg doesn't hurt anymore.' She looked cheerful about this.

Except for his mother's death, this was the only time Smoothbore could remember crying. Sweet Pea's leg did not trouble her because the nerves were already dead. Her entire leg had turned black, and she had run a high fever for two days. Smoothbore could not bear to follow Brother Teeth's orders any longer, and he carried Sweet Pea to the hospital. The doctors informed him that it was already too late: the girl had blood poisoning. She passed away late the next night, consumed by fever.

From that moment on, Smoothbore's blood ran cold, and just as Mr K predicted, it never warmed again. Killing others became a pleasure for

Smoothbore, more addictive than any drug. He lived to smash the delicate jade vessels called 'humans', to watch the red liquid contained within gush out and cool to room temperature. That alone was the truth – that all the warmth in that liquid was only ever a charade.

Without conscious intent, Smoothbore had burned a pixel-perfect image of the gash on Sweet Pea's leg into his memory. Later, the image had manifested itself on Brother Teeth's torn abdomen, a precise copy of the original wound.

*

The junkwoman stood, slung her oversized sack over her shoulder, and slowly turned to leave. It was not Smoothbore's arrival that prompted her departure. She had not noticed what he held in his hand, and could not imagine that this well-dressed man might bear any relation to herself. It was simply time for her to go. As the Elder Brothers' ship sank below the western horizon, Smoothbore stood motionless on the landfill, watching her figure vanish into the fading blue twilight.

Smoothbore returned his gun to its holster. He drew out his cellphone and dialed Zhu Hanyang's number: 'I want to meet with you. There is something I need to ask.'

'Nine o'clock tomorrow, same place.' Zhu Hanyang's answer was unfazed and concise, as if he had expected Smoothbore's call.

*

As he entered the Presidential Hall, Smoothbore discovered that the entire thirteen-person standing committee of the Council for Liquidation of Social Wealth was already assembled there, their stern gazes focused upon his own person.

'Please ask what you came to ask,' said Zhu Hanyang.

'Why do you want to kill these three people?' asked Smoothbore.

'You have violated the ethics of your profession,' Zhu observed drily, slicing the cap off a cigar with an elegant cigar cutter.

'Yes, and it will cost me. But I need to know the reason, or I cannot do this job.'

Zhu lit the cigar with a long match and nodded slowly: 'I cannot help but think that you only accept work that targets the wealthy. If this is the case, then you are not a true professional hitman, just a thug with a penchant for petty class vengeance, a psychopath who has killed forty-one people in three years, who is being desperately pursued by the police at this very moment. Your reputation will come crashing down around you.'

'You could call the police right now,' Smoothbore replied calmly.

'Has this task touched upon a bit of personal history?' asked Xu Xueping.

Smoothbore could not help but admire her keen insight. His silence answered for him.

'Was it the woman?'

Smoothbore did not reply. The conversation had veered too far off course.

'Very well.' Zhu exhaled a lungful of white smoke. 'This task is important, and we cannot find anyone more suited to it on such short notice. We have no choice but to accept your terms and tell you the reason, but know that it will exceed your wildest dreams. We, the wealthiest few in this society, desire to kill its poorest and weakest members, and this has made us deranged, hateful creatures in your eyes. Before we explain our motivations, we must first correct this impression.'

'I'm not interested in issues of light and dark.'

'But the facts say otherwise. Come with us, please.' Tossing away his barely smoked cigar, Zhu stood and walked out of the room.

Smoothbore exited the hotel in the company of the full standing committee of the Council for Liquidation of Social Wealth. Something strange was occurring overhead, and pedestrians anxiously craned their heads towards the sky. The Elder Brothers' spaceship was sweeping past in low orbit. In the light of the rising sun, it seemed especially visible against the early morning skies. The ship scattered a trail of shining silver stars in its wake at even intervals, which stretched behind it to the horizon. The ship's length had shortened significantly, and as it released star after star its bulk grew jagged, like a broken stick. Smoothbore had learned from the news that the Elder Brothers' enormous spaceship was actually assembled from thousands of smaller vessels. Now it seemed that the composite whole was splitting apart into an armada.

'Attention, everyone!' Zhu beckoned to the committee. 'You can see the situation has developed, and there may not be much time. We must accelerate our efforts. Each team should report immediately to their assigned liquidation area and continue yesterday's work.'

As he finished, he and Xu Xueping climbed into a truck and called for Smoothbore to join them.

Only then did Smoothbore notice that the vehicles waiting outside the hotel were not the billionaires' usual limousines, but a line of Isuzu trucks.

'So we can transport more cargo,' explained Xu, reading the confusion on Smoothbore's face. Smoothbore looked into the bed of the truck and saw that it was neatly packed with small, identical black suitcases. The cases looked elegant and expensive, and he estimated there were over a hundred of them.

There was no driver, and Zhu himself pulled the vehicle out onto the main road. The truck soon turned onto a tree-lined avenue and reduced its speed. Smoothbore realized that Zhu was driving slowly alongside a pedestrian – a vagrant. Although in this day and age the homeless did not necessarily dress in rags, there was always something that gave them away. This man had tied a plastic bag around his waist, and its contents rattled with every step.

Smoothbore knew that the mystery behind the vanishing homeless and junkmen was about to unravel, but he did not believe Zhu and Xu would dare to kill the man right here. In all likelihood, they would first lure their target into the truck and dispose of him at another location. Given their status, it was wholly unnecessary for them to dirty their hands with this sort of work. Perhaps they were setting an example for him? Smoothbore had no inclination to interrupt them, but he certainly would not help them either. This was not in his contract.

The tramp was quite unconscious of the fact that the truck had slowed for him until Xu Xueping called out to him.

'Hello!' said Xu, rolling down the window. The man stopped and turned his head to look at her. His face had the anesthetized look common to that class. 'Do you have a place to live?' Xu asked, smiling.

'In the summer, I can live anywhere,' said the man.

'And in the winter?'

'Hot air vents. Some restrooms are heated, too.'

'How long have you lived like this?'

'Don't really remember. Came to the city after my land requisition payments ran out, lived like this ever since.'

'Would you like a three bedroom house in the city? A home?'

The tramp stared blankly at the billionaire. There was not an inkling of comprehension on his face.

'Can you read?' asked Xu. After the man nodded, she pointed to a large billboard in front of the truck. 'Look over there—' The billboard displayed a grassy knoll dotted with cream-colored buildings, like an idyllic paradise. 'That's an advertisement for commercial housing.' The man turned his head to the billboard, and then looked back at Xu. He did not have the faintest clue what she meant. 'Okay, now take a case from the truck.'

He obediently walked to the rear of the truck, picked out a case, and walked back to the passenger door. Pointing at the case, Xu told him, 'Inside is one million yuan. Use five hundred thousand to buy yourself a house like the ones on the billboard, and use the rest to live in comfort. Of course, if you can't spend all that money yourself, you can do what we're doing and give it someone poorer.'

The tramp's eyes moved back and forth rapidly, but he remained expressionless, and did not let go of the box. He knew there had to be a catch.

'Open it and see for yourself.'

He fumbled at the lid with one grimy hand. He opened the case just a crack, and then snapped it shut again, the layer of apathy frozen to his face finally shattered. He looked like he had seen a ghost.

'Do you have an ID card?' Zhu Hanyang asked.

The man nodded mechanically, holding the case as far away from himself as possible, as if it was a bomb.

'Then make a deposit at the bank. It'll be more convenient.'

'What…do you want me to do?' asked the tramp.

'We just need you to do us one little favor: the aliens are coming. If they ask you, tell them you have this much money. That's all. Can you promise to do this?'

The man nodded.

Xu stepped down from the truck and bowed deeply to the tramp. 'Thank you.'

'Thank you,' added Zhu from the truck.

What shocked Smoothbore most was that their gratitude seemed sincere.

They drove on, losing sight of the newly-minted millionaire in the rear view windows. Not far down the road, the truck stopped at a corner. Smoothbore spotted three migrant day-laborers squatting on the curb, waiting for work. Each man had a small metal trowel, and a small cardboard sign on the ground read: 'Scrapers.' The three men ran over as soon as the truck pulled up and clamored for work: 'Got a job for us, boss?'

Zhu Hanyang shook his head. 'No. Has business been good lately?'

'No business to be had. Everybody uses that new thermal spray coating nowadays, no need for scrapers anymore.'

'Where are you from?'

'Henan.'

Zhu rattled off several questions: 'The same village? Is it poor? How many households?'

'It's up in the hills, there are maybe fifty families. Everyone's poor. It never rains. Boss, you wouldn't believe it – we have to irrigate our plants one by one with a watering can.'

'Don't bother with farming. Do you have bank accounts?'

All three shook their heads.

'You'll have to take cash, then. They're heavy, but I'll still trouble you to take a dozen cases from the back.'

'A dozen?' It was the scrapers' only question as they unloaded the cases from the bed of the truck and piled them on the sidewalk. They did not pause to consider Zhu's instructions – work was work.

'It doesn't matter, take as many as you like.'

Fifteen cases soon lay on the ground. Pointing to the stack, Zhu told them, 'Each box contains one million yuan, fifteen million in total. Go home and share the money with your whole village.'

One of the men laughed at this, as if Zhu had cracked a joke. One of his companions crouched down and opened one of the cases. The men stared at its contents, the same flabbergasted expression as the tramp creeping over their faces.

'The cases are heavy, so you should hire a car to return to Henan. Actually, if one of you can drive, buy a car. It will be more convenient,' said Xu Xueping.

The three scrapers gaped at the two people in front of them, unsure if they were angels or devils. Like clockwork, one of the men raised the same question as the tramp before him: 'What do you want with us?'

The answer was the same: 'We just need you to do us one little favor: the aliens are coming. If they ask you, tell them you have this much money. That's all. Can you promise to do this?'

The three men nodded in assent.

'Thank you.'

'Thank you.' The two plutocrats bowed in sincere appreciation and drove off, leaving the three baffled scrapers standing next to the stack of cases.

'You must be wondering if they will keep the money all for themselves,' Zhu said to Smoothbore, his eyes still on the steering wheel. 'Perhaps in the beginning, but they will soon share their wealth with the less fortunate, just as we have done.'

Smoothbore kept silent. Confronted with such absurdity, he felt it was best to say nothing at all. His intuition told him that the world as he knew it was about to undergo a fundamental change.

'Stop the car!' cried Xu. She called to a small, filthy child who was rummaging through a trash can for tin cans and cola bottles: 'Kid, come here!' The urchin dashed over, dragging his half-filled sack of cans and bottles behind him as if afraid of losing it. 'Take a case from the truck bed.' The boy obliged. 'Look inside.' He opened the case and peered inside. He was surprised, but not as shocked as the four adults had been. 'What is it?' prompted Xu.

'Money,' replied the boy, lifting his head to gaze at her.

'One million yuan. Take it home and give it to your parents.'

'So it's true?' The boy blinked, turning his head to look at the cases still stacked high in the truck bed.

'What do you mean?'

'I heard people were giving away money all over the city. Like throwing away scrap paper.'

Xu continued: 'You have to promise something before you can keep it. The aliens are coming. If they ask you, you must tell them you have this much money – you do have this much money, right? That's all we want. Will you do it?'

'Yes!'

'Then take your money and go home, boy. No one will ever be poor again,' said Zhu as he started the truck.

'No one will ever be rich again, either,' said Xu, a dark look on her face.

'Pull yourself together. It's a bad situation, but we have a responsibility to stop it from getting worse,' said Zhu.

'You really think there is a point to this little game of ours?'

Zhu slammed the brakes and brought the truck to a lurching halt. Gesticulating wildly over the steering wheel, he shouted, 'Yes, of course it has a point! Or do you want to live the rest of your life like these people? Starving and homeless?'

'I don't even want to go on living anymore.'

'Your sense of duty will sustain you. In these dark days, it's the only thing that keeps me going. Our wealth demands that we devote ourselves to this mission.'

'Our wealth what?' shrieked Xu. 'We never stole, we never coerced, every yuan we earned was clean. Our wealth pushed society forward. Society should thank us!'

'Try telling that to the Elder Brothers,' said Zhu, stepping down from the truck. He tilted his face to the sky and heaved a long sigh.

'Now do you see that we're not psycho killers with a grudge against the poor?' The question was addressed to Smoothbore, who had followed him outside. 'No, on the contrary, we've been spreading our wealth amongst the very poorest, like you just witnessed. In this city and many others, in our nation's most impoverished areas, the employees of our companies are doing the same thing. They are utilizing every resource available to our conglomerate – billions of checks, credit cards, savings accounts, truckload upon truckloads of cash – to eliminate poverty.'

Just then, Smoothbore noticed the curious spectacle in the sky: the line of silver stars now stretched from one horizon to the other. The Elder Brothers' mother ship had completely disintegrated, and thousands of smaller ships had formed a gleaming halo around Earth.

'Earth is surrounded,' said Zhu. 'Each of those ships is the size of an aircraft carrier, and the weapons of just one of them could destroy the whole planet.'

'Last night, they destroyed Australia,' interjected Xu.

'Destroyed? What do you mean destroyed?' asked Smoothbore, his head craning towards the sky.

'They swept a laser over the Australian continent from space. It pierced right through buildings and bunkers, and every human and large mammal was dead within the hour. Insects and plants were left unscathed, though, and porcelain in shop windows wasn't so much as scratched.'

Smoothbore glanced momentarily at Xu, and then turned his gaze back to the sky. He was better equipped to deal with this sort of terror than most.

'It was a show of force. They chose Australia because it was the first country to explicitly reject the "reservation" plan,' added Zhu.

'What plan?' Smoothbore asked.

'Let me start from the beginning,' began Zhu. 'The Elder Brothers have come to our solar system as refugees, unable to survive on First Earth. "We have lost our homeland"— those were the words they used. They have not elaborated on the causes. They want to occupy our Earth, Fourth Earth, and use it as a new habitat. As for this Earth's inhabitants, they will be relocated to a human "reservation", located in what used to be Australia. Every other territory will belong to the Elder Brothers… An announcement will be made in tonight's news.'

'Australia? It's a big chunk of rock in the middle of the ocean.' Smoothbore considered it for a moment. 'Actually, it is pretty suitable. The Australian outback is one big desert – if they squeeze five billion people on the island, starvation will set in before the week is out.'

'Things aren't that bleak. Human agriculture and industry will not exist on the reservation. There will be no need to engage in production to survive.'

'How will they live?'

'The Elder Brothers will support us – they will provide for humanity. In the future, everything humans need to live will be provided by the Elder Brothers and distributed evenly among us. Every person will receive the same amount. In the future, wealth inequality will cease to exist in human society.'

'But how will they determine how much to allocate each person?'

'You've grasped the key issue at hand,' replied Zhu. 'According to the reservation plan, the Elder Brothers will conduct a comprehensive census of humanity, the goal of which is to determine the absolute minimum standard of living that humans can tolerate. The Elder Brothers will then allocate resources according to the results.'

Smoothbore lowered his head and thought for a moment, and then suddenly chuckled, 'I think I get it. At least, I think I see the big picture now.'

'You understand the plight that humanity currently faces?'

'Actually, the Elder Brothers' plan is very fair to humanity.'

'What? You think it's fair?! You—' Xu sputtered.

'He's right, it is fair,' Zhu calmly interrupted. 'If there is no gap between poor and rich, no difference between the lowest and highest standards of living, then the reservation will be paradise on Earth.'

'But now . . .'

'Now, what we must do is simple: before the Elder Brothers conduct their census, we must rapidly level the sharp divide between rich and poor.'

'So this is "social wealth liquidation"?' asked Smoothbore.

'Precisely. At present, society's wealth has solidified. It has its ups and downs, like the high-rises on this street or a mountain towering over a plain. But once it has been liquefied, it will become like the smooth surface of the ocean.

'But what you are doing now will only create chaos.'

'True,' nodded Zhu. 'We are merely making a gesture of goodwill on behalf of people of means. The real liquidation of wealth will soon commence under the unified leadership of national governments and the United Nations. A sweeping campaign to eliminate poverty is about to begin. Rich countries will pour capital into the Third World, rich people will shower the poor with money – and it will be carried out with perfect sincerity.'

Smoothbore gave a cynical laugh. 'Things may not be that simple.'

'What do you mean, you bastard?' Xu snarled through clenched teeth. She jabbed a finger at Smoothbore's nose, but Zhu instantly stopped her.

'He's a smart fellow. He figured it out,' said Zhu, tilting his head in Smoothbore's direction.

'Yes, I have figured it out. There are poor people who don't want your money.'

Xu glowered at Smoothbore, then lowered her head and fell silent. Zhu nodded. 'Right. There are those who do not want money. Can you imagine? Scrounging in the garbage for scraps of food, but refusing an offer of one million yuan? Yes, you hit the nail on the head.'

'But those people must surely be a tiny minority,' said Smoothbore.

'Of course, but even if they account for just one in every hundred thousand poor people, they will be counted as a separate social class. According to the Elder Brothers' advanced survey methods, their standard of living will be identified as humanity's minimum standard of living, which in turn will be adopted as the criterion for the Elder Brothers' resource allocation to the reservation! Do you get it? Just one thousandth of one percent!'

'What percentage of the population do they account for at present?'

'About one in every thousand.'

'Perverted, despicable traitors!' Xu cursed loudly at the sky.

'So you contracted me to kill them.' At the moment, Smoothbore did not feel like using professional jargon.

Zhu nodded.

Smoothbore stared at Zhu with a queer expression, and then threw his head back and burst into laughter. 'I'm killing for the benefit of humankind!'

'You are benefiting humanity. You are rescuing human civilization.'

'Actually,' mused Smoothbore, 'death threats would do the trick.'

'That's no guarantee!' Xu leaned towards Smoothbore and whispered in a low voice. 'We are dealing with lunatics, twisted with class hatred. Even if they did take the money, they would still swear to the Elder Brothers that they are penniless. We have to wipe them off the planet as soon as possible.'

'I understand,' nodded Smoothbore.

'So what's your plan now? We have explained our reasoning just as you asked us. Of course, money will soon be meaningless, and you certainly don't care about helping humanity.'

'Money was never of great concern to me, and I've never considered the latter . . . But I will fulfill the contract – by midnight tonight. Please prepare whatever you need to verify its completion.' As he finished speaking, Smoothbore stepped down from the truck and began to leave.

'I have one question,' Zhu called after Smoothbore's retreating back. 'Perhaps it's impolite, so you don't have to answer. If you were poor, would you refuse our money?'

'I am not poor,' Smoothbore answered, without looking back. He took a few more steps, and then paused and turned. He fixed the pair with a hawkish gaze. 'If were . . . then yes, I would not take it.' Then he strode away.

*

'Why did you refuse their money?' Smoothbore asked his first mark. He had last seen the homeless man in Blossom Plaza; now, they stood in a grove of trees in a nearby park. Two types of light filtered through the canopy. The first was the eerie blue glow that emanated from the ring of the Elder Brothers' ships, casting dappled shadows across the ground. The second was the shifting, kaleidoscopic brilliance of the metropolis itself, wavering wildly as it slanted through the trees, as if terrified of the blue glow.

The tramp snickered. 'They were begging me. All those rich people were begging me! One woman even cried! If I took their money, they wouldn't care about me, and it felt so refreshing to be begged for a change.'

'Yes, very refreshing,' said Smoothbore, as he pulled Snubnose's trigger.

The tramp was an enterprising thief. He had seen at a glance that the man who had called him into the grove was holding something wrapped beneath his coat, and he was curious to discover what it was. He saw a sudden flash from beneath the man's coat, like the wink of some strange creature within, and he was plunged into endless darkness.

The job was processed and cooled almost instantly. The rapidly spinning bullet severed most of the unit's head above the brow. The gunshot was muffled under layers of clothing. No one noticed.

*

Returning to the landfill, Smoothbore discovered that only his mark remained –the other junkmen had evidently claimed their new fortunes and left.

Under the blue light of the ring of starships, Smoothbore picked his way across the warm, springy waste heap with purposeful strides, heading straight for his target. He had reminded himself a hundred times beforehand that this was not Sweet Pea, and there was no need to repeat the warning again. His blood ran cold, and it would not be warmed by a handful of youthful memories. The scavenger girl had not even noticed his arrival when Smoothbore fired his gun. There was no need to silence his weapon on the landfill. Freed from his coat, the shot rang clear, and the flash lit up the garbage around him like a small bolt of lightning. The range gave the bullet time to sing as it tumbled through the air, its whine like the wailing of spirits.

This job was also processed and cooled almost instantly. In an instant, the bullet shredded the unit's heart like the whirling blade of a buzz-saw. She was dead before she hit the ground. Her body was instantly swallowed into the landfill, and the blood that might have testified to her existence was quickly sopped up by the garbage.

Without warning, Smoothbore became aware of a presence behind him. He spun on his heel to face the itinerant artist. The man's long hair fluttered in the evening breeze, like blue flames in the light of the ring of stars.

'They had you kill her?' asked the artist.

'Merely honoring a contract. Did you know her?'

'Yes. She often came to look at my art. She couldn't read much, but she understood the paintings. She liked them, just like you.'

'I've been contracted to kill you, too.'

The artist dipped his head in calm acknowledgment. He did not betray a hint of fear. 'I thought so.'

'Out of curiosity, why did you refuse the money?'

'My paintings describe poverty and death. If I became a millionaire overnight, my art would die.'

Smoothbore nodded. 'Your art will live on. I truly do like your painting.' He raised his gun.

'Wait a moment. You said you were fulfilling a contract. Can I sign one with you?'

Smoothbore nodded again. 'Of course.'

'My death doesn't matter, but I want you to avenge her.' The artist pointed to where the scavenger lay amid the garbage.

'Let me rephrase your request in the language of my profession: you want to contract me to process an order of work, the same units that contracted me to process you and this other unit.'

The artist responded with a nod. 'Just like that.'

Smoothbore gravely assented, 'Not a problem.'

'I have no money.'

Smoothbore laughed, 'You sold me that painting far too cheaply. It has already paid for this job.'

'Then, thank you.'

'You're welcome. I am merely honoring a contract.'

Snubnose's muzzle spat deadly fire once more. The bullet twisted, caterwauling through the air, and struck the artist in the heart. Blood sprayed from his chest and his back as he fell. Seconds later, the droplets showered the ground like a hot, red rain.

'There was no need for that.'

The voice came from behind Smoothbore. He whirled around again and saw a person standing in the center of the landfill, a man. He wore a leather jacket almost identical to Smoothbore's own, and he looked young but otherwise unremarkable. The blue light from the ring of stars glinted in his eyes.

Smoothbore lowered his gun and trained it away from the newcomer, but he lightly squeezed the trigger. Snubnose's hammer rose unhurriedly to the fully-cocked position, ready to fire at the slightest touch.

'Are you police?' Smoothbore asked casually.

The stranger shook his head.

'Then go call them.'

The man stood still.

'I will not shoot you in the back. I only process work specified in my contract.'

'Currently, we are not to intervene in human affairs,' the man replied evenly.

His words struck Smoothbore like a bolt of lightning. His grip slackened, and the hammer of his revolver fell back into place. He peered closely at the stranger. In the glow of the starships, he was, by all appearances, an ordinary man.

'You've…already landed, then?' Smoothbore asked, an uncommon waver in his voice.

'We landed quite some time ago.'

Standing atop a landfill somewhere on Fourth Earth, a long silence settled over the two individuals from different worlds. The thick, warm air suddenly felt stifling. Smoothbore wanted to say something, anything, and the events of the past few days prompted a question: 'Are there poor people and rich people where you come from?'

The First Earthling smiled and said, 'Of course. I am poor.' He gestured towards the ring of stars above them. 'As are they.'

'How many people are up there?'

'If you mean those of us in the ships you can see now, about five hundred thousand. But we are just the vanguard. Ten thousand more ships will arrive in a few years from now, carrying one billion.'

'A billion?' wondered Smoothbore. 'They…can't all be poor, can they?'

'Every last one,' confirmed the alien.

'How many people are there on First Earth?'

'Two billion.'[1]

'How can so many people on one world be poor?'

'Why can't so many people on one world be poor?' countered the alien.

'I would think,' Smoothbore said, 'that too many poor people would destabilize a world, which would make things difficult for the middle and upper classes as well.'

'At this stage of Fourth Earth's development, that is true.'

1　此句与原文略有出入，本书保留译文的处理方法。——编者注

'But it won't always be true?'

The First Earthling bowed his head and considered this, and then replied, 'Why don't I tell you the story of the rich and poor of First Earth?'

'I'd like to hear it.' Smoothbore tucked Snubnose back into his underarm holster.

'Our two human civilizations are remarkably similar,' began the alien. 'The paths you follow now, we travelled before you, and we, too, lived through an era similar to your present. Although the distribution of wealth was uneven, our society struck a certain balance. The population, rich and poor alike, was a manageable size, and it was commonly believed that wealth inequality would disappear as society progressed. Most people looked forward to an age of perfect prosperity and great harmony. But we soon discovered that things were far more complicated than we had imagined, and the balance we had achieved would soon be destroyed.'

'Destroyed by what?'

'Education. You know that in the present age of Fourth Earth, education is the sole means of social ascendancy. If society is an ocean, stratified by differences in temperature and salinity, then education is a pipe that connects the ocean floor to the surface, and prevents the complete isolation of each layer.'

'So you're saying that fewer and fewer poor people could afford to attend university?'

'Yes. The cost of higher education grew increasingly expensive, until it became a privilege reserved for the sons and daughters of the social elite. However, the price of traditional education did have limits, even if they were only crude market considerations, so while the pipe grew gossamer-thin, it did not vanish completely. But one day, the appearance of a dramatic new technology fundamentally changed education.'

Smoothbore hazarded a guess. 'Do you mean the ability to transmit knowledge directly to the brain?'

'Yes, but the direct infusion of knowledge was only part of it. A supercomputer, with a capacity that far exceeded that of the brain itself, could be implanted in a human brain; the inventoried knowledge of the computer could then be recalled by the implantee as distinct memories.' The alien continued, 'But this was only one of the computer's secondary functions. It was an amplifier of intelligence, an amplifier of understanding, and it could raise human thought to a whole new level. Suddenly, knowledge, intelligence, depth of thought – even perfection of mind, character, and aesthetic judgment – were commodities that could be purchased.'

'Must have been expensive,' observed Smoothbore.

'Incredibly so. Expressed in your current monetary terms, the cost of this premium education for a single person was equivalent to buying two or three one hundred fifty square meter apartments in one of Shanghai or Beijing's prime neighborhoods.'

'Even if it cost that much, there would still be a few who could afford it.'

'Yes,' the First Earthling admitted, 'but they were a tiny segment of the upper class. The pipeline from the bottom of society to the top was completely severed. Those who received this premium education were vastly more intelligent than those who did not. The cognitive differences between these educated elites and ordinary humans were as large as those between humans and dogs, and these differences manifested themselves in every aspect of human life – even artistic sensibility, for example. This super-intelligentsia formed a new culture – a culture as incomprehensible to the rest of humanity as a symphony is incomprehensible to a dog. They could master hundreds of languages, and on any given occasion, they would use the particular language that etiquette demanded. From the perspective of these super-intellects, conversing with ordinary people seemed as condescending as cooing to puppies. And so, quite naturally, something happened. You're smart, you should be able to guess.'

Smoothbore hesitated. 'Rich people and poor people were no longer the same... the same...'

'The rich and the poor were no longer the same species. The rich were as different to the poor as the poor were to animals. The poor were no longer people.'

Smoothbore gasped. 'That must have changed everything.'

'It changed many things. First, the factors you mentioned that maintained a balance of wealth and limited the poor population, ceased to exist. Even if animals outnumbered humans, they would be unable to destabilize the foundations of human society. At worst, the disruption would be a nuisance but unthreatening. Sympathy for poor people hinged on one shared characteristic – personhood. When the poor ceased to be people, and all commonalities between rich and poor vanished, sympathy followed suit. This was humanity's second evolution. When we first split from apes, it was due to natural selection. When we split from the poor, it was due to an equally sacred law: the inviolability of private property.'

'Property is sacred in our world, too.'

'On First Earth, it was upheld by something called the Social Machine,' explained the alien. 'The Social Machine was a powerful enforcement system, and its Enforcers could be found in every corner on the planet. Some of these units no bigger than mosquitoes, but they were capable of killing hundreds in single strike. They were not governed by the Three Laws proposed by your Asimov, but by the fundamental principle of the First Earth Constitution, that private property shall be inviolable. But it would be inaccurate to say they brought about autocracy. They enforced the law with absolute impartiality, and showed no favor to the wealthy. If the pitiful property of some poor fellow came under threat, they would protect it in strict accordance with the constitution.

'Under the powerful protection of the Social Machine, the wealth of First Earth flowed relentlessly towards the pockets of an elite minority. To make matters worse, technological development eliminated the reliance of the propertied classes on the propertyless. On your world, the rich still need the poor, because factories still need workers. On First Earth, machines no longer needed human operators, and high-efficiency robots could perform any required task. The poor could not even sell their labor, and they sank into absolute destitution as a result. This transformed the economic reality of First Earth, vastly accelerating the concentration of wealth in just a few people's hands.

'I would not be able to explain the highly complex process of wealth concentration to you,' the alien said, 'but in essence it resembles the movements of capital on your world. During my great-grandfather's lifetime, sixty percent of the wealth on First Earth was controlled by ten million people. During my grandfather's lifetime, eighty percent of our world's wealth was controlled by ten thousand people. During my father's lifetime, ninety percent of the wealth belonged to just forty two people. When I was born, capitalism had reached its apex on First Earth, and had worked an unbelievable miracle: ninety-nine percent of the planet's wealth was held by a single person! This person became known as the Last Capitalist.

'While disparities in standards of living still existed among the other two billion, they controlled just one percent of the world's wealth in total. That is to say, First Earth had become a world with one rich person and two billion impoverished people. All the while, the constitutional inviolability of private property remained in effect, and the Social Machine faithfully carried out its duty to protect the property of a sole individual.

'Do you want to know what the Last Capitalist owned?' The alien raised his voice. 'He owned First Earth! Every continent and ocean on the planet became his parlor rooms and private gardens. Even the atmosphere of First Earth was among his personal property.

'The remaining two billion individuals inhabited fully enclosed dwellings – miniature, self-contained life-support units. They lived sealed away in their own tiny worlds, sustained by their own paltry supplies of water, air, soil, and other resources. The one resource that did not belong to the Last Capitalist, and the only thing they could lawfully take from the outside world, was sunlight.

'My home sat next to a small river, edged by green grass. The meadows stretched down to the riverbed and beyond, sweeping all the way to the emerald foothills in the distance. From inside, we could hear the sounds of birds twittering and fish leaping from the water, and we could see unhurried herds of deer drinking water by the riverbanks, but it was the sight of the grass rippling in the breeze that I found particularly bewitching.

'But none of this belonged to us. My family was strictly cut off from the outside world, and we could only watch from airtight portholes that could never be opened. To go outside, it was necessary to pass through an airlock, as if we were exiting a spaceship into outer space. In truth, our home was very much like a spaceship – the difference was the hostile environment was on the inside! We could only breathe the foul air supplied by our life-support system, could only drink the water that had been re-filtered a million times over, could only choke down food produced using our own raw excrement. And all the while, only a single wall separated us from the vast, bountiful world of nature. When we stepped outside, we dressed like astronauts and brought our own food and water. We even brought our own oxygen tanks, because the air, after all, belonged not to us, but to the Last Capitalist.

'Of course, we could afford the occasional splurge. On weddings or holidays, we would leave our closed little home and luxuriate in the great outdoors. That first breath of natural air was positively intoxicating. It was faintly sweet – sweet enough to make you cry. It wasn't free, though. We had to swallow pill-sized air meters before we went out, which measured exactly how much air we breathed. Every time we inhaled, a fee was deducted from our bank account. This was a luxury for most of the poor, something they could afford once or twice a year. We never dared to exert ourselves while outdoors. We mostly just sat and controlled our breathing. Before we returned home, we had to carefully scrape the soles of our shoes, because the soil outside was not ours to keep.'

The First Earthling paused for a moment. 'I will tell you how my mother died,' he said slowly. 'In order to cut down on expenditures, she refrained from leaving the house for three years. She could not bear to go out even on holidays. On the night it happened, she managed to slip past the airlock doors in her sleep. She had to have been dreaming about nature. When she was discovered by an Enforcer, she had already wandered quite far. It saw that she had not swallowed an air meter, so it dragged her back home, cuffing her about the neck with a metal claw. It never intended to strangle her. By preventing her from breathing, it only meant to protect another citizen's inviolable private property – the air. She was dead by the time she arrived home. The Enforcer dropped her corpse and informed us that she had committed larceny. We were fined, but we could not pay, so my mother's body was confiscated instead. You should know that a corpse is a precious thing for a poor family – seventy percent of its weight is water, plus a few other resources. The value of my mother's corpse, however, could not cover the fine, and the Social Machine siphoned off an amount of air that corresponded to the remainder of the debt.

'The air supply in our family's life-support system was already critically low, as we lacked the funds to replenish it. The removal of more air put our very survival at risk. In order to replace the lost oxygen, the life-support system was forced to separate some of its water resources through electrolysis. Unfortunately, this operation caused the entire system to deteriorate sharply. The main control computer issued an alarm: if we did not add fifteen liters of water to the system, it would crash in exactly thirty hours. The crimson glow of the warning lights filled every room.

'We considered stealing water from the river outside, but soon abandoned the plan. We would not make it back home with the water without being shot dead by the omnipresent Enforcers. My father thought for a while, and then told me not to worry and to go to bed. Though I was terrified, oxygen deprivation crept in, and I slept. I do not know how much time had passed when a robot nudged me awake. It had entered via the resource conversion vehicle that was docked to my home. It pointed to a bucket of crystal clear water and told me: "This is your father."

'Resource conversion vehicles were mobile installations that converted human bodies into resources that could be utilized by household life-support systems. My father had utilized the service to extract every last drop of water from his own body, while not one hundred meters from our house, that pretty little river burbled in the moonlight. The resource conversion truck also extracted a few other useful things from his body for our life-support system: a container of grease, a bottle of calcium tablets, even a piece of iron as large as a coin.'

The alien paused again to collect himself. 'The water from my father rescued our life-support system, and I lived on alone. I grew up day by day, and soon five years had passed. One fall evening, as I looked through the porthole at the world outside, I suddenly noticed someone jogging along the riverbank. I was astonished: who was so extravagant that they would dare breathe like that outside?! Upon a closer look, I realized it was the Last Capitalist himself!

'He slowed his pace to a stroll, and then sat down on a rock by the river's edge, dipping one bare foot into the water. He looked like a trim middle-aged man, but in reality, he was over two thousand years old. Genetic engineering guaranteed that he would live for at least another two millennia, perhaps even forever. But he seemed perfectly ordinary to me.

'Two years later, my home's life-support system functions deteriorated once more. Small-scale ecosystems like that were bound to have limited lifespans. Eventually, the whole system broke down. As the oxygen content in the air supply dwindled, I swallowed an air meter and walked out the door before I fell into an anoxic coma. Like every other person whose life-support system had failed, I stoically accepted my fate: I would breathe away the last of the pitiful savings in my account, and then I would be suffocated or shot by an Enforcer.

'I found there were many other people outside. The mass failures of household life-support systems had begun. A gargantuan Enforcer hovered above us and broadcast a final warning: "Citizens, you have intruded into someone else's home. You have committed an act of trespassing. Please leave immediately! Otherwise . . ."

'Leave? Where could we go? There was no air left to breathe in our homes. Together with the others, I bounded through the green grass along the river, letting the fresh, sweet spring breeze rush over our pallid faces, looking to go out in a blaze of glory . . .

'I don't know how long we ran before we realized we had long since breathed up the last of our savings, and yet the Enforcers had not taken action. Just then, the Last Capitalist's voice boomed forth from the massive Enforcer floating in the air.

Hello, everyone. Welcome to my humble home!

I am pleased to have so many guests, and I hope you have enjoyed yourselves in my garden. You will have to forgive me, however, but there are just too many of you. As of this moment, almost one billion people worldwide have left their own homes as their life-support systems failed, and have walked into mine. Another billion may be close behind. You have trespassed on my private property and violated the habitation and privacy rights of your fellow citizen. The Social Machine is lawfully empowered to take action to end your lives, and if I had not dissuaded it from doing just that, you would all have been vaporized by the Enforcers' lasers long ago. In any case, I did dissuade it. I am a gentleman who has received the best education available, and I treat guests in my home – even unlawful intruders – with courtesy and respect. But you must imagine things from my perspective. Two billion guests is a few too many for even the most thoughtful host, and I am someone who enjoys quiet solitude. Therefore, I must ask you all to leave. I recognize, of course, that there is nowhere on Earth for you to go, but I have taken it upon myself to prepare a fleet of twenty thousand spaceships for you.

Each ship is the size of a medium city, and can travel at one percent of the speed of light. While the ships are not equipped with complete life-support systems, there are enough cryogenic chambers onboard to hold all two billion of you for fifty thousand years. This is the only planet in our solar system, so you will have to search for a new homeland among the stars, but I am certain you will find such a place. In the vastness of the cosmos, is it really necessary to crowd this little cottage of mine? You have no cause to resent me. I obtained my home through perfectly reasonable and legitimate means. I got my start as the manager of a small feminine hygiene products company, and to this day, I have relied only on my own business savvy. I am a law-abiding citizen, so the Social Machine has protected and will continue to protect me and my legal property. It will not tolerate your wrongdoing, however, so I advise everyone to get going as soon as possible.

Out of respect for our common evolutionary origin, I will remember you, and I hope you will remember me. Take care.

'And that is how we came to Fourth Earth,' concluded the First Earthling. 'Our voyage lasted for thirty thousand years. We lost nearly half our fleet while wandering endlessly through the stars. Some disappeared amidst interstellar dust; some were swallowed by black holes . . . But ten thousand ships survived, and one billion of us reached this world. And that is the story of First Earth, the story of two billion poor people and one rich man.'

'If you did not intervene, would our world repeat this tale?' Smoothbore asked after the First Earthling finished his narration.

'I do not know. Perhaps, but perhaps not. The course of a civilization is like the fate of an individual – fickle and impossible to predict.' The alien paused. 'I should go now. I am only an ordinary census taker, and I must work for my living.'

'I have things to attend to as well,' replied Smoothbore.

'Farewell, little brother.'

'Farewell, elder brother.'

Under the light of the ring of stars, two men from two different worlds parted in two different directions.

*

As Smoothbore entered the Presidential Hall, the thirteen members of the standing committee of the Council for Liquidation of Social Wealth turned to face him. Zhu Hanyang spoke first: 'We have verified your work, and you have done well. The second half of your payment has been transferred into your account, although it will not be of use for much longer.' He trailed off. 'There is something else you must already know: the Elder Brothers' census takers have landed on Earth. Our work is meaningless now, and we have no further tasks to give you.'

'Actually, I've taken another commission.'

As he spoke, Smoothbore drew his pistol with one hand and stretched his opposite hand forward, fist clenched.

Bang, bang, bang, bang, bang, bang, bang – seven glinting bullets fell to the table in front of him. Together with the six shots in Snubnose, that made thirteen in all.

Thirteen faces, shaped by the weight of their immense wealth, twisted in unison as shock and horror flashed across their refined features. Then a calm settled. Maybe they felt relief.

Outside, a hail of massive meteors split the sky. Their brilliant light pierced through the heavy curtains and eclipsed the crystal chandelier, and the ground shook violently. The ships of First Earth had entered the atmosphere.

'Have you had dinner?' Xu Xueping asked Smoothbore. She pointed towards a heap of instant noodles on the table. 'Let's eat first.'

They stacked a large silver punch basin atop three crystal ashtrays, and added water to the basin. Then, they lit a fire beneath it with one hundred yuan notes. Everyone took turns feeding bills into the fire, gazing absently at the yellow and green flames that leapt like a small joyful creature.

After the fire consumed 1.35 million yuan, the water began to boil.

让日常阅读成为砍向我们内心冰封大海的斧头。

时间移民

刘慈欣 _ 著

[美]刘宇昆(Ken Liu)等 _ 译

北京联合出版公司

Beijing United Publishing Co.,Ltd.

编者按

在翻开这本书之前，你或许已经浸淫在科幻故事中多年，或许只是匆匆过客，或许已经读过书中个别篇目，又或许与之素未谋面。前者也好，后者也罢，单纯从阅读的维度来看，这套书无疑会带你进入一场全新的旅途。

你即将读到的 21 篇经典中短篇小说的英译版出自两本科幻作品集：*To Hold Up the Sky* 和 *The Wandering Earth*。这两本沉甸甸的精装书于 2020 年到 2021 年相继面世，是由托尔出版公司对刘慈欣经典科幻中短篇小说进行全新选编而成的。

华语科幻的译介是一场漫漫征途，将英译版作品重新引入国内则是"照镜子"一般的历程。文字的意义是流动的，不同语言、不同译者的文本往往呈现出极具差异化的风貌。编辑过程中，编者在最大限度地保持英译本的独立性和完整性的基础上，对一些规范性的内容进行了统一，与此同时，也在有必要提示之处插入了简短的注释，尽可能减少困惑，消除阅读障碍。

值得注意的修订有：

其一，*To Hold Up the Sky* 和 *The Wandering Earth* 两本书在英文符号的使用上有所不同，为了方便中文读者阅读，在编辑过程中对个别篇目的标点符号进行了修订，做到了统一。

其二，如果你在中英文对照阅读的过程中，发现某些地方英文比中文描述得更详尽，请不必感到困惑，考虑到译者本身的文字风格以及英语表述习惯，对于不影响文意的润色和增减，编者在编辑稿件时尽可能地保留了。

其三，在《带上她的眼睛》一辑中，《吞食者》和《诗云》的故事存在交集，文字和人物也均有"串场"，两位译者对个别人物、段落的表述不同，编辑无意在两个版本中做取舍，于是在文内相应位置添加了脚注，供读者阅读赏析。

其四，对于英译稿存在明显误读的地方，编者进行了修订；除了技术性偏误之外，一些误读是文化传播中出现的认知偏差所致，一些则是顾及文化差异、"入乡随俗"的有心之举——如《梦之海》中改变了主人公的性别。对于上述两类情况，编者分别以直接修订和添加脚注的方式做了处理，尽可能将译介过程中微妙的文意变化呈现出来。

阅读是一场走进心灵的旅途，希望这套作品能够陪伴你探索认知的边界，聆听华语科幻在世界舞台上律动的音符。

公子政

2022.1.18

目录

时间移民

THE TIME MIGRATION

前不见古人

后不见来者

念天地之悠悠

独怆然而涕下

——题记

移民

告全民书

迫于环境和人口已无法承受的压力，政府决定进行时间移民，首批移民人数为 8000 万，移民距离为 120 年。

要走的只剩下大使一个人了，他脚下的大地是空的，那是一个巨大的冷库，里面冷冻着 40 万人。在这个世界上，有 200 个这样的冷库，其实它们更像——大使打了一个寒战——坟墓。

桦不同他走，她完全符合移民条件，并拿到了让人羡慕的移民卡。与那些向往未来新生活的人不同，她认为现世和现实是最值得留恋的。她留下了，让大使一个人走向120年之后的未来。

1小时之后，大使走了，接近绝对零度的液氦淹没了他，凝固了他的生命。他率领着这个时代的8000万人，沿着时间踏上了逃荒之路。

跋涉

无知觉中，时光流逝，太阳如流星般划过长空，出生、爱情、死亡、狂喜、悲伤、失落，追求、奋斗、失败，一切的一切，如迎面而来的列车，在外部世界中呼啸着掠过……

……10年……20年……40年……60年……80年……100年……120年。

第一站：黑色时代

绝对零度下的超睡中，意识随机体完全凝固，完全感觉不到时间的存在，以至于大使醒来时，以为是低温系统出现故障，出发后不久临时解冻的。但对面原子钟巨大的等离子显示告诉他，120年过去了，一个半人生过去了，他们已是时代的流放者。

100人的先遣队在一星期前醒来并出动与这个时代联系。队长这时站在大使旁边，大使的体力还没有恢复到能说话的程度，在他探询的目光下，先遣队队长摇摇头，苦笑了一下。

国家元首在冷冻室大厅里迎接他们。他看上去是一个饱经风霜的人，同他一起来的人也一样。在 120 年之后，这很奇怪。大使把自己时代政府的信交给他，并转达自己时代人民对未来的问候。元首没说太多的话，只是紧紧握住大使的手。元首的手同他的脸一样粗糙，使大使感到一切的变化并不像他想象的那么大，他有一种温暖的感觉。

但这种感觉在走出冷冻室后立刻消失了。外面是黑色的：黑色的大地，黑色的树林，黑色的河流，黑色的流云。他们乘坐的悬浮车扬起了黑色的尘土。路上向反方向行驶的坦克纵队已成了一排行驶的黑块，空中低低掠过的直升机群也像一群黑色的幽灵，特别是现在的直升机听不到一点声音。一切像被天火烧了一遍一样。他们驶过了一个大坑，那坑太大了，像大使时代的露天煤矿。

"弹坑。"元首说。

"……弹坑？"大使没说出那个骇人的字。

"是的，这颗当量大约 15000 吨级。"元首淡淡地说，苦难对他已是淡淡的了。

在两个时代的会面中，空气凝固了。

"战争什么时候开始的？"

"这次是 2 年前。"

"这次？"

"你们走后还有过几次？"

元首避开了这个话题。他不像是 120 年后的晚辈，倒像大使时代的长辈，这样的长辈出现在那个时代的工地和农场里，用自己宽阔的胸怀包容一切苦难，不让它溢出一点。"我们将接收所有的移民，并且保证他们在和平环境中生活。"

"这可能吗，在现在这种情况下？"大使的一个随员问道，他本人则沉默着。

"这届政府和全体人民将不惜一切代价做到这点，这是责任。"元首说，"当然，移民还要努力适应这个时代，这有些困难，120年来变化很大。"

"有什么变化？"大使说，"一样的没有理智，一样的战争，一样的屠杀……"

"您只看到了表面。"一位穿迷彩服的将军说，"以战争为例，现在两个国家这样交战：首先公布自己各类战术与战略武器的数量和型号，根据双方各种武器的对毁率，计算机可以给出战争的结果。武器是纯威慑性质的，从来不会动用。战争就是计算机中数学模型的演算，以结果决定战争的胜负。"

"如何知道对毁率呢？"

"有一个国际武器试验组织，他们就像你们时代的……国际贸易组织。"

"战争已经像经济一样正规和有序了？"

"战争就是经济。"

大使看了一眼车窗外的黑色世界，"但现在，世界好像不仅仅是在演算。"

元首用深沉的目光看着大使，"算过了，但我们不相信结果真能决定胜败。"

"所以我们发起了你们那样的战争，流血的战争，'真'的战争。"将军说。

"我们现在去首都，研究一下移民解冻的问题。"元首再次避开了这个话题。

"返回。"大使说。

"什么？！"

"返回。你们已无法承受更多的负担了，这个时代不适合移民，我们再向前走一段吧。"

悬浮车返回了 1 号冷冻室。告别前，元首递给了大使一本精装的书。"这是 120 年的编年史。"他说。

这时，一位政府官员带来一位 123 岁的老人，他是现在能找到的唯一一个与移民同时代生活过的人，他坚持要见见大使。"好多的事，你们走后，好多的事啊！"老人拿出两个碗，大使时代的碗，又给碗里满上了酒，"我的父母是移民，这酒是我 3 岁时他们走之前留给我的，让我存到他们解冻时喝。我见不到他们了！我也是你们见到的最后一个同时代的人了。"

喝了酒后，大使望着老人平静干涸的双眼，正想着这个时代的人似乎已不会流泪了，老人的眼泪流了下来。他跪了下来，抓住大使的双手。

"前辈保重，西出阳关无故人啊！"

大使在被液氦的超低温凝固之前，桦突然出现在他那残存的意识中，他看到她站在秋日的落叶上，之后落叶变黑，出现了一块墓碑，那是她的墓碑吗？

跋涉

无知觉中，太阳如流星般划过长空，时光在外部世界飞速掠过……

……120 年……130 年……150 年……180 年……200 年……250 年……300 年……350 年……400 年……500 年……600 年。

第二站：大厅时代

"怎么这么久才叫醒我？！"大使吃惊地看着原子钟。

"先遣队已以百年为间隔醒来并出动了 5 次，最长的一次是我们曾在一个时代生活了 10 年，但每次都无法实现移民，所以没有唤醒您。这个原则是您自己确定的。"先遣队队长说。大使这才发现他比上次见面老了许多。

"又遇到战争了？"

"没有，战争永远消失了。前三个时代生态环境继续恶化，直到 200 年前才开始好转，但后两个时代拒绝接收移民。这个时代同意接收，最后需要您和委员会来决定。"

冷冻室大厅里没有人。在巨大的密封门隆隆开启时，先遣队队长低声对大使说："变化远远超出您的想象，要有精神准备。"

大使踏进这个时代的第一步，脚下响起了一阵音乐声，梦幻般——像过去时代的风铃声。他低下头，看到自己踏在水晶状的地面上，水晶的深处有彩色的光影在变幻，水晶看上去十分坚硬，踏上去却像地毯般柔软。踏到的位置响起那风铃般的乐声，同时有一圈圈同心的彩色光环以踏点为中心扩散开来，如同踏在平静水面上激起的水波。大使抬头望去，发现目力所及之处，整个平原都是水晶状了。

"全球所有的陆地都铺上了这种材料，以至于整个世界都像人造的一样。"先遣队队长说，看着大使惊愕的样子，他笑了，好像在说：这才刚刚开始呢！大使又注意到自己在水晶地面上的影子，有好几个，以他为中心向四面散开。他抬起头来……

6个太阳。

"现在是深夜，但200年前就没有夜晚了，您看到的是同步轨道上的6个反射镜把阳光反射到地球夜晚的一面，每个镜面有几百平方千米的面积。"

"山呢？"大使发现地平线处连绵的群山不见了，大地与蓝天的相接处如拿着尺子画出的一般平直。

"没有山了，全被平掉了，全球各大洲都是这样的平原。"

"为什么？！"

"不知道。"

大使觉得那6个太阳如大厅里的6盏灯。大厅！对了，他有了一种朦胧的感觉。进一步，他发现这是一个干净得出奇的时代，整个世界没有尘土，令人难以置信，一点都没有。大地如同一个巨大的桌面一样干净。天空同样一尘不染，呈干净的纯蓝色，但由于6个太阳的存在，天空已失去了过去时代的那种广阔和深邃，像大厅的拱顶。大厅！他的感觉更确定了，整个世界变成了一个大厅！铺着柔软的发出风铃声的水晶地毯，有着6个吊灯的大厅！这是个精致的、干净的时代，同上次的黑色时代形成了鲜明对比。以后的移民编年史中，他们把它叫大厅时代。

"他们不来迎接我们吗？"大使看着眼前空旷的平原问道。

"我们得自己到首都去见他们。虽然有精致的外表，这却是个没有礼仪的时代，甚至连好奇心也没有了。"

"他们对移民是什么态度？"

"同意接收，但移民只能在与社会隔绝的保留区生活。至于保留区的位置，在地球还是其他行星上，或在太空专建一个城市，由我们决定。"

"这绝对不能接受！"大使愤怒地说，"全体移民必须融入现在的社会，融入现在的生活，移民不是二等公民，这是时间移民最基本的原则！"

"这不可能。"先遣队队长摇摇头。

"是他们的看法？"

"也是我的。哦，请听我把话说完。您刚解冻，而这之前我已在这个时代生活了半年多。请相信我，现实远比您看到的更离奇，就是发挥最疯狂的想象力，您也无法想象出这个时代的十分之一，与此相比，旧石器时代的原始人理解我们的时代倒容易多了！"

"移民开始时已经考虑了适应的问题，所以移民的年龄都在25岁以下。我们会努力学习，努力适应这一切的！"大使说。

"学习？"先遣队队长笑着摇摇头，"您有书吗？"他指着大使的手提箱问，"什么书都行。"大使不解地拿出一本伊·亚·冈察洛夫在19世纪末写的《环球航海游记》，这是他出发前看到一半的书。先遣队队长看了一眼书名说："随便翻到一页，告诉我页数。"大使照办了，翻到第239页。先遣队队长流利地背诵起航海家在非洲的见闻，令人难以置信，一字不差。

"看到了吗，根本不需要学习，他们就像我们往磁盘上拷数据一样向大脑中输入知识！人的大脑能达到记忆的极限。如果这还不够，看这个……"先遣队队长从耳后取下一个助听器大小的东西，"这是量子级的存储器，人类有史以来所有的书籍都可以存在里面，愿意的话可以连一个账本都不放过！大脑可以像计算机访问内存一样提取它的信息，比大脑本身的记忆还快。看到了吗，我自己就是人类全部知识的载体，如果愿意，您在不到 1 小时的时间内也能做到。对他们来说，学习是一种古老的不可理解的神秘仪式。"

"他们的孩子一出生就马上得到一切知识？"

"孩子？"先遣队队长又笑了，"他们没有孩子。"

"那孩子呢？"

"我说过没有。家庭在更早的时候就没有了。"

"就是说，他们是最后一代人了。"

"也没有代，代的概念不存在了。"

大使的惊奇现在变成了茫然，但他还是努力去理解，并多少理解了一些。"你是说，他们永远活着？！"

"身体的一个器官失效，就更换一个新的，大脑失效，就把其中的信息拷贝出来，再拷到一个新培植的脑中去。当这种更换在进行了几百年后，每个人唯一留下的是自己的记忆。你能说清他们是孩子还是老人吗？也许他们更倾向于把自己当成老人，所以不来接我们。当然，愿意的话，也会有孩子的——用克隆或是更传统的方法，但不多了。这一代长生者现在已生存了 300 多年，还会继续生存下去。这一切会产生出一个什么样的社会形态，您能想象得出吗？我们所梦想的东西：博学、美貌、长生，在这个时代都是轻而易举能得到的东西。"

"那么这是理想社会了？他们还有想要而得不到的东西吗？"

"没有，但正因为他们能得到一切，同时也就失去了一切。对我们来说这很难理解，对他们来说却是真实的感受。现在远不是理想社会。"

大使的茫然又变成了沉思。天空中的 6 个太阳已斜向西方，很快落到地平线下。当西天只剩下 2 个太阳时，启明星出现了，接着，真正的太阳在东方映出霞光。那柔和的霞光使大使感到了一丝慰藉，宇宙间总有永恒不变的东西。

"500 年，时间不算长，怎么会有这么大的变化呢？"大使像在问先遣队队长，又像在问整个世界。

"人类的发展是一个加速度发展的过程，我们时代那 50 年的发展，可与过去 500 年相比，而现在的 500 年，也许与过去的 5 万年相当了！您还认为移民能适应这一切吗？"

"加速到最后会是什么样？"大使半闭起双眼。

"不知道。"

"你所拥有的全人类的知识也不能回答这个问题吗？"

"我游历这几个时代得到的最深感受是：知识能解释一切的时代过去了。"

……

"我们继续朝前走！"大使做出了决定，"带上那块芯片，还有他们向人脑输入知识的机器。"

在进入超睡前的朦胧中，大使又见到了桦，桦越过 620 年的漫漫长夜向他看了一眼，那让人心醉又心碎的眼神，使大使在孤独的时间流浪中有了家园的感觉。大使梦见水晶大地上出现了一阵缥缈的飞尘，那是桦的骨骼变成的吗？

跋涉

无知觉中，太阳如流星般划过长空，时光在外部世界飞速掠过……

……600 年……620 年……650 年……700 年……750 年……800 年……850 年……900 年……950 年……1000 年。

第三站：无形时代

冷冻室巨大的密封门隆隆地开启，大使第三次站在未知时代的门槛前，这次他做好了看到一个全新时代的精神准备，但出门后发现，变化没有他想象的那么大。

水晶地毯仍然存在，铺满大地；6 个太阳也在天空中发着光。但这个世界给人的感觉与大厅时代全然不同。首先，水晶地毯似乎已经"死"了，深处的光影还有，但暗了许多，在上面走动时不再发出风铃声，也没有美丽的波纹出现。天空中的 6 个太阳，有 4 个已暗淡无光，它们发出的暗红色光只能标明自己的位置，而不能照亮下面的世界。最引人注意的变化是，这世界有尘土了！尘土在水晶地面上薄薄地落了一层。天空不再纯净，有灰色的流云。地平线也不那么清晰笔直了。所有的一切给人这样一个感觉：大厅时代的大厅已人去屋空，外部的大自然慢慢渗透进来。

"两个世界都拒绝接收移民。"先遣队队长说。

"两个世界？"

"有形世界和无形世界。有形世界就是我们熟知的世界，尽管已很不相同。有同我们一样的人，但对很大一部分人来说，有机物已不是他们的主要组成部分了。"

"同上次一样，平原上还是看不到一个人。"大使极目远望。

"有几百年人们不用那么费力地在地面上行走了。您看——"先遣队队长指指空中的某个位置，大使透过尘土和流云，隐约看到一些飞行物，距离很远，看上去只是一群小黑点，"那些东西，也许是一架飞机，也许就是一个人。任何机器都可能是一个人的身体，比如海上的一艘巨轮可能就是一个人的身体，操纵巨轮的电脑的存储器是这个人大脑的拷贝。一般来说每个人有几个身体，这些身体中总有一个是同我们一样的有机体，这是人们最重视的一个身体，虽然也是最脆弱的，这也许是由于来自过去的情感吧。"

"我们是在做梦吗？"大使喃喃地问。

"与有形世界相比，无形世界更像一个梦。"

"我已经能想象出那是什么，人们连机器的身体也不要了。"

"是的。无形世界就是一台超级电脑的内存，每个人是内存中的一个软件。"

先遣队队长指了指前方，地平线上有一座山峰，孤独地立在那里，在阳光下闪着蓝色的金属光泽。"那就是无形世界中的一个大陆。您还记得上次我们带回的那些小小的量子芯片吧，而您看到的是量子芯片堆成的高山。由此可以想象，或根本无法想象，这台超级电脑的容量。"

"在它里面，是一种什么样的生活呢？在内存里人们什么都不是，只是一些量子脉冲的组合罢了。"大使说。

"正因为如此，您可以真正随心所欲，创造您想要的一切。您可以创造一个有千亿人口的帝国，在那里您是国王；您可以经历 1000 次各不相同的浪漫史，在 1 万次战争中死 10 万次。那里每个人都是一个世界的主宰，比神更有力量。您甚至可以为自己创造一个宇宙，那宇宙里有上亿个星系，每个星系有上亿个星球，每个星球都是各不相同的您渴望或不敢渴望的世界。不要担心没有时间享受这些，超级电脑的速度使那里的 1 秒钟有外面的几个世纪长。在那里，唯一的限制就是想象力。无形世界中，想象与现实是一个东西，当您的想象出现时，想象同时也就变为现实了，当然，是量子芯片内的现实，用您的说法，就是脉冲的组合。这个时代的人们正在渐渐转向无形世界，现在生活在无形世界中的人数已超过有形世界。虽然可以在两个世界都有一份大脑的拷贝，但无形世界的生活如毒品一样，一旦经历过那种生活，谁也无法再回到有形世界里来，我们充满烦恼的世界对他们来说如同地狱一般。现在，无形世界已掌握了立法权，正在渐渐控制整个世界。"

跨过 1000 年的两个人，梦游似的看着那座量子芯片堆成的高山，忘记了时间，直到真正的太阳像过去亿万年的每一天那样点亮了东方，才回到了现实。

"再以后会是什么呢？"大使问。

"无形世界中，作为一个软件，您可以轻易地拷贝多个自我，如果对自己性格的某些方面不喜欢，比如您认为在受着感情和责任心的折磨，您也可以把这两种情感都去掉，或把它们做一个备份，需要时再连接到您的自我上。您也可以把一个自我分裂成多个，分别代表您个性的某个方面。进一步，您可以和别人合为一体，形成一个由两者精神和记忆组合而成的新自我。再进一步，还可以组合几个、几十个或几百个人……够了，我不想让您发疯，但这一切在无形世界中随时都在发生。"

"再以后呢？"

"只能猜测，现在最明显的迹象是，无形世界中的个体可能会消失，最终所有人合为一个软件。"

"再以后呢？"

"不知道。这已是个哲学问题了，经过了这几次解冻，我已经害怕哲学了。"

"我则相反，已是个哲学家了。你说得对，这是个哲学问题，必须从哲学的深度来思考。对这次移民，我们早就该这样思考，但现在也不晚。哲学是一层纸，现在对于我，至少这层纸被捅破了，突然间——几乎突然间，我知道我们以后的路了。"

"我们必须在这个时代结束移民，再走下去，移民将更难适应目的时代的环境。"先遣队队长说，"我们应该起义，争得自己的权利。"

"这不可能，也没必要。"

"我们难道还有别的选择？"

"当然有，而且这个选择就像前面正在升起的太阳一样清晰和光明。请把总工程师叫来。"

总工程师是同大使一起被解冻的，现在正在冷冻室中检查和维护设备。由于他的解冻很频繁，已由出发时的青年变成老人了。当茫然的先遣队队长把他叫来后，大使问："冷冻还能维持多长时间？"

"现在绝热层良好，聚变堆的工作情况也正常。在大厅时代，我们按当时的技术更换了全部的制冷设备，并补充了聚变燃料，现在看来，所有 200 个冷冻室，即使以后不更换任何设备和不进行任何维护，也可维持 1.2 万年。"

"好极了。立刻在原子钟上设定最终目的地，全体人员进入超睡，在到达最终目的地之前，不再有任何人解冻。"

"最终目的地定在……"

"1.1 万年。"

……

桦又进入了大使超睡前的残存意识中，这一次最真实：她的长发在寒风中飘动，大眼睛含着泪，在呼唤他。在进入无知觉的冥冥中之前，大使对她喊："桦，我们要回家了！我们要回家了！！！"

跋涉

无知觉中，太阳如流星般划过长空，时光在外部世界飞速掠过……

……1000 年……2000 年……3500 年……5500 年……7000年……9000 年……1 万年……1.1 万年。

第四站：回家

这一次，甚至在超睡中也能感觉到时光的漫长了。在1万年的漫漫长夜中，在100个世纪的超长等待中，连忠实地控制着全球200个超级冷冻室的电脑都要睡着了。在最后的1000年中，它的部件开始损坏，无数只由传感器构成的眼睛一只只地闭上，集成块构成的神经一根根瘫痪，聚变堆的能量相继耗尽。在最后的几十年中，冷冻室仅靠着绝热层维持着绝对零度。之后，温度开始上升，很快到了危险的程度，液氢开始蒸发，超睡容器内的压力急剧增高，1.1万年的跋涉似乎都将在一声爆破中无知觉地完结。但就在这时，电脑唯一还睁着的那双眼看到了原子钟的时间，这最后1秒钟的流逝唤醒了它古老的记忆，它发出了一个微弱的信号，苏醒系统启动了。在核磁脉冲的作用下，先遣队队长和100名先遣队员的身体中接近绝对零度的细胞液在不到百分之一秒的时间内融化，然后升到正常体温。一天后，他们走出了冷冻室。一个星期后，大使和移民委员会的全体委员都苏醒了。

当冷冻室的巨门刚刚开启一条缝时，一股风吹了进来。大使闻到了外面的气息，这气息同前三个时代不同，它带着嫩芽的芳香，这是春天的气息、家的气息。大使现在几乎已经肯定，他在1万年前的决定是正确的。

大使同委员会所有的人一起跨进了他们最后到达的时代。

大地是土的，但土是看不见的，因为上面长满了一望无际的绿草。冷冻室的门前有一条小河，河水清澈，可以看到河底美丽的花石和几条悠闲的小鱼。几个年轻的先遣队员在小河边洗脸，他们光着脚，脚上有泥，轻风隐隐送来了他们的笑声。只有一个太阳，蓝天上有雪白的云朵。一只鹰在懒洋洋地盘旋，有小鸟的叫声。远远望去，1万年前大厅时代消失了的山脉又出现在天边，山上盖满了森林……

对经历过前三个时代的大使来说，眼前的世界太平淡了，他为这种平淡流下热泪。经过1.1万年流浪的他和其他所有人需要这平淡的一切，这平淡的世界是一张温暖而柔软的天鹅绒，他们把自己疲惫破碎的心轻轻放上去。

平原上没有人类活动的迹象。

先遣队队长走过来，大使和委员们的目光集中在他脸上，那是最后审判日里人类的目光。

"都结束了。"先遣队队长说。

谁都明白这话的含义。在神圣的蓝天绿草之间，人类沉默着，平静地接受了这个现实。

"知道原因吗？"大使问。

先遣队队长摇摇头。

"由于环境？"

"不，不是由于环境，也不是战争，不是我们能想到的任何原因。"

"有遗迹吗？"大使问。

"没有，什么都没留下。"

委员们围过来，开始急促地发问。

"有星际移民的迹象吗？"

"没有，近地行星都恢复到未开发状态。也没有恒星际移民的迹象。"

"什么都没留下？一点点，一点点都没有？"

"是的，什么都没有。以前的山脉都被恢复了，是从海洋中部取的岩石和土壤。植被和生态也恢复得很好，但都看不到人工的痕迹。古迹只保留到公元前 1 世纪，以后的时代痕迹全无。生态系统自行运转估计有 5000 年了，现在的自然环境类似于新石器时代，但物种不如那时丰富。"

"什么都没留下，怎么可能？！"

"他们没什么话要说了。"

最后这句话使大家再次陷入沉默。

"这一切您都预料到了，是吗？"先遣队队长问大使，"那么，您应该想到原因了？"

"我们能想到，但永远无法理解。原因要在哲学的深度上找。在对存在思考到终极时，他们认为不存在是最合理的并选择了它。"

"我说过，我怕哲学！"

"那好，我们暂时离开哲学吧。"大使走远几步，面向委员们。

"移民到达，全体解冻！"

200 个聚变堆发出最后的强大能量，核磁脉冲在解冻着 8000 万人。一天后，人类从冷冻室中走出，并在沉寂了几千年的各个大陆上扩散开来。在 1 号冷冻室所在的平原上，聚集了几十万人，大使站在冷冻室门前巨大的台阶上面对他们，只有很少一部分人能听到他的讲话，但他们把听到的话像水波一样传开去。

"公民们，本来计划走 120 年的我们，走了 1.1 万年，最后到达这里。现在的一切你们都看到了，他们消失了，我们是仅存的人类。他们什么都没有留下，但又留下了一切。这几天，所有的人一直在努力寻找，渴望找到他们留下的只言片语，但没有，什么都没有。他们真没什么可说的吗？不！他们有，而且说了！看这蓝天，这草地，这山脉，这森林，这整个重新创造的大自然，就是他们要说的话！看看这绿色的大地，这是我们的母亲！是我们力量的源泉！是我们存在的依据和永恒的归宿！以后人类还会犯错误，还会在苦难和失望的荒漠中跋涉，但只要我们的根不离开我们的大地母亲，我们就不会像他们那样消失。不管多么艰难，人类和生活将永远延续！公民们，现在这世界是我们的了，我们开始了人类新的轮回。我们现在一无所有，但又拥有人类有过的一切！"

大使把那个来自大厅时代的量子芯片高高举起，把全人类的知识高高举起。突然，他像石像一样凝固了，他的眼睛盯着人海中一个飞快移动的小黑点，近了，他看清了那束在梦中无数次出现的长发，那双他认为在100个世纪前已化为尘土的眼睛。桦没留在1.1万年前，她最后还是跟他来了，跟他跨越了这漫长的时间沙漠！当他们拥抱在一起时，天、地、人合为一体了。

"新生活万岁！"有人高呼。

"新生活万岁！！！"这呼声响彻了整个平原，群鸟欢唱着从人海上空飞过。

在一切都结束之后，一切都开始了。

镜子

MIRROR

随着探索的深入，人们发现量子效应只是物质之海表面的涟漪，是物质更深层规律扰动的影子。当这些规律渐渐明朗时，在量子力学中飘忽不定的实在图像再次稳定下来，确定值重新代替了概率，新的宇宙模型中，本认为已经消失了的因果链再次浮现并清晰起来。

追捕

办公室中竖立着国旗和党旗，宽大的办公桌两旁有两个人。

"我知道首长很忙，但这事必须向您汇报，说真的，我从来没遇到过这种事。"桌前一个身着二级警监警服的人说。他年近 50 岁，但身躯挺拔，脸上线条刚劲。

"继峰啊，我清楚你最后这句话的分量，毕竟是 30 年的老刑侦了。"首长说。他说话的时候看着手中的一支缓缓转动的红蓝铅笔，仿佛在专心评价笔尖削出的形状。大多数时间他都是这样将自己的目光隐藏起来，在过去的岁月中，陈继峰能记起的首长直视自己不超过三次，每一次都是自己一生的关键时刻。

"每次采取行动之前目标总能逃脱，他肯定预先知道。"

"这事，你不会没遇到过吧？"

"当然，要只是这个倒没什么，我们首先能想到的就是内部问题。"

"你手下的这套班子，不太可能。"

"是不可能，按您的吩咐，这个案子的参与范围已经压缩到最小，组里只有四个人，真正知道全部情况的人只有两个。不过我还是怕万一，就计划召开一次会议，对参加人员逐个儿排查。我让沉兵召集会议，您认识的，十一处很可靠的那个，宋诚的事就是他办的……但这时，邪门的事出现了……您，可别以为我是在胡扯，我下面说的绝对是真的。"陈继峰笑了笑，好像对自己的辩解很不好意思似的，"就在这时，他来了电话！我们追捕的目标给我来了电话！我在手机里听到他说：你们不用开这个会，你们没有内奸。而这个时刻，距我向沉兵说出开会的打算不到 30 秒！"

首长手中的铅笔停止了转动。

"您可能想到了窃听，但不可能，我们的谈话地点是随意选的，在一个机关礼堂中央，礼堂里正在排演国庆合唱，说话凑到耳根才能听清。后来这样的怪事接连发生，他给我们来过 8 次电话，每次都谈到我们刚刚说过的话或做过的事。最可怕的是，他不仅能听到一切，还能看到一切！有一次，沉兵决定搜查他父母家，组里的两个人刚起身，还没走出局里的办公室呢，就接到他的电话。他在电话里说你们搜查证拿错了，我的父母都是细心人，可能以为你们是骗子呢。沉兵掏出搜查证一看，首长，他真的拿错了。"

首长轻轻地将铅笔放在桌上，沉默着等陈继峰继续说下去，但后者好像已经说不出什么了。首长拿出一支烟，陈继峰忙拍拍衣袋找打火机，但没有找到。

桌上两部电话中的一部响了。

"是他……"陈继峰扫了一眼来电显示后低声说。首长沉着地示意了一下，他按下免提键，立刻有话音响起，声音听上去很年轻，有一种疲惫无力感。

"您的打火机放在公文包里。"

陈继峰和首长对视了一下，拿起桌上的公文包翻找起来，一时找不到。

"夹在一份文件中了，就是那份关于城市户籍制度改革的文件。"目标在电话中说。

陈继峰拿出那份文件，啪的一下，打火机掉到桌面上。

"好东西，法国都彭牌的，两面各镶有 30 颗钻石，整体用钯金制成，价格……我查查，是 39960 元。"

首长没动，陈继峰却抬头打量了一下办公室，这不是首长的办公室，而是事先在这座大办公楼上任意选的一间。

目标在继续显示着自己的力量："首长，您那盒中华烟还剩 5 根，您上衣衣袋中的降血脂麦非奇罗片只剩 1 片了，让秘书再拿些吧。"

陈继峰从桌上拿起烟盒，首长则从衣袋中掏出药的包装盒，都证实了目标所说是对的。

"你们别再追捕我了，我现在也很难，不知道该怎么办。"目标继续说。

"我们能见面谈谈吗？"首长问。

"请您相信，那对我们双方都是一场灾难。"说完电话挂断了。

陈继峰松了一口气，现在他的话得到了证实，而让首长认为他在胡扯，比这个对手的诡异更令他不安。"见了鬼了……"他摇摇头说。

"我不相信鬼，但看到了危险。"首长说。有生以来第四次，陈继峰看到那双眼睛直视着自己。

犯人和被追捕者

市近郊第二看守所。

宋诚被押解着走进这间已有六个犯人的监室中，这里大部分是待审期较长的犯人。宋诚面对着一双双冷眼，看守人员出去后刚关上门，有一个瘦小的家伙就站起来走到他面前。

"板油！"他冲宋诚喊，看到后者迷惑的样子，他解释道，"这儿按规矩分成大油、二油、三油……板油，你就是最板的那个。喂，别以为是爷们儿欺负你来得晚。"他用大拇指向后指了指斜靠在墙根的一个满脸胡子的人，"鲍哥刚来三天，已经是大油了。像你这种烂货，虽然以前官儿不小，但现在是最板的！"

他转向那人，恭敬地问："鲍哥，怎么接待？"

"立体声。"那人懒洋洋地说。

几个躺着的犯人呼啦一下站了起来，抓住宋诚将他头朝下倒提起来，悬在马桶的上方，慢慢下降，使他的脑袋大部分伸进了马桶里。

"唱歌儿，"瘦猴命令道，"这就是立体声，就来一首歌曲，《左右手》什么的！"

宋诚不唱，那几个人松了手，他的脑袋完全扎进了马桶中。

宋诚挣扎着将头从恶臭的马桶中抽出来，紧接着大口呕吐起来，他现在知道，诬陷者给予他的这个角色，在犯人中都是最受鄙夷的。

周围兴高采烈的犯人们突然散开，飞快地闪回到自己的铺位上去。门开了，刚才那名看守警察又走了进来，他厌恶地看着蹲在马桶前的宋诚说："到水龙头那儿把脑袋冲冲，有人探视你。"

宋诚冲完头后跟着看守来到了一间宽大的办公室，探视者在那里等着他。来人很年轻，面容清瘦，头发纷乱，戴着一副宽框眼镜，拎着一个很大的手提箱。宋诚冷冷地坐下了，没有看来人一眼，被获准在这个时候探视他，而且不去有玻璃隔断的探视室，直接到这里面对面，宋诚已基本猜出了来人是哪一方面的。但对方的第一句话让他吃惊地抬起头，大感意外。

"我叫白冰，气象模拟中心的工程师，他们在到处追捕我，和你一样的原因。"来人说。

宋诚看了来人一眼，觉得他此时的说话方式有问题：这种话应该是低声说出的，而他的声音正常高低，好像他所谈的事根本不用避开人。

白冰似乎看出了他的疑惑，说："两小时前我给首长打了电话，他约我谈谈，我没答应。然后他们就跟踪上了我，一直跟到看守所前。之所以没有抓我，是对我们的会面很好奇，想知道我要对你说些什么。现在，我们的谈话都在被窃听。"

宋诚将目光从白冰身上移开，又看着天花板，他很难相信这人，同时对这事也不感兴趣。即使他在法律上能侥幸免于一死，对他精神上的死刑却已经被执行，他的心已死了，此时不可能再对什么感兴趣了。

"我知道事情的全部真相。"白冰说。

宋诚的嘴角隐现一丝冷笑，没人知道真相，除了他们，但他懒得说出来了。

"你是7年前到省纪委工作的，提拔到这个位置还不到1年。"

宋诚仍沉默着，他很恼火，白冰的话又将他拉回到他好不容易躲开的回忆中。

大案

自从21世纪初郑州市政府首先以一批副处级岗位招聘博士以来，很多城市都效仿这种做法，后来这种招聘上升到一些省份的省政府一级，而且不限毕业年限，招聘的职位也更高。这种做法确实向外界显示了招聘者的大度和远见，但实质上只是一种华而不实的政绩工程。招聘者确实深谋远虑，他们清楚地知道，这些只会谋事不会谋人的年轻高知没有任何从政经验，一旦进入陌生险恶的政界，就会陷在极其复杂的官场迷宫中不知所措，根本不可能立足，这样到最后在职缺上不会有什么损失，产生的政绩效益却是可观的。就是这个机会，使当时已是法学教授的宋诚离开平静的校园和书斋投身政界。与他一同来的那几位不到1年就全军覆没，垂头丧气地离去，唯一的收获就是对现实的幻灭。但宋诚是个例外，他不但在政界待了下来，而且走得很好。这应归功于两个人，其一是他的大学同学吕文明。本科毕业那年宋诚考研，吕文明则考上了公务员，依靠优越的家庭背景和自己的奋斗，10多年后成为国内最年轻的省纪委书记。是他力劝宋诚弃学从政的，这位单纯的学者刚来时，他不是手把手，而是手把脚地教他走路，每一步踏在哪儿都细心指点，终于使宋诚绕过只凭自己绝对看不出来的各处雷区，一路向上地走到今天。他要感谢的另一个人就是首长……想到这里，宋诚的心抽搐了一下。

"得承认，这一切都是你自己的选择，不能说人家没给你退路。"白冰说。

宋诚点点头，是的，人家给退路了，而且是一条光明的康庄大道。

白冰接着说："首长和你在几个月前有过一次会面，你一定记得很清楚。那是在远郊阳河边的一幢别墅里，首长一般是不在那里接见外人的。你一下车就发现他在门口迎接，这是很高的礼遇了。他热情地同你握手，并拉着你的手走进客厅。别墅客厅布置给你的第一印象一定是简单和简朴，但你错了，那套看上去有些旧的红木家具价值百万元；墙上唯一的一幅不起眼的字画更陈旧，细看还有虫蛀的痕迹，那是明朝吴彬的《宕壑奇姿》，从香港佳士得拍卖行以 800 万港元购得；还有首长亲自给你泡的那杯茶，那是中国星级茶王赛评出的五星级茶王，500 克的价格是 90 万元。"

宋诚确实想起了白冰说的那杯茶，碧绿的茶液晶莹透明，几根精致的茶叶在那小小的清纯空间中缓缓漂行，仿佛一首古筝奏出的悠扬仙乐……他甚至回忆起自己当时的随感：要是外面的世界也这么纯净该多好啊。宋诚意识中那层麻木的帷帐一下子被掀去了，模糊的意识又聚焦起来，他瞪大双眼震惊地盯着白冰。

他怎么知道这些？！这件事处于秘密之井的最底端，是隐秘中的隐秘，这个世界上知道的人加上自己不超过四个！

"你是谁？！"他第一次开口了。

白冰笑笑说："我刚才自我介绍过，只是个普通人，但坦率地告诉你，我不仅仅是知道得很多，我什么都知道，或者说什么都能知道，正因为这个他们也要除掉我，就像除掉你一样。"

白冰接着讲下去："首长当时坐得离你很近，一只手放在你的膝盖上，他看着你的慈祥目光能令任何一个晚辈感动。据我所知（记住，我什么都知道），他从未与谁表现得这样亲近。他对你说：'年轻人，不要紧张，大家都是同志，有什么事情，只要真诚地以心换心，总是谈得开的……你有思想、有能力、有责任感和使命感，特别是后两项，在现在的年轻干部里面真如沙漠中的清泉一样珍贵啊。这也是我看重你的原因，从你身上，我看到了自己年轻时的影子啊。'这里要说明一下，首长的这番话可能是真诚的。以前在工作中你与他交往的机会不是太多，但有好几次，在机关大楼的走廊上偶然相遇，或在散会后，他都主动与你攀谈几句。他很少与下级，特别是年轻的下级这样的，这些人们都看在眼里。虽然在组织会议上他从没有为你说过什么话，但他的那些姿态对你的仕途是起了很大作用的。"

宋诚又点点头，他知道这些，并曾经感激万分，一直想找机会报答。

"首长抬手向后示意了一下，立刻进来一个人，将一大摞文件材料轻轻地放到桌子上。你一定注意到，那个人不是首长平时的秘书。首长抚着那摞材料说：'就说你刚刚完成的这项工作吧，充分证明了你的那些宝贵素质：如此巨量而艰难的调查取证，资料充分而翔实，结论深刻，很难相信这些只用半年时间就完成了。你这样出类拔萃的纪检干部要多一些，真是党的事业之大幸啊……'你当时的感觉，我就不用说了吧。"

当然不用说，那是宋诚一生中最惊恐的时刻，那份材料先是令他如触电似的颤抖了一下，然后像石化般僵住了。

"这一切都是从一宗中纪委委托调查的非法审批国有土地案开始的。嗯……我记得你童年的时候，曾与两个小伙伴一起到一个溶洞探险。当地人叫它老君洞，那洞口只有半米高，弯着腰才能进去，但里面却是一个宏伟的黑暗大厅，手电光照不到高高的穹顶，只有纷飞的蝙蝠不断掠过光柱，每一个小小的响动都能激起遥远的回声，阴森的寒气浸入你的骨髓……这就是这次调查的生动写照：你沿着那条看似平常的线索向前走，它把你引到的地方令你越来越不敢相信自己的眼睛。随着调查的深入，一张全省范围的腐败网络气势磅礴地展现在你的面前，这张网上的每一根经络都通向一个地方、一个人。现在，这份本来要上报中纪委的绝密纪检材料，竟在这个人的手中！对这项调查，你设想过各种最坏的情况，但眼前发生的事是你万万没有想到的。你当时完全乱了方寸，结结巴巴地问：'这……这怎么到了您手里？！'首长从容地一笑，又轻轻抬手示意了一下，纪委书记吕文明走进了客厅，你立刻得到了答案。

"你站起身，怒视着吕文明说：'你，你怎么能这样？！你怎么能这样违反组织原则和纪律？'吕文明挥手打断你，用同样的愤怒质问道：'这事为什么不向我打个招呼？'你回答说：'你到中央党校学习的 1 年期间，是我主持纪委工作，当然不能打招呼，这是组织纪律！'吕文明伤心地摇摇头，好像要难过得流出泪似的说：'如果不是我及时截下了这份材料，那……那是什么后果嘛！宋诚啊，你这个人最要命的缺陷就是总要分出个黑和白，但现实全是灰色的！'"

宋诚长长地叹息了一声，他记得当时他呆呆地看着同学，不相信这话是从他嘴里说出的，因为以前他从未表露过这样的思想。难道那一次次深夜的促膝长谈中表现出的对党内腐败的痛恨，那一次次触动雷区后面对上下左右压力时的坚定不移，那一次次彻夜工作后面对朝阳发出的对党和国家前途充满使命感的忧虑，都是伪装？

"不能说吕文明以前欺骗了你，只能说他的心灵还从来没有向你敞开到那么深，他就像那道著名的叫火焙阿拉斯加的菜，那道爆炒冰激凌，其中的火热和冰冷都是真实的……首长没有看吕文明，而是猛拍了一下桌子，说：'什么灰色？文明啊，我就看不惯你这一点！宋诚做得非常优秀，无可指责，在这点上他比你强！'接着他转向你说：'小宋啊，就应该这样。一个人，特别是年轻人，失去了信念和使命感，就完了，我看不起那样的人。'"

宋诚当时感触最深的是：虽然他和吕文明同岁，但首长只称他为年轻人，而且反复强调。其含意很明显：跟我斗，你还是个孩子。而宋诚现在也不得不承认这一点。

"首长接着说：'但，年轻人，我们也应该成熟起来。举个例子来说，你这份材料中关于恒宇电解铝基地的问题，确实存在，而且比你已调查出来的还严重，除了国内，还涉及外资方伙同政府官员的严重违法行为。一旦处理，外资肯定撤走，这个国内最大的电解铝企业就会瘫痪。为恒宇提供氧化铝原料的桐山铝矾土矿也要陷入困境。然后是橙林核电厂，由于前几年电力紧张时期建设口子放得太大，现在国内电力严重过剩，这座新建核电厂发出的电主要供电解铝基地使用，恒宇一倒，橙林核电厂也将面临破产。接下来，为橙林核电厂提供浓缩铀的照西口化工厂也将陷入困境……这些，将使近 700 亿元的国家投资无法收回，三四万人失业。这些企业就在省城近郊，这个中心城市将立刻陷入不稳定之中……上面说的恒宇的问题还只是这个案件的一小部分，这庞大的案情涉及正省级 1 人、副省级 3 人、厅局级 215 人、处级 614 人，再往下不计其数。省内近一半经营出色的大型企业和最有希望的投资建设项目都被划到了这个范围里，盖子一旦揭开，这就意味着全省政治经济的全面瘫痪！而涉及范围如此之广的巨大动作，会产生什么其他更可怕的后果，还不得而知，也无法预测。省里好不容易形成的政治稳定和经济良性增长的局面将荡然无存，这难道对党和国家就有利？年轻人，你现在不能延续法学家的思维，只要法律正义得到伸张，哪管他洪水滔天！这是不负责任的。平衡，历史都是在各种因素间建立的某种平衡中发展到今天的，不顾平衡一味走极端，在政治上是极其幼稚的表现。'

"首长沉默后，吕文明接着说：'这个事情，中纪委那方面我去办。你，关键要做好项目组那几个干部的工作。下星期我会中断党校学习，回来协助你……'

　　"'混账！'首长再次猛拍桌子，把吕文明吓得一抖。'你是怎么理解我的话的？你竟然以为是我让小宋放弃原则和责任？！文明啊，这么多年了，你从心里讲，我是这么一个没有党性、没有原则的人吗？你什么时候变得这么圆滑了，真让人伤心啊。'然后首长转向你：'年轻人，在这件事上，你们前面的工作做得十分出色，一定要顶住干扰和压力坚持下去，让腐败分子得到应有的惩罚！案情触目惊心啊，放过他们，无法向人民交代，天理也不容！我刚才讲的你绝不能当成负担，我只是以一个老党员的身份提醒你，要慎重，避免出现不可预测的严重后果。但有一点十分明确，那就是这个腐败大案必须一查到底！'首长说着，拿出了一张纸，郑重地递给你，'这个范围，你看够吗？'"

　　宋诚当时知道，他们也设下了祭坛，要往上放牺牲品了。他看了一眼那个名单，够了，真的够了，无论从级别上还是人数上，都真的够了。这将是一个震惊全国的腐败大案，而他宋诚，将随着这个案件的最终告破而成为国家级反腐英雄，将作为正义和良知的化身而被人民敬仰。但他心里清楚，这只是蜥蜴在危急时刻自断的一条尾巴，蜥蜴跑了，尾巴很快还会长出来。他当时看着首长盯着自己的样子，一时间真想到了蜥蜴，浑身一颤。但宋诚也知道他害怕了，自己使他害怕了，这让宋诚感到自豪。正是这自豪，一时间使他大大高估了自己的力量，更由于一个理想主义学者血液中固有的某种东西，他做出了致命的选择。

　　"你站起身来，伸出双手拿起了那摞材料，对首长说：'根据党内监督条例规定，纪委有权对同级党委的领导人进行监督，按组织纪律，这材料不能放在您这里，我拿走了。'吕文明想拦你，但首长轻轻制止了他。你走到门口时听到同学在后面阴沉地说：'宋诚，过分了。'首长一直把你送到车上，临别时他握着你的手慢慢地说：'年轻人，慢走。'"

宋诚后来才真正理解这句话的深长意味：慢走，你的路不多了。

宇宙大爆炸

"你到底是谁？！"宋诚充满惊恐地看着白冰，他怎么知道这么多？绝对没人能知道这么多！

"好了，我们不回忆那些事了。"白冰一挥手中断了讲述，"我说说事情的来龙去脉吧，以解开你的疑问——你……你知道宇宙大爆炸吗？"

宋诚呆呆地看着白冰，他的大脑一时还难以理解白冰最后那句话。后来，他终于做出了一般人的正常反应，笑了笑。

"是的是的，我知道太突兀了，但请相信我没有毛病，要想把事情讲清楚，真的得从宇宙诞生的大爆炸讲起！这……怎么才能向你说清楚呢，还是回到大爆炸吧。你可能多少知道一些，我们的宇宙诞生于200亿年前的一次大爆炸。在一般人的想象中，那次创世爆炸像漆黑空间中一团怒放的烟火，但这个图像是完全错误的：大爆炸之前什么都没有，包括时间和空间，都没有，只有一个奇点，一个没有大小的点，这个奇点急剧扩张开来，形成了我们今天的宇宙。现在一切的一切，包括我们自己，都来自这个奇点的扩张，它是万物的种子！这理论很深，我也搞不太清楚，与我们这事有关的是这一点：随着物理学的进步，随着弦论之类的超级理论的出现，物理学家们渐渐搞清了那个奇点的结构，并且给出了它的数学模型。与这之前量子力学的模型不同，如果奇点爆炸前的基本参数确定，所生成的宇宙中的一切也就都确定了，一条永不中断的因果链贯穿了宇宙中的一切过程……哎，真是，这些怎么讲得清呢。"

白冰看到宋诚摇摇头，那意思或是听不懂，或是根本不想听下去。

白冰说："我说，还是暂时不要想你那些痛苦的经历吧。其实，我的命运比你好不到哪里去。刚才介绍过，我是一个普通人，但现在被追杀，下场可能比你还惨，就因为我什么都知道。如果说你是为使命和信念而献身，我……纯粹是倒霉！倒了八辈子霉！！！所以比你更惨。"

宋诚悲哀的目光表达了一个明确的意思：没有人会比我更惨。

诬陷

在与首长会面一个星期后，宋诚被捕了，罪名是故意杀人。

其实，宋诚知道他们会采用非常规手段对付自己，对于一个知道得这样多又在行动中的人，一般的行政和政治手段就不保险了，但他没有想到对手动作这样快，出手又这样狠。

死者罗罗是一个夜总会的舞男，死在宋诚的汽车里。车门锁着，从内部无法打开，车内有两罐打火机用的丙烷气，罐皮都被割开了口子，里面的气体全部蒸发，受害人就是在车里的高浓度丙烷气里中毒而死的。死者被发现时，手中握着已经破碎的手机，显然是试图用它来砸破车窗玻璃。

警方提供的证据很充分，有长达两个小时的录像证明宋诚与罗罗已有 3 个多月的不正常交往，最为有力的证据是罗罗死前给 110 打的一个报警电话：

罗罗："快！快来！！！我打不开车门！我喘不上气，我头疼……"

110："你在哪里？把情况再说清楚些！"

罗罗："宋……宋诚要杀我……"

…………

事后在死者手机里发现了一小段通话录音，录下了宋诚和受害人的对话。

宋诚："我们既然已走到了这一步，你就和许雪萍断了吧。"

罗罗："宋哥，这何必呢？我和许姐只是男女关系嘛，影响不了咱们的事，说不定还有帮助呢。"

宋诚："我心里觉得别扭，你别逼我采取行动。"

罗罗："宋哥，我有我的活法儿。"

…………

这是十分专业的诬陷，其高明之处就在于，警方掌握的证据几乎百分之百是真实的。

宋诚确实与罗罗有长时间的交往，这种交往是秘密的，要说不正常也可以，那两段录音都不是伪造的，只是后面那段被曲解了。

宋诚认识罗罗是由于许雪萍的缘故。许是昌通集团的总裁，与腐败网络的许多节点都有着密切的经济关系，对其背景和内幕了解很深。宋诚当然不可能直接从她嘴里得到任何东西，但他发现了罗罗这个突破口。

　　罗罗向宋诚提供情况绝不是出于正义感，在他眼里，世界早就是一张擦屁股纸了，他是为了报复。

　　这个笼罩在工业烟尘中的内地都市，虽然人均收入排在全国同等城市的最后，却拥有多家国内最豪华的夜总会。首都的那些高干子弟，在京城多少要注意一些影响，不可能像民间富豪那样随意享乐，就在每个周末驱车沿高速公路疾驶四五个小时，来到这座城市度过荒淫奢靡的两天一夜，再在星期天晚上驱车赶回北京。罗罗所在的蓝浪夜总会是最豪华的一处，这里点一首歌最低3000元，几千元一瓶的马爹利和轩尼诗一夜能卖出两三打。但蓝浪出名的真正原因并不在于此，而是它是一个只接待女客的夜总会。

　　与其他的同伴不同，罗罗并不在意其服务对象给的多少，而在意给的比例。如果是一个年收入仅二三十万元的外资白领（在蓝浪，她们是罕见的穷人），给个几百元他也能收下。但许姐不同，她那几十亿元的财富在过去的几年中威震江南，现在到北方来发展也势如破竹，但在交往几个月后扔给他40万元就把他打发了。让许姐看上不容易，要放到同伴们身上，用罗罗的话说他们要美得肝儿疼。但罗罗不行，他对许雪萍充满了仇恨。那名高级纪检官员的到来让他看到了报复的希望，他极力施展自己这方面的能力，又和许姐联系上了。平时许雪萍对罗罗嘴也很严，但他们在一起喝多或吸多了时就不一样了。同时，罗罗是个很有心计的人，在许多个黎明前最黑暗的时候，他会从熟睡的许姐身边无声地爬起来，在她的随身公文包和抽屉里寻找自己和宋诚需要的东西，用数码相机拍下来。

警方手中那些证明宋诚和罗罗交往的录像，大都是在蓝浪的大舞厅拍的，往往首先拍的是舞台，上面一群妖艳的年轻男孩在疯狂地摇滚着，镜头移动，显示出那些服饰华贵的女客人，在幽暗中凑在一起，对着台上指指点点，不时发出暧昧的低笑。最后镜头总是落到宋诚和罗罗身上，他们往往坐在最后面的角落里，头凑在一起密谈着，显得很亲密。作为唯一的男客，宋诚自然显得很突出……宋诚实在没有办法，大多数时间他只能在蓝浪找到罗罗。舞厅的光线总是很暗，但这些录像十分清晰，显然使用了高级的微光镜头，这种设备不是一般人能拥有的。这么说，他们从一开始就注意到自己了，这令宋诚觉得与对手相比自己是何等不成熟。

这天罗罗约宋诚通报最新的情况，宋诚在夜总会见到罗罗时，他一反常态，要到宋诚的车里谈，谈完后，他说现在身体不舒服，不想上去了，上去后老板肯定要派事儿，想在宋诚的车里休息一会儿。宋诚以为他的毒瘾又来了，但也没有办法，只好将车开回机关，到办公室去处理一些白天没干完的工作，把车停在机关大楼外面，罗罗就待在车里。40多分钟后他下来时，已经有人发现罗罗死在充满丙烷气味的车里。车门只有宋诚能从外面打开，后来，公安系统参与此案侦查的一位密友告诉宋诚，他的车门门锁没有任何被破坏的痕迹，从其他方面也确实能够排除还有其他凶手的可能性。这样，人们理所当然地认为是宋诚杀了罗罗，而宋诚则知道只有一个可能：那两个丙烷罐是罗罗自己带进车里的。

这让宋诚彻底绝望了，他放弃了洗清自己的努力——如果一个人以自己的生命为武器来诬陷他，那他是绝对逃不掉的。

其实罗罗的自杀并不让宋诚觉得意外，他的 HIV 化验呈阳性。但罗罗以死来陷害自己，显然是受人指使的，那么罗罗得到了什么样的报酬？那些钱对他还有什么意义？他是为谁挣那些钱？也许报酬根本就不是钱，那是什么？除了报复许雪萍，还有什么更强烈的诱惑或恐惧能征服他吗？这些宋诚永远不可能知道了，但他由此进一步看到了对手的强大和自己的稚嫩。

这就是他为人所知的一生了：一个高级纪检干部，生活腐化变态，因同性恋情杀被捕，他以前在男女交往方面的洁身自好在人们眼里反倒成了证据之一……像一只被人群踏死的臭虫，他的一切很快就将消失得干干净净，即使偶尔有人想起他，也不过是想起了一只臭虫。

现在宋诚知道，他以前之所以做好了为信念和使命牺牲的准备，是因为根本就不明白牺牲意味着什么。他想当然地把死作为一条底线，现在才发现，牺牲的残酷远在这条底线之下。在进行搜查时他被带回家一次，当时妻子和女儿都在家，他向女儿伸出手去，孩子厌恶地惊叫一声，扑在妈妈的怀里缩到墙角。她们投向自己的那种目光他只见过一次，那是一天早晨，他发现放在衣柜下的捕鼠夹夹住了一只老鼠，他拿起夹子让她们看那只死鼠……

"好了，我们暂时把大爆炸和奇点这些抽象的东西放到一边。"白冰打断了宋诚痛苦的回忆，将那个大手提箱提到桌面上，"看看这个。"

超弦计算机、终极容量和镜像模拟

"这是一台超弦计算机，是我从气象模拟中心带出来的，你说偷出来的也行，我全凭它摆脱了追捕。"白冰拍着那个箱子说。

宋诚将目光移到箱子上，显得很迷惑。

"这是很贵的东西，目前在省里还有两台。根据超弦理论，物质的基本粒子不是点状物，而是无限细的一维弦，在十一维空间中振动。现在，我们可以操纵这根弦，沿其一维长度存储和处理信息，这就是超弦计算机的原理。

"在传统的电子计算机中的一块 CPU 或一条内存，在超弦机中只是一个原子！超弦电路是基于粒子的十一维微观空间结构运行的，这种超空间微观矩阵，使人类拥有了几乎无限的运算和存储能力。将过去的巨型计算机同超弦机相比，就如我们的 10 根手指头同那台巨型机相比一般。超弦机具有终极容量。终极容量啊，就是说，它可以将已知宇宙中的每一个基本粒子的状态都存储起来并进行运算。就是说，如果是基于三维空间和一维时间，超弦机能够在原子级别上模拟整个宇宙……"

宋诚交替地看着箱子和白冰，与刚才不同，他似乎在很认真地听白冰的话，其实他是在努力寻找一种解脱，让这个神秘来人的这番不着边际的话，将自己从那痛苦的回忆中解脱出来。

白冰说："很抱歉我说了这么多莫名其妙的话，大爆炸、奇点、超弦计算机什么的，与我们面对的现实好像八竿子打不着，但要把事情解释清楚，就绕不开这些东西。下面谈谈我的专业吧，我是个软件工程师，主要搞模拟软件，也就是建立一个数学模型，在计算机里让它运行，模拟现实世界中的某种事物或过程。我是学数学的，所以建模和编程都搞，以前搞过沙尘暴模拟、黄土高原水土流失模拟、东北能源经济发展趋势模拟等，现在搞大范围天气模拟。我很喜欢这个工作，看着现实世界的某一部分在计算机内存中运动演化，真是一件很有意思的事。"

白冰看看宋诚，后者的双眼一动不动地盯着他，似乎仍在注意听着，于是他接着说下去。

"你知道，物理学在近年来连续得到大突破，很像上世纪初那阵儿。现在，只要给定边界条件，我们就可以拨开量子效应的迷雾，准确地预测单个或一群基本粒子的运动和演化。注意我说的一群，如果群里粒子的数量足够大，它就构成了一个宏观物体，也就是说，我们现在可以在原子级别上建立一个宏观物体的数学模型。这种模拟被称为镜像模拟，因为它能以百分之百的准确率再现模拟对象的宏观过程，如同为宏观模拟对象建立了一个数字镜像。打个比方吧，如果用镜像模拟方式为一个鸡蛋建立数学模型，也就是将组成鸡蛋的每一个原子的状态都输入模型的数据库，当这个模型在计算机中运行时，如果给出的边界条件合适，内存中的那个虚拟鸡蛋就会孵出小鸡来，而且那只内存中的虚拟小鸡，与现实中的那个鸡蛋孵出的小鸡一模一样，连每一根毛尖都不会差一丝一毫！你往下想，如果这个模拟目标比鸡蛋再大些呢？大到一棵树、一个人，甚至很多人；大到一座城市、一个国家，甚至大到整个地球呢？"白冰说到这里激动起来，开始手舞足蹈，"我是一个狂想爱好者，热衷于在想象中把一切都推向终极，这就让我想到，如果镜像模拟的对象是整个宇宙会怎么样？！"白冰进入一种不能自已的亢奋中，"想想，整个宇宙！奶奶的，在一个计算机内存中运行的宇宙！从诞生到毁灭……"

白冰突然中断了兴奋的讲述，警觉地站了起来。这时门无声地开了，走进两个神色阴沉的男人，其中一位稍年长些的对着白冰抬抬双手，示意他照着做。白冰和宋诚都看到了他敞开的夹克中的手枪皮套。白冰顺从地举起双手，年轻的那位上前在他的身上十分仔细地上下轻拍了一遍，然后对稍年长者摇摇头，同时将那个大手提箱从桌子上提开，放到离白冰远一些的地方。

稍年长者走到门口，对外面做了一个"请"的手势，又进来三个人，第一个是市公安局局长陈继峰，第二个是省纪委书记吕文明，最后进来的是首长。

年轻人拿出了一副手铐，但吕文明冲他摇了摇头。陈继峰则将头向门的方向微微偏了一下，两个便衣警察便向门口走去，其中的一人走时还从办公桌桌腿上取下一个小东西放进衣袋，显然是窃听器。

初始条件

白冰脸上丝毫没有意外的表情，他淡淡一笑说："你们终于抓到我了。"

"准确地说是自投罗网，得承认，如果你真想逃，我们是很难抓到你的。"陈继峰说。

吕文明表情复杂地看了宋诚一眼，欲言又止。首长则缓缓地摇摇头，语气沉重地沉吟道："宋诚啊，你，怎么堕落到这一步呢……"他双手撑着桌沿长久地默立着，眼睛有些湿润，谁看到都不会怀疑他的悲哀是装出来的。

"首长，在这儿就不必演戏了吧。"白冰冷眼看着这一切说。

首长没有动。

"诬陷他是您策划的。"

"证据？"首长仍没有动，从容地问。

"那次会面后，关于宋诚您只说过一句话，是对他说的。"白冰指指陈继峰，"继峰啊，宋诚的事你当然知道意味着什么，还是认真办一办吧。"

"这能证明什么？"

"从法律意义上当然证明不了什么，这是您的精明和老练之处，即使是密谈也深藏不露。但他，"白冰又指了指陈继峰，"都领会得很准确。他对您的意思一直领会得很准确，对宋诚的诬陷是他指示刚才那两个人中的一个具体干的。那人叫沉兵，是他手下最得力的人，整个过程可是一个复杂的大工程，我就不用细说了吧。"

首长缓缓转过身来，在办公桌边的一把椅子上坐下，两眼看着地板说："年轻人，必须承认，你的突然出现有许多令人吃惊的地方，用陈局长的话说叫见鬼了。"他沉默了一会儿后，语气变得真诚起来，"说明你的真实身份吧，如果你真是上级派来的，请相信，我们是会协助工作的。"

"不是，我多次声明自己是个普通人，身份就是你们已经查明的那样。"

首长点点头，看不出白冰的话让他感到欣慰还是更加忧虑。

"坐，都坐吧。"首长对仍站着的吕、陈二人挥挥手，然后俯身靠近白冰，郑重地说，"年轻人，今天，我们把一切都彻底讲清楚，好吗？"

白冰点点头："这也是我的打算。我，从头说起吧。"

"不，不用，你刚才对宋诚说的那些我们都听到了，就从中断处接着说吧。"

白冰语塞，一时想不起刚才说到哪儿了。

"在原子级别模拟整个宇宙。"首长提醒他，但是白冰仍然不知如何说起，他便自己接着说下去，"年轻人，我认为你这个想法是不可能实现的。不错，超弦计算机具有终极容量，为这种模拟运算提供了硬件基础，但，你想过初始状态的问题吗？对宇宙的镜像模拟必须从某个初始状态开始，也就是说，要在模拟开始时的某个时间断面上，将宇宙的全部原子的状态一个一个地输入计算机，以在原子级别上构建一个初始宇宙模型，这可能吗？别说是宇宙了，就是你说的那个鸡蛋都不可能，构成它的原子数比有史以来出现过的所有鸡蛋的数量都要大几个数量级；甚至一个细菌都不可能，它的原子数也是令人望而生畏的。退一步说，就算动用了难以想象的人力和物力，将细菌甚至鸡蛋这类小物体的初始状态从原子级别上输入计算机，那么它们运动和演化所需要的边界条件呢？比如鸡蛋孵出小鸡所需要的温度、湿度等，这些边界条件在原子级别上的资料量同样大得不可想象，甚至可能要大于模拟对象本身。"

"您能对技术问题进行如此描述，我很敬佩。"白冰由衷地说。

"首长是高能物理专业的高才生，是改革开放恢复学位后国内的第一批物理学硕士之一。"吕文明说。

白冰对吕文明点点头，又转向首长："但您忘了，存在着那样一个时间断面，宇宙是十分简单的，甚至比鸡蛋和细菌都简单，比现实中最简单的东西都简单，因为它那时的原子数是零，没有大小，没有结构。"

"大爆炸奇点？"首长飞快接上话，几乎没有空隙，显示出他沉稳迟缓的外表下灵敏快捷的思维。

"是的，大爆炸奇点。超弦理论已经建立了完善的奇点模型，我们只需要将这个模型用软件实现，输入计算机运算就可以了。"

"是这样，年轻人，真是这样。"首长站起身，走到白冰身边拍拍他的肩膀，显示出了少有的兴奋。对刚才的那番对话不甚了了的陈继峰和吕文明则用迷惑的目光看着他。

"这是你从那个科研中心拿出来的超弦计算机吗？"首长指着那个大手提箱问。

"偷出来的。"白冰说。

"呵，没关系，宇宙大爆炸的镜像模拟软件一定在里面吧？"

"是的。"

"做做看。"

创世游戏

白冰点点头，把箱子提到桌面上打开了。除了显示设备外，箱子中还装着一个圆柱体容器，超弦计算机的主机其实只有一个烟盒大小，但原子电路需要在超低温下运行，所以主机浸在这个绝热容器里的液氮中。白冰将液晶显示器支起来，动了一下鼠标，处于休眠状态下的超弦计算机立刻苏醒过来，液晶屏亮起来，像睁开了一只惺忪的睡眼，显示出一个很简单的接口，仅由一个下拉文本框和一个小小的标题组成，标题是：请选择创世起爆参数。

白冰点了一下文本框旁边的箭头，下拉出一行行资料组，每组有十几个数据项，各行看上去差别很大。"奇点的性质由18个参数确定，参数的组合原则上是无限的，但根据超弦理论的推断，能够产生创世爆炸的参数组的数量是有限的，但有多少组目前还是个谜。这里显示的是其中的一小部分，我们随便选一组吧。"

白冰选中一组参数后，屏幕立刻变成了乳白色，正中凸显了两个醒目的大按钮：

"引爆""取消"。

白冰点了"引爆"按钮，屏幕上只剩下一片乳白。"这白色象征虚无，这时没有空间，时间也还没有开始，什么都没有。"

屏幕的左下角出现了一个红色数字"0"。

"这个数字是宇宙演化的时间，0的出现说明奇点已经生成，它没有大小，所以我们看不到。"

红色数字开始飞快增长。

"注意，宇宙大爆炸开始了。"

屏幕中央出现了一个蓝色的小点，很快增大为一个球体，发出耀眼的蓝光。球体急剧膨胀，很快占满了整个屏幕，软件将视野拉远，球体重新缩为遥远处的一点，但爆炸中的宇宙很快又充满了整个屏幕。这个过程反复重复着，频率很快，仿佛是一首宏伟乐曲的节拍。

"宇宙现在正处于暴胀阶段，它的膨胀速度远超过光速。"

随着球体膨胀速度的降低，视野拉开的频率渐渐慢下来，随着能量密度的降低，球体的颜色由蓝向黄红渐变，后来宇宙的色彩在红色上固定下来，并渐渐变暗，屏幕上的视野不再拉远，变成黑色的球体在屏幕上很缓慢地膨胀着。

"好，现在距大爆炸已经 100 亿年了，这个宇宙处于稳定的演化阶段，我们进去看看吧。"白冰说完动了动鼠标，球体迅速前移，屏幕完全黑了下来，"好，现在我们就在这个宇宙的太空中了。"

"什么也没有啊！"吕文明说。

"我们看看……"白冰说着，按动鼠标右键弹出了一个很复杂的接口，一个程序开始统计这个宇宙中的物质总量，"呵，这个宇宙中只有 11 个基本粒子。"他又调出了一大堆信息仔细读着，"有 10 个粒子结成了 5 个粒子对，互相环绕对方运行，不过每个粒子对中的 2 个粒子相距几千万光年，要上百万年才能相对运动 1 毫米；还有 1 个粒子是自由的。"

"11 个基本粒子？！说了半天还是什么都没有。"吕文明说。

"有空间啊，近千亿光年直径的空间！还有时间，100 亿年的时间！时空是最实在的存在！要说这个宇宙，还是创造得比较成功的，以前创造的相当多的宇宙连空间都很快湮灭了，只剩时间。"

"无聊。"陈继峰哼了一声，转身不再看屏幕。

"不，很有意思，"首长高兴地说，"再来一次。"

白冰退回到引爆接口，重选了一组参数，再次启动了大爆炸。这个新宇宙诞生的过程看上去与刚才基本相同，也是一个在膨胀中渐渐暗下来的球体。在创世后的 150 亿年，球体完全变黑，宇宙的演化稳定下来，白冰让视点进入宇宙内部，这时，连最不感兴趣的陈继峰也惊叹起来。广漠的黑色太空下，一张银色的大膜向各个方向延伸至无穷远处，大膜上点缀着各种色彩的小球体，像滚动在广阔镜面上的多彩露珠。

白冰又调出了分析接口，看了一会儿后说："运气好，这是一个丰富多彩的宇宙，半径约 400 亿光年，其中一半是液体一半是空间。也就是说，这个宇宙就是一个深度和表面半径都是 400 亿光年的大洋！宇宙中的固体星球就浮在洋面上！"白冰将画面推向洋面，可以看到银色的洋面在缓缓波动着，画面中出现了一个星球的近景。"这个漂浮着的星球有……我看看，木星那么大吧。哇，它还在自转耶！看它表面的那些山脉，在出水和入水时是何等壮观！我们就把这液体叫水吧。看那被山脉甩到轨道上的水，在洋面形成了一个半圆的彩虹环耶！"

"是很美，但这个宇宙是违反物理学基本定律的。"首长看着屏幕说，"别说 400 亿光年深的海洋，就是 4 光年，那水体也早在引力下坍缩成黑洞了。"

白冰摇摇头说："您忘了最基本的一点，这不是我们的宇宙，这个宇宙有自己的一套物理定律，与我们宇宙中的完全不同。在这个宇宙中，万有引力常数、普朗克常数、光速等基本物理常数与我们的宇宙完全不同；在这个宇宙中，1 加 1 甚至都不等于 2。"

在首长的鼓励下，白冰继续做下去，第三个宇宙被创造出来，进入其中后屏幕上出现了一堆极其混乱的色彩和形状，白冰立刻将它关掉了。"这是一个六维宇宙，我们无法观察它。其实大多数情况都是这样，我们创造的前两个都是三维宇宙，只是运气好而已，宇宙从高能状态冷却后，被释放到宏观的维数为 3 的概率只有 3：11。"

第四个宇宙出现时，所有的人都很迷惑：宇宙呈现一个无际的黑色平面，有无数根银光闪闪的直线与黑色平面垂直相交。看过分析资料后，白冰说："这个宇宙与上面相反，维数比我们的低，是一个 2.5 维的宇宙。"

"2.5 维？"首长很吃惊。

"您看，这个黑色的没有厚度的二维平面就是这个宇宙的太空，直径约 5000 亿光年；那些与平面垂直的亮线就是太空中的恒星，它们都有几亿光年长，但无限细，只有一维。分数维的宇宙很少见，我要把这组创世参数记下来。"

"有个问题，"首长说，"如果你用这组参数再次启动大爆炸，所得到的宇宙与这个完全一样吗？"

"是的，而且其演化过程也完全一样，一切在大爆炸时就决定了。您看，物理学穿过量子迷雾之后，宇宙又显示出了因果链和决定论的本性。"白冰依次看看每个人，郑重地说，"我请各位都牢记这一点，如果要理解我们后面将要面对的那些可怕的事，这是关键。"

"真的很有意思，做上帝的体验，超脱而空灵，很长时间没有这种感觉了。"首长感叹道。

"我的感觉同您一样，"白冰离开了计算机，站起来来回走着，"所以，我就一遍又一遍地玩着创世游戏，到现在为止，我已经启动了 1000 多次大爆炸，那 1000 多个宇宙，其神奇壮观，很难用语言形容，我像吸毒似的上了瘾……本来我可以这样一直玩儿下去，我们之间将永远素不相识，不会有任何关系，我们双方的生活都会按正常的轨道进行下去，但……唉……那是今年年初一个下雪的晚上，已经凌晨两点了，很静很静，我启动了那天的最后一次大爆炸，在超弦计算机中诞生了第 1207 号宇宙，就是这一个……"

白冰回到计算机前，将文本框下拉到底，选择了最后一组创世参数，启动了宇宙大爆炸。新生的宇宙在蓝光中急剧膨胀后熄灭为黑色。白冰移动鼠标，在创世之后的 190 亿年进入了这个编号为第 1207 号的宇宙。

这一次，屏幕上出现了灿烂的星海。

"1207 的半径约为 200 亿光年，宏观维数是 3。这个宇宙中，万有引力常数是 $6.67 \times 10^{-11} N \cdot m^2 / kg^2$，真空中的光速是每秒 30 万千米；这个宇宙中，电子电量是 1.602×10^{-19} 库仑；这个宇宙中，普朗克常数是 6.626……"白冰凑近首长，用令人胆寒的目光逼视着他，"这个宇宙中，1 加 1 等于 2。"

"这是我们的宇宙。"首长点点头，他仍很沉着，但额头有些潮湿了。

历史检索

"得到 1207 号宇宙后，我花了 1 个多月的时间做了一个搜索引擎，以模式识别为基础的。然后，我就从天文资料中查到银河系与仙女座、大小麦哲伦等相邻星系的几何构图，在全宇宙范围内查询这种构图，得到了 8 万多个结果。下一步我就在这个范围内，用银河系和邻近星系本身的形状进行查询，很快在宇宙中定位了银河系。"以漆黑的太空为背景，一个银色的大旋涡在屏幕上显示出来，"太阳的定位就更容易了，我们已经知道它在银河系中的大致范围——"白冰用鼠标在大旋涡的一个旋臂顶端拉出一个小矩形框，"仍用模式识别的方法，在这个范围中很快就定位了太阳。"屏幕上出现了一个耀眼的光球，光球周围环绕着一个雾蒙蒙的大环，"哦，这时太阳系的行星还没有诞生，这个星际尘埃构成的环就是构成它们的原材料。"白冰在屏幕下方调出了一个滚动条，"看，用这个来移动时间，"他将滑块缓缓前移，越过了 2 亿年的漫漫时光，太阳周围的尘埃环消失了，"现在八大行星已经诞生。这是真实尺度的图像，不是天象演示，所以找到地球还要费些事，我把以前存储的坐标调出来吧。"于是原始地球在屏幕上出现了，一个灰蒙蒙的球体，白冰转动鼠标的滚轮，"我们降低高度，好，现在，大约是 1 万米高吧。"下面大陆仍笼罩在迷雾之中，但雾中纵横交错的发着红光的网线显现出来，像胚胎上的血管，白冰指着那些网线说，"这是岩浆河。"他继续转动鼠标滚轮，穿过浓浓的酸雾，褐色的海面出现了，紧接着视点扎入海中，一片浑浊，有几个微小的悬浮物，它们大多是圆形的，也有其他较复杂的形状，与其他悬浮物最明显的区别是，它们自己在运动，而不是随水流漂移。"生命，刚出现的生命。"白冰用鼠标点点那些微小的东西说。他很快反向转动滚轮，将视点重新升到太空中，再次显示出古地球的全貌，然后移动时间滚动条，亿万年时光又飞逝而过，笼罩在地球表面的浓雾消失了，海洋在变蓝，大陆在变绿。后来，巨大的冈瓦纳古陆像初春的冰块分崩离析，"如果愿意，我们可以看到生命进化的全过程，包括几次大灭绝和随之而来的生命大爆发。但是算了吧，省些时间，我们就要看到关系到咱们命运的谜底了。"古陆的各个碎块继续漂移，终于，一幅熟悉的世界构图出现了。白冰改变了时间滚动条的比例，开始以较慢的速度移动时间，并在一点停住了，"好了，在这里，人类出现了。"他又将滑块小心地向前移动一小段，"现在，文明出现了。"

"对于上古的历史，一般只能宏观地看看，检索具体事件不太容易，具体人物就更难了。一般的历史检索是靠两个参数：地点和时间，这两点在上古历史记载中很难准确，我们做一次看看吧。来，我们下去了！"白冰说着，将鼠标在地中海范围的一个位置双击了一下，视点高度令人目眩地急剧降低，最后，一个荒凉的海滩出现了，黄沙的尽头，是一片连绵的橄榄丛。

"古希腊时代的特洛伊海岸。"白冰说。

"那……你能移到木马屠城的时间吗？"吕文明兴奋地问。

"从来就没有过什么木马。"白冰淡淡地说。

陈继峰点点头："那种东西像儿戏，在实际的战争中是不可能出现的。"

"从来没有过特洛伊战争。"白冰说。

首长很惊奇："这么说，特洛伊城是出于别的原因毁灭的？"

"从来没有过特洛伊城。"

另外三个人惊奇地互相看看。

白冰指着屏幕说："现在显示的就是应该发生那场战争时特洛伊海岸的真实情景，我们再前后移动 500 年……"白冰小心地微移鼠标，屏幕上的海岸在白昼和黑夜的高频转换中急剧闪动，树丛的形状也在飞快变化，沙滩的尽头出现过几个小棚屋，时而还能看到一闪而过的几个小小的人影，棚屋时多时少，但最多时也没有超过一个村庄的规模，"看到了吗，伟大的特洛伊城只在那些游吟诗人的想象中存在过。"

"怎么会呢？"吕文明惊叫起来，"本世纪初有考古发现证实啊！当时还挖出了……阿伽门农的黄金面具。"

"阿伽门农的面具？"白冰大笑一声。

"随着历史记载的增多和更加准确，往后的检索就越来越容易，再做一次。"

白冰将视点升回地球轨道，这次他没有使用鼠标，而是手动输入了时间和地理坐标，视点向亚洲西部降落。很快，屏幕上显示出一片沙漠，在一处红柳丛的阴影下躺着几个人，他们穿着破旧的粗布袍，皮肤黝黑，头发很长，且被沙尘和汗水弄成一缕一缕的，远远看去像一堆破烂的废弃物。白冰说："这里离村庄不远，但鼠疫流行，他们不敢去。"有一个身形瘦长的人坐了起来，四下看看，确认别人都睡熟了后，拿起旁边一个人的羊皮水囊喝了一通，又从另一个人的破行囊中拿出一块饼，掰下三分之一放到自己的包里，随后满意地躺下了。

"我用正常速度运行了两天，看到他五次偷别人的水喝，三次偷别人的饼。"白冰用鼠标点着那个刚躺下的人说。

"他是谁？"

"马可·波罗。检索到他可不容易，关押他的那个热那亚监狱的地点和时间都比较准确，我在那里定位了他，随后向回跟踪他经历了那次海战，提取了一些特征点，又向回跳过一大段时间跟到这里，这是在那时的波斯、现在的伊朗巴姆市附近，不过都白费劲儿了。"

"那他是在去中国的路上了，你应该能跟着他进入忽必烈的宫殿。"吕文明说。

"他没有进入过任何宫殿。"

"你是说，他在中国期间只是在民间待着？"

"马可·波罗根本就没有来过中国，前面更加险恶的漫漫长路吓住了他，他们就在西亚转悠了几年，后来这人把从那里道听途说来的传闻讲给了那位作家狱友，后者写成了那本伟大的游记。"

三个人再次惊奇得面面相觑。

"再往后，检索具体的人和事就更加容易了，再来一次，到近代吧。"

在一间很暗的大屋子里，一张很宽的木桌子上铺着一张大地图，桌旁围着几个身着清朝武官服的人，由于很暗，看不清他们的面容。

"这是北洋海军提督府的一次会议。"

有一个人在说话，画面传出的声音很模糊，且南方口音重，听不懂。白冰解释说："这个人说，在近海防御中，不要一味追求大炮巨舰，就这么点儿钱，与其从西洋购买大吨位铁甲舰，不如买更多数量的蒸汽鱼雷快艇，每艘艇上可装载 4—6 枚瓦斯鱼雷，构成庞大的快艇攻击群，用灵活机动的航线避开日舰舰炮火力，抵近攻击……我曾请教过多位海军专家和战史研究者，他们一致认为，如果在当时这人的想法得以实施，北洋水师将是甲午海战中的胜利者。这人的高明和超前之处在于，他是海战史上最早从新式武器的出现发现传统大炮巨舰主义缺陷的人。"

"他是谁？邓世昌？"陈继峰问。

白冰摇摇头："方伯谦。"

"什么？就是那个在黄海大海战中临阵脱逃的怕死鬼？"

"就是他。"

"直觉告诉我，这些才像真实的历史。"首长沉思着说。

白冰点点头："是啊，到这一步，超脱和空灵消失了，我开始陷入郁闷中，我发现，我们基本上被自己所知道的历史骗了：那些名垂青史的英雄，有一大半也许是卑鄙的骗子和阴谋家，用他们的权势为自己树碑立传且成功了。而那些为正义和真理献身的人，三分之二都默默地惨死在历史的尘埃中，没有人知道他们的存在；剩下的三分之一则在强有力的诬陷下遗臭万年，就像现在宋诚的命运；他们中只有极少数的人得到了历史正确的记忆，其比例连冰山的一角都不到。"

这时，人们才注意到一直沉默的宋诚，看到他已经悄悄振作起来，两眼放出光芒，像一个已经倒地的战士又站了起来，拿起武器并跨上一匹新的战马。

现实检索

"然后，你就进入了1207宇宙中的现实，是吗？"首长问。

"是的，我在那个镜像中将时间调到现在。"白冰说着，同时将屏幕上时间滑标上的滑块推到尽头，这时视点又回到了太空中，蓝色的地球看上去与古代并没有什么不同，"这就是1207镜像中的现实：我们这个内地省份，经过了几十年不间断的能源和资源输出，除了矿产开采和电力之外，至今也未能建立起一个像样的工业体系，只留下了污染，农村的大片地区仍处于贫困线下，城市失业严重，治安状况恶化……我自然想看看领导和指挥着这一切的人是怎样工作的，最后看到了什么，我就不用说了。"

"你这样做的目的呢？"首长问。

白冰苦笑着摇摇头："别以为我有他那样崇高的目的，"他指指宋诚，"我只是个普通老百姓，自得其乐地过日子，你们干什么，和我有什么关系？我本来根本不想惹你们的，但……我为这个超级模拟软件费了这么大劲儿，自然想通过它得些实惠，于是，我就给你们中的几个人打电话，想小小地敲一笔钱……"他说着突然变得恼怒起来，"你们干吗反应这么过激？！干吗非要除掉我？！其实我那笔钱不就完了嘛……好了，现在我把一切都讲清楚了。"

五个人陷入了长时间的沉默，他们都默默地盯着屏幕上的地球，这是现实中的地球的数字镜像，他们也在镜像中。

"你真的能够在这台计算机中观察到世界上发生过的一切？"陈继峰打破沉默问。

"是的，历史和现实的所有细节，都是这台计算机中运行的资料，资料是可以随意解析的，不管多么隐秘的事情，观察它们不过是从数据库中提取一些资料进行处理，这个数据库以原子级别存储着整个世界的镜像，所有资料都是可以随意提取的。"

"能证明一下吗？"

"这很容易，你出去，随便到什么地方，随便干一件什么事，然后回来。"

陈继峰依次看了看首长和吕文明，转身走出了房间，2分钟后，他回来了，无言地看着白冰。

白冰移动鼠标，使视点从太空急剧下降，悬在这城市上空，城市一览无余地展现在屏幕上。白冰移动画面仔细寻找，很快找到了近郊的第二看守所，找到了他们所在的这幢三层楼房。视点随即进入了楼房内，在二楼空荡的走廊中移动，画面上出现了坐在走廊长椅子上的两个便衣警察，其中的沉兵正在点一支烟。最后，画面中出现了他们所在的办公室的门。

"现在的模拟画面，只比正在发生的现实滞后 0.1 秒，让我们后退几分钟。"白冰将时间滑标向后移了一点点。

屏幕上，门开了，陈继峰走了出来，坐在长椅上的两个人看到他后立刻站了起来，陈向他们摆摆手示意没事，就向另一个方向走去，视点紧跟着他，像有人用摄像机在跟踪拍摄。镜像画面上，陈继峰进了卫生间，从裤子口袋中掏出手枪，拉了一下枪栓后装回裤袋，白冰将这个画面定住，并使其像三维动画一样旋转至各个方位。陈继峰走出卫生间，画面跟着他回到了办公室，并显示出了正在等待中的另外四人。

首长不动声色地看着屏幕，吕文明则抬头警觉地看了陈继峰一眼。

"这东西确实厉害。"吕文明阴沉着脸说。

"下面我为您演示它更厉害的地方。"白冰说着，使屏幕上的画面静止了，"由于镜像模拟的宇宙是以原子级别存储的，所以我们可以检索到这个宇宙中的每一个细节。下面，让我们看看陈局长上衣口袋中装着什么。"

白冰在静止画面上拉出一个方框，圈住陈继峰的上衣口袋范围，然后弹出一个处理接口，经过一系列操作，上衣口袋外侧的布被去除了，显示出放在口袋中的一张折叠起来的小纸片。白冰使用拷贝键将纸片复制下来，然后启动了一个三维模型处理软件，将拷贝的资料粘贴到软件的处理桌面上，又经过几项操作，那折叠的纸片被展开来，那是一张外汇支票，数额是 25 万美元。

"下面，我们就追踪这张支票的来源。"白冰说着关闭了图像处理软件，又回到四个人的静止画面上来，白冰在陈继峰上衣口袋中那张已被选定的支票上按右键调出功能选项，选择了trace项，支票闪动起来，画面也立刻活动起来了，时间在逆向流动，显示首长一行三人退出了办公室，又退出了大楼，退回到一辆汽车上，其中的陈继峰和吕文明戴上了耳机，显然是在监听白冰和宋诚的谈话。跟踪检索继续进行，场景不断变换，但那张闪动的支票作为检索键值一直处于画面的中央，陈继峰仿佛被它吸附着，穿过一个又一个场景。终于，那张支票跳出了陈的上衣口袋，钻进了一个小篮子，那个篮子又从陈的手中跳到了另一个人的手中，在这个时刻，白冰使画面静止了。

"就从这里开始放吧。"白冰说着，启动了画面，以正常速度播放。这好像是在陈继峰家的客厅里，屏幕上一个穿黑西装的中年人拎着那个水果篮站在那里，好像刚进来，陈继峰则坐在沙发上。

"陈局长，温总托我来看看您，也是表示一下上次的谢意。他本想亲自来的，但觉得为了免去一些闲话，这种走动还是少些好。"

陈继峰说："你回去告诉温雄，现在他条件好了，一定要走正道，总是出格对谁都没好处，也别怪我不客气！"

"是，是，温哥怎么能忘记陈局的教诲呢。他现在不但为社会积极贡献，在贫困地区建了四所小学，政治上也要求进步，已经当选市人大代表了！"来人说着，将果篮放到茶几上。

"东西拿走。"陈继峰挥挥手说。

"哪敢带什么好东西，那不是成心惹陈局长生气嘛，一点水果，表表心意。您是不知道，温总一说起您，就眼泪汪汪的，说您是我们的再生父母啊。"

来人走后，陈继峰关上门后回到茶几旁，将果篮的水果全倒出来，从篮底拿出那张支票放进上衣口袋。

首长和吕文明都冷冷地看了陈继峰一眼，这些他们显然也都不知晓。温雄是利成集团的总裁，这是个包含着餐饮、长途客运等众多业务的庞大公司，其原始积累来自温雄黑社会体系的贩毒利润，他们使这座城市成为云南至俄罗斯毒品管道上一个重要的枢纽，现在温雄在合法商业上发展顺利，他的黑道毒品业务也在前者的补充滋养下更快地膨胀起来，致使这座内地城市毒品泛滥，治安恶化。而陈继峰这个后台是其生存的重要保证。

"收的是美元？一定是要给儿子汇去吧。"白冰笑着说，"您儿子在美国读书的钱可全是温雄出的……对了，想不想看看他现在在地球那一边干什么？很容易的，现在波士顿是午夜，不过上两次我看到他时，他都还没有睡觉。"白冰将视点升到太空，将地球旋转了180度，然后将北美大陆放大，在大西洋海岸找到了那座灯火灿烂的城市，然后很快定位了他以前显然找到过的一座公寓，视点进入公寓卧室后，显示出一幅令人尴尬的画面：那个黄皮肤男孩正在和一白一黑两个妓女鬼混。

"陈局长，看到儿子是怎样花你的钱了吗？"

陈继峰恼怒地将液晶显示屏反扣到箱子上。

被深深震撼了的几个人再次陷入长时间的沉默中，然后吕文明问："这些天，你为什么只是逃跑，没有想过通过更……正当的方式摆脱困境吗？"

"您是说我到纪委去举报？真是个好主意，我开始也这么想过，于是便在镜像中对纪委领导班子进行查询。"白冰抬头看了看吕文明，"您应该知道我都看到了什么，我不想落到您老同学这样的下场。那么我能去检察院和反贪局吗？郭院长和常局长对大部分重大举报肯定会严格秉公办理，对一小部分会小心地绕开，而我将举报的那些，一说出口他们就会同你们一起要了我的命。那么还能去哪儿呢？让媒体将这一切曝光吗？省里新闻媒体的那几个关键人物我想你们都清楚，首长的政绩不就是他们捧出来的吗？那些记者与妓女的唯一区别就是出卖的部位不同……这是一张互相联结在一起的大网，哪一根线都动不得啊，我没地方可去。"

"你可以去中央。"首长仔细观察着白冰，不动声色地说。

白冰点点头说："这是唯一的选择了，但我是个普通的小人物，所以首先来见见宋诚，找到一个稳妥可靠的渠道，也顾不得你们的追杀了。"白冰犹豫了一下，接着说，"但这个选择并不轻松，你们都是聪明人，知道这样做最终意味着什么。"

"意味着这项技术将公之于世。"

"很对。那时，笼罩在历史和现实上的所有迷雾将一扫而光，一切的一切，在明处和暗处的，过去和现在的，都将赤裸裸地展现于光天化日之下。到那时，光明与黑暗将不得不进行一场史无前例的大决斗，世界将陷入一片混乱……"

"但最后的结果，是光明取得胜利。"一直沉默的宋诚终于说话了，他走到白冰面前，直视着他说，"知道黑暗的力量来自哪里吗？就是来自黑暗，也就是说来自它的隐蔽性，一旦暴露在明处，它的力量就消失了，如腐败之类的，大多如此。而你的镜像，就是使所有黑暗完全暴露的强光。"

首长和陈、吕二人互相交换了一下目光。

沉默，超弦计算机的屏幕上，原子级别的地球镜像静静地悬浮在太空中。

"有一个机会，"首长突然站起身，对吕、陈二人说，"好像有一个机会。"

首长接着抚着白冰的肩膀说："为什么不将镜像中的时间标尺移向未来？"

白冰和陈、吕二人不解地看着首长。

"如果我们能够准确地预见未来，就能够在现在改变它，这样我们就能控制未来历史的走向，也就控制了一切……年轻人，你认为这没有可能吗？也许，我们能够一起肩负起创造历史的使命。"

白冰明白过来，苦笑着摇摇头，站起身走到计算机前，用鼠标将时间标尺拉长，在零时标后面拉出了一个未来时段，然后对首长说："您自己来试试吧。"

单程递归

首长扑向计算机，谁都没有见过他那么敏捷，如饥饿的鹰见到地面上的小鸡，令人恐惧。他熟练地移动鼠标，将时间滑标滑过零时点，在滑标进入未来时段的瞬间，一个错误提示窗口跳了出来：

Stack over flow……

白冰从首长手中拿过鼠标，"让我们启动错误跟踪程序，Step by step 吧。"

　　模拟软件退回到出错前，开始分步运行。当现实中的白冰将滑块移过零时点，镜像中虚拟的白冰也正在做着同样的事。错误跟踪程序立刻放大了镜像中的那台超弦计算机的屏幕，可以看到，在那台虚拟计算机的屏幕上，第二层的虚拟白冰也正在将滑块移过零时点。于是，错误跟踪程序又放大了第三层虚拟中的那台超弦计算机的屏幕……就这样，跟踪程序一层层地深入，每一层的白冰都在将滑块移过零时点。这是一个依次向下包容的永无休止的魔盒。

　　"这是递归，一种程序自己调用自己的算法，正常情况下，当调用进行到有限的某一层时会得到答案，多层自我调用的程序再逐层按原路返回。而我们现在看到的是无限调用自己、永远得不到答案的单程递归，由于每次调用时都需将上层的现场资料存入堆栈，就造成了刚才看到的堆栈内存溢出。由于是无限递归调用，即使是超弦计算机的终极容量，也会被耗尽的。"

　　"哦。"首长点点头。

　　"所以，虽然这个宇宙中的一切过程早在大爆炸发生时就已经决定，但未来对我们来说仍是未知的，对讨厌由因果链而产生的决定论的人来说，这也是一个安慰吧。"

　　"哦——"首长又点点头，他"哦"的这一声很长很长。

镜像时代

白冰发现，首长发生了奇怪的变化，仿佛他身上的什么东西被抽走了似的，整个身躯在萎缩，似乎失去支撑自身的力量而摇摇欲坠。他脸色苍白，呼吸急促起来，双手撑着椅子慢慢地坐下，动作艰难而小心翼翼，好像怕压断自己的哪根骨头。

"年轻人，你，毁了我的一生。"首长缓缓地说，"你们赢了。"

白冰看看陈继峰和吕文明，发现他们也与自己一样不知所措，而宋诚，则昂然挺立在他们中间，脸上充满了胜利的光彩。

陈继峰缓缓站起来，从裤子口袋中抽出握枪的手。

"住手。"首长说，声音不高，但威严无比，使陈继峰手中的枪悬在半空不动了，"把枪放下。"首长命令道，但陈仍然不动。

"首长，到了这一步，必须果断，他们死在这儿说得过去，不过是因拒捕和企图逃跑被击毙……"

"放下枪，你这条疯狗！"首长低沉地喝道。

陈继峰拿枪的手垂了下来，慢慢地转向首长道："我不是疯狗，是条好狗，一条知道报恩的狗！一条永远也不会背叛您的狗！！！像我这样从最低层一步步爬上来的，对让自己有今天的上级，就具有值得信任的狗的道德，脑子当然没有那些一帆风顺的知识分子活。"

"你什么意思？"好长时间没有说话的吕文明站了起来。

"我的意思谁都明白，我不像有些人，每走一步都看好两三步的退路，我的退路在哪儿？到这个时刻我不自卫能靠谁？！"

白冰平静地说："杀我没用的，如果你想把镜像公之于世，这是最快捷的办法。"

"傻瓜都能想到这类自卫措施，你真的失去理智了。"吕文明低声对陈继峰说。

陈继峰说："我当然知道这小子不会那么傻，但我们也有自己的技术力量，投入全力是有可能彻底销毁镜像的。"

白冰摇摇头："没有可能。陈局长，这是网络时代，隐藏和发布信息是很简单的事，我在暗处，跟我玩这个你赢不了的，就算你动用最出色的技术专家都赢不了。我就是告诉你那些镜像的备份在哪儿，我死后它如何发布，你也没办法。至于那组创世参数，就更容易隐藏和发布了，打消那个念头吧。"

陈继峰慢慢地将手枪放回裤袋，颓然地坐下了。

"你以为自己已经站在历史的山巅上了，是吗？"首长无力地对宋诚说。

"是正义站在历史的山巅了。"宋诚庄严地说。

"不错，镜像把我们都毁了，但它的毁灭性远不止于此。"

"是的，它将毁灭所有罪恶。"

首长缓缓地点点头。

"然后毁灭所有虽不是罪恶但肮脏和不道德的东西。"

首长又点点头，说："它最后毁灭的，是整个人类文明。"

他这话使其他人都微微一愣，宋诚说："人类文明从来就没有面对过如此光明的前景，这场善恶大搏斗将洗去它身上的一切灰尘。"

"然后呢？"首长轻声问。

"然后，伟大的镜像时代将到来，全人类将面对着一面镜子，每个人的一举一动都能在镜像中精确地查到，没有任何罪行可以隐藏，每一个有罪之人，都不可避免地面临最后审判，那是没有黑暗的时代，阳光将普照到每个角落，人类社会将变得水晶般纯洁。"

"换句话说，那是一个死了的社会。"首长抬头直视着宋诚说。

"能解释一下吗？"宋诚带着对失败者的嘲笑说。

"设想一下，如果 DNA 从来不出错，永远精确地复制和遗传，现在地球上的生命世界会是什么样子？"

在宋诚思考之际，白冰替他回答了："那样的话，现在的地球上根本没有生命，生命进化的基础——变异，正是由 DNA 的错误产生的。"

首长对白冰点点头："社会也是这样，它的进化和活力，是以种种偏离道德主线的冲动和欲望为基础的，清水无鱼，一个在道德上永不出错的社会，其实已经死了。"

"你为自己的罪行进行的这种辩解是很可笑的。"宋诚轻蔑地说。

"也不尽然。"白冰紧接着说，他的话让所有人都有些吃惊，他犹豫了几秒钟，好像下了决心似的说下去，"其实，我不愿意将镜像模拟软件公之于世，还有另一个原因，我……我也不太喜欢有镜像的世界。"

"你像他们一样害怕光明吗？"宋诚质问道。

"我是个普通人，没什么阴暗的罪行。但说到光明，那也要看是什么样的光明，如果半夜窗外有探照灯照你的卧室，那样的光明叫光污染……举个例子吧：我结婚才两年，已经产生了那种……审美疲劳，于是与单位新来的一个女大学生有了……那种关系，老婆当然不知道，大家过得都很好。如果镜像时代到来，我就不可能这样生活了。"

"你这本来就是一种不道德、不负责任的生活！"宋诚说，语气有些愤怒。

"但大家不都是这么过的吗？谁没有些见不得人的地方？这年头儿要想快乐，有时候就得人不人鬼不鬼的，像您这样一尘不染的圣人，能有几个？如果镜像使全人类都成了圣人，一点出轨的事儿都不能干，那……那还有什么劲儿啊！"

首长笑了起来，连一直脸色阴沉的吕、陈二人都露出了些笑容。首长拍着白冰的肩膀说："年轻人，虽然没有上升到理论高度，但你的思想比这位学者要深刻得多。"他说着转向宋诚，"我们肯定是逃不掉的，所以你现在可以将对我们的仇恨和报复欲望放到一边，作为一个社会哲学知识博大精深的人，你不会真浅薄到认为历史是善和正义创造的吧？"

首长这话像强力冷却剂，使处于胜利狂热中的宋诚沉静下来，"我的职责就是惩恶扬善，匡扶正义。"他犹像了一下说，语气和缓了许多。

首长满意地点点头："你没有正面回答，很好，说明你确实还没有浅薄到那个程度。"

首长说到这里，突然打了一个激灵，仿佛被冷水从头浇下，使他从恍惚中猛醒过来，虚弱一扫而光，那刚失去的某种力量似乎又回到了他的身上。他站起身，郑重地扣上领扣，又将衣服上的皱褶处仔细整理了一下，然后极其严肃地对吕文明和陈继峰说："同志们，从现在起，一切已在镜像中了，请注意自己的行为和形象。"

吕文明神情凝重地站了起来，像首长一样整理了一下自己的仪容，长叹一声说："是啊，从此以后，苍天在上了。"

陈继峰一动不动地低头站着。

首长依次看看每个人，说："好，我要回去了，明天的工作会很忙。"他转向白冰，"小白啊，你明天下午 6 点钟到我办公室来一趟，把超弦计算机带上。"然后转向陈、吕二人，"至于二位，好自为之吧。继峰你抬起头来，我们罪不可赦，但不必自惭形秽，比起他们，"他指指宋诚和白冰，"我们所做的真不算什么了。"

说完，他打开门，昂头走了出去。

生日

第二天对于首长来说确实是很忙的一天。

一上班，他就先后召见省里主管工业、农业、财政、环保等领域的主要负责人，向他们交代了下一步的工作。虽然同每位领导谈的时间都很短，但是凭借丰富的工作经验，首长还是言简意赅地讲明了工作重点和最需要注意的问题，同时，他以老到的谈话技巧，让每个人都以为这只是一次普通的工作交代，没发现任何异常之处。

上午 10 点半，送走了最后一位主管领导，首长静下心来，开始写一份材料，向上级阐明自己对本省经济发展和解决省内国有大中型企业面临的问题的意见。材料不长，不到 2000 字，但浓缩了自己这几十年的工作经验和思考。那些熟悉首长理念的人看到这份材料应该很吃惊，这与他以前的观点有很大差别。这是他在权力高端的这么长时间里，第一次纯粹从党和国家的最高利益的角度，在完全不掺杂私心的情况下发表自己的意见。

材料写完后已经是中午 12 点多了，首长没有吃饭，只是喝了一杯茶，便接着工作。

这时，镜像时代的第一个征兆出现了，首长得知陈继峰在自己的办公室里开枪自杀；吕文明则变得精神恍惚，不断地系领口的扣子，整理自己的衣服，好像随时都有人给他拍照似的。对这两件事，首长一笑置之。

镜像时代还没有到来，黑暗已经在崩溃了。

首长命令反贪局立刻成立一个项目组，在公安和工商有关部门的配合下，立刻查封自己的儿子拥有的大西商贸集团和儿媳拥有的北原公司的全部账目和经营资料，并依法控制这些实体的法人。对自己其他亲戚和亲信拥有的各类经济实体也照此办理。

下午 4 点半，首长开始草拟一份名单。他知道，镜像时代到来后，省内各系统落马的处级以上干部将数以千计，现在最紧要的是物色各系统重要岗位的合适接任人选，他的这份名单就是向省委组织部和上级提出的建议。其实，在镜像出现之前，这份名单在他的心中已存在了很长时间，那都是他计划清除、排挤和报复的人。

这时已是下午 5 点半，该下班了，他感到从未有过的欣慰，自己至少做了一天的人。

宋诚走进了办公室，首长将一份厚厚的材料递给他："这就是你那份关于我的调查材料，尽快上报中纪委吧。也附上了我昨天晚上写的一份自首材料，里面除了确认你们调查的事实外，还对一些遗漏做了补充。"

宋诚接过材料，神情严肃地点点头，没有说话。

"过一会儿，白冰要来这里，带着超弦计算机。你应该告诉他，镜像软件马上就要上报上级，一开始，上级领导会考虑到各方面的因素谨慎使用它，要防止镜像软件提前泄露到社会上，那样会产生很大的副作用和危险。基于这个原因，你让他立刻将自己所有的备份，在网上或其他什么地方的，全部删除；还有那个创世参数，如果告诉过其他人，让他列出名单。他相信你，会照办的。一定要确认他把备份删除干净。"

"这正是我们想要做的。"宋诚说。

"然后，"首长直视着宋诚的眼睛，"杀了他，并毁掉那台超弦机。现在，你不会认为我这还是为自己着想吧。"

宋诚愣过后，摇头笑了起来。

首长也露出笑容："好了，我该说的都说完了，以后的事情与我无关。镜像已经记下了我说的这些话，在遥远的未来，也许有那么一天，会有人认真听这些话的。"

首长对宋诚挥了挥手让他走，然后头靠在椅子的靠背上长长地出了一口气，沉浸在一种释然和解脱中。

宋诚走后，下午6点整，白冰准时走进了办公室，他的手里提着那个箱子，装着历史和现实的镜像。

首长招呼他坐下，看着放在办公桌上的超弦计算机说："年轻人，我有一个请求，能不能让我在镜像中看看自己的一生？"

"当然可以，这很容易的！"白冰说着，打开箱子启动了计算机。镜像模拟软件启动后，他首先将时标设定到现在，定位了这间办公室，屏幕上显示出两个人的实时影像后，白冰复制了首长的影像，按动鼠标右键启动了跟踪功能。这时，画面急剧变幻起来，速度之快使整块屏幕看起来一片模糊，但作为跟踪键值的首长的影像一直处于屏幕中央，仿佛是世界的中心。虽然这影像也在急剧变化，但可以看到人越变越年轻。"现在是逆时跟踪搜索，模式识别软件不可能根据您现在的形象识别和定位早年的您，它需要根据您随年龄逐渐变化的形象一步步追踪到那时。"

几分钟后，屏幕停止了闪动，显示出一个初生儿湿漉漉的脸蛋儿，产科护士刚刚把他从盘秤上取下来。这个小生命不哭不闹，睁着一双动人的小眼睛好奇地打量着这个世界。

"呵呵，这就是我了，母亲多次说过，我一生下来就睁开眼睛了。"首长微笑着说，他显然在故作轻松地掩盖自己心中的波澜，但这次很例外地，他做得不太成功。

"您看这个，"白冰指着屏幕下方的一个功能条说，"这些按钮是对图像的焦距和角度进行调整的。这是时间滚动条，镜像软件将一直以您为键值进行显示，您如果想检索某个时间或事件，就如同在文字处理软件中查阅大文件时使用滚动条差不多，先用较大时间跨度走到大概的位置，再进行微调，借助于您熟悉的场景前后移动滚动条，一般总能找到的，这也类似于影碟的快进、快退操作，当然这张碟正常播放将需……"

"近 5 万小时吧。"首长替白冰算出来，然后接过鼠标，将图像的焦距拉开，显示出产床上的年轻母亲和整间病房，这里摆放着那个年代式样朴素的床柜和灯，窗子是木制的，引起他注意的是墙上的一块橘红色光斑，"我出生时是傍晚，时间和现在差不多，这可能是最后一抹夕阳了。"

首长移动时间滚动条，画面又急剧闪动起来，时光在飞逝，他在一个画面上停住了。一盏从天花板上吊下的裸露的电灯照着一张小圆桌，桌旁，他那戴着眼镜、衣着俭朴的母亲正在辅导四个孩子学习，还有一个更小的孩子，三四岁的样子，显然是他本人，正笨拙地捧着一个小木碗吃饭。"我母亲是小学教师，常常把学习差的学生带回家里来辅导，这样就不误从幼儿园接我了。"首长看了一会儿，一直看到幼年的自己不小心将木碗中的粥倒了一身，母亲赶紧起身拿毛巾擦时，才再次移动了时间滚动条。

　　时光又跳过了许多年，画面突然亮起了一片红光，好像是一个高炉的出钢口，几个穿着满是尘污的石棉工作服的人影在晃动，不时被炉口的火焰吞没又重现，首长指着其中的一个说："我父亲，一名炉前工。"

　　"可以把画面的角度调一下，调到正面。"白冰说着，要从首长手中拿过鼠标，但被首长谢绝了。

　　"哦，不不，这年厂里创高产加班，那时要家属去送饭，我去的，这是第一次看到父亲工作，就是从这个角度，之后，他炉火前的这个背影在我脑子里印得很深。"

　　时光又随着滚动条的移动而飞逝，在一个晴朗的日子停止了，一面鲜红的队旗在蓝天的背景上飘扬，一个身穿白衣蓝裤的男孩在仰视着它，一双手给男孩系上红领巾，孩子右手扬上头顶，激动地对世界宣布他时刻准备着，他的眼睛很清澈，如同那天如洗的碧空。

　　"我入队了，小学二年级。"

　　时光跳过，又一面旗帜出现了，是团旗，背景是一座烈士纪念碑，一小群少年对着团旗宣誓，他站在后排，眼睛仍像童年那样清澈，但多了几分热诚和渴望。

"我入团，初一。"

滚动条移动，他一生中的第三面红色旗帜出现了，这次是党旗。这好像是在一间很大的阶梯教室中，首长将焦距调向那六个宣誓中的年轻人中间的那个，让他的脸庞充满了画面。

"入党，大二。"首长指指画面，"你看看我的眼睛，能看出些什么？"

那双年轻的眼睛中，仍能看到童年的清澈、少年的热诚和渴望，但多了一些尚不成熟的睿智。

"我觉得，您……很真诚。"白冰看着那双眼睛说。

"说得对，直到那时，我对那个誓词还是真诚的。"首长说完，在眼睛上抹了一下，动作很轻微，没有被白冰注意到。

时间滚动条又移动了几年，这次移得太过了，经过几次微调，画面上出现了一个林荫道，他站在那里看着一位刚刚转身离去的姑娘，那姑娘回头看了他一眼，眼睛含着晶莹的泪，一副让人心动的冰清玉洁的样子，然后在两排高大的白杨间渐行渐远……白冰知趣地站起身想离开，但首长拦住了他。

"没关系，这是我最后一次见到她了。"说完，他放下了鼠标，目光离开了屏幕，"好了，谢谢，把机器关了吧。"

"您为什么不继续看呢？"

"值得回忆的就这么多了。"

"……我们可以找到现在的她，就是现在的，很容易！"

"不用了，时间不早了，你走吧，谢谢，真的谢谢。"

白冰走后，首长给保卫处打了个电话，让机关院内道岗的哨兵到办公室来一下。很快，那名武警哨兵进来，敬礼。

"你是……哦，小杨吧？"

"首长记性真好。"

"我叫你上来，也没什么事，就是想告诉你，今天是我的生日。"

哨兵立刻变得手足无措起来，话也不会说了。

首长宽容地笑笑："向战士们问好，去吧。"在哨兵敬礼后转身要走之际，他像突然想起来什么似的说，"哦，把枪留下。"

哨兵愣了一下，还是抽出手枪，走过去小心地放在宽大的办公桌的一端，再次敬礼后走出去。

首长拿起枪，取出弹夹，把子弹一颗颗地退出来，只留下一颗在弹夹里，再把弹夹推上枪。下一个拿到这把枪的人可能是他的秘书，也可能是天黑后进来打扫的勤杂工，那时空枪总是安全些。

他把枪放到桌面上，把退出来的子弹在玻璃板上摆成一小圈，像生日蛋糕上的蜡烛。然后，他踱到窗前，看着城市尽头即将落下的夕阳，它在市郊的工业烟尘后面呈一个深红色的圆盘，他觉得它像镜子。

他做的最后一件事，就是将自己胸前的"为人民服务"的小标牌摘下来，轻轻地放到桌面上小面国旗和党旗的基座上。

然后，他在办公桌旁坐下，静静地等候着最后一抹夕阳照进来。

未来

当天夜里，宋诚来到气象模拟中心的主机房，找到了白冰，他正一个人静静地看着已经启动的超弦计算机的屏幕。

宋诚走过去拍拍他的肩说："小白，我已经向你的单位领导打了招呼，马上有一辆专车送你去北京，你把超弦计算机交给一位中央领导，听你汇报的除了这位领导，可能还有几名这方面的技术专家。由于这项技术非同寻常的性质，让人完全理解和相信可不是一件容易的事，你讲解和演示的时候要耐心……白冰，你怎么了？"

白冰没有转过身来，仍静坐在那里，屏幕上的镜像宇宙中，地球在太空中悬浮着，它的极地冰盖形状有些变化，海洋的颜色也由蓝转灰了些，但这些变化并不明显，宋诚是看不出来的。

"他是对的。"白冰说。

"什么？"

"首长是对的。"白冰说着，缓缓转身面对宋诚，他的双眼布满血丝。

"这是你思考了一天一夜的结果？"

"不，我完成了镜像的未来递归运算。"

"你是说……镜像能模拟未来了？！"

白冰无力地点点头："只能模拟很遥远的未来。我在昨天晚上想出了一种全新的算法，避开较近的未来，这样就避免了因得知未来而改变现实对因果链的破坏，使镜像直接跳到遥远未来。"

"那是什么时间？"

"3.5万年后。"

宋诚小心翼翼地问："那时的社会是什么样子？镜像在起作用吗？"

　　白冰摇摇头："那时没有镜像了，也没有社会了，人类文明消亡了。"

　　震惊使宋诚说不出话来。

　　屏幕上，视点急剧下降，在一座沙漠中的城市上空悬停。

　　"这就是我们的城市，是一座空城，已死去2000多年了。"

　　死城给人的第一印象是一个正方形的世界，所有的建筑都是标准的正立方体，且大小完全一样，这些建筑都横竖整齐地排列着，构成了一个标准的正方形城市。只有方格状的街道上不时扬起的黄色沙尘，才使人不至于将城市误认为是画在教科书上的抽象几何图形。

　　白冰移动视点，进入了一幢正立方体建筑内部的一个房间，里面的一切已经被漫长岁月积累的沙尘埋没了，在窗边，积沙呈一个斜坡升上去，已接上了窗台。沙中有几个鼓包，像是被埋住的家电和家具，从墙角伸出几根枯枝似的东西，那是已经大部分锈蚀的金属衣帽架。白冰将图像的一部分拷贝下来，粘贴到处理软件中，去掉了上面厚厚的积沙，露出了锈蚀得只剩空架子的电视和冰箱，还有一张写字台样的桌子，桌上有一个已放倒的相框，白冰调整视点，使相框中的那张小照片充满了屏幕。

　　这是一张三口之家的合影，但照片上的三人外貌和衣着几乎完全一样，仅能从头发的长短看出男女，从身高看出年龄。他们穿着样式完全一样的类似于中山装的衣服，整齐而呆板，扣子都是一直扣到领口。宋诚仔细看看，发现他们的容貌还是有差别的，之所以产生一样的感觉，是因为他们那完全一致的表情，一种麻木的平静，一种呆滞的庄严。

"我发现的所有照片和残存的影像资料上的人都是这样的表情，没有见过其他表情，更没有哭或笑的。"

宋诚惊恐地说："怎么会这样呢？你能查查留下来的历史资料吗？"

"查过了，我们以后的历史大略是这样的：镜像时代在 5 年后就开始了，在前 20 年，镜像模拟只应用于司法部门，但已经对社会产生了实质性的影响，人类社会的形态发生了重大变化。以后，镜像渗透到社会生活的各个角落，历史上称为镜像纪元。在新纪元的头 5 个世纪，人类社会还是在缓慢发展之中。完全停滞的迹象最初出现在镜像 6 世纪中叶，首先停滞的是文化。由于人性已经像一汪清水般纯洁，没有什么可描写和表现的，文学首先消失了，接着是整个人类艺术都停滞和消失了。接下来，科学和技术也陷入了彻底的停滞。这种停滞的状态持续了 3 万年，这段漫长的岁月，史称'光明的中世纪'。"

"以后呢？"

"以后就很简单了，地球资源耗尽，土地全部沙漠化，人类仍没有进行太空移民的技术能力，也没有能力开发新的资源，在5000 年时间里，一切都慢慢结束了……就是我们现在显示的这个状态，各大陆仍有人在生活，不过也没什么看头了。"

"哦——"宋诚发出了像首长那样的长长的一声叹息，过了很长时间，他才用发颤的声音问道，"那……我们该怎么办？我是说现在，销毁镜像吗？"

白冰抽出两支烟，递给宋诚一支，将自己的点着后深深地吸了一口，将白色的烟雾吐在屏幕上那三个呆滞的人像上："镜像我肯定要销毁，留到现在就是想让你看看这些。不过，现在我们干什么都无所谓了，有一点可以自我安慰：以后发生的一切与我们无关。"

"还有别人生成了镜像？"

"它的理论和技术都具备了，而根据超弦理论，创世参数的组合虽然数量巨大，但是有限的，不停试下去总能碰上那一组……3万多年后，直到文明的最后岁月，人们还在崇拜和感谢一个叫尼尔·克里斯托夫的人。"

"他是谁？"

"按历史记载：虔诚的基督教徒，物理学家，镜像模拟软件的创造者。"

5个月后，普林斯顿大学宇宙学实验中心。

当灿烂的星海在50块屏幕中的一块上出现时，在场的科学家和工程师们都欢呼起来。这里放置着5台超弦计算机，每台中又设置了10台虚拟机，共有50个创世模拟软件在日夜不停地运行，现在诞生的虚拟宇宙是第32961号。

只有一个中年男人不动声色，他浓眉大眼，气宇轩昂，胸前那枚银色的十字架在黑色的套衫上格外醒目，他默默地画了一个"十"字，问：

"万有引力常数？"

"$6.67 \times 10^{-11} N \cdot m^2 /kg^2$！"

"真空光速？"

"每秒29.98万千米！"

"普朗克常数？"

"6.626！"

"电子电量？"

"1.602×10^{-19} 库仑。"

"1 加 1？"他庄重地吻了一下胸前的十字架。

"等于 2，这是我们的宇宙，克里斯托夫博士！"

2018年四月一日

2018
04
01

又是犹豫的一天，这之前我已经犹豫了两三个月，犹豫像一潭死滞的淤泥，我感觉自己的生命正在其中以几十倍于从前的速度消耗着，这里说的从前是我没产生那个想法的时候，是基延还没有商业化的时候。

从写字楼顶层的窗子望出去，城市在下面扩展开来，像一片被剖开的集成电路，我不过是那密密麻麻的纳米线路中一个奔跑的电子，真的算不了什么，所以我做出的决定也算不了什么，所以决定就可以做出了……像以前多少次一样，决定还是做不出，犹豫还在继续。

强子又迟到了，带着一股风闯进办公室，他脸上有瘀青，脑门儿上还贴着一块创可贴，但他显得很自豪，仰着头，像贴着一枚勋章。他的办公桌就在我对面，他坐下后没开电脑，直勾勾地看着我，显然在等我发问，但我没那个兴趣。

"昨晚从电视里看到了吧？"强子兴奋地说。

他显然是指"生命水面"袭击市中心医院的事，那也是国内最大的基延中心。医院雪白的楼面上出现了两道长长的火烧的痕迹，像如玉的美人的脸被脏手摸了一下，触目惊心。"生命水面"是众多反基延组织中规模最大的一个，也是最极端的一个，强子就是其中的一员，但我没在电视中看到他，当时，医院外面的人群像愤怒的潮水。

"刚开过会，你知道公司的警告，再这样你的饭碗就没了。"我说。

基延是通过基因改造延长生命技术的简称，通过去除人类基因中产生衰老时钟的片段，可将人类的正常寿命延长至 300 岁。这项技术在 5 年前开始商业应用，现在却演化为一场波及全世界的社会和政治灾难，原因是它太贵了，在这里，一个人的基延价格相当于一座豪华别墅，只有少数人能消费得起。

"我不在乎。"强子说，"对于一个连 100 岁都活不到的人来说，我在乎什么？"说着，他点上一支烟，办公室里严禁吸烟，他看来是想表示自己真的不在乎。

"忌妒，忌妒是一种有害健康的情绪。"我挥手驱散眼前的烟雾，说，"以前也有很多人因为交不起医疗费而减少寿命的。"

"那不一样，那时，看不起病的人是少数，而现在，99% 的人眼巴巴地看着那 1% 的有钱人活 300 岁！我不怕承认忌妒，是忌妒在维护着社会公平。"他从办公桌上探身凑近我，"你敢拍胸脯说自己不忌妒？加入我们吧。"

强子的目光让我打了个寒战，一时间真怀疑他看透了我。是的，我就要成为一个他忌妒的对象，我就要成为一个基延人了。

其实我没有多少钱，30多岁一事无成，还处于职场的最低层。但我是财务人员，有机会挪用资金。经过长期的策划，一切都已完成，现在我只要点一下鼠标，基延所需的那500万元新人民币就能进入我的秘密账户，然后再转到基延中心的账户上。在这方面我是个很专业的人，我在迷宫般的财务系统中设置了层层掩护，至少要半年时间，这笔资金的缺口才有可能被发现。那时，我将丢掉工作，将被判刑，被没收全部财产，将承受无数鄙夷的目光……

但那时的我已经是一个能活300岁的人了。

可我还在犹豫。

我仔细研究过法律，按贪污罪量刑，500万元最多判20年。20年后，我前面还有200多年的诱人岁月。现在的问题是，这么简单的算术题，难道只有我会做吗？事实上，只要能进入基延一族，现有法律中除死刑之外的所有罪行都值得一犯。那么，有多少人和我一样处于策划和犹豫中？这想法催我尽快行动，同时也使我畏缩。

但最让我犹豫的还是简简，这已经属于理性之外了。在遇到简简之前，我不相信世界上有爱情这回事；在遇到她之后，我不相信世界上除了爱情还有什么。离开她，我活2000年又有什么意思？现在，在人生的天平上，一边是两个半世纪的寿命，另一边是离开简简的痛苦，天平几乎是平的。

部门主管召集开会。从他脸上的表情我就能猜出来，这个会不是安排工作，而是针对个人。果然，主管说他今天想谈谈某些员工的"不能被容忍的"社会行为。我没有转头看强子，但知道他要倒霉了，可主管说出的却是另一个人的名字。

"刘伟，据可靠消息，你加入了 IT 共和国？"

刘伟点点头，像走上断头台的路易十六般高傲："这与工作无关，我不希望公司干涉个人自由。"

主管严肃地摇摇头，冲他竖起一根手指："很少有事情是与工作无关的，不要把你们在大学中热衷的那一套带到职场上来，如果一个国家可以在大街上骂总统，那叫民主，但要是都不服从老板，那这个国家肯定会崩溃的。"

"虚拟国家就要被承认了。"

"被谁承认？联合国？还是某个大国？别做梦了。"

其实主管最后这句话中并没有多少自信。现在，人类社会拥有的领土分为两部分，一部分是地球各大陆和岛屿，另一部分则是互联网广阔的电子空间。后者以快百倍的速度重复着文明史，在那里，经历了几十年无序的石器时代之后，国家顺理成章地出现了。虚拟国家主要有两个起源，一是各种聚集了大量 ID 的 BBS，二是那些玩家已经上亿的大型游戏。虚拟国家有着与实体国家相似的元首和议会，甚至拥有只在网上出现的军队。与实体国家以地域和民族划分不同，虚拟国家主要以信仰、爱好和职业为基础组建，每个虚拟国家的成员都遍布全世界，多个虚拟国家构成了虚拟国际，现已拥有 20 亿人口，并建立了与实体国际对等的虚拟联合国，成为叠加在传统国家之上的巨大的政治实体。

IT 共和国就是虚拟国际中的一个超级大国，人口 8000 万，还在迅速增长中。这是一个主要由 IT 工程师组成的国家，有着咄咄逼人的政治诉求，也有着对实体国际产生作用的强大力量。我不知道刘伟在其中的公民身份是什么。据说 IT 共和国的元首是某个 IT 公司的普通小职员；相反，也有不止一个实体国家的元首被爆是某个虚拟国家的普通公民。

主管对大家进行严重警告，任何人不得拥有第二国籍，并阴沉地让刘伟到总经理办公室去一趟，然后宣布散会。我们还没有从座位上起身，一直待在电脑屏幕前的郑丽丽让人头皮发炸地大叫起来，说出大事儿了，让大家看新闻。

我回到办公桌前，把电脑切换到新闻频道，看到紧急插播的重要新闻。播音员一脸阴霾，他宣布，在联合国否决 IT 共和国要求获得承认的 3617 号决议被安理会通过后，IT 共和国向实体国际宣战，半个小时前已经开始了对世界金融系统的攻击。

我看看刘伟，他对这事好像也感到很意外。

画面切换到某个大都市，高楼间的街道上，长长的车流拥堵着，人们从车中和两旁的建筑物中纷纷涌出，像是发生了大地震一般。镜头又切换到一家大型超市，人群像黑色的潮水般涌入，疯狂地争抢货物，一排排货架摇摇欲坠，像被潮水冲散的沙堤……

"这是干什么？"我惊恐地问。

"还不明白吗？！"郑丽丽继续尖叫道，"要均贫富了！所有的人都要一文不名了！快抢吃的呀！！！"

我当然明白，但不敢相信噩梦已成现实。传统的纸币和硬币已在 3 年前停止流通，现在即使在街边小货亭买盒烟也要刷卡。在这个全信息化时代，财富什么的，说到底不过是计算机存储器中的一串串脉冲和磁印。以这座华丽宏伟的写字楼来说，如果相关部门中所有的电子记录都被删除，公司的总裁即使拿着房产证，也没有谁承认他的所有权。钱是什么？钱不再是王八蛋了，钱只是一串比细菌还小的电磁印记和转瞬即逝的脉冲，对于 IT 共和国来说，实体世界中近一半的 IT 从业者都是其公民，抹掉这些印记是很容易的。

　　程序员、网络工程师、数据库管理员，这几类人构成了 IT 共和国的主体，这个阶层是 19 世纪的产业大军在 21 世纪的再现，只不过劳作的部分由肢体变成大脑，繁重程度却有增无减。在浩如烟海的程序代码和迷宫般的网络软硬件中，他们如 200 多年前的码头搬运工般背起重负，彻夜赶工。信息技术的发展一日千里，除了部分爬到管理层的幸运儿，其他人的知识和技能很快过时，新的 IT 专业毕业生如饥饿的白蚁般成群涌来，老的人（其实不老，大多 30 岁出头）被挤到一边，被代替和抛弃，但新来者没有丝毫得意，因为他们明白，这也是他们中大多数人不算遥远的前景……这个阶层被称作技术无产阶级。

　　"不要说我们一无所有，我们要把世界格式化！"这是被篡改的《国际歌》歌词。

　　我突然像遭雷劈一样，天哪，我的钱，那些现在还不属于我，但即将为我买来两个多世纪生命和生活的钱，要被删除了吗？！但如果一切都格式化了，结果不是都一样吗？我的钱、我的基延、我的梦想……我眼前发黑，像无头苍蝇般在办公室中来回走着。

　　一阵狂笑使我停下脚步，笑声是郑丽丽发出的，她在那里笑得蹲下了。

　　"愚人节快乐。"冷静的刘伟扫了一眼办公室一角的网络交换机说。我顺着他的目光看去，发现交换机与公司网络断开了，郑丽丽的笔记本电脑接在上面，充当了服务器，这个婊子！为了这个愚人节笑话她肯定费了不少劲，主要是做那些新闻画面，但在这个一个人猫在屋里就能用 3D 软件做出一部大片的时代，这也算不了什么。

别人显然并不觉得郑丽丽的玩笑过分了，强子又用那种眼光看着我说："咋啦，这应该是他们发毛才对啊，你怕什么？"他指指高管们所在的上层。

我又出了一身冷汗，怀疑他是不是真看透我了，但我最大的恐惧不在于此。

世界格式化，真的只是 IT 共和国中极端分子的疯话？真的只是一个愚人节玩笑？吊着这把悬剑的那根头发还能支撑多久？

一瞬间，我的犹豫像突然打开的强光灯下的黑暗那样消失了，我决定了。

晚上我约了简简，当我从城市灯海的背景上辨认出她的身影时，我坚硬的心又软了下来，她那小小的剪影看上去那么娇弱，像一束随时都会被一阵微风吹灭的烛苗，我怎么能伤害她？！当她走近，我看到她的眼睛时，心中的天平已经完全倾向另一个方向，没有她，我要那 200 多年有什么用？时间真会抚平创伤？那可能不过是两个多世纪漫长的刑罚而已。爱情使我这个极端自私的人又崇高起来。

但简简先说话了，说出的居然是我原来准备向她说的话，一字不差："我犹豫了好长时间，我们还是分手吧。"

我茫然地问她为什么。

"很长时间后，当我还年轻时，你已经老了。"

我好半天才理解了她的意思，随即也读懂了她那刚才还令我心碎的哀怨目光，我本以为是她已经看透了我或猜到了些什么。我轻轻笑了起来，很快变成仰天大笑。我真是傻，傻得不透气，也不看看这是个什么时代，也不看看我们前面浮现出了怎样的诱惑。笑过之后，我如释重负，浑身轻松得像要飘起来，不过在这同时，我还是真诚地为简简高兴。

"你哪来那么多钱？"我问她。

"只够我一个人的。"她低声说，眼睛不敢看我。

"我知道，没关系，我是说你一个人也要不少钱的。"

"父亲给了我一些，100年时间是够的。我还存了一些钱，到那时利息应该不少了。"

我知道自己又猜错了，她不是要做基延，而是要冬眠。这是另一项已经商业化的生命科学成果，在 -50℃左右的低温状态，通过药物和体外循环系统使人体的新陈代谢速度降至正常状态的百分之一，使人在冬眠中度过 100 年时间，生理年龄仅长 1 岁。

"生活太累了，也无趣，我只是想逃避。"简简说。

"到一个世纪后就不用面对了吗？那时你的学历已经不被承认，也不适应那时的社会，能过得好吗？"

"时代总是越来越好的，实在不行我到时候再接着冬眠，还可以做基延，到那时基延一定很便宜了。"

我和简简默默地分别了。也许，一个世纪后我们还能再相会，但我没向她承诺什么，那时的她还是她，但我已经是一个经历了 130 多年沧桑的人了。

简简的背影消失后，我没再犹豫片刻，拿出手机登录到网银系统，立刻把那 500 万元新人民币转到基延中心的账户上。虽然已近午夜，我还是很快收到了中心主任的电话，他说明天就可以开始我的基因改良操作，顺利的话一周就能完成。他还郑重地重复了中心的保密承诺（身份暴露的基延族中，已经有三人被杀）。

"你会为自己的决定庆幸的。"主任说,"因为你将得到的不只是两个多世纪的寿命,可能是永生。"

我明白这点,谁也不知道两个世纪后会出现什么样的技术,也许,到时可以把人的意识和记忆拷贝出来,做成永远不丢失的备份,随时可以灌注到一个新的身体中;也许根本不需要身体,我们的意识在网络中像神一般游荡,通过数量无限的传感器感受着世界和宇宙,这真的是永生了。

主任接着说:"其实,有了时间就有了一切,只要时间足够,一只乱敲打字机的猴子都能打出莎士比亚全集,而你有的是时间。"

"我?不是我们吗?"

"我没有做基延。"

"为什么?"

对方沉默良久后说:"这世界变化太快了,太多的机会、太多的诱惑、太多的欲望、太多的危险,我觉得头晕目眩,毕竟岁数大了。不过你放心,"他接着说出了简简那句话,"时代总是越来越好的。"

现在,我坐在自己狭小的单身公寓中写着这篇日记,这是我有生以来记的第一篇日记,以后要坚持记下去,因为我总要留下些东西。时间也会让人失去一切,我知道,长寿的并不是我,两个世纪后的我肯定是另一个陌生人了。其实仔细想想,自我的概念本来就很可疑,构成自我的身体、记忆和意识都在不断地变化,与简简分别之前的我,以犯罪的方式付款之前的我,与主任交谈之前的我,甚至在打出这个"甚至"之前的我,都已经不是同一个人了,想到这里,我很释然。

但我总是要留下些东西。

窗外的夜空中，黎明前的星星在发出它们最后的寒光，与城市辉煌的灯海相比，星星如此暗淡，刚能被辨认出来，但它们是永恒的象征。就在这一夜，不知有多少与我一样的新新人类上路了，不管好坏，我们将是第一批真正触摸永恒的人。

太原之恋

CURSE
5.0

诅咒 1.0 诞生于 2009 年 12 月 8 日。

这是金融危机的第二年，人们本来以为危机已快要结束了，没想到只是开始，所以社会处于一种焦躁的情绪中，每个人都需要发泄，并积极创造发泄的方式，诅咒的诞生也许与这种氛围有关。

诅咒的作者是一个女孩，18—28 岁，关于她，后来的 IT 考古学家们能知道的就这么多。诅咒的对象是一个男孩，20 岁，他的情况却都被记载得很清楚，他叫撒碧，在太原工业大学上大四。他和那女孩之间发生的事儿没什么特别的，也就是少男少女之间每天都在发生的那些个事儿，后来有上千个版本，这里面可能有一个版本是真实的，但人们不知道是哪一个。反正他们之间的事情结束后，那女孩对那男孩是恨透了，于是编写了诅咒 1.0。

女孩是个编程高手，真的不知道她是怎样学来的这个本事。

在这个 IT 从业者人数急剧膨胀的年代，真正精通系统底层编程的人却并未增加，因为能用的工具太多了，也太方便了，没必要像苦力似的一行行编代码，大部分都可以用工具直接生成。即使像女孩要做的编写病毒这样的活计也是一样，有众多的功能强大的黑客工具。所谓编写病毒，不过是把几个现成模块组装起来就行，或更简单些，对单个模块修改一下即可。在诅咒之前大规模流行的最后一个病毒"熊猫烧香"就是这么弄出来的。但这个女孩却是从头做起，没有借助任何工具，自己一行一行地写代码，像勤劳的农家女用原始的织布机把棉线一根一根织成布。想象她伏在电脑前咬牙切齿敲键盘的样子，我们不由得想起海涅的《西里西亚织工》中的两句诗：老德意志，我们在织你的尸布，我们织！我们织！！！

诅咒 1.0 是历史上在传播方面最成功的计算机病毒，它成功的主要原因在两个方面。第一个原因，诅咒不对感染者进行任何破坏（其实其他的病毒大部分也没有破坏企图，极少的破坏是由于其低劣的传播或表现技术所导致，诅咒在避免传播中的副作用方面做得很完善）。它的表现也很克制，在大部分被感染的电脑上没有任何表现，只有当系统条件组合符合某一条件时（大约占总感染数的 1/10），才会表现，且每台机器只表现一次。具体的表现方式是在被感染的电脑上弹出一行字：

撒碧去死吧！！！

如果点击这行字，就会出现关于撒碧更进一步的信息，告诉你这个被诅咒者是中国山西省太原市太原工业大学 × × 系 × × 专业 × × 班 × × 宿舍楼 × × 寝室的。如果不点击，这行字将在 3 秒钟内消失，且永不在这台电脑上重新出现。因为被记忆的有硬件信息，所以即使重装系统后也一样。

诅咒 1.0 成功传播的第二个原因在于系统拟态技术，这倒不是女孩的发明，但这项技术被她熟练地运用到了极致。系统拟态就是把病毒代码的很多部分做成与系统代码相同，且采用与系统进程类似的行为方式，杀毒软件在杀灭该病毒时，极有可能把系统也破坏掉，最后不得不使其投鼠忌器。其实，瑞星、Norton 等都曾盯上过诅咒 1.0，但却发现惹上了越来越多的麻烦，甚至发生过比 Norton 在 2007 年误删 Windows XP 系统文件更恶劣的后果。加上诅咒 1.0 在传播中没出现任何破坏行为，且所占系统资源也微不足道，就先后把它从病毒特征库中删掉了。

诅咒诞生之日，正是写科幻的刘慈欣第 264 次因公来太原之时。尽管这是他最讨厌的一座城市，但每次来时还都要逛街，都是到柳巷的一个小店去为他那老掉牙的 Zippo 打火机买一瓶专用汽油，这是目前极少数不能从淘宝或易贝邮购的东西之一。前两天刚下过雪，像每次下雪一样，这时的雪地被轧成了黑乎乎的冰，他摔了一跤，屁股的疼让他忘了在进火车站时把那一小瓶汽油从旅行包中拿出来装到衣袋中，结果过安检时被查了出来，被没收后又罚款 200 元。

他更讨厌这座城市了。

诅咒 1.0 流传下去，5 年，10 年，它仍然在日益扩展的网络世界静悄悄地繁衍生息。

这期间，金融危机过去了，繁荣再次到来。随着石油资源的渐渐枯竭，煤炭在世界能源中的比重迅速增加，地下的黑金为山西带来了滚滚财源，使其成为亚洲的阿拉伯，省会太原自然也就成了新的迪拜。这是一个具有煤老板性格的城市，过去穷怕了，即使在 21 世纪初仍处于贫寒的日子里，也是下面穿露屁股的破裤子，上身着名牌西装，在下岗工人成天堵大街的情况下建起国内最豪华的歌厅和洗浴中心。现在成了真正的暴发户，更是在歇斯底里的狂笑中穷奢极欲，迎泽大街两旁的超高建筑群令上海浦东相形见绌，而这条除长安街外全国最宽直的大街则成了终日难见阳光的深谷。有钱和没钱的人怀着梦想和欲望涌入这座城市，立刻忘记了自己是谁和想要什么，只是跌入繁华喧闹的旋涡旋转着，一年转 365 圈。

这天，第 397 次来太原的刘慈欣又到柳巷去买汽油，忽见街上有一位飘逸帅哥，他的长发中那一缕雪白格外引人注目，他就是先写科幻后写奇幻再后来科奇都写的潘大角。被太原的繁荣所吸引，大角抛弃上海移居太原。大刘和大角当初分别处于科幻的硬、软两头儿，此时相见不亦乐乎。在一家头脑店（头脑是本地的一种传统美食）酒酣耳热之时，刘慈欣眉飞色舞地说出了自己下一步的宏伟创作计划：计划写一部 10 卷 300 万字的科幻史诗，描写 200 个文明的 2000 次毁灭和多次因真空衰变而发生的宇宙格式化，最后以整个已知宇宙漏入一个抽水马桶般的超级黑洞结束。大角很受感染，认为两人有合作的可能：同一个史诗构思，刘慈欣写硬得不能再硬的科幻版，面向男读者；大角写软得不能再软的奇幻版，面向女孩们。大刘、大角一拍即合，立刻抛弃一切俗务投身创作。

在诅咒 1.0 10 岁生日时，它的末日也快到了。Vista 以后，微软实在难以找到对操作系统频繁升级的理由，这多少延长了诅咒 1.0 的寿命。但操作系统就像暴发户的老婆，升级总是不可避免的，诅咒 1.0 代码的兼容性越来越差，很快就将沉入网络海洋的底部，成为死亡的沙子，销声匿迹。但正在这时，诞生了一门新的学科：IT考古学。按说网络世界的历史还不到半个世纪，没什么古可考，可仍然有很多怀旧的人热衷此道。IT考古主要是发掘那些仍活在网络世界某些犄角旮旯儿的东西，比如10年来都没有点击过但仍能点开的网页，20年没有人光顾但仍能注册发帖的BBS等。这些虚拟古董中，来自"远古"的病毒是IT考古学家们最热衷寻找的，如果能找到一个10多年前诞生的仍在网上活着的病毒，就有在天池中发现恐龙一般的感觉。

诅咒1.0被发现了，发现者把病毒的全部代码升级到新的操作系统下，这样就能保证它再存活10年。这人并没有张扬，也许这是为了他（她）所珍爱的这件古董更顺利地存活下去。这就是诅咒2.0。人们把10年前诅咒1.0的创造者叫诅咒始祖，把这个IT考古学家叫诅咒升级者。

诅咒2.0在网上出现的那一刻，在太原火车站附近的一个垃圾桶旁，大刘和大角正在争抢刚从桶中翻找到的半袋方便面。他们卧薪尝胆五六年，各自写出两部300万字的10卷本科幻和奇幻史诗，书名分别为《三千体》和《九万洲》。两人对这两部巨作充满信心，但找不到出版者，于是一起变卖了包括房子在内的全部家产并预支了所有退休金自费出版，最后，《三千体》和《九万洲》的销量分别是15本和27本，总数42本，科幻迷都知道这是个吉利的数字。在太原举行了同样是自费的隆重签售仪式后，两人就开始了流浪生涯。

太原是一个最适合流浪的城市，在这个穷奢极欲的大都市里，垃圾桶里的食品是取之不尽的，最次也能找到几粒被丢弃的工作丸（见后文）。住的地方也问题不大，太原模仿迪拜，在每一个公交候车亭里都装上了冷暖空调。如果暂时厌倦街头，还可以去救助站待几天，那里不仅有吃有住，而且太原久已繁荣的性服务业还响应政府的号召，把每周日定为对弱势群体的性援助日，救助站就是那些来自红灯区的志愿者们开展活动的地方之一。在城市各阶层幸福指数调查中，盲流、乞丐位列榜首，所以大刘和大角都后悔没有早些投入这种生活。

两人最惬意的时候是《科幻大王》编辑部每周一次的请客，一般都是去唐都这样的高级地方。太原的《科幻大王》杂志深得科幻的精髓，知道这种文学体裁的灵魂就是神奇感和疏离感，而现在高技术幻想已经没有这种感觉了，技术奇迹是最平淡不过的事儿，每天都在发生。倒是低技术具有神奇感和疏离感，于是他们创立了幻想未来低技术时代的反浪潮科幻，取得了巨大成功，迎来了世界科幻的第二个黄金时代。为了彰显反浪潮科幻的理念，《科幻大王》编辑部拒绝一切电脑和网络，只接收手写稿件，用铅字排版印刷，还用每匹相当于一辆宝马车的价格买回几十匹蒙古马，并在编辑部旁建设豪华的马厩，杂志社人员出行一律骑着绝对没有上网的骏马，城市某处如果听到嘚嘚的清脆马蹄声，那就是 SFK 编辑部的人来了。他们常请刘慈欣和大角吃饭，除了他们以前写过科幻外，还因为虽然他们现在写的科幻已经很不科幻了，但他们自己按照反浪潮科幻的理念却是十分科幻的，因为他们上不起网，技术也很低。

SFK、大刘和大角都不知道，他们的这个共同特点将会救他们的命。

诅咒 2.0 又流传了 7 年，这时，一个后来被称为"诅咒武装者"的女人发现了它。她仔细研究了诅咒 2.0 的代码，即使经过升级，她仍能感受到 17 年前诅咒始祖的仇恨和怨念。她与始祖有着相同的经历，也处于每天像牙痛般咒恨某个男人的阶段，但她觉得那个 17 年前的女孩既可怜又可笑：这么做有何意义？真能动那个臭男人一根汗毛吗？这就像百年前的怨女们在写了名字的小布人儿上扎针的愚蠢游戏一样，解决不了任何问题，结果只能使自己更郁闷。还是让姐姐来帮帮你吧（正常情况下诅咒始祖应该活着，但诅咒武装者肯定要叫她阿姨了）。

17 年后的今天已经完全是一个新时代了，这时，世界上的一切都落网了。这么说是因为在 17 年前网络上的东西只能在电脑上看到，但今天的网络就像一棵超级圣诞树，这世界上的几乎所有东西都挂在上面闪闪发光。以家庭为例，家里所有通电的东西都联上了网并受其控制，甚至连指甲刀和开瓶器也不例外，前者可通过剪下来的指甲判断你是否缺钙并通过短信或 E-mail 告知你；后者可判断酒是否真品并发出中奖通知，而对于过度酗酒者，则间隔很长时间才能开一次瓶……在这种情况下，通过诅咒病毒直接操纵硬件世界成为可能。

诅咒武装者给诅咒 2.0 增加了一个功能：如果撒碧坐出租车，就撞死他！

其实对于这个时代的一个 AI 编程高手来说，这点并不难做到。现在的汽车已经全部无人驾驶，网络就是驾驶员，乘客上出租车时要刷卡，这时新的诅咒就可通过信用卡识别他的身份。只要上了车并被识别，杀他的方法数不胜数，最简单的就是径直撞向路边的建筑物，或从桥上开下去。但诅咒武装者想了想，并不愿简单地撞死撒碧，而是为他选择了一个更为浪漫的死法，完全配得上他对 17 年前的那个妹妹做的事（其实诅咒武装者和别人一样，根本不知道撒碧对始祖做错了什么，也可能错根本不在这男孩）。经她升级的诅咒在得知目标上车后，就不理会他设定的目的地，疯狂猛开，从太原一直开到张家口，那里再向前就是一片沙漠了，车就停在沙漠深处，并切断与外界的一切通信联系（这时诅咒已经驻留车内电脑，不需网络了）。这辆出租车被发现的可能性很小，即使偶尔有人或车靠近，它也会立刻躲到沙漠的另一处。无论过去多长时间，车门从内部是绝对打不开的。这样，如果在冬天，撒碧将被冻死；如果在夏天，撒碧将被热死；如果在春天、秋天，撒碧将被渴死、饿死。

就这样，诅咒 3.0 诞生了，这是真正的诅咒。

诅咒武装者是此方面的艺术家，这也是一族新新人类，他们通过操纵网络做出一些没有实际意义但具有美感（当然这个时代的美感与十几年前的不是一回事了）的行为艺术，比如让全城的汽车同时鸣笛并奏出某种旋律，让大酒店的亮灯窗口组成某个图形等。诅咒 3.0 就是一件这样的作品，不管它是否真能实现其功能，它本身就构成了一件卓越的艺术品，因而在 2026 年上海现代艺术双年展上得到好评。虽然因其人身伤害内容被警方宣布为非法的，但其仍在网上进一步流传开来，众多的 AI 艺术家加入了对这一作品的集体创作，诅咒 3.0 飞快进化，越来越多的功能被添加进来：

如果撒碧在家，煤气熏死他！这也比较容易，因为每家的厨房都由网络控制，这样户主们就可以在外面遥控厨房做饭，这当然包括打开煤气的功能，而诅咒 3.0 当然可以使房间里的有害气体报警器失效。

如果撒碧在家，放火烧死他！很容易，包括煤气在内，家里有很多可以点火的东西，如摩丝、发胶什么的，都联在网上（可通过网络由专业发型师做头发），火焰报警器和灭火器当然也可以失效。

如果撒碧洗澡，放开水烫死他！如上，很容易。

如果撒碧去医院看病，开药毒死他！这个稍有些复杂，给目标开特定的药是很容易的，因为现在医院的药房全部是自动取药，且药库系统都联网。关键是药品的包装问题，撒碧不是SB，要让他拿到药后愿意吃才行。要做到这点，诅咒3.0需要追溯到制药厂的生产包装和销售环节，要有一盒表里不一的药只卖给目标。真的有些复杂，但能做到，而且对于AI艺术来说，越复杂，作品的观赏价值就越高。

如果撒碧坐飞机，摔死他！这不容易，比出租车操作难多了，因为被诅咒的只有撒碧一人，诅咒3.0不能杀死其他人，而撒碧大概没有专机，所以摔死他是不可能的。但可以这样：目标所乘的飞机舱内突然在高空失压（用开舱门或别的什么办法），这时，在所有乘客都戴上的氧气面罩中，只有撒碧的面罩中没有氧气。

如果撒碧吃饭，噎死他！这个看似荒唐，其实十分简单。现代社会的超快节奏催生了超快餐食品，就是一粒小小的药丸，名叫工作丸。工作丸密度很大，拿在手中沉甸甸的，像一颗子弹头，服下后会在胃中膨化，类似于以前的压缩饼干。关键是在生产的过程中，工作丸的膨化速度是可以控制的，诅咒3.0可以用与开药类似的方式在生产过程中做手脚，生产出一粒超快速膨化的工作丸，再控制销售过程专卖给撒碧，他在进工作餐时，喝水把工作丸送下去，结果小丸在嗓子眼就膨化了。

…………

但诅咒 3.0 从来没有找到目标，也没有杀死过任何人。早在诅咒 1.0 诞生时，撒碧受到了不小的骚扰，还有媒体记者因此采访过他，使他不得不改了名，甚至连姓也改了。姓撒的人本来就很少，加上这个名字不雅的谐音，在这个城市里面没有重名。同时，病毒中记录的撒碧的工作单位和住址仍是他十几年前所上的大学，使得定位他更不可能。诅咒曾经拥有进入公安厅电脑追溯目标改名记录的功能，但没有成功。所以在以后的 4 年中，诅咒 3.0 仍然只是一件 AI 艺术品。

但诅咒通配者出现了，他们是大刘和大角。

通配符是一个古老的概念，源自导师时代（这是对操作系统的上古时代——DOS 操作系统时代的称呼），最常见的通配符有"*"和"？"两种，用于泛指字符串中的一切字符，其中"？"指代单一字串，"*"指代的字符数量不限，也最常用。比如：刘*，指姓刘的所有人；山西*，指以山西打头的所有字串，而如果只有一个 *，则指代一切。所以在导师时代，del*.* 是一个邪恶的命令（del 是删除命令，而 DOS 系统下的文件全名分为文件名和扩展名两部分，用 . 隔开）。在以后的操作系统演进中，通配符功能一直存在，只是系统进入图形界面后人们很少使用命令行操作，一般人就渐渐把它淡忘了，但在包括诅咒 3.0 在内的各种软件中，它是可用的。

这天是中秋节，但明月在太原城的璀璨灯火中像个脏兮兮的烧饼。大刘、大角在五一广场的一张长椅子上坐下来，摆开他们下午从垃圾桶中翻出的五半瓶酒、两半袋平遥牛肉、几乎一整袋晋祠驴肉和三粒工作丸，准备庆祝一番。天刚黑的时候，大刘还从一个垃圾桶中翻出一台破笔记本电脑，他声称自己能把它修好，否则这辈子计算机工作就算是白干了。他蹲在长椅旁紧张地鼓捣起来，同时和大角意犹未尽地回味着下午救助站的援助。大刘热情地请大角把三粒工作丸都吃了，这样可为自己省下不少酒肉，但大角并不上当，一粒也没吃，只是喝酒吃肉。

电脑很快能用了，屏幕发出幽幽的蓝光，大角发现无线上网功能竟然也恢复了，就立刻抢过电脑，先上 QQ，他的号已经不能用了；再上九州网站、天空之城、豆瓣、水木清华、大江东去……那些链接都早已消失。最后他扔下电脑长叹一声："唉！昔人已乘黄鹤去。"

大刘拿过半瓶酒喝起来，看了看屏幕："此地连黄鹤楼也没留下。"

然后大刘便细细查看电脑中的东西，发现里面安装了大量的黑客工具和病毒样本，这可能是一个黑客的笔记本电脑，也许是在逃避 AI 警察的追捕时匆忙扔到垃圾桶中的。他顺手打开了一个桌面上的文件，是一个已经被编译出来的 C 程序，他认出了，这正是诅咒 3.0。他随意翻阅着代码，回忆着自己编写电子诗人的时光，酒劲上来时翻到了目标识别参数那部分。

大角在一边喋喋不休地回忆着当年峥嵘的科幻岁月，大刘很快也受了感染，推开本本一同回忆起来。想当年，自己那上帝视角的充满阳刚之气的毁灭史诗曾引起多少男人的共鸣啊，曾让他们中的多少人心中充满了万丈激情！可现在，15 本，仅仅卖出 15 本！他又灌下去一大口，那还是一瓶老白汾，这酒的味道在这个年代已经面目全非，有点儿像威士忌了，但酒精度一点没减。他开始恨男读者，进而恨所有的男人，他两眼直勾勾地看着屏幕上诅咒 3.0 的目标参数，说："很转的圆润木妖怪……胡东奇（现在的男人没一个好东西）。"顺手把姓名由"撒碧"换成"*"，工作单位和住址也由"太原工业大学，××系，××专业，××宿舍楼，××寝室"换成了"*，*，*，*，*"，只有性别参数仍为"男"。

大角也处于一把鼻涕一把泪的感慨中。想当初，自己那色彩斑斓、意境悠远的美文如诗如梦，曾经迷倒多少 MM，连自己也成为她们的偶像。可现在，看看旁边经过的那些妙龄 MM，居然没一个人朝自己这边看一眼，这太让人失落了！他扔出一个已空的酒瓶，喃喃说道："圆润木素胡东奇，雨润豆素（男人不是好东西，女人就是）？"说着，把目标参数中的性别由"男"改成"女"。

大刘不干了，觉得这没女人什么事，自己那些粗陋的小说从来也不指望获得女读者的青睐，就又把性别参数改回"男"，大角再改成"女"。两人为惩罚自己的忘恩负义的读者群争执起来，太原也在他俩的幻想中成为寡妇城市和光棍城市的可能性之间摇摆不定。大刘、大角最后抢起酒瓶打了起来，直到一个巡警制止了他们。两人摸着脑袋上的鼓包，达成了一个协议，把目标的性别参数改成了"*"，完成了诅咒 3.0 的通配。也许是因为打架的干扰，或由于已经烂醉，他们谁也没动"太原市、山西省、中国"这三个参数。这样，诅咒 4.0 诞生了。

太原被诅咒了。

新版诅咒诞生之际，立刻意识到了自己肩负的宏伟使命，由于这个操作太宏大了，诅咒 4.0 没有立刻行动，而是留下足够的时间让自己充分繁殖，以达到操作所需的足够数量，同时互相联系，慢慢生成一个统一行动的总体规划，计划的总原则是，对诅咒目标的清除首先从软操作开始，然后过渡到硬操作并逐步升级。

10小时后晨曦初露时，操作开始。

软操作主要针对敏感的、神经脆弱的和冲动型的目标，特别是那些患有抑郁症和狂躁症的男人女人。在这个心理病和心理咨询泛滥的时代，诅咒4.0很容易找到这类人。在第一批操作中，有3万名刚从医院完成检查的人被告知患有肝癌、胃癌、肺癌、脑癌、肠癌、淋巴癌、白血病，最多的是食道癌（本地区高发癌症），另有2万名刚化验过血的人被告知HIV呈阳性。这些结果并非来自简单的伪造诊断结果，而是由诅咒4.0直接操纵B超、CT、核磁共振仪、血液化验仪等医疗检查设备得出的"真实"结果，即使去不同医院复查，结果也一样。这5万人中，大部分都选择了治疗，但有400多人本来就活腻歪了，得知诊断结果后立刻一了百了，之后还有陆续做此选择的。随后，5万名敏感的、抑郁的或狂躁的男女都接到了配偶或情人的电话，男人们听到他们的女人说："你看你那个熊样，屁本事没有，你还像个男人吗？我已经和某某好了，我们很和谐、很幸福，你去死吧！"男人们对他们的女人说："你已人老珠黄，其实你当初就是恐龙，我瞎了眼，怎么看上你的？现在我和小三在一起，我们很和谐、很幸福，你去死吧！"这个诅咒4.0编造的情敌大都是目标本来就最讨厌的人。这5万人中，大部分都通过直接找对方质问而消除了误会，但也有约百分之一的人选择了他杀或自杀，其中的一部分两者同时做了。还有另外一些软操作，比如在已经势不两立、剑拔弩张的几大黑帮之间挑起大规模械斗，或把被判无期或有期徒刑的罪犯的判决书改成死刑并立即执行等。但总的来说，软操作效率很低，总共清除的目标也就是几千人。不过诅咒 4.0 有着正确的心态，知道大事情是从一点一滴做起的，不以恶小而不为，所有的手段一定都要试到。

在软操作中，诅咒 4.0 清除了自己最初的创造者。在创造诅咒以后的岁月中，诅咒始祖一直对男人倍加提防，20 年来一直用最现代化的手段监视老公，几乎成为谍报专家。但突然接到一直安分守己的老公的一个电话，致使心脏病突发，她被送医院后又被输入进一步加剧心肌梗死的药物，死于自己的诅咒下。

5 天后，硬操作开始了。之前的软操作在城市中激发的超常的自杀或他杀率已经引起了高度恐慌，但诅咒 4.0 仍需避免政府的分析走上正确的轨道，所以硬操作的第一阶段仍进行得很隐蔽。首先，吃错药的病人数量急剧增加，这些药的包装都正常，但吃下去后大部分一剂致命。同时，吃饭噎死的人也大量出现，都是工作丸在嗓子眼儿膨化所致；还有少部分是撑死的，因为工作丸的压缩密度大大超标，那些食客掂着沉甸甸的小丸，还以为物超所值呢。

第一次大规模清除操作是对自来水系统的操作。即使对于一切受控于网络人工智能的城市，把氰化物或芥子气加入自来水也是不可能的，诅咒 4.0 选择了两种无害的转基因细菌，它们混合后则产生毒性。这两种细菌并不是同时加入自来水系统中，而是先加一种，待其基本排净后再加第二种，两种物质的混合其实是在人体内进行的，后一种细菌与前一种在胃和血液中的残留部分发生作用生成毒性。如果这时仍不致命，那目标去医院取到的药物再与体内已有的两种细菌发生反应，做完最后的事。

这时，省公安厅和国家 AI 安全部已经定位了灾难的来源，针对诅咒 4.0 的专杀工具正在紧急开发中。于是，诅咒操作急剧加速和升级，由隐藏的暗流变为惊天动地的噩梦。

这天早晨的交通高峰时段，从城市的地下传来一连串沉闷的爆炸声，这是地铁相撞的声音。太原市的地铁建成较晚，设计时正值城市成为暴发户的时候，所以十分先进，磁悬浮在真空隧道中运行，以高速闻名，被称为准时空门，意思是从起点进去后很快就能从终点走出。因此它们的相撞也格外惨烈，地面因爆炸隆起一座座冒出浓烟的小山包，像城市突然长出的恶疮。

这时，城市中的大部分汽车已被诅咒控制（这个时代，所有的汽车都能在网络 AI 的控制下自动行驶），成为进行诅咒操作的最有力的工具。一时间，全城的上百万辆汽车像做布朗运动的分子那样横冲直撞，但这种撞击并非杂乱无章，而是遵循着经过严密优化计算的规律和顺序，每辆车首先尽可能多地清除车外行走的目标，所以在混乱的开始，发生撞击的车辆并不多，每辆车都在追逐并冲撞行人，车与车之间密切配合，对行人围追堵截，并在空地和广场上形成包围圈。最大的包围圈在五一广场，几千辆汽车围成一圈向中心撞击，一下子就清除了上万个目标。当外面的行人几乎都被清除或躲入建筑物时，汽车开始撞向附近的建筑物，以清除车内的目标。这种撞击同样是经过精密组织的，对于人口密集的大型建筑物，车辆会集中撞击，后面冲来的车会蹿到前面已撞毁的车上面，就这样一层层堆起来。在市里最高建筑300 层的煤交会大厦下面，撞来的车辆堆到 10 多层楼高，疯狂燃烧着，像是围在大厦周围的一圈火化的柴堆。在大撞击的前夜，市里出现出租车集体排长队加油的奇观，在撞击时它们的油箱都是满的。与此同时，从城市两个机场强行起飞的上百架民航飞机也纷纷在市区着陆，像一堆巨型燃烧弹，加剧了火势。

政府发出紧急通告，宣布城市处于危急状态，呼吁人们待在家中。这个决定最初看来是正确的，因为与大型建筑相比，居民大楼遭到的袭击并不严重，居民区的道路显然不像城市主要街道那么宽敞，大撞击开始后不久就堵塞了。但很快，诅咒 4.0 把每一户人家都变成死亡的陷阱，煤气和液化气全部开放，达到爆燃浓度后即点火引爆，一座座居民楼在爆炸中被火焰吞没，有的整座建筑都被炸飞了。

政府的下一步措施是全城断电，但这时城市中已经没电了，诅咒 4.0 失去了作用，但它们已经成功了。

整座城市陷入一片火海，火势迅速增大，其猛烈程度相当于"二战"时期德累斯顿大轰炸的效应：城内的氧气被火焰耗尽，人即使逃离火区也难逃一死。

由于很少接触上网的东西，同其他盲流哥们儿一样，大刘和大角逃过了诅咒最初的操作。在后期操作开始后，他们凭着在城市中长期步行练就的技巧，以与其高龄不相称的灵活躲过了多次汽车的冲撞，又凭着对市区道路的熟悉，在大火的初期幸存下来。但情况很快变得险恶了，整座城市变成火海时，他们正在还算宽阔的大营盘十字路口中心，窒息的热浪开始笼罩一切，周围高层建筑中的火焰像巨型蜥蜴的长舌般舔过来。描写过无数次宇宙毁灭的大刘此时惊慌失措，而作品充满人文主义温情的大角却镇定自若。

大角抚须环视着周围的火海，用悠长的语调说："早知毁灭如此壮观，当初何不写之？"

大刘两腿一软坐到地上："早知毁灭这么恐怖，当初写它真是吃饱撑的！唉，俺这个乌鸦嘴，这下可好……"

最后他们达成了一致：只有牵涉自个儿的毁灭才是最刺激的毁灭。

这时，他们听到一个银铃般的声音，像这火海中的一块冰晶："刘和角，快走！！！"循声望去，只见两匹快马如精灵般穿出火海，马上是 SFK 编辑部最漂亮的两个长发 MM，她们把大刘、大角拉上马背，骏马在火海的间隙中闪电般穿行，飞越过一排排燃烧的汽车残骸。不一会儿，眼前豁然开阔，马已奔上了汾河大桥。大刘和大角深吸清凉的空气，抱着 MM 的纤腰，脸被她们的长发轻拂着，觉得这逃生之路还是太短了。

过了桥就基本进入安全地带，他们很快和 SFK 编辑部的其他人会合。他们都骑着高头大马，这威武的马队向晋祠方向开去，吸引着路边步行逃生者们惊羡的目光。大刘、大角和 SFK 编辑部的人都看到，幸存者的队伍中还有一个骑自行车的人。之所以注意到他，是因为这年代自行车也都由网络控制，诅咒早就把所有的自行车完全锁死了。骑车的是一个上了年纪的男人，他是撒碧。

由于早年被诅咒病毒骚扰，撒碧对网络产生了本能的恐惧和厌恶，在生活中尽可能减少与网络的接触，比如他骑的自行车就是一件 20 年前的老古董。他住的地方在汾河岸边，靠近城市边缘，在大撞击开始时，他就骑着这辆绝对没有上网的自行车逃了出来。其实，撒碧是这个时代少有的知足的人，对自己艳遇不断的一生很满足，这时就是死了也无怨无悔。

马队和撒碧最后上了山，大家站在山顶呆呆地看着下面燃烧的城市，这里狂风呼啸，这风掠过周围的群山，从四面八方刮向太原盆地，补充那里因热力而上升的空气。

距他们不远，省政府和市政府的主要成员正从载着他们逃离火海的直升机上走下来。市长的口袋里还装着一份发言稿，那是即将到来的城庆日的发言稿。确定太原城的诞生日期颇费了番周折，专家们称：公元前497年古晋阳城问世，历经春秋、战国至唐、五代等10多个朝代，太原一直是中国北方的一个军事重镇。从公元979年赵宋毁太原起，新兴的太原又先后在宋、金、元、明、清等数朝中崛起，不仅是军事重镇，而且发展成为著名的文化古城和商业都会。于是提出了城庆口号：热烈庆祝太原建市2500年！现在，历经了25个世纪的城市正在火海中化为灰烬。

这时，同行的军用电台终于取得了与中央的联系，得知救援大军正在从全国四面八方赶来，但通信很快又中断了，只听到一片干扰声。1小时后接到报告，各救援队伍停止前进，空中的救援机群也转向或返回。

省AI安全局的一名负责人打开笔记本电脑，上面显示着最新编译的诅咒5.0的代码。在目标参数中，"太原市""山西省""中国"也换成了"*""*""*"。

坍缩 CONTRACTION

坦缩将在凌晨 1 时 24 分 17 秒发生。

对坦缩的观测将在国家天文台最大的观测厅进行，这个观测厅接收在同步轨道上运行的太空望远镜发回的图像，并把它投射到一个面积有一个篮球场大小的巨型屏幕上。现在，屏幕上还是空白。到场的人并不多，但都是理论物理学、天体物理学和宇宙学的权威，对即将到来的这一时刻，他们是这个世界上少数真正能理解其含义的人。此时他们静静地坐着，等着那一时刻，就像刚刚用泥土做成的亚当、夏娃等着上帝那一口生命之气一样。只有天文台的台长在焦躁地来回踱着步。巨型屏幕出了故障，而负责维修的工程师到现在还没来，如果她来不了的话，来自太空望远镜的图像只能在小屏幕上显示，那这一伟大时刻的气氛就差多了。丁仪教授走进了大厅。

科学家们都提前变活了，他们一齐站了起来。除了半径 200

光年的宇宙，能让他们感到敬畏的就是这个人了。

　　丁仪同往常一样目空一切，没有同任何人打招呼，也没有坐到那把为他准备的大而舒适的椅子上去，而是信步走到大厅的一角，欣赏起那里放在玻璃柜中的一个大陶土盘。这个陶土盘是天文台的镇台之宝，是价值连城的西周时代的文物，上面刻着几千年前已化为尘土的眼睛所看到的夏夜星图。这个陶土盘经历了沧海桑田的漫长岁月已到了崩散的边缘，上面的星图模糊不清，但大厅外面的星空却丝毫没变。

　　丁仪掏出一个大烟斗，向一个上衣口袋里挖了一下，就挖出了满满一斗烟丝，然后旁若无人地点上烟斗抽了起来。大家都很惊诧，因为他有严重的气管炎，以前是不抽烟的，别人也不敢在他面前抽烟。再说，观测大厅里严禁吸烟，而那个大烟斗产生的烟比10支香烟都多。

　　但，丁教授是有资格做任何事情的。他创立了统一场论，实现了爱因斯坦的梦。他的理论对宇宙大尺度空间所做的一系列预言都得到了实际观测的精确证实。后来，使用统一场论的数学模型，上百台巨型计算机不间断地运行了3年，得出了令人难以置信的结论：已膨胀了200亿年的宇宙将在两年后转为坍缩。

　　现在，这两年时间只剩不到1个小时了。白色的烟雾在丁仪的头上聚集盘旋，形成梦幻般的图案，仿佛是他那不可思议的思想从大脑中飘出……台长小心翼翼地走到丁仪身边，说："丁老，今天省长要来，请到他不容易，请您一定对省长施加一些压力，让他给我们多少拨一些钱。本来不该用这些事使您分心的，但台里的经费状况已到了山穷水尽的地步，国家今年不可能再给钱，只能向省里要了。我们是国内主要的宇宙学观测基地，可您看我们到了什么地步，连射电望远镜的电费都拿不出。现在，我们已经开始打它的主意了。"台长指了指丁仪正欣赏的古老的星图盘，"要不是有文物法，我们早就卖掉它了！"

这时，省长同两名随行人员一起走进了大厅，他们的脸上露出忙碌的疲惫，把一缕尘世的气息带进这超脱的地方。"对不起，哦，丁老您好，大家好，对不起来晚了。今天是连续暴雨后的第一个晴天，洪水形势很紧张，长江已接近1998年的最高水位了。"

台长激动地说了许多欢迎的话，然后把省长领到丁仪面前："下面请丁老为您介绍一下宇宙坍缩的概念……"他同时向丁仪使了个眼色。

"这样好不好，我先说说自己对这个概念的理解，然后请丁老和各位科学家指正。首先，哈勃发现了宇宙的红移现象，是哪一年我记不清了。我们所能观测到的所有星系的光谱都向红端移动，根据多普勒效应，这显示所有的星系都在离我们远去。由以上现象我们可以得出结论：宇宙在膨胀之中。由此又得出结论：宇宙是在200亿年前的一次大爆炸中诞生的。如果宇宙的总质量小于某一数值，宇宙将永远膨胀下去；如果总质量大于某一数值，则万有引力逐渐使膨胀减速，最后使其停止，之后，宇宙将在引力作用下走向坍缩。以前宇宙中所能观测到的物质总量使人们倾向于第一个结论，但后来发现中微子具有质量，并且在宇宙中发现了大量的以前没有观测到的暗物质，这使宇宙的总质量大大增加，使人们又转向了后一个结论，认为宇宙的膨胀将逐渐减慢，最后转为坍缩，宇宙中的所有星系将向一个引力中心聚集。这时，同样由于多普勒效应，在我们眼中所有星系的光谱将向蓝端移动，即蓝移。现在，丁老的统一场论计算出了宇宙由膨胀转为坍缩的精确时间。"

"精彩！"台长恭维地拍了几下手，"像您这样对基础科学有如此了解的领导是不多的，我想，丁老也是这么认为的。"他又向丁仪使了个眼色。

"他说得基本正确。"丁仪慢慢地把烟灰磕到干净的地毯上。

"对，对，如果丁老都这么认为……"台长高兴得眉飞色舞。

"正确到足以显示他的肤浅。"丁仪又从上衣口袋里挖出一斗烟丝。

台长的表情凝固了，科学家们那边传来了低低的几声笑。

省长很宽容地笑了笑："我也是学的物理专业，但之后这30年，我都差不多忘光了，同在场的各位相比，我的物理学和宇宙学知识怕是连肤浅都达不到。唉，我现在只记得牛顿三大定律了。"

"但离理解它还差得很远。"丁仪点上了新装的烟丝。

台长哭笑不得地摇摇头。

"丁老，我们生活在两个完全不同的世界里。"省长感慨地说，"我的世界是一个现实的、无诗意的、烦琐的世界，我们整天像蚂蚁一样忙碌，目光也像蚂蚁一样受到局限。有时深夜从办公室里出来，抬头看看星空，已是难得的奢侈了。您的世界充满着空灵与玄妙，您的思想跨越上百光年的空间和上百亿年的时间，地球对于您只是宇宙中的一粒灰尘，现世对于您只是永恒中短得无法测量的一瞬，整个宇宙似乎都是为了满足您的好奇心而存在的。说句真心话，丁老，我真有些嫉妒您。我年轻时做过那样的梦，但进入您的世界太难了。"

"但今天晚上并不难，您至少可以在丁老的世界中待一会儿，一起目睹这个世界最伟大的一瞬间。"台长说。

"我没有这么幸运。各位，很对不起，长江大堤已出现多处险情，我得马上赶到防总去。在走之前，我还有个问题想请教丁老，这些问题在您看来可能幼稚可笑，但我苦想了很长时间也没有弄明白。第一个问题，坍缩的标志是宇宙由红移转为蓝移，我们将看到所有星系的光谱同时向蓝端移动。但目前能观测到的最远的星系距我们200亿光年，按您的计算，宇宙将在同一时刻坍缩，那样的话，我们要过200亿年才能看到这些星系的蓝移出现。即使最近的半人马座，也要在4年之后才能看到它的蓝移。"

丁仪缓缓地吐出一口烟雾，那烟雾在空中飘浮，像微缩的旋涡星系。"很好，能看到这一点，使您有点像一个物理系的学生了，尽管仍是一个肤浅的学生。是的，我们将同时看到宇宙中所有星系光谱的蓝移，而不是在从4年到200亿年的时间上依次看到。这源于宇宙大尺度范围内的量子效应，它的数学模型复杂，是物理学和宇宙学中最难表述的概念，没希望您能理解。但由此您已得到第一个启示，它提醒您，宇宙坍缩产生的效应远比人们想象的复杂。您有问题吗？哦，您没有必要马上走，您要去处理的事情并不像您想象的那样紧迫。"

"同您的整个宇宙相比，长江的洪水当然微不足道了。但丁老，神秘的宇宙固然令人神往，现实生活也还是要过的。我真的该走了，谢谢丁老的教海，祝各位今晚看到你们想看的。"

"您不明白我的意思，"丁仪说，"现在长江大堤上一定有很多人在抗洪。"

"但我有我的责任，丁老，我必须回去。"

"您还是不明白我的意思，我是说大堤上的人们一定很累了，您可以让他们也离开。"

所有的人都惊呆了。

"什么……离开？！干什么，看宇宙坍缩吗？"

"如果他们对此不感兴趣，可以回家睡觉。"

"丁老，您真会开玩笑！"

"我是认真的，他们干的事已没有意义。"

"为什么？"

"因为坍缩。"

沉默了好长时间，省长指了指大厅一角陈列的那个古老的星图盘说："丁老，宇宙一直在膨胀，但从上古时代到今天，我们所看到的宇宙没有什么变化。坍缩也一样，人类的时空同宇宙时空相比，渺小到可以忽略不计，除了纯理论的意义外，我不认为坍缩会对人类生活产生任何影响。甚至，我们可能在1亿年之后都不会观测到坍缩使星系产生的微小位移，如果那时还有我们的话。"

"15亿年，"丁仪说，"如果用我们目前最精密的仪器，15亿年后我们才能观测到这种位移，那时太阳早已熄灭，大概没有我们了。"

"而宇宙完全坍缩要200亿年，所以，人类是宇宙这棵大树上的一滴小露珠，在它短暂的寿命中，是绝对感觉不到大树的成长的。您总不至于同意互联网上那些可笑的谣言，说地球会被坍缩挤扁吧！"

这时，一位年轻姑娘走了进来，她脸色苍白，目光暗淡，她就是负责巨型显示屏的工程师。

"小张，你也太不像话了！你知道这是什么时候吗？！"台长气急败坏地冲她喊道。

"我父亲刚在医院去世。"

台长的怒气立刻消失了："真对不起，我不知道，可你看……"

工程师没再说什么，只是默默地走到大屏幕的控制计算机前，开始埋头检查故障。丁仪叼着烟斗慢慢走了过去。

"哦，姑娘，如果你真正了解宇宙坍缩的含义，父亲的死就不会让你这么悲伤了。"

丁仪的话激怒了在场的所有人，工程师猛地站起来，她苍白的脸由于愤怒而涨红，双眼充满泪水。

"您不是这个世界上的人！也许，同您的宇宙相比，父亲不算什么，但父亲对我很重要，对我们这些普通人很重要！而您的坍缩，不过是夜空中那弱得不能再弱的光线频率的一点点变化而已，这变化，甚至那光线，如果不是由精密仪器放大上万倍，谁都看不到！坍缩是什么？对普通人来说什么都不是！宇宙膨胀或坍缩，对我们有什么区别？！但父亲对我们是很重要的，您明白吗？！"

当工程师意识到自己是在向谁发火时，她克制了自己，转身继续她的工作。

丁仪叹息着摇摇头，对省长说："是的，如您所说，两个世界。我们的世界，"他挥手把自己和那一群物理学家和宇宙学家画到一个圈里，然后指指物理学家们，"小的尺度是亿亿分之一毫米，"又指指宇宙学家们，"大的尺度是百亿光年。这是一个只能用想象来把握的世界；而你们的世界，有长江的洪水，有紧张的预算，有逝去的或还活着的父亲……一个实实在在的世界。但可悲的是，人们总要把这两个世界分开。"

"可您看到它们是分开的。"省长说。

"不！基本粒子虽小，却组成了我们；宇宙虽大，我们身在其中。微观和宏观世界的每一个变化都牵动着我们的一切。"

"可即将发生的宇宙坍缩牵动着我们的什么吗？"

丁仪突然大笑起来，这笑除了神经质外，还包含着一种神秘的东西，让人毛骨悚然。

"好吧，物理系的学生，请背诵您所记住的时间、空间和物质的关系。"

省长像一个小学生那样顺从地背了起来："由相对论和量子力学所构成的现代物理学已证明，时间和空间不能离开物质而独立存在，没有绝对时空，时间、空间和物质世界是融为一体的。"

"很好，但有谁真正理解呢？您吗？"丁仪问省长，然后转向台长，"您吗？"接着转向埋头工作的工程师，"您吗？"又转向大厅中的其他技术人员，"你们吗？"最后转向科学家们，"甚至你们？！不，你们都不理解。你们仍按绝对时空来思考宇宙，就像脚踏大地一样自然，绝对时空就是你们思想的大地，离开它你们对一切都无从把握。谈到宇宙的膨胀和坍缩，你们认为那只是太空中的星系在绝对的时间、空间中散开和汇聚。"他说着，踱到那个玻璃陈列柜前，伸手打开柜门，把那个珍贵的星图盘拿了出来，放在手上抚摩着、欣赏着。台长万分担心地抬起两只手在星图盘下护着，这件宝物放在那儿20多年，还没有人敢动一下。台长焦急地等着丁仪把星图盘放回原位，但他没有，而是一抬手，把星图盘扔了出去！

价值连城的古老珍宝，在地毯上碎成了无数陶土块。

空气凝固了，大家呆若木鸡。只有丁仪还在悠然地踱着步，是这僵住的世界中唯一活动的因素，他的话音仍不间断地响着。

"时空和物质是不可分的，宇宙的膨胀和坍缩包括整个时空，是的，朋友们，包括整个时间和空间！"

又响起了破裂声，一只玻璃水杯从一名物理学家手中掉下去。引起他们震惊的原因同其他人不一样，不是星图盘，而是丁仪话中的含义。

"您是说……"一名宇宙学家死死地盯住丁仪，话卡在喉咙里说不出来。

"是的。"丁仪点点头，然后对省长说，"他们明白了。"

"那么，这就是统一场数学模型的计算结果中那个负时间参量的含义？！"一名物理学家恍然大悟地说。丁仪点点头。

"为什么不早些把它公布于世？！您太不负责任了！"另一名物理学家愤怒地说。

"有什么用？只能引起全世界范围的混乱，对时空，我们能做些什么？"

"你们都在说些什么？！"省长一头雾水地问。

"坍缩……"台长，同时是一名天体物理学家，做梦似的喃喃地说。

"宇宙坍缩会对人类产生影响，是吗？"

"影响？不，它将改变一切。"

"能改变什么呢？"

科学家们都在匆匆地整理着自己的思绪，没人回答他。

"你们就告诉我，坍缩时，或宇宙蓝移开始时，会发生什么？"省长着急地问。

"时间将反演。"丁仪回答。

"……反演？"省长迷惑地望望台长，又望望丁仪。

"时光倒流。"台长简短地解释。

巨型屏幕这时修好了，壮丽的宇宙出现在大家面前。为了使坍缩的出现更为直观，太空望远镜发回的图像由计算机进行变频处理，并对频率变化所产生的色彩效应进行了视觉上的夸张。现在所有的恒星和星系发出的光在大屏幕上都呈红色，象征着目前膨胀中宇宙的红移。当坍缩开始时，它们将同时变为蓝色。屏幕的一角显示出蓝移出现的倒计时：150 秒。

"我们的时间随宇宙膨胀了 200 亿年，但现在，这膨胀的时间只剩不到 3 分钟了，之后，时间将随宇宙坍缩，时光将倒流。"丁仪走到木然的台长面前，指指摔碎的星图盘，"不必为这件古物而痛心，蓝移出现后不久，碎片就会重新复原，它会回到陈列柜中去，多少年以后，回到土中深埋，再过几千年的时间，它将回到燃烧的窑中，然后作为一团潮泥回到那位上古天文学家的手中……"他走到那位年轻的女工程师身边，"也不要为你的父亲悲伤，他将很快复活，你们很快就会见面。如果父亲对你很重要，你应该感到安慰，因为在坍缩的宇宙中，他比你长寿，他将看着你作为婴儿离开这个世界。是的，我们这些老人都是刚刚踏上人生旅途，而你们年轻人则已近暮年，或说幼年。"他又走到省长面前，"如果过去没有，那么长江的洪水未来永远不会在您的任期内越出江堤，因为现在宇宙中的未来只剩 100 秒了。坍缩宇宙中的未来就是膨胀宇宙中的过去。最大的险情要到 1998 年才会出现，但那时您的生命已接近幼年，那不是您的责任了。还有 1 分钟，现在无论做什么，都不会对将来产生后果，大家可以做各自喜欢的事情而不必顾虑将来，在这个时间里已经没有将来了。至于我，我现在只是干我喜欢但以前由于气管炎而不能干的一件小事。"丁仪又用大烟斗从口袋里挖了一斗烟丝点上，悠然地抽了起来。

蓝移倒计时 50 秒。

"这不可能！"省长叫道，"从逻辑上这说不通，时间反演？一切都将反过来进行，难道我们倒着说话吗？这太难以想象了！"

"您会适应的。"

蓝移倒计时 40 秒。

"也就是说，以后的一切都是重复，那历史和人生变得多么乏味。"

"不会的，您将在另一个时间里，现在的过去将是您的未来，我们现在就在那时的未来里。您不可能记住未来，蓝移开始时，您的未来一片空白，对它，您什么都不记得，什么都不知道。"

蓝移倒计时 20 秒。

"这不可能！"

"您将会发现，从老年走向幼年，从成熟走向幼稚是多么合理多么理所当然。如果有人谈起时间还有另一个流向，您会认为他是痴人说梦。快了，还有十几秒，十几秒后，宇宙将通过一个时间奇点，在那一点时间不存在。然后，我们将进入坍缩宇宙。"

蓝移倒计时 8 秒。

"这不可能！真的不可能！！！"

"没关系，您很快就会知道的。"

蓝移倒计时 5 秒，4、3、2、1、0！

宇宙中的星光由使人烦躁的红色变为空洞的白色……

……时间奇点……

……星光由白色变为宁静美丽的蓝色，蓝移开始了，坍缩开始了。

……

……

。了始开缩坍，了始开移蓝，色蓝的丽美静宁为变色白由光星……

……点奇间时……

……色白的洞空为变色红的躁烦人使由光星的中宙宇

！0、1、2、3、4，秒 5 时计倒移蓝

"。的道知会就快很您，系关没"

"！！！能可不的真！能可不这"

。秒 8 时计倒移蓝

"。宙宇缩坍人进将们我，后然。在存不间时点一那在，点奇间时个一过通将宙宇，后秒几十，秒几十有还，了快。梦说人痴是他为认会您，向流个一另有还间时起谈人有果如。然当所理么多……"

赡养上帝

TAKING CARE OF GOD

一

　　上帝又惹秋生一家不高兴了。

　　这本来是一个很好的早晨，西岑村周围的田野上，在一人多高处悬着薄薄的一层白雾，像是一张刚刚变空白的画纸，这宁静的田野就是从那张纸上掉出来的画儿；第一缕朝阳照过来，今年的头道露珠们那短暂的生命进入了最辉煌的时期……但这个好早晨全让上帝给搅了。

　　上帝今天起得很早，自个儿到厨房去热牛奶。赡养时代开始后，牛奶市场兴旺起来，秋生家就花了1万元出头儿买了一头奶牛，学着人家的样儿把奶兑上水卖，而没有兑水的奶也成了本家上帝的主要食品之一。上帝热好奶后，就端着去堂屋看电视了，液化气也不关。刚清完牛圈和猪圈的秋生媳妇玉莲回来了，闻到满屋的液化气味，赶紧用毛巾捂着鼻子到厨房关了气，打开窗和换气扇。

"老不死的，你要把这一家子害死啊！"玉莲回到堂屋大嚷着。用上液化气也就是领到赡养费以后的事，秋生爹一直反对，说这玩意儿不如蜂窝煤好，这次他又落着理了。

像往常一样，上帝低头站在那里，那扫把似的雪白长胡须一直拖到膝盖以下，脸上堆着胆怯的笑，像一个做错了事儿的孩子。"我……我把奶锅儿拿下来了啊，它怎么不关呢？"

"你以为这是在你们飞船上啊？"正在下楼的秋生大声说，"这里的什么东西都是傻的，我们不像你们什么都有机器伺候着，我们得用傻工具劳动，才有饭吃！"

"我们也劳动过，要不怎么会有你们？"上帝小心翼翼地回应道。

"又说这个，又说这个，你就不觉得没意思？有本事走，再造些个孝子贤孙养活你。"玉莲一摔毛巾说。

"算了算了，快弄吃的吧。"像每次一样，又是秋生打圆场。

兵兵也起床了，他下楼时打着哈欠说："爸、妈，这上帝，又半夜咳，闹得我睡不着。"

"你知足吧小祖宗，我俩就在他隔壁还没发怨呢。"玉莲说。

上帝像是被提醒了，又咳嗽起来，咳得那么专心致志，像在做一项心爱的运动。

"唉，真是倒了八辈子的霉了。"玉莲看了上帝几秒钟，气鼓鼓地说，转身进厨房做饭去了。

上帝再也没吱声，默默地在桌边儿和一家人一块儿就着酱菜喝了一碗粥，吃了半个馒头，这期间一直承受着玉莲的白眼，不知是因为液化气的事儿，还是又嫌他吃得太多了。

饭后，上帝像往常一样，很勤快地收拾碗筷，到厨房去洗了起来。玉莲在外面冲他喊："不带油的不要用洗洁精！那都是要花钱买的，就你那点赡养费，哼。"上帝在厨房中连续"唉唉"地表示知道了。

小两口上地里去了，兵兵也去上学了，这个时候秋生爹才睡起来，两眼迷迷糊糊地下了楼，咕噜咕噜喝了两大碗粥后，点上一袋烟，才想起上帝的存在。

"老家伙，别洗了，出来杀一盘！"他冲厨房里喊道。

上帝用围裙擦着手出来，殷勤地笑着点点头。同秋生爹下棋对上帝来说也是个苦差事，输赢都不愉快。如果上帝赢了，秋生爹肯定暴跳如雷：你个老东西是个什么东西？！赢了我就显出你了是不是？！屁！你是上帝，赢我算个屁本事！你说说你，进这个门儿这么长时间了，怎么连个庄户人家的礼数都不懂？！如果上帝输了，这老头儿照样暴跳如雷：你个老东西是个什么东西？！我的棋术，方圆百里内没的比，赢你还不跟捏个臭虫似的，用得着你让着我？！你这是……用句文点儿的话说吧，对我的侮辱！！！反正最后的结果都一样，老头儿把棋盘一掀，棋子儿满天飞。秋生爹的臭脾气是远近闻名的，这下子可算找着了一个出气筒。不过这老头儿不记仇，每次上帝悄悄把棋子儿收拾回来再悄悄摆好后，他就又会坐下同上帝下起来，并重复上面的过程。当几盘下来两人都累了时，就已近中午了。

这时上帝就要起来去洗菜，玉莲不让他做饭，嫌他做得不好，但菜是必须洗的。一会儿小两口下地回来，如果发现菜啊什么的没弄好，她又是一通尖酸刻薄的数落。他洗菜时，秋生爹一般都踱到邻家串门去了。这是上帝一天中最清静的时候，中午的阳光充满了院子里的每一个砖缝，也照亮了他那幽深的记忆之谷。这时他往往开始发呆，忘记了手中的活儿，直到村头传来从田间归来的人声，他才猛醒过来，加紧干着手中的活儿，同时总是长叹一声。

唉——日子怎么过成了这个样子呢！

这不仅是上帝的叹息，也是秋生、玉莲和秋生爹的叹息，是地球上 50 多亿人和 20 亿上帝的叹息。

二

这一切都是从 3 年前那个秋日的黄昏开始的。

"快看啊，天上都是玩具耶！！！"兵兵在院子里大喊，秋生和玉莲从屋里跑出来，抬头看到天上真的布满了玩具，或者说，天空中出现的那无数物体，其形状只有玩具才能具有。这些物体在黄昏的苍穹中均匀地分布着，反射着已落到地平线下的夕阳的光芒，每个都有满月那么亮，这些光合在一起，使地面如正午般通明，而这光亮很诡异，它来自天空所有的方向，不会给任何物体投下影子，整个世界仿佛处于一个巨大的手术无影灯下。

开始，人们以为这些物体的位置都很低，位于大气层内，这样想是由于它们都清晰地显示出形状来，后来知道这只是由于其体积巨大产生的错觉，实际上它们都处于 3 万多千米高的地球同步轨道上。

到来的外星飞船共有 21513 艘，均匀地停泊在同步轨道上，形成了一层地球的外壳。这种停泊是以一种令人类观察者迷惑的极其复杂的队形和轨道完成的，所有的飞船同时停泊到位，这样可以避免飞船质量引力在地球海洋上产生致命的潮汐，这让人类多少安心了一些，因为它或多或少地表明了外星人对地球没有恶意。

以后的几天，人类世界与外星飞船的沟通尝试均告失败，后者对地球发出的询问信息保持着完全的沉默。与此同时，地球变成了一个没有夜晚的世界，太空中那上万艘巨大飞船反射的阳光，使地球背对太阳的一面亮如白昼；而在面向太阳的这一面，大地则周期性地笼罩在飞船巨大的阴影下。天空中的恐怖景象使人类的精神承受力达到了极限，因而也忽视了地球上正在发生的一件奇怪的事情，更不会想到这事与太空中外星飞船群的联系。

在世界各大城市中，陆续出现了一些流浪的老者，他们都有一些共同特点：年纪都很大，都留着长长的白胡须和白头发，身着一样的白色长袍。在开始的那些天，在这些白胡须、白头发和白长袍还没有被弄脏时，远远看去他们就像一个个雪人似的。这些老流浪者的长相介于各色人种之间，好像都是混血人种。他们没有任何能证明自己国籍和身份的东西，也说不清自己的来历，只是用生硬的各国语言温和地向路人乞讨，都说着同样的一句话：

"我们是上帝，看在创造了这个世界的分儿上，给点儿吃的吧——"

如果只有一个或几个老流浪者这么说，把他们送进收容所或养老院，与那些无家可归的老年妄想症患者放到一起就是了，但要是有上百万个流落街头的老头儿、老太太都这么说，那就是另一回事了。事实上，这种老流浪者在不到半个月的时间里增长到了3000多万人，在纽约、北京、伦敦和莫斯科的街头上，到处是这种步履蹒跚的老家伙，他们成群结队地堵塞了交通，看上去比城市的原住居民都多。最可怖的是，他们都说着同一句话：

"我们是上帝，看在创造了这个世界的分儿上，给点儿吃的吧——"

直到这时，人们才把注意力从太空中的外星飞船转移到地球上的这些不速之客上来。最近，各大洲上空都多次出现了原因不明的大规模流星雨，每次壮观的流星雨过后，相应地区老流浪者的数量就急剧增加。经过仔细观察，人们发现了这个令人难以置信的事实：老流浪者是自天而降的，他们来自那些外星飞船。他们都像跳水似的孤身跃入大气层，每人身上都穿着一件名叫"再入膜"的密封服，当这种绝热的服装在大气层中摩擦燃烧时，会产生经过精确调节的减速推力，在漫长的坠落过程中，这种推力产生的过载始终不超过4个G，在这些老家伙的承受范围内。当老流浪者接触地面时，他们的下落速度接近于零，就像是从一张板凳上跳下差不多，即使这样，还是有很多人在着陆时崴了脚。而在他们接触地面的同时，身上穿的再入膜也正好蒸发干净，不留下一点残余。

天空中的流星雨绵绵不断，老流浪者以越来越大的流量降临地球，他们的人数已接近1亿。

各国政府都试图在他们中找出一个或一些代表，但他们声称，所有的"上帝"都是绝对平等的，他们中的任何一个人都能代表全体。于是，在为此召开的紧急特别联合国大会上，从时代广场上随意找来的一个英语已讲得比较好的老流浪者进入了会场。他显然是最早降临地球的那一批，长袍脏兮兮的，破了好几个洞，大白胡子落满了灰，像一把墩布，他的头上没有神圣的光环，倒是盘旋着几只忠实追随的苍蝇。他挂着那根当作拐杖的顶端已开裂的竹竿，颤巍巍地走到大圆会议桌旁，在各国首脑的注视下慢慢坐下，抬头看着秘书长，露出了他们特有的那种孩子般的笑容：

"我，呵，还没吃早饭呢。"

于是有人给他端上来一份早餐。全世界的人都在电视中看着他狼吞虎咽，好几次被噎住。面包、香肠和一大盘沙拉很快被风卷残云般吃光，他又喝下一大杯牛奶。然后，他又对秘书长露出了天真的笑：

"呵呵，有没有……酒？一小杯就行。"

于是有人给他端上一杯葡萄酒，他小口地抿着，满意地点点头："昨天夜里，暖和的地铁出风口让新下来的一帮老家伙占了，我只好睡广场上，现在喝点儿，关节就灵活些，呵呵……你，能给我捶捶背吗？稍捶几下就行。"在秘书长开始捶背时，他摇摇头长叹一声，"唉——给你们添麻烦了。"

"你们从哪里来？"美国总统问。

老流浪者又摇摇头："一个文明，只有在它是个幼儿时才有固定的位置。行星会变化，恒星也会变化，文明不久就得迁移，到青年时代它已迁移过多次，这时肯定发现，任何行星的环境都不如密封的飞船稳定，于是它就以飞船为家，行星反而成为临时住所。所以，任何长大成人的文明都是星舰文明，在太空进行着永恒的流浪，飞船就是它的家。从哪里来？我们从飞船上来。"他说着，用一根脏乎乎的指头向上指指。

"你们总共有多少人？"

"20 亿。"

"你们到底是谁？"秘书长的这个问题问得有道理，他们看上去与人类没有任何不同。

"说过多少次了，我们是上帝。"老流浪者不耐烦地摆了一下手说。

"能解释一下吗？"

"我们的文明，呵，就叫它上帝文明吧，在地球诞生前就已存在了很久，在上帝文明步入衰落的暮年时，我们就在刚形成不久的地球上培育了最初的生命，然后，上帝文明在接近光速的航行中跨越时间，在地球生命世界进化到适当的程度时，按照我们远祖的基因引入了一个物种，并消灭了它的天敌，细心地引导它进化，最后在地球上形成了与我们一模一样的文明种族。"

"如何让我们相信您所说的呢？"

"这很容易。"

于是，开始了历时半年的证实行动。人们震惊地看到了从飞船上传输来的地球生命的原始设计蓝图，看到了地球远古的图像。按照老流浪者的指点，在各大陆和各大洋底深深的岩层中挖出了那些令人惊恐的大机器，那是在过去漫长的岁月中一直监测和调节着地球生命世界的仪表……

人们终于不得不相信，至少对于地球生命而言，他们确实是上帝。

三

在第三次紧急特别联大上，秘书长终于代表全人类，向上帝提出了那个关键的问题：他们到地球来的目的是什么？

"我回答这个问题之前，你们首先要对文明有一个正确的认识。"上帝代表捋着胡子说，他还是半年前光临第一届紧急联大的那一位。"你们认为，随着时间的延续，文明会怎样演化？"

"地球文明正处于快速发展时期，如果没有来自大自然的不可抗拒的灾难和意外，我们想，它会一直发展下去。"秘书长回答说。

"错了，你想想，每个人都会经历童年、青年、中年和老年，最终走向死亡，恒星也一样，宇宙中的任何事物都一样，甚至宇宙本身也有终结的那一天。为什么唯有文明能够一直成长呢？不，文明也都有老去的那一天，当然也都有死亡的那一天。"

"这个过程具体是怎么发生的呢？"

"不同的文明有着不同的衰老和死亡方式，像不同的人死于不同的疾病或无疾而终一样。具体到上帝文明，个体寿命的延长是文明步入老年的第一个标志。那时，上帝文明中的个体寿命已延长至近 4000 个地球年，而他们的思想在 2000 岁左右就已完全僵化，创造性消失殆尽。这样的个体掌握了社会的绝大部分权力，而新的生命很难出生和成长，文明就老了。"

"以后呢？"

"文明衰老的第二个标志是机器摇篮时代。"

"嗯？"

"那时，我们的机器已经完全不依赖于它们的创造者而独立运行，能够自我维护、更新和扩展，这样的智能机器能够提供一切我们所需要的东西，这不只是物质需要，也包括精神需要，我们不需为生存付出任何努力，完全靠机器养活了，就像躺在一个舒适的摇篮中。想一想，假如当初地球的丛林中充满了采摘不尽的果实，到处是伸手就能抓到的小猎物，猿还能进化成人吗？机器摇篮就是这样一个富庶的丛林，渐渐地，我们忘却了技术和科学，文化变得懒散而空虚，人们失去了创新能力和进取心，文明加速老去，你们所看到的，就是这样一个进入了风烛残年的上帝文明。"

"那么，您现在是否可以告诉我们上帝文明来到地球的目的？"

"我们无家可归了。"

"可——"秘书长向上指指。

"那都是些老飞船。虽然，飞船上的生态系统比包括地球在内的任何自然形成的生态系统都强健稳定，但飞船都太老了，老得让你们无法想象，机器的部件老化失效，漫长时间内积聚的量子效应产生出越来越多的软件错误，系统的自我维护和修复功能遇到了越来越多的障碍。飞船中的生态环境在渐渐恶化，每个人能够得到的生活必需品配给日益减少，现在只够勉强维持生存。在飞船中的 2 万多个城市中，弥漫着污浊的空气和绝望的情绪。"

"没有补救的办法吗？比如更新飞船的硬件和软件？"

上帝摇摇头："上帝文明已到垂暮之年，我们是 20 亿个 3000 多岁的老朽之人。其实，早在我们之前，已有上百代人生活在舒适的机器摇篮之中，技术早就被遗忘干净了。现在，我们不会维修那已经运行了几千万年的飞船。其实在技术和学习能力上我们连你们都不如，我们连点亮一盏灯的电路都不会接，连一元二次方程都不会解……终于有一天，飞船说，它们已经到了报废的边缘，航行动力系统已没有能力将飞船推进到接近光速，上帝文明只能进行不到光速 1/10 的低速航行，飞船上的生态循环系统已接近崩溃，它们无法继续养活 20 亿人了，请我们自寻生路。"

"以前，你们没有想到过会有这一天吗？"

"当然想到过，在 2000 年前，飞船就开始对我们发出警告，于是，我们采取了措施，在地球上播种生命，为养老做准备。"

"您是说，在 2000 年前？"

"是的，当然，那是我们的航行时间，从你们的时间坐标来看，那是在 35 亿年前，那时地球刚刚冷却。"

"这就有个问题：你们已经失去了技术能力，但播种生命不需要技术吗？"

"哦，在一个星球上启动生命进程其实只是个很小的工程，播下种子，生命就自己繁衍起来。这种软件在机器摇篮时代之前就有了，只要运行软件，机器就能完成一切。创造一个行星规模的生命世界，进而产生文明，最基本的需要只是时间，几十亿年漫长的时间。接近光速的航行能使我们几乎无限地拥有另一个世界的时间，但现在，上帝文明的飞船发动机已老化，再也不可能接近光速，否则我们还可以创造更多的生命和文明世界，这时也就拥有更多的选择。此时，我们已被禁锢在低速，这些都无法实现了。"

"这么说，你们是想到地球上来养老。"

"哦，是的是的，希望你们尽到对自己创造者的责任，收留我们。"上帝拄着拐杖颤巍巍地向各国首脑鞠躬，差点儿向前跌倒。

"那么，你们打算如何在地球上生活呢？"

"如果我们在地球上仍然集中生活，那还不如在太空中了却残生呢。我们想融入你们的社会，进入你们的家庭。在上帝文明的童年时代，我们也曾有过家庭，你知道，童年是最值得珍惜的，你们现在正好处于文明的童年时代，如果我们能够回到这个时代，在家庭的温暖中度过余生，那真是最大的幸福。"

"你们有 20 亿，地球社会中的每个家庭都要收留你们中的一至两人。"秘书长说完，会场陷入了长时间的沉默。

"是啊是啊，给你们添麻烦了……"上帝连连鞠躬，同时偷偷看秘书长和各国首脑的表情，"当然，我们会给你们一定的补偿的。"他挥了一下拐杖，又有两个白胡子上帝走进了会场，吃力地抬着一个银色的金属箱子。"你们看，这是大量的高密度信息存储体，系统地存储着上帝文明在各个学科和技术领域的所有资料，它将使地球文明飞跃进化，相信你们会喜欢的。"

秘书长看着金属箱，与在场的各国首脑一样极力掩盖着心中的狂喜，说："赡养上帝应该是人类的责任，虽然这还需要世界各国进一步磋商，但我想，原则上……"

"给你们添麻烦了，给你们添麻烦了……"上帝一时老泪纵横，又连连鞠躬。

当秘书长和各国首脑走出会议大厅时，发现联合国大厦外面聚集了几万名上帝，看上去一片白花花的人山人海，天地之间充斥着一片嗡嗡的话音，秘书长仔细听了听，听出他们都在用不同的地球语言反复说着同一句话：

"给你们添麻烦了，给你们添麻烦了……"

四

20 亿上帝降临到了地球，他们大多是穿着再入膜坠入大气层的，那段时间，天空中缤纷的彩雨在白天都能看到。这些上帝着陆后，分散进入了人类社会的 15 亿家庭中。由于得到了上帝的科技资料，人们都对未来充满了历史上从未有过的希冀和憧憬，似乎人类在一夜之间就能进入世世代代梦想中的天堂。在这种心情下，每个家庭都真诚地欢迎上帝的到来。

这天，秋生一家同村里的其他乡亲一起，早早地等在村口，迎接分配到本村的上帝。

"今儿真是个晴天啊！"玉莲兴奋地说。

她的这种感觉并非完全是心情使然，因为那布满天空的外星飞船在一夜之间完全消失了，天空重新变得空旷开阔起来。人类一直没有机会登上那些飞船中的任何一艘，上帝对地球人的这种愿望不持异议，但飞船自己不允许。对于人类发射的那些接近它们的简陋原始的探测器，它们不理不睬，紧闭舱门。当最后一批上帝跃入地球大气层后，2 万多艘飞船同时飞离了地球同步轨道。但它们并没有走远，在小行星带飘浮着。这些飞船虽然陈旧不堪，但古老的程序仍在运行，它们唯一的终极使命就是为上帝服务，因而不可能远离上帝，当后者需要时，它们会招之即来的。

乡里的两辆大轿车很快开来，送来了分配到西岑村的 106 名上帝。秋生和玉莲很快领到了分配给自己家的那个上帝，两口子亲热地挽着上帝的胳膊，秋生爹和兵兵乐呵呵地跟在后面，在上午明媚的阳光下朝家走去。

"老爷子，哦，上帝老爷子，"玉莲把脸贴在上帝的肩上，灿烂地笑着说，"听说，你们送的那些技术，马上就能让我们实现共产主义了！到时候是按需分配，什么都不要钱，去商店拿就行了。"

上帝笑着冲她点点满是白发的头，用还很生硬的汉语说："是的，其实，按需分配只是满足了一个文明最基本的需要，我们的技术将给你们带来的生活，其富裕和舒适，是你完全想象不出来的。"

玉莲的脸笑成了一朵花："不用不用，按需分配就成了，我就满足了。嘻嘻！"

"嗯！"秋生爹在后面重重地点点头。

"我们还能像您这样长生不老？"秋生问。

"我们并不能长生不老，只是比你们活得长些而已，现在不是都老了吗？其实人要活过3000岁，感觉和死了也差不多，对一个文明来说，个体太长寿是致命的危险。"

"哦，不用3000岁，300岁就成啊！"秋生爹也像玉莲一样笑得合不拢嘴，"想想，那样的话我现在还是个小伙儿，说不定还能……呵呵呵呵……"

这天，村里像过大年一样，家家都张罗了丰盛的宴席为上帝接风，秋生家也不例外。秋生爹很快让老花雕灌得有三分迷糊了，他冲上帝竖起了大拇指。

"你们行！能造出这所有的活物来，神仙啊！"

上帝也喝了不少，但脑子还清醒，他冲秋生爹摆摆手："不，不是神，是科学，生物科学发展到一定层次，就能像制造机器一样制造出生命来。"

"话虽这么说，可在我们眼里，你们还是跟下凡的神仙没两样啊。"

上帝摇摇头："神应该是不会出错的，但我们，在创世过程中错误不断。"

"你们造我们时还出过错？"玉莲吃惊地瞪大了双眼，因为在她的想象里，创造万千生灵就像她8年前生兵兵一样，是出不得错的。

"出过很多，以较近的来说，由于创世软件对环境判断的某些失误，地球上出现了像恐龙这类体积大而适应性差的动物，后来为了你们的进化，只好又把它们抹掉。再说更近的事：自古爱琴海文明消亡后，创世软件认为已经成功地创建了地球文明，就再也没有对人类的进程进行监视和微调，就像把一个上好了发条的钟表扔在那里任它自己走动，这就出现了更多的错。比如，应该让古希腊文明充分地独立发展，马其顿的征服，还有后来罗马的征服都应被制止，虽然这两个力量都不是希腊文明的对立面而是其继承者，但希腊文明的发展方向被改变了……"

秋生家没人能听懂这番话，但都很敬畏地探头恭听。

"再到后来，地球上出现了汉朝和古罗马两大力量，与前面提到的希腊文明相反，不应该让这两大力量在相互隔绝的状态下发展，而应该让它们充分接触……"

"你说的汉朝，是刘邦、项羽的汉朝吧？"秋生爹终于抓住了自己知道的一点儿，"那古罗马？"

"好像是那时洋人的一个大国，也很大的。"秋生试着解释道。

秋生爹不解地问："什么？洋人在清朝就把我们收拾成那样儿了，你还让他们早在汉朝就同我们见面？！"

上帝笑着说："不不，那时，汉朝的军事力量绝不比古罗马差。"

"那也很糟，这两强相遇要打起来，可是大仗，血流成河啊！"

上帝点点头，伸了筷子去夹红烧肉："有可能，但东西方两大文明将碰撞出灿烂的火花，将人类大大向前推进一步……唉，要是避免那些错误的话，地球人现在可能已经殖民火星，你们的恒星际探测器已越过天狼星了。"

秋生爹举起酒碗敬佩地说："说上帝们在摇篮里把科学忘了，其实你们还是很有学问的嘛。"

"为了在摇篮中过得舒适，还是需要知道一些哲学、艺术、历史之类的，只是些常识而已，算不得什么学问，现在地球上的很多学者，思想都比我们深刻得多。"

…………

上帝文明进入人类社会的最初一段时间，是上帝们的黄金时光。那时，他们与人类家庭相处得十分融洽，仿佛回到了上帝文明的童年时代，融入了那早已被他们忘却的家庭温暖之中，对于他们那漫长的一生来说，这应该是再好不过的结局了。

秋生家的上帝，在这个秀美的江南小村过着宁静的田园生活，每天到竹林环绕的池塘中钓钓鱼，同村里的老人聊聊天、下下棋，其乐融融。但他最大的爱好是看戏，有戏班子到村里或镇里时，他场场不误。上帝最爱看的是《梁祝》，看一场不够，竟跟着那个戏班子走了 100 多里地，连看了好几场。后来秋生从镇子里为他买回一张这戏的 VCD，他就一遍遍放着看，再后来也能哼几句像模像样的黄梅戏了。

有天玉莲发现了一个秘密，她悄悄地对秋生和公公说："你们知道吗，上帝老爷子每次看完戏，总是从里面口袋中掏出一张小片片看，边看边哼曲儿。我刚才偷看了一眼，那是张照片，上面有个好漂亮的姑娘耶！"

傍晚，上帝又放了一遍《梁祝》，掏出那张美人像边看边哼起来，秋生爹悄悄凑过去："上帝老爷子啊，你那是……从前的相好儿？"

上帝吓了一跳，赶紧把照片塞进怀里，对秋生爹露出孩子般的笑："呵呵，是，是，她是我 2000 多年前的爱。"

在旁边偷听的玉莲撇了撇嘴，还 2000 多年前的爱呢，这么大岁数了，真酸得慌。

秋生爹本想看看那张照片，但看到上帝护得那么紧，也不好意思强要，只能听着上帝的回忆。

"那时我们都还很年轻，她是极少数没有在机器摇篮中沉沦的人之一，发起了一次宏伟的探险航行，要航行到宇宙的尽头。哦，这你不用细想，很难搞明白的……她期望用这次航行唤醒机器摇篮中的上帝文明，当然，这不过是一个美好的愿望罢了。她让我同去，但我不敢，那无边无际的宇宙荒漠吓住了我，那是200 亿光年的漫漫长程啊。她就自己去了，在以后的 2000 多年里，我对她的思念从来就没间断过啊。"

"200 亿光年？照你以前说的，就是光要走 200 亿年？！乖乖，那也太远了，这可是生离死别啊。上帝老爷子，你就死了那个心吧，再也见不着她的面儿啰。"

上帝点点头，长叹一声。

"不过嘛，她现在也是你这岁数了吧。"

上帝从沉思中醒过来，摇摇头："哦，不不，这么远的航程，那艘探险飞船会很贴近光速地航行，她应该还很年轻，老的是我……宇宙啊，你真不知道它有多大，你们所谓的沧海桑田、天长地久，不过是时空中的一粒沙啊……话说回来，你感觉不到这些，有时候还真是一种幸运呢！"

五

上帝与人类的蜜月很快结束了。

人们曾对从上帝那里得到的科技资料欣喜若狂，认为它们能使人类的梦想在一夜之间变为现实。借助于上帝提供的接口设备，那些巨量的信息被很顺利地从存储器中提取出来，并开始被源源不断地译成英文，为了避免纷争，世界各国都拷贝了一份。但人们很快发现，要将这些技术变成现实，至少在本世纪内是不可能的事。其实设想一下，如果有一个时间旅行者将现代技术资料送给古埃及人会是什么情况，就能够理解现在人类面临的尴尬处境了。

在石油即将采尽的今天，能源技术是人们最关心的技术。但科学家和工程师们很快发现，上帝文明的能源技术对现代人类毫无用处，因为他们的能源是建立在正反物质湮灭的基础上的。即使读懂所有相关资料，最后制造出湮灭发动机和发电机（在这一

148

代人中这基本上不可能），一切还是等于零，因为这些能源机器的燃料——反物质，需要远航飞船从宇宙中开采。据上帝的资料记载，距地球最近的反物质矿藏在银河系至仙女座星云之间的黑暗太空中，有55万光年之遥！而接近光速的星际航行几乎涉及所有的学科，其中的大部分理论和技术对人类而言高深莫测，人类学者即使对其基础部分有个大概的了解，可能也需半个世纪的时间。科学家们曾满怀希望地查询受控核聚变的技术信息，但根本没有，这很好理解：人类现代的能源科学并不包含钻木取火的技巧。

在其他的学科领域，如信息技术和生命科学（其中蕴含着使人类长生的秘密）也一样，最前沿的科学家也完全无法读懂那些资料，上帝科学与人类科学的理论距离目前还是一道无法跨越的鸿沟。

来到地球上的上帝们无法给科学家们提供任何帮助，正如那一位所说，现在在他们中间，会解一元二次方程的人都很少了。而那群飘浮在小行星带的飞船，对人类的呼唤毫不理睬。现在的人类就像一群刚入学的小学生，突然被要求研读博士研究生的课程，而且没有导师。

另外，地球上突然增加了20亿人口，这些人都是不能创造任何价值的超老人，其中大半疾病缠身，给人类社会造成了前所未有的压力。各国政府要付给每个接收上帝的家庭一笔可观的赡养费，医疗和其他公共设施也已不堪重负，世界经济到了崩溃的边缘。

上帝和秋生一家的融洽关系不复存在，他渐渐被这家人看作一个天外飞来的负担，遭到越来越多的嫌弃，而每个嫌弃他的人各有各的理由。

玉莲的理由最现实也最接近问题的实质，那就是上帝让她家的日子过穷了。在这家人中，她是最令上帝烦恼的一个，那张尖酸刻薄的刀子嘴，比太空中的黑洞和超新星更令他恐惧。她的共产主义理想破灭后，就不停地在上帝面前唠叨，说在他来之前他们家的日子是多么富裕、多么滋润，那时什么都好，现在什么都差，都是因为他，摊上他这么个老不死的真是倒了大霉！每天只要一有机会，她就这样对上帝恶语相向。上帝有很重的气管炎，这虽不是什么花大钱的病，但需要长期去治和养，钱自然是要不断地花。终于有一天，玉莲不让秋生带上帝去镇医院看病，也不给他买药了。这事让村支书知道了，很快找上门来。

　　支书对玉莲说："你家上帝的病还是要用心治，镇医院跟我打招呼了，说他的气管炎如果不及时治疗，有可能转成肺气肿。"

　　"要治村里或政府给他治，我家没那么多钱花在这上面！"玉莲冲村支书嚷道。

　　"玉莲啊，按《上帝赡养法》，这种小额医疗是要由接收家庭承担的，政府发放的赡养费已经包括这费用了。"

　　"那点儿赡养费顶个屁用！"

　　"话不能这么说，你家领到赡养费后买了奶牛，用上了液化气，还换了大彩电，就没钱给上帝治病？大伙都知道这个家是你在当，我把话说在这儿，你可别给脸不要脸，下次就不是我来劝你了，会是乡里、县里、上委（上帝赡养委员会）的人来找你，到时让你吃不了兜着走！"

　　玉莲没办法，只好恢复了对上帝的医疗，但日后对他就更没好脸了。

　　有一次上帝对玉莲说："不要着急嘛，地球人很有悟性，学得也很快，只需 1 个世纪左右，上帝科学技术中层次较低的一部分就能在人类社会得到初步应用，那时生活会好起来的。"

"切，1 个世纪，还只需，你这叫人话啊？"正在洗碗的玉莲头也不回地说。

"这时间很短啊。"

"那是对你们，你以为我能像你似的长生不老啊，1 个世纪过去，我的骨头都找不着了！不过我倒要问问，你觉得自个儿还能活多少时间呢？"

"唉！风烛残年了，再能活三四百个地球年就很不错了。"

玉莲将一摞碗全摔到了地上："咱这到底是谁给谁养老、谁给谁送终啊？！啊，合着我累死累活伺候你一辈子，还得搭上我儿子孙子甚至往下十几辈不成？！说你老不死，你还真是啊！"

…………

至于秋生爹，则认为上帝是个骗子。其实，这种说法在社会上也很普遍，既然科学家看不懂上帝的科技文献，就无法证实它们的真伪，说不定人类真让上帝给耍了。对于秋生爹而言，他这方面的证据更充分一些。

"老骗子，行骗也没你这么猖狂的。"他有一天对上帝说，"我懒得揭穿你，你那一套真不值得我揭穿，甚至不值得我孙子揭穿呢！"

上帝问他有什么地方不对。

"先说最简单的一个吧：我们的科学家知道，人是由猴儿变来的，对不对？"

上帝点点头："准确地说是由古猿进化来的。"

"那你怎么说我们是你们造的呢？既然造人，直接造成我们这样儿不就行了，为什么先要造出古猿，再进化什么的，这说不通啊！"

"人要以婴儿出生再长大为成人，一个文明也一样，必须从原始状态进化发展而来，其中的漫长历程是不可省略的。事实上，对于人类这一物种分支，我们最初引入的是更为原始的东西，古猿已经经过相当长时间的进化了。"

"我不信你故弄玄虚的那一套，好好，再说个更明显的吧，告诉你，这还是我孙子看出来的：我们的科学家说地球上30多亿年前就有生命了，这你是认可的，对吧？"

上帝点点头："他们估计得基本准确。"

"那你有30多亿岁？"

"按你们的时间坐标，是的；但按上帝飞船的时间坐标，我只有3500岁。飞船以接近光速飞行，时间的流逝比你们的世界要慢得多。当然，有少数飞船会不定期脱离光速，降至低速来到地球，对地球上的生命进化进行一些调整。但这只需很短的时间，这些飞船很快就会重新进入太空进行接近光速的航行，继续跨越时间。"

"扯——"秋生爹轻蔑地说。

"爹，这可是相对论，也是咱们的科学家证实了的。"秋生插嘴说。

"相对个屁！你也给我瞎扯，哪有那么玄乎的事儿？时间又不是香油，还能流得快慢不同？！我还没老糊涂呢！倒是你，那些书把你看傻了！"

"我很快就能向你们证明，时间能够以不同的速度流逝。"上帝一脸神秘地说，同时从怀里掏出了那张 2000 年前的情人的照片，把它递给秋生，"仔细看看，记住她的每一个细节。"

秋生看那照片的第一眼时，就知道自己肯定能够记住每一个细节，想忘都不容易。同其他的上帝一样，她综合了各色人种的特点，皮肤是温润的象牙色，那双会唱歌的大眼睛绝对是活的，一下子就把秋生的魂儿勾走了。她是上帝中的姑娘，她是姑娘中的上帝，那种上帝之美，如第二个太阳，人类从未见过，也根本无法承受。

"瞧你那德行样儿，口水都流出来了！"玉莲一把从已经有些傻呆的秋生手中抢过照片，还没拿稳，就让公公抢去了。

"我来我来。"秋生爹说着，那双老眼立刻凑到照片上，近得不能再近了，好长时间一动不动，好像那能当饭吃。

"凑那么近干吗？"玉莲轻蔑地问。

"去去，我不是没戴老花镜嘛。"秋生爹脸伏在照片上说。

玉莲用不屑的目光斜视了公公几秒钟，撇撇嘴，转身进厨房了。

上帝把照片从秋生爹手中拿走了，后者的双手恋恋不舍地护送照片走了一段。上帝说："记好细节，明天的这个时候再让你们看。"

整整一天，秋生爷俩少言寡语，都在想着那位上帝姑娘，他们心照不宣，惹得玉莲脾气又大了许多。终于等到了第二天的同一个时候，上帝好像忘了那事，经秋生爹的提醒才想起来，他掏出那张让爷俩想念了一天的照片，首先递给秋生："仔细看看，她有什么变化？"

"没啥变化呀。"秋生全神贯注地看着，过了好一会儿，终于看出点东西来，"哦，对，她嘴唇儿张开的缝比昨天好像小了一些，小得不多，但确实小了一些，看嘴角儿这儿……"

"不要脸的，你看得倒是细！"照片又让媳妇抢走了，同样又让他爹抢到手里了。

"还是我来——"秋生爹今天拿来了老花镜，戴上细细端详着，"是，是，是小了些。还有很明显的一点你怎么没看出来呢？这小缕头发嘛，比昨天肯定向右飘了一点点的！"

上帝将照片从秋生爹手中拿过来，举到他们面前："这不是一张照片，而是一台电视接收机。"

"就是……电视机？"

"是的，电视机，现在它接收的，是她在那艘飞向宇宙边缘的探险飞船上的实况画面。"

"实况？就像转播足球赛那样？！"

"是的。"

"这，这上面的她居然……是活的！"秋生目瞪口呆地说，连玉莲的双眼都睁得像核桃那么大。

"是活的，但比起地球上的实况转播，这个画面有时滞，探险飞船大约已经飞出了 8000 万光年，那么时滞就是 8000 万年，我们看到的，是 8000 万年前的她。"

"这小玩意儿能收到那么远的地方传来的电波？"

"这样的超远程宇宙通信，只能使用中微子或引力波，我们的飞船才能收到，放大后再转发到这台小电视机上。"

"宝物，真是宝物啊！"秋生爹由衷地赞叹道，不知是指的那台小电视，还是电视上那个上帝姑娘。反正一听说她居然是"活的"，秋生爷俩的感情就上升了一个层次，秋生伸手要去捧小电视，但老上帝不给。

"电视中的她为什么动得那么慢呢？"秋生问。

"这就是时间流逝速度不同的结果，从我们的时空坐标上看，接近光速飞行的探险飞船上的时间流逝得很慢很慢。"

"那……她就能跟你说话了是吗？"玉莲指指小电视问。

上帝点点头，按动了小屏幕背面的一个开关，小电视立刻发出了一个声音，那是一个柔美的女声，但是音节恒定不变，像是歌唱结束时永恒拖长的尾声。上帝用充满爱意的目光凝视着小屏幕："她正在说呢，刚刚说出'我爱你'三个字，每个字说了 1 年多的时间，已说了 3 年半，现在正在结束'你'字，完全结束可能还需要 3 个月左右吧。"上帝把目光从屏幕上移开，仰视着院子上方的苍穹，"她后面还有话，我会用尽残生去听的。"

兵兵和本家上帝的好关系倒是维持了一段时间，老上帝们或多或少都有些童心，与孩子们谈得来，也能玩到一块儿。但有一天，兵兵闹着要上帝的那块大手表，上帝坚决不给，说那是和上帝文明通信的工具，没有它，自己就无法和本种族联系了。

"哼，看看看看，还想着你们那个文明啊种族啊，从来就没有把我们当自家人！"玉莲气鼓鼓地说。

从此以后，兵兵也不和上帝好了，还不时搞些恶作剧来捉弄他。

家里唯一还对上帝保持着尊敬和孝心的就是秋生。秋生高中毕业，加上平时爱看书，村里除去那几个考上大学走了的，他就是最知书达理的人了。但秋生在家是个地地道道的软蛋角色，平时看老婆的眼色行事，听爹的训斥过活，要是遇到爹和老婆对他的指示不一致，就只会抱头蹲在那儿流眼泪了。他这个熊样儿，在家里自然无法维护上帝的权益了。

六

上帝与人类的关系终于恶化到不可挽回的地步。

秋生家与上帝关系的彻底破裂，是因为方便面那事。这天午饭前，玉莲就搬着一个纸箱子从厨房出来，问她昨天刚买的一整箱方便面怎么一下子少了一半。

"是我拿的，我给河那边送过去了，他们快断粮了。"上帝低着头小声回答说。

他说的河那边，是指村里那些离家出走的上帝的聚集点。近日来，村里虐待上帝的事屡有发生，其中最刁蛮的一户人家，对本家的上帝又打又骂，还不给饭吃，逼得那个上帝跳到村前的河里寻短见，幸亏让人救起。这事惊动面很大，来处理的不是乡和县里的人，而是市公安局的刑警，还跟着 CCTV 和省电视台的一帮记者，把那两口子一下子都铐走了。按照《上帝赡养法》，他们犯了虐待上帝罪，最少要判 10 年的，而这个法律是唯一一个在世界各国都通用并且统一量刑的法律。这以后村里的各家收敛了许多，至少在明里不敢对上帝太过分了，但同时，也更加剧了村里人和上帝之间的隔阂。开始有上帝离家出走，其他的上帝纷纷效仿，截至目前，西岑村近 1/3 的上帝离开了收留他们的家庭。这些出走的上帝在河对岸的田野上搭起帐篷，过起了艰苦的原始生活。

在国内和世界的其他地方，情况也好不到哪里去，城市中的街道上再次出现了成群的流浪上帝，且数量还在急剧增加，重演了 3 年前那噩梦般的一幕。这个人和上帝共同生活的世界面临着巨大的危机。

"好啊，你倒是大方！你个吃里爬外的老不死的！"玉莲大骂起来。

"我说老家伙，"秋生爹一拍桌子站了起来，"你给我滚！你不是惦记着河那边的吗？滚到那里去和他们一起过吧！"

上帝低头沉默了一会儿，站起身，到楼上自己的小房间去，默默地把属于他自己的不多的几件东西装到一个小包袱里，拄着那根竹拐杖缓缓出了门，向河的方向走去。

秋生没有和家里人一起吃饭，一个人低头蹲在墙角默不作声。

"死鬼，过来吃啊，下午还要去镇里买饲料呢！"玉莲冲他喊，见他没动，就过去揪他的耳朵。

"放开。"秋生说，声音不高，但玉莲还是触电似的放开了，因为她从来没有见过自己的男人有那种阴沉的表情。

"甭管他，爱吃不吃，傻小子一个。"秋生爹不以为然地说。

"呵，你惦记老不死的上帝了是不是？那你也滚到河那边野地里跟他们过去吧！"玉莲用一根手指捅着秋生的脑袋说。

秋生站起身，上楼到卧室里，像刚才上帝那样整理了不多的几件东西，装到以前进城打工用过的那个旅行包中，背着下了楼，大步向外走去。

"死鬼，你去哪儿啊？！"玉莲喊道，秋生不理会，只是向外走，她又喊，声音有些胆怯了，"多会儿回来？！"

"不回来了。"秋生头也不回地说。

"什么？！回来！你小子是不是吃大粪了？！回来！"秋生爹跟着儿子出了屋，"你咋的？就算不要老婆孩子，爹你也不管了？！"

秋生站住了，头也不回地说："凭什么要我管你？"

"哎，这话说的？我是你老子！我养大了你！你娘死得那么早，我把你姐弟俩拉扯大容易吗？！你浑了你！"

秋生回头看了他爹一眼说："要是创造出咱们祖宗的祖宗的祖宗的人都让你一脚踢出了家门，我不养你的老也算不得什么大罪过。"说完自顾自地走了，留下他爹和媳妇在门边目瞪口呆地站着。

秋生从那座古老的石拱桥上过了河，向上帝们的帐篷走去。他看到，在撒满金色秋叶的草地上，几个上帝正支着一口锅煮着什么，他们的大白胡子和锅里冒出的蒸汽都散映着正午的阳光，很像一幅上古神话中的画面。秋生找到自家的上帝，憨憨地说："上帝老爷子，咱们走吧。"

"我不回那个家了。"上帝摆摆手说。

"我也不回了，咱们先去镇里我姐家住一阵儿，然后我去城里打工，咱们租房子住，我会养活您一辈子的。"

"你是个好孩子啊——"上帝拍拍秋生的肩膀说，"可我们要走了。"他指指自己手腕上的表，秋生这才发现，他和所有上帝的手表都发出闪动的红光。

"走？去哪儿？"

"回飞船上去。"上帝指了指天空，秋生抬头一看，发现空中已经有了两艘外星飞船，反射着银色的阳光，在蓝天上格外醒目。其中一艘已经呈现出很大的轮廓和清晰的形状，另一艘则处在后面深空的远处，看上去小了很多。最令秋生震惊的是，从第一艘飞船上垂下了一根纤细的蛛丝，从太空直垂到远方的地面！随着蛛丝缓慢的摆动，耀眼的阳光在蛛丝不同的区段上窜动，看上去像蓝色晴空中细长的闪电。

"太空电梯，现在在各个大陆上已经建起了100多条，我们要乘它离开地球回到飞船上去。"上帝解释说。秋生后来知道，飞船在同步轨道上放下电梯的同时，向着太空的另一侧也要有相同的质量来平衡，后面那艘深空中的飞船就是作为平衡配重的。当秋生的眼睛适应了天空的光亮后，发现更远的深空中布满了银色的星星，那些星星分布均匀整齐，构成一个巨大的矩阵。秋生知道，那是正在从小行星带飞向地球的其余2万多艘上帝文明的飞船。

七

2万艘外星飞船又布满了地球的天空，在以后的2个月中，有大量的太空舱沿着垂向各大陆的太空电梯上上下下，接走在地球上生活了1年多的20亿上帝。那些太空舱都是银色的球体，远远看去，像是一串串挂在蛛丝导轨上的晶莹露珠。

西岑村的上帝走的这天，全村的人都去送，所有的人对上帝都亲亲热热，让人想起1年前上帝来的那天，好像上帝前面受到的那些嫌弃和虐待与他们毫无关系似的。

村口停着两辆大轿车，就是1年前送上帝来的那两辆，这100多个上帝要被送到最近的太空电梯下垂点搭乘太空舱，从这里能看到的那根蛛丝，与陆地的接点其实有几百千米之遥。

秋生一家都去送本家的上帝，一路上大家默默无语，快到村口时，上帝停下了，拄着拐杖对一家人鞠躬："就送到这儿吧，谢谢你们这 1 年的收留和照顾，真的谢谢，不管飞到宇宙的哪个角落，我都会记住这个家的。"说着，他把那块球形的大手表摘下来，放到兵兵手里，"送给你啦。"

"那……你以后怎么同其他上帝通信呢？"兵兵问。

"都在飞船上，用不着这东西了。"上帝笑着说。

"上帝老爷子啊，"秋生爹一脸伤感地说，"你们那些船可都是破船了，住不了多久了，你们坐着它们能去哪儿呢？"

上帝抚着胡子平静地说："飞到哪儿算哪儿吧，太空无边无际，哪儿还不埋人呢？"

玉莲突然哭出声儿来："上帝老爷子啊，我这人……也太不厚道了，把过日子攒起来的怨气全撒到您身上，真像秋生说的，一点良心都没了……"她把一个竹篮子递到上帝手中，"我一早煮了些鸡蛋，您拿着路上吃吧。"

上帝接过了篮子，说道："谢谢！"他拿出一个鸡蛋剥开壳津津有味地吃了起来，白胡子上沾了星星点点的蛋黄，同时口齿不清地说着，"其实，我们到地球来，并不只是为了活下去，都是活了两三千岁的人了，死有什么可在意的？我们只是想和你们在一起，我们喜欢和珍惜你们对生活的热情、你们的创造力和想象力，这些都是上帝文明早已失去的，我们从你们身上看到了上帝文明的童年。但真没想到给你们带来了这么多的麻烦，实在对不起了。"

"你留下来吧爷爷，我不会再不懂事了！"兵兵流着眼泪说。

上帝缓缓摇摇头："我们走，并不是因为你们待我们怎么样，能收留我们，已经很满足了。但有一件事让我们没法待下去，那就是，上帝在你们的眼中已经变成了一群老可怜虫，你们可怜我们了，你们竟然可怜我们了。"

上帝扔下手中的蛋壳，抬起白发苍苍的头仰望长空，仿佛透过那湛蓝的大气层看到了灿烂的星海。

"上帝文明怎么会让人可怜呢？你们根本不知道这是一个怎样伟大的文明，不知道它在宇宙中创造了多少壮丽的史诗、多少雄伟的奇迹！记得那是银河 1857 纪元吧，天文学家们发现，有大批的恒星加速了向银河系中心的运动，这恒星的洪水一旦被银心的超级黑洞吞没，产生的辐射将毁灭银河系中的一切生命。于是，我们那些伟大的祖先，在银心黑洞周围沿银河系平面建起了一个直径 1 万光年的星云屏蔽环，使银河系中的生命和文明延续下去。那是一项多么宏伟的工程啊，整整延续了 1400 万年才完成……紧接着，仙女座和大麦哲伦两个星系的文明对银河系发动了强大的联合入侵，上帝文明的星际舰队跨越几十万光年，在仙女座与银河系的引力平衡点迎击入侵者。当战争进入白热化的时候，双方数量巨大的舰队在缠斗中混为一体，形成了一个直径有太阳系大小的旋涡星云。在战争的最后阶段，上帝文明毅然将剩余的所有战舰和巨量的非战斗飞船投入了这个高速自旋的星云，使得星云总质量急剧增加，引力大于了离心力，这个由星际战舰和飞船构成的星云居然在自身引力下坍缩，生成了一颗恒星！由于这颗恒星中的重元素比例很高，在生成后立刻变成了一颗疯狂爆发的超新星，照亮了仙女座和银河系之间漆黑的宇宙深渊！我们伟大的先祖就是以这样的气概和牺牲消灭了入侵者，把银河系变成一个和平的生命乐园……现代文明是老了，但不是我们的错，无论怎样努力避免，一个文明总是要老的。谁都有老的时候，你们也一样。我们真的不需要你们可怜。"

"与你们相比，人类真算不得什么。"秋生敬畏地说。

"也不能这么说，地球文明还是个幼儿。我们盼着你们快快长大，盼望地球文明能够继承它的创造者的光荣。"上帝把拐杖扔下，两手一高一低地放在秋生和兵兵肩上，"说到这里，我最后有些话要嘱咐你们。"

"我们不一定听得懂，但您说吧。"秋生郑重地点点头说。

"首先，一定要飞出去！"上帝对着长空伸开双臂，他身上宽大的白袍随着秋风飘舞，像一面风帆。

"飞？飞到哪儿？"秋生爹迷惑地问。

"先飞向太阳系的其他行星，再飞向其他的恒星，不要问为什么，只是尽最大的力量向外飞，飞得越远越好！这样要花很多钱死很多人，但一定要飞出去。任何文明，待在它诞生的世界不动就等于自杀！到宇宙中去寻找新的世界新的家，把你们的后代像春雨般撒遍银河系！"

"我们记住了。"秋生点点头，虽然他和自己的父亲、儿子、媳妇一样，都不能真正理解上帝的话。

"那就好。"上帝欣慰地长出一口气，"下面，我要告诉你们一个秘密，一个对你们来说是天大的秘密——"他用蓝幽幽的眼睛依次盯着秋生家的每个人看，那目光如飕飕寒风，让他们心里发毛，"你们，有兄弟。"

秋生一家迷惑不解地看着上帝，是秋生首先悟出了上帝这话的含意："您是说，你们还创造了其他的地球？"

上帝缓缓地点点头："是的，还创造了其他的地球，也就是其他的人类文明。目前除了你们，这样的文明还存在着三个，距你们都不远，都在 200 光年的范围内，你们是地球四号，是年龄最小的一个。"

　　"你们去过那里吗？"兵兵问。

　　上帝又点点头："去过，在来你们的地球之前，我们先去了那三个地球，想让他们收留我们。地球一号还算好，在骗走了我们的科技资料后，只是把我们赶了出来；地球二号，扣下了我们中的 100 万人当人质，让我们用飞船交换，我们付出了 1000 艘飞船，他们得到飞船后发现不会操作，就让那些人质教他们，发现人质也不会，就将他们全杀了；地球三号也扣下了我们的 300 万人质，让我们用几艘飞船分别撞击地球一号和二号，因为他们之间处于一种旷日持久的战争状态中，其实只需一艘反物质动力飞船的撞击就足以完全毁灭一个地球上的全部生命，我们拒绝了，他们也杀了那些人质……"

　　"这些不肖子孙，你们应该收拾他们几下子！"秋生爹愤怒地说。

　　上帝摇摇头："我们是不会攻击自己创造的文明的。你们是这四个兄弟中最懂事的，所以我才对你们说了上面那些话。你们那三个哥哥极具侵略性，他们不知爱和道德为何物，其凶残和嗜杀是你们根本无法想象的。其实我们最初创造了六个地球，另外两个分别与地球一号和三号在同一个行星系，都被他们的兄弟毁灭了。这三个地球之所以还没有互相毁灭，只是因为他们分属不同的恒星，距离较远。他们三个都已经得知了地球四号的存在，并有太阳系的准确坐标，所以，你们必须先去消灭他们，免得他们来消灭你们。"

"这太吓人了！"玉莲说。

"暂时还没那么可怕，因为这三个哥哥虽然文明进化程度都比你们先进，但仍处于低速宇航阶段，他们最高的航行速度不超过光速的1/10，航行距离也超不出30光年。这是一场生死赛跑，看你们中谁最先贴近光速航行，这是突破时空禁锢的唯一方式，谁能够首先达到这个技术水平，谁才能生存下来，其他稍慢一步的都必死无疑。这就是宇宙中的生存竞争，孩子们，时间不多了，要抓紧！"

"这些事情，地球上那些最有学问、最有权力的人都知道了吧？"秋生爹战战兢兢地问。

"当然知道，但不要只依赖他们，一个文明的生存要靠其每个个体的共同努力，当然也包括你们这些普通人。"

"听到了吧兵兵，要好好学习！"秋生对儿子说。

"当你们以近光速飞向宇宙，解除了那三个哥哥的威胁，还要抓紧办一件重要的事：找到几颗比较适合生命生存的行星，把地球上的一些低等生物，如细菌、海藻之类的，播撒到那些行星上，让它们自行进化。"

秋生正要提问，却见上帝弯腰拾起了地上的拐杖，于是一家人同他一起向大轿车走去，其他的上帝已在车上了。

"哦，秋生啊，"上帝想起了什么，又站住了，"走的时候没经你同意就拿了你几本书，"他打开小包袱让秋生看，"你上中学时的数理化课本。"

"啊，拿走好了，可您要这个干什么？"

上帝系起包袱说："学习呗，从解一元二次方程学起，以后太

164

空中的漫漫长夜里，总得找些办法打发时间。谁知道呢，也许有那么一天，我真的能试着修好我们那艘飞船的反物质发动机，让它重新接近光速飞行呢！"

"对了，那样你们又能跨越时间了，就可以找个星球再创造一个文明给你们养老了！"秋生兴奋地说。

上帝连连摇头："不不不，我们对养老已经不感兴趣了，该死去的就让它死去吧。我这么做，只是为了自己最后一个心愿，"他从怀里掏出了那台小电视机，屏幕上，他那 2000 年前的情人还在慢慢说着那三个字中的最后一个，"我只想再见到她。"

"这念头儿是好，但也就是想想罢了。"秋生爹摇摇头说，"你想啊，她已经飞出去 2000 多年了，以光速飞的，谁知道飞到什么地方去了，你就是修好了船，也追不上她了。你不是说过，没什么能比光走得更快吗？"

上帝用拐杖指指天空："这个宇宙，只要你耐心等待，什么愿望都有可能实现，虽然这种可能性十分渺茫，但总是存在的。我对你们说过，宇宙诞生于一场大爆炸，现在，引力使它的膨胀速度慢了下来，然后宇宙的膨胀会停下来，转为坍缩。如果我们的飞船真能再次接近光速，我就让它无限逼近光速飞行，这样就能跨越无限的时间，直接到达宇宙的末日时刻。那时，宇宙已经坍缩得很小很小，会比兵兵的皮球还小，会成为一个点。那时，宇宙中的一切都在一起了，我和她，自然也在一起了。"一滴泪滑出上帝的眼眶，滚到胡子上，在上午的阳光中晶莹闪烁着，"宇宙啊，就是《梁祝》最后的坟墓，我和她，就是墓中飞出的两只蝶啊——"

八

一个星期后，最后一艘外星飞船从地球的视野中消失，上帝走了。

西岑村恢复了以前的宁静。夜里，秋生一家坐在小院中看着满天的星星。已是深秋，田野里的虫鸣已经消失了，微风吹动着脚下的落叶，感觉有些寒意了。

"他们在那么高的地方飞，多大的风啊，多冷啊——"玉莲喃喃自语道。

秋生说："哪有什么风啊，那是太空，连空气都没有呢！冷倒是真的，冷到了头儿，书上叫绝对零度。唉，那黑漆漆的一片，不见底也没有边，那是噩梦都梦不见的地方啊！"

玉莲的眼泪又出来了，但她还是找话说加以掩饰："上帝最后说的那两件事儿，地球的三个哥哥我倒是听明白了，可他后面又说，要我们向别的星球撒细菌什么的，我想到现在也不明白。"

"我明白了。"秋生爹说。在这灿烂的星空下，他愚拙了一辈子的脑袋终于开了一次窍，他仰望着群星，头顶着它们过了一辈子，他发现自己今天才真切地看到它们的样子，一种从未有过的感觉充满了他的血液，使他觉得自己仿佛与什么更大的东西接触了一下，虽远未融为一体，但这感觉还是令他震惊不已。

他对着星海长叹一声，说：

"人啊，该考虑养老的事了。"

赡养人类 FOR THE BENEFIT OF MANKIND

业务就是业务，与别的无关。这是滑膛所遵循的铁的原则，但这一次他遇到了一些困惑。

　　首先客户的委托方式不对，他要与自己面谈，在这个行业中，这可是件很稀奇的事。3 年前，滑膛听教官不止一次地说过，他们与客户的关系，应该是前额与后脑勺的关系，永世不得见面，这当然是为了双方的利益考虑。见面的地点更令滑膛吃惊，是在这座大城市中最豪华的五星级酒店中最豪华的总统大厅里，那可是世界上最不适合委托这种业务的地方。据对方透露，这次委托加工的工件有三个，这倒无所谓，再多些他也不在乎。

　　服务生拉开了总统大厅包金的大门，滑膛在走进去前，不为人察觉地把手向夹克里探了一下，轻轻拉开了左腋下枪套的暗扣。其实这没有必要，没人会在这种地方对他干太意外的事。

　　大厅金碧辉煌，仿佛是与外面现实毫无关系的另一个世界，巨型水晶吊灯就是这个世界的太阳，猩红色的地毯就是这个世界的草原。这里初看很空旷，但滑膛还是很快发现了人，他们围在大厅一角的两个落地窗前，撩开厚重的窗帘向外面的天空看，滑膛扫了一眼，立刻数出竟有 13 个人。客户是他们而不是他，也出乎滑膛的预料。教官说过，客户与他们还像情人关系——尽管可能有多个，但每次只能与他们中的一人接触。

滑膛知道他们在看什么，哥哥飞船又移到南半球上空了，现在可以清晰地看到。上帝文明离开地球已经 3 年了，那次来自宇宙的大规模造访，使人类对外星文明的心理承受能力增强了许多，况且，上帝文明有铺天盖地的 2 万多艘飞船，而这次到来的哥哥飞船只有一艘。它的形状也没有上帝文明的飞船那么奇特，只是一个两头圆的柱体，像是宇宙中的一粒感冒胶囊。

看到滑膛进来，那 13 个人都离开窗子，回到了大厅中央的大圆桌旁。滑膛认出了他们中的大部分，立刻感觉这间华丽的大厅变得寒陋了。这些人中最引人注目的是朱汉扬，他的华软集团的"东方 3000"操作系统正在全球范围内取代老朽的 Windows。其他的人，也都在《福布斯》《财富》500 强排行的前 50 内。这些人每年的收益，可能相当于一个中等国家的 GDP，滑膛处于一个小型版的全球财富论坛中。

这些人与齿哥是绝对不一样的，滑膛暗想，齿哥是一夜的富豪，他们则是三代修成的贵族。虽然真正的时间远没有那么长，但他们确实是贵族，财富在他们这里已转化成内敛的高贵。就像朱汉扬手上的那枚钻戒，纤细精致，在他修长的手指上若隐若现，只是偶尔闪一下温润的柔光，但它的价值，也许能买几十个齿哥手指上那颗核桃大小金光四射的玩意儿。

但现在，这 13 名高贵的财富精英聚在这里，却是要雇职业杀手杀人，而且要杀 3 个人。据首次联系的人说，这还只是第一批。

其实滑膛并没有去注意那枚钻戒，他看的是朱汉扬手上的那 3 张照片，那显然就是委托加工的工件了。朱汉扬起身越过圆桌，将 3 张照片推到他面前。扫了一眼后，滑膛又有微微的挫折感。教官曾说过，对于自己开展业务的地区，要预先熟悉那些有可能被委托加工的工件，至少在这个大城市，滑膛做到了。但照片上这 3 个人，滑膛是绝对不认识的。这 3 张照片显然是用长焦距镜头拍的，上面的脸孔蓬头垢面，与眼前这群高贵的人简直不是一个物种。细看后才发现，其中有一个是女性，还很年轻，与其他两人相比，她要整洁些，头发虽然落着尘土，但细心地梳过。她的眼神很特别，滑膛很注意人的眼神，他这个职业的人都这样，他平时看到的眼神有两类：充满欲望焦虑的和麻木的，但这双眼睛充满少见的平静。滑膛的心微微动了一下，但转瞬即逝，像一缕随风飘散的轻雾。

"这桩业务，是社会财富液化委员会委托给你的，这里是委员会的全体常委，我是委员会的主席。"朱汉扬说。

社会财富液化委员会？好奇怪的名字，滑膛只明白了，这是一个由顶级富豪构成的组织，并没有去思考它名称的含义，他知道这是属于那类如果没有提示不可能想象出其真实含义的名称。

"他们的地址都在背面写着，不太固定，只是一个大概范围，你得去找，应该不难找到的。钱已经汇到你的账户上，先核实一下吧。"朱汉扬说，滑膛抬头看看他，发现他的眼神并不高贵，属于充满焦虑的那一类，但令他微微惊奇的是，其中的欲望已经无影无踪了。

滑膛拿出手机，查询了账户，数清了那串数字后面零的个数后，他冷冷地说："第一，没有这么多，按我的出价付就可以；第二，预付一半，完工后付清。"

"就这样吧。"朱汉扬不以为意地说。

滑膛按了一阵手机后说："已经把多余款项退回去了，您核实一下吧。先生，我们也有自己的职业准则。"

"其实现在做这种业务的很多，我们看重的就是您的这种敬业和荣誉感。"许雪萍说。这个女人的笑很动人，她是远源集团的总裁，远源是电力市场完全放开后诞生的亚洲最大的能源开发实体。

"这是第一批，请做得利索些。"海上石油巨头薛桐说。

"快冷却还是慢冷却？"滑膛问，同时加了一句，"需要的话我可以解释。"

"我们懂，这些无所谓，你看着做吧。"朱汉扬回答。

"验收方式？录像还是实物样本？"

"都不需要，你做完就行，我们自己验收。"

"我想就这些了吧？"

"是，您可以走了。"

滑膛走出酒店，看到高厦间狭窄的天空中，哥哥飞船正在缓缓移过。飞船的体积大了许多，运行的速度也更快了，显然降低了轨道高度。它光滑的表面涌现着绚丽的花纹，那花纹在不断地缓缓变化，看久了对人有一种催眠作用。其实飞船表面什么都没有，只是一层全反射镜面，人们看到的花纹，只是地球变形的映像。滑膛觉得它像一块钝银，很美。他喜欢银，不喜欢金，银很静、很冷。

3 年前，上帝文明在离去时告诉人类，他们共创造了六个地球，现在还有四个存在，其他三个兄弟都在距地球 200 光年的范围内。上帝敦促地球人类全力发展技术，必须先去消灭那三个兄弟，免得他们来消灭自己。但这信息来得晚了。

那三个遥远地球世界中的一个——地球一号，在上帝船队走后不久就来到了太阳系，他们的飞船泊入地球轨道。他们的文明历史比太阳系人类长两倍，所以这个地球上的人类应该叫他们哥哥。

滑膛拿出手机，又看了一下账户中的金额。齿哥，我现在的钱和你一样多了，但总还是觉得少什么。而你，总好像是认为自己已经得到了一切，所做的就是竭力避免它们失去……滑膛摇摇头，想把头脑中的影子甩掉，这时候想起齿哥，不吉利。

齿哥得名，源自他从不离身的一把锯，那锯薄而柔软，但极其锋利，锯柄是坚硬的海柳做的，有着美丽的浮世绘风格的花纹。他总是将锯像腰带似的绕在腰上，没事儿时取下来，拿一把提琴弓在锯背上划动，借助于锯身不同宽度产生的音差，加上将锯身适当地弯曲，居然能奏出音乐来。乐声飘忽不定，音色忧郁而阴森，像一个幽灵在呜咽。这把利锯的其他用途滑膛当然听说过，但只有一次看到过齿哥以第二种方式使用它。那是在一间旧仓库中的一场豪赌中，一个叫半头砖的二老大输了个精光，连他父母的房子都输掉了，眼红得冒血，要把自己的两条胳膊押上翻本。齿哥手中玩着骰子对他微笑了一下，说："胳膊不能押的，来日方长啊，没了手，以后咱们兄弟不就没法玩了吗？押腿吧。"
于是半头砖就把两条腿押上了。他再次输光后，齿哥当场就用那
把锯把他的两条小腿齐膝锯了下来。滑膛清楚地记得利锯划过肌
腱和骨骼时的声音，当时齿哥一脚踩着半头砖的脖子，所以他的
惨叫声发不出来，宽阔阴冷的大仓库中只回荡着锯拉过骨肉的声
音，像欢快的歌声，在锯到膝盖的不同位置时呈现出丰富的音色
层次，雪白雪白的骨末撒在鲜红的血泊上，形成的构图呈现出一
种妖艳的美。滑膛当时被这种美震撼了，他身上的每一个细胞都
加入了锯和血肉的歌声中，这才叫生活！那天是他 18 岁生日，
绝好的成年礼。完事后，齿哥把心爱的锯擦了擦缠回腰间，指着
已被抬走的半头砖和两条断腿留下的血迹说："告诉砖儿，后半
辈子我养活他。"

　　滑膛虽年轻，也是自幼随齿哥打天下的元老之一，见血的差
事每月都有。当齿哥终于在血腥的社会阴沟里完成了原始积累，
由黑道转向白道时，一直追随着他的人都被封了副董事长、副总
裁之类的，唯有滑膛只落得给齿哥当保镖。但知情的人都明白，
这种信任非同小可。齿哥是个非常小心的人，这可能是源于他干
爹的命运。齿哥的干爹也是非常小心的，用齿哥的话说恨不得把
自己用一块铁包起来。许多年的平安无事后，那次干爹乘飞机，
带了两个最可靠的保镖，在一排座位上，他坐在两个保镖中间。
在珠海降落后，空姐发现这排座上的三个人没有起身，坐在那里
若有所思的样子，接着发现他们的血已淌过了 10 多排座位。有
许多根极细的长钢针从后排座位透过靠背穿过来，两个保镖每人
的心脏都穿过了 3 根，至于干爹，足足被 14 根钢针穿透，像一
个被精心钉牢的蝴蝶标本。这 14 肯定是有说头的，也许暗示着

他不合规则吞下的 1400 万元，也许是复仇者 14 年的等待……与干爹一样，齿哥出道的征途，使得整个社会对于他来说除了暗刃的森林就是陷阱的沼泽，他实际上是将自己的命交到了滑膛手上。

但很快，滑膛的地位就受到了老克的威胁。老克是俄罗斯人。那时，在富人们中有一个时髦的做法：聘请前克格勃人员做保镖，有这样一位保镖，与拥有一个影视明星情人一样值得炫耀。齿哥周围的人叫不惯那个拗口的俄罗斯名，就叫这人克格勃，时间一长就叫老克了。其实老克与克格勃没什么关系，真正的前克格勃机构中，大部分人不过是坐办公室的文职人员，即使是那些处于秘密战最前沿的，对安全保卫也都是外行。老克是那时中央警卫局的保卫人员，是这个领域货真价实的精英。而齿哥以相当于公司副董事长的高薪聘请他，完全不是为了炫耀，真的是出于对自身安全的考虑。老克一出现，立刻显出了他与普通保镖的不同。这之前那些富豪的保镖，在饭桌上比他们的雇主还能吃能喝，还喜欢在主人谈生意时乱插嘴，真正出现危险情况时，他们要么像街头打群架那样胡来，要么溜得比主人还快。而老克，不论是在宴席还是谈判时，都静静地站在齿哥身后，他那魁梧的身躯像一堵厚实坚稳的墙，随时准备挡开一切威胁。老克并没有机会遇到他的保护对象受到威胁的危险情况，但他的敬业和专业使人们都相信，一旦那种情况出现时，他将是绝对称职的。虽然与别的保镖相比，滑膛更敬业一些，也没有那些坏毛病，但他从老克的身上看到了自己与他的差距。过了好长时间他才知道，老克不分昼夜地戴着墨镜，并不是扮酷，而是为了掩藏自己的视线。

虽然老克的汉语学得很快，但他和包括自己雇主在内的周围人都没什么交往，直到有一天，他突然把滑膛请到自己简朴的房间里，给他和自己倒上一杯伏特加后，用生硬的汉语说："我，想教你说话。"

"说话？"

"说外国话。"

于是滑膛就跟老克学外国话，几天后他才知道老克教自己的不是俄语而是英语。滑膛也学得很快，当他们能用英语和汉语交流后，有一天老克对滑膛说："你和别人不一样。"

"这我也感觉到了。"滑膛点点头。

"30年的职业经验，使我能够从人群中准确地识别出具有那种潜质的人，这种人很稀少，但你就是，第一眼看到你时我就打了个寒战。冷血一下并不难，但冷下去的血再温起来就很难了，你会成为那一行的精英，可别埋没了自己。"

"我能做什么呢？"

"先去留学。"

齿哥听到老克的建议后，倒是满口答应，并许诺费用的事他完全负责。其实有了老克后，他一直想摆脱滑膛，但公司中又没有空位子了。

于是，在一个冬夜，一架喷气客机载着这个自幼失去父母、从黑社会最低层中成长起来的孩子，飞向遥远的陌生国度。

开着一辆很旧的桑塔纳，滑膛按照片上的地址去踩点。他首先去的是春花广场，没费多少劲儿就找到了照片上的人，那个流浪汉正在垃圾桶中翻找着，然后提着一个鼓鼓的垃圾袋走到一张长椅处。他的收获颇丰，一盒几乎没怎么动的盒饭，还是菜饭分放的那种大盒，一根只咬了一口的火腿肠，几块基本完好的面包，还有大半瓶可乐。滑膛本以为流浪汉会用手抓着盒饭吃，但看到他从这初夏仍穿着的脏大衣口袋中掏出了一个小铝勺。他慢慢地吃完晚餐，把剩下的东西又扔回垃圾桶中。滑膛四下看看，广场四周华灯初上，他很熟悉这里，但现在觉得有些异样。很快，他弄明白了这个流浪汉轻易填饱肚子的原因。这里原是城市流浪者聚集的地方，但现在他们都不见了，只剩下他的这个目标。他们去哪里了？都被委托"加工"了吗？

滑膛接着找到了第二张照片上的地址。在城市边缘一座交通桥的桥孔下，有一个用废瓦楞和纸箱搭起来的窝棚，里面透出昏黄的灯光。滑膛将窝棚的破门小心地推开一道缝，探进头去，出乎意料，他竟进入了一个色彩斑斓的世界。原来窝棚里挂满了大小不一的油画，形成了另一层墙壁。顺着一团烟雾，滑膛看到了那个流浪画家，他像一头冬眠的熊一般躺在一个破画架下，头发很长，穿着一件涂满油彩像长袍般肥大的破T恤衫，抽着5毛一盒的玉蝶烟。他的眼睛在自己的作品间游移，目光充满了惊奇和迷惘，仿佛他才是第一次到这里来的人。他的大部分时光大概都是在这种对自己作品的自恋中度过的。这种穷困潦倒的画家在20世纪90年代曾有过很多，但现在不多见了。

"没关系，进来吧。"画家说，眼睛仍扫视着那些画，没朝门口看一眼。听他的口气，就像这里是一座帝王宫殿似的。在滑膛走进来之后，他又问，"喜欢我的画吗？"

滑膛四下看了看，发现大部分的画只是一堆零乱的色彩，就是随意将油彩泼到画布上都比它们显得有理性。但有几幅画面却很写实，滑膛的目光很快被其中的一幅吸引了：占满整幅画面的是一片干裂的黄土地，从裂缝间伸出几株干枯的植物，仿佛已经枯死了几个世纪。而在这个世界上，水也似乎从来就没有存在过。在这干旱的土地上，放着一个骷髅头，它也干得发白，表面布满裂纹，但从它的口洞和一个眼窝中居然长出了两株活生生的绿色植物，它们青翠欲滴，与周围的酷旱和死亡形成鲜明对比，其中一株植物的顶部还开着一朵娇艳的小花。这个骷髅头的另一个眼窝中，有一只活着的眼睛，清澈的眸子瞪着天空，目光就像画家的眼睛一样，充满惊奇和迷惘。

"我喜欢这幅。"滑膛指指那幅画说。

"这是《贫瘠》系列之二，你买吗？"

"多少钱？"

"看着给吧。"

滑膛掏出皮夹，将里面所有的百元钞票都取了出来，递给画家，但后者只从中抽了两张。

"只值这么多，画是你的了。"

滑膛发动了车子，然后拿起第三张照片看上面的地址，旋即将车熄了火，因为这个地方就在桥旁边，是这座城市最大的一个垃圾场。滑膛取出望远镜，透过挡风玻璃从垃圾场上那一群拾荒者中寻找着目标。

这座大都市中靠拾垃圾为生的拾荒者有 30 万人，已形成了一个阶层，而他们内部也有明确的等级。最高等级的拾荒者能够进入高档别墅区，在那里如艺术雕塑般精致的垃圾桶中，每天都能拾到只穿用过一次的新衬衣、袜子和床单，这些东西在这里是一次性用品；垃圾桶中还常常出现只有轻微损坏的高档皮鞋和腰带，以及只抽了 1/3 的哈瓦纳雪茄和只吃了一角的高级巧克力……但进入这里捡垃圾要重金贿赂社区保安，所以能来的只是少数人，他们是拾荒者中的贵族。拾荒者的中间阶层都集中在城市中众多的垃圾中转站里，那是城市垃圾的第一个集中地。在那里，垃圾中最值钱的部分：废旧电器、金属、完整的纸制品、废弃的医疗器械、被丢弃的过期药品等，都被捡拾得差不多了。那里也不是随便就能进去的，每个垃圾中转站都是某个垃圾把头控制的地盘，其他拾荒者擅自进入，轻者被暴打一顿赶走，重者可能丢了命。经过中转站被送往城市外面的大型堆放和填埋场的垃圾已经没有多少"营养"了，但靠它生存的人最多，他们是拾荒者中的最低层，就是滑膛现在看到的这些人。留给这些生活底层拾荒者的，都是不值钱又回收困难的碎塑料、碎纸等，再就是垃圾中的腐烂食品，可以以每千克 1 分钱的价格卖给附近农民当猪饲料。在不远处，大都市如一块璀璨的巨大宝石闪烁着，它的光芒传到这里，给恶臭的垃圾山镀上了一层变幻的光晕。其实，就是从拾到的东西中，拾荒者们也能体会到那不远处大都市的奢华：在他们收集到的腐烂食品中，常常能依稀认出只吃了 4 条腿的烤乳猪、只动了一筷子的石斑鱼、完整的鸡……最近整只乌骨鸡多了起来，这源自一道刚时兴的名叫乌鸡白玉的菜。这道菜是把豆腐放进乌骨鸡的肚子里炖出来的，真正的菜就是那几片豆腐，鸡虽然美味，但只是包装，如果不知道吃了，就如同吃粽子连芦苇叶一起吃一样，会成为有品位的食客的笑柄……

这时，当天最后一趟运垃圾的环卫车来了，当自卸车厢倾斜着升起时，一群拾荒者迎着山崩似的垃圾冲上来，很快在飞扬的尘土中与垃圾山融为一体。这些人似乎完成了新的进化，垃圾山的恶臭、毒菌和灰尘似乎对他们都不产生影响。当然，这是只看到他们如何生存而没见到他们如何死亡的普通人产生的印象，正像普通人平时见不到虫子和老鼠的尸体，因而也不关心它们如何死去一样。事实上，这个大垃圾场多次发现拾荒者的尸体，他们静悄悄地死在这里，然后被新的垃圾掩埋了。

在场边一盏泛光灯昏暗的灯光中，拾荒者们只是一群灰尘中模糊的影子，但滑膛还是很快在他们中发现了自己要找的目标。这么快找到她，滑膛除了借助自己锐利的目光外，还有一个原因：与春花广场上的流浪者一样，今天垃圾场上的拾荒者人数明显减少了。这是为什么？

滑膛在望远镜中观察着目标，她初看上去与其他的拾荒者没有太大大区别，腰间束着一根绳子，手里拿着大编织袋和顶端装着耙勺的长杆，只是她看上去比别人瘦弱，挤不到前面去，只能在其他拾荒者的圈外捡拾着，她翻找的，已经是垃圾中的垃圾了。

滑膛放下望远镜，沉思片刻，轻轻摇摇头。世界上最离奇的事正在他的眼前发生：一个城市流浪者，一个穷得居无定所的画家，加上一个靠拾垃圾为生的女孩子，这三个世界上最贫穷、最弱势的人，在什么地方威胁到那些处于世界财富之巅的超级财阀呢？这种威胁甚至于迫使他们雇用杀手将其置于死地！

后座上放着那幅《贫瘠》系列之二，骷髅头上的那只眼睛在黑暗中凝视着滑膛，令他如芒在背。

垃圾场那边发出了一阵惊叫声，滑膛看到，车外的世界笼罩在一片蓝光中，蓝光来自东方地平线，那里，一轮蓝太阳正在快速升起，那是运行到南半球的哥哥飞船。飞船一般是不发光的，晚上，自身反射的阳光使它看上去像一轮小月亮，但有时它也会突然发出照亮整个世界的蓝光，这总是令人们陷入莫名的恐惧之中。这一次飞船发出的光比以往都亮，可能是轨道更低的缘故。蓝太阳从城市后面升起，使高楼群的影子一直拖到这里，像一群巨人的手臂，但随着飞船的快速上升，影子渐渐缩回去了。

在哥哥飞船的光芒中，垃圾场上那个拾荒女孩被看得更清楚了。滑膛再次举起望远镜，证实了自己刚才的观察，就是她，她蹲在那里，编织袋放在膝盖上，仰望的眼睛有一丝惊恐，但更多的还是他在照片上看到的平静。滑膛的心又动了一下，但像上次一样，这触动转瞬即逝，他知道这涟漪来自心灵深处的某个地方，为再次失去它而懊悔。

飞船很快划过长空，在西方地平线落下，在西天留下了一片诡异的蓝色晚霞，然后，一切又没入昏暗的夜色中，远方的城市之光又灿烂起来。

滑膛的思想又回到那个谜上来：世界最富有的 13 个人要杀死最穷的 3 个人，这不是一般的荒唐，这真是对他的想象力最大的挑战。但思路没走多远就猛地刹住，滑膛自责地拍了一下方向盘，他突然想到自己已经违反了这个行业的最高精神准则，校长的那句话浮现在他的脑海中，这是行业的座右铭：

瞄准谁，与枪无关。

到现在，滑膛也不知道他是在哪个国家留学的，更不知道那所学校的确切位置。他只知道飞机降落的第一站是莫斯科，那里有人接他，那人的英语没有一点儿俄罗斯口音，他被要求戴上一副不透明的墨镜，伪装成一个盲人，以后的旅程都是在黑暗中度过的。又坐了 3 个多小时的飞机，再坐一天的汽车，才到达学校，这时是否还在俄罗斯境内，滑膛真的说不准了。学校地处深山，围在高墙中，学生在毕业之前绝对不准外出。被允许摘下墨镜后，滑膛发现学校的建筑明显地分为两大类：一类是灰色的，外形毫无特点；另一类的色彩和形状都很奇特。他很快知道，后一类建筑实际上是一堆巨型积木，可以组合成各种形状，以模拟变化万千的射击环境。整所学校，基本上就是一个设施精良的大靶场。

开学典礼是全体学生唯一的一次集合，他们的人数刚过 400。校长一头银发，一副令人肃然起敬的古典学者风度，他讲了如下一番话：

"同学们，在以后的 4 年中，你们将学习一个我们永远不会讲出其名称的行业所需的专业知识和技能，这是人类最古老的行业之一，同样会有光辉的未来。从小处讲，它能够为做出最后选择的客户解决只有我们才能解决的问题；从大处讲，它能够改变历史。

"曾有不同的政治组织出高价委托我们训练游击队员，我们拒绝了，我们只培养独立的专业人员。是的，独立，除钱以外独立于一切。从今以后，你们要把自己当成一支枪，你们的责任，就是实现枪的功能，在这个过程中展现枪的美感，至于瞄准谁，与枪无关。A 持枪射击 B，B 又夺过同一支枪射击 A，枪应该对这每一次射击一视同仁，都以最高的质量完成操作，这是我们最基本的职业道德。"

在开学典礼上，滑膛还学会了几个最常用的术语：该行业的基本操作叫加工，操作的对象叫工件，死亡叫冷却。

学校分 L、M 和 S 三个专业，分别代表长、中、短三种距离。

L 专业是最神秘的，学费高昂，学生人数很少，且基本不和其他专业的人交往。滑膛的教官也劝他们离 L 专业的人远些："他们是行业中的贵族，是最有可能改变历史的人。"L 专业的知识博大精深，他们的学生使用的狙击步枪价值几十万美元，装配起来有 2 米多长。L 专业的加工距离均超过 1000 米，据说最长可达到 3000 米！1500 米以上的加工操作是一项复杂的工程，其中的前期工作之一就是沿射程按一定间距放置一系列的"风铃"，这是一种精巧的微型测风仪，它可将监测值以无线发回，显示在射手的眼镜显示器上，以便他（她）掌握射程不同阶段的风速和风向。

M 专业的加工距离在 10 米至 300 米之间，是最传统的专业，学生也最多，他们一般使用普通制式步枪。M 专业的应用面最广，但也是平淡和缺少传奇的。

滑膛学的是 S 专业，加工距离在 10 米以下，对武器要求最低，一般使用手枪，甚至还可能使用冷兵器。在三个专业中，S 专业无疑是最危险的，但也是最浪漫的。校长就是这个专业的大师，亲自为 S 专业授课，他首先开的课程竟然是——英语文学。

"你们首先要明白 S 专业的价值。"看着迷惑的学生们，校长庄重地说，"在 L 和 M 专业中，工件与加工者是不见面的，工件都是在不知情的状态下被加工并冷却的。这对他们当然是一种幸运，但对客户却不是，相当一部分客户，需要让工件在冷却之前得知他们被谁、为什么委托加工的，这就要由我们来告知工件。这时，我们已经不是自己，而是客户的化身，我们要把客户传达的最后信息向工件庄严完美地表达出来，让工件在冷却前受到最大的心灵震慑和煎熬，这就是Ｓ专业的浪漫和美感之所在。工件冷却前那恐惧绝望的眼神，将是我们在工作中最大的精神享受。但要做到这些，就需要我们具有相当的表达能力和文学素养。"

于是，滑膛学了一年的文学。他读《荷马史诗》，背莎士比亚，读了很多经典和现代名著。滑膛感觉这一年是自己留学生涯中最有收获的一年，因为后面学的那些东西他以前多少都知道一些，以后迟早也能学到，但深入地接触文学，这是他唯一的机会。通过文学，他重新发现了人，惊叹人原来是那么一种精致而复杂的东西，以前杀人，在他的感觉中只是打碎盛着红色液体的粗糙陶罐，现在惊喜地发现自己击碎的原来是精美绝伦的玉器，这更增加了他杀戮的快感。

接下来的课程是人体解剖学。与其他两个专业相比，Ｓ专业的另一大优势是可以控制被加工后的工件冷却到环境温度的时间，术语叫快冷却和慢冷却。很多客户是要求慢冷却的，冷却的过程还要录像，以供他们珍藏和欣赏。当然这需要很高的技术和丰富的经验，人体解剖学当然也是不可缺少的知识。

然后，真正的专业课才开始。

垃圾场上拾荒的人渐渐走散，只剩下包括目标在内的几个人。滑膛当即决定，今晚就把这个工件加工了。按行业惯例，一般在勘察时是不动手的，但也有例外，合适的加工时机稍纵即逝。

滑膛将车开离桥下，经过一阵颠簸后在垃圾场边的一条小路旁停下。滑膛观察到这是抬荒者离开垃圾场的必经之路，这里很黑，只能隐约看到荒草在夜风中摇曳的影子，是很合适的加工地点，他决定在这里等着工件。

滑膛抽出枪，轻轻放在驾驶台上。这是一支外形粗陋的左轮，7.6口径，可以用大黑星[1]的子弹，按其形状，他叫它大鼻子，是没有牌子的私造枪，他从西双版纳的一个黑市上花3000元买到的。枪虽然外形丑陋，但材料很好，且各个部件的结构都加工正确，最大的缺陷就是最难加工的膛线没有做出来，枪管内壁光光的。滑膛有机会得到名牌好枪，他初做保镖时，齿哥给他配了一支32发的短乌齐，后来，又将一支七七式当作生日礼物送给他，但那两支枪都被他压到箱底，从来没带过，他只喜欢大鼻子。现在，它在城市的光晕中冷冷地闪亮，将滑膛的思绪又带回了学校的岁月。

专业课开课的第一天，校长要求每个学生展示自己的武器。当滑膛将大鼻子放到那一排精致的高级手枪中时，很是不好意思。但校长却拿起它把玩着，由衷地赞赏道："好东西。"

"连膛线都没有，消声器也拧不上。"一名学生不屑地说。

"S专业对准确性和射程要求最低，膛线并不重要；消声器嘛，垫个小枕头不就行了？孩子，别让自己变得匠气了。在大师手中，这把枪能产生出你们这堆昂贵的玩意儿产生不了的艺术效果。"

校长说得对，由于没有膛线，大鼻子射出的子弹在飞行时会

1　黑社会对五四手枪的称呼。

翻跟头，在空气中发出正常子弹所没有的令人恐惧的尖啸，在射入工件后仍会持续旋转，像一柄锋利的旋转刀片，切碎沿途的一切。

"我们以后就叫你滑膛吧！"校长将枪递还给滑膛时说，"好好掌握它，孩子，看来你得学飞刀了。"滑膛立刻明白了校长的话：专业飞刀是握着刀尖出刀的，这样才能在旋转中产生更大的穿刺动量，这就需要在到达目标时刀尖正好旋转到前方。校长希望滑膛像掌握飞刀那样掌握大鼻子射出的子弹！这样，就可以使子弹在工件上的创口产生丰富多彩的变化。经过长达 2 年的苦练，消耗了近 3 万发子弹，滑膛竟真的练成了这种在学校最优秀的射击教官看来都不可能实现的技巧。

滑膛的留学经历与大鼻子是分不开的。在第四学年，他认识了同专业的一个名叫火的女生，她的名字也许来自那头红发。在这里当然不可能知道她的国籍，滑膛猜测她可能来自西欧某个国家。这里不多的女生，几乎个个都是天生的神枪手，但火的枪打得很糟，匕首根本不会用，真不知道她以前是靠什么吃饭的。但在一次勒杀课程中，她从自己手上那枚精致的戒指中抽出一根肉眼看不见的细线，熟练地套到用作教具的山羊脖子上，那根如利刃般的细线竟将山羊的头齐齐地切了下来。据火介绍，这是一段纳米丝，这种超高强度的材料未来可能被用来建造太空电梯。

火对滑膛没什么真爱可言，那种东西也不可能在这里出现。她同时还与外系一个名叫黑冰狼的北欧男生交往，并在滑膛和黑冰狼之间像斗蛐蛐似的反复挑逗，企图引起一场流血争斗，以便为枯燥的学习生活带来一点儿消遣。她很快成功了，两个男人决定以俄罗斯轮盘赌的形式决斗。这天深夜，全班同学将靶场上的巨型积木摆放成罗马斗兽场的形状，决斗就在斗兽场中央进行，使用的武器是大鼻子。火做裁判，她优雅地将一颗子弹塞进大鼻子的空弹仓，然后握住枪管，将弹仓在她那如常春藤般的玉臂上来回滚动了十几次，然后，两个男人谦让了一番，火微笑着将大鼻子递给滑膛。滑膛缓缓举起枪，当冰凉的枪口吻到太阳穴时，一种前所未有的空虚和孤独向他袭来，他感到无形的寒风吹透了世界万物，漆黑的宇宙中只有自己的心是热的。一横心，他连扣了 5 下扳机，击锤点了 5 下头，弹仓转动了 5 下，枪没响。"咔咔咔咔咔"，这 5 声清脆的金属声敲响了黑冰狼的丧钟。全班同学欢呼起来，火更是快活得流出了眼泪，对着滑膛高呼她是他的了。这中间笑得最轻松的是黑冰狼，他对滑膛点点头，由衷地说："东方人，这是自柯尔特[1]以来最精彩的赌局了。"然后转向火，"没关系亲爱的，人生于我，一场豪赌而已。"说完他抓起大鼻子对准自己的太阳穴，一声有力的闷响，血花和碎骨片溅得很潇洒。

之后不久滑膛就毕业了，他又戴上了那副来时戴的墨镜离开了这所没有名称的学校，回到了他长大的地方。他再也没有听到过学校的一丝消息，仿佛它从来就没有存在过似的。

回到外部世界后，滑膛才听说世界上发生了一件大事：上帝文明来了，要接受他们培植的人类的赡养，但在地球的生活并不如意，他们只待了 1 年多时间就离去了，那 2 万多艘飞船已经消失在茫茫宇宙中。

回来后刚下飞机，滑膛就接到了一桩加工业务。

1　左轮手枪的发明者。

齿哥热情地欢迎滑膛归来，摆上了豪华的接风宴，滑膛要求和齿哥单独待在宴席上，他说自己有好多心里话要说。其他人离开后，滑膛对齿哥说：

"我是在您身边长大的，从内心里，我一直没把您当大哥，而是当成亲生父亲。您说，我应当去干所学的这个专业吗？就一句话，我听您的。"

齿哥亲切地抚着滑膛的肩膀说："只要你喜欢，就干嘛，我看得出来你是喜欢的，别管白道黑道，都是道儿嘛，有出息的人，哪条道上都能出息。"

"好，我听您的。"

滑膛说完，抽出手枪对着齿哥的肚子就是一枪，飞旋的子弹以恰到好处的角度划开一道横贯齿哥腹部的大口子，然后穿进地板中。齿哥透过烟雾看着滑膛，眼中的震惊只是一掠而过，随之而来的是恍然大悟后的麻木，他对着滑膛笑了一下，点点头。

"已经出息了，小子。"齿哥吐着血沫说完，软软地倒在地上。

滑膛接的这桩业务是1小时慢冷却，但不录像，客户信得过他。滑膛倒上一杯酒，冷静地看着地上血泊中的齿哥，后者慢慢地整理着自己流出的肠子，像码麻将那样，然后塞回肚子里，滑溜溜的肠子很快又流出来，齿哥就再整理好将其塞回去……当这工作进行到第12遍时，他咽了气，这时距枪响正好1小时。

滑膛说把齿哥当成亲生父亲是真心话。在他5岁时的一个雨天，输红了眼的父亲逼着母亲把家里全部的存折都拿出来，母亲不从，便被父亲殴打致死，滑膛因阻拦也被打断鼻梁骨和一条胳膊，随后父亲便消失在雨中。后来滑膛多方查找也没有消息，如果找到，他也会让其享受一次慢冷却的。

事后，滑膛听说老克将自己的全部薪金都退给了齿哥的家人，返回了俄罗斯。他走前说：送滑膛去留学那天，他就知道齿哥会死在他手里，齿哥的一生是从刀尖上走过来的，却不懂得一个纯正的杀手是什么样的人。

垃圾场上的拾荒者一个接一个离开了，只剩下目标一人还在那里埋头刨找着。她力气小，垃圾来时抢不到好位置，只能借助更长时间的劳作来弥补了。这样，滑膛就没有必要等在这里了，于是他拿起大鼻子塞到夹克口袋中，走下了车，径直朝垃圾中的目标走去。他脚下的垃圾软软的，还有一股温热，他仿佛踏在一只巨兽的身上。当距目标四五米时，滑膛抽出了握枪的手……

这时，一阵蓝光从东方射过来，哥哥飞船已绕地球一周，又转到了南半球，仍发着光。这突然升起的蓝太阳同时吸引了两人的目光，他们都盯着蓝太阳看了一会儿，然后互相看了对方一眼。当两人的目光相遇时，滑膛身上发生了一名职业杀手绝对不会发生的事：手中的枪差点滑落了。震撼令他一时感觉不到手中枪的存在，他几乎失声叫出：

"果儿——"

但滑膛知道她不是果儿，14 年前，果儿就在他面前痛苦地死去了。但果儿在他心中一直活着，一直在成长，他常在梦中见到已经长成大姑娘的果儿，就是眼前她这样儿。

齿哥早年一直在做着他永远不会对后人提起的买卖：他从人贩子手中买下一批残疾儿童，将他们放到城市中去乞讨，那时，人们的同情心还没有疲劳，这些孩子收益颇丰，齿哥就是借此完成了自己的原始积累。

一次，滑膛跟着齿哥去一个人贩子那里接收新的一批残疾孩子，到那个旧仓库中，看到有五个孩子，其中的四个是先天性畸形，但另一个小女孩却是完全正常的。那女孩就是果儿，她当时6岁，长得很可爱，大眼睛水灵灵的，同旁边的畸形儿形成鲜明对比。她当时就用这双后来滑膛一想起来就心碎的大眼睛看看这个看看那个，全然不知等待着自己的是怎样的命运。

"这些就是了。"人贩子指指那四个畸形儿说。

"不是说好五个吗？"齿哥问。

"车厢里闷，有一个在路上完了。"

"那这个呢？"齿哥指指果儿。

"这不是卖给你的。"

"我要了，就按这些的价儿。"齿哥用一种不容商量的语气说。

"可……她好端端的，你怎么拿她挣钱？"

"死心眼，加工一下不就得了？"

齿哥说着，解下腰间的利锯，朝果儿滑嫩的小腿上划了一下，划出了一道贯穿小腿的长口子，血在果儿的惨叫声中涌了出来。

"给她裹裹，止住血，但别上消炎药，要烂开才好。"齿哥对滑膛说。

滑膛于是给果儿包扎伤口，血浸透了好几层纱布，直流得果儿脸色惨白。滑膛背着齿哥，还是给果儿吃了些利菌沙和抗菌优之类的消炎药，但是没有用，果儿的伤口还是发炎了。

两天以后，齿哥就打发果儿上街乞讨，果儿可爱而虚弱的小样儿，她的伤腿，都立刻产生了超出齿哥预期的效果，头一天就挣了 3000 多块。以后的一个星期里，果儿挣的钱每天都不少于 2000 块，最多的一次，一对外国夫妇一下子就给了 400 美元。但果儿每天得到的只是一盒发馊的盒饭，这倒也不全是由于齿哥吝啬，他要的就是孩子挨饿的样子。滑膛只能在暗中给她些吃的。

一天傍晚，他上果儿乞讨的地方去接她回去，小女孩附在他的耳边悄悄地说："哥，我的腿不疼了呢。"一副高兴的样子。在滑膛的记忆中，这是他除母亲惨死外唯一一次流泪，果儿的腿是不疼了，那是因为神经都已经坏死，整条腿都发黑了，她已经发了两天的高烧。滑膛再也不顾齿哥的禁令，抱着果儿去了医院，医生说已经晚了，孩子的血液中毒。第二天深夜，果儿在高烧中去了。

从此以后，滑膛的血变冷了，而且像老克说的那样，再也没有温起来。杀人成了他的一项嗜好，比吸毒更上瘾，他热衷于打碎那一个个叫作人的精致器皿，看着它们盛装的红色液体流出来，冷却到与环境相同的温度，这才是它们的真相，以前那些红色液体里的热度，都是伪装。

完全是下意识地，滑膛以最高的分辨率真切地记下了果儿小腿上那道长伤口的形状，后来在齿哥腹部划出的那一道，就是它准确的拷贝。

拾荒女站起身，背起那个对她而言显得很大的编织袋慢慢离去。她显然并非因滑膛的到来而走，她没注意到他手里拿的是什么，也不会想到这个穿着体面的人的到来与自己有什么关系，她只是该走了。哥哥飞船在西天落下，滑膛一动不动地站在垃圾中，看着她的身影消失在短暂的蓝色黄昏里。

滑膛把枪插回枪套，拿出手机拨通了朱汉扬的电话："我想见你们，有事要问。"

"明天 9 点，老地方。"朱汉扬简洁地回答，好像早就预料到了这一切。

走进总统大厅，滑膛发现社会财富液化委员会的 13 个常委都在，他们将严肃的目光聚集在他身上。

"请提你的问题。"朱汉扬说。

"为什么要杀这三个人？"滑膛问。

"你违反了自己行业的职业道德。"朱汉扬用一个精致的雪茄剪切开一根雪茄的头部，不动声色地说。

"是的，我会让自己付出代价的，但必须清楚原因，否则这桩业务无法进行。"

朱汉扬用一根长火柴转着圈点着雪茄，缓缓地点点头："现在我不得不认为，你只接针对有产阶级的业务。这样看来，你并不是一个真正的职业杀手，只是一名进行狭隘阶级报复的凶手，一名警方正在全力搜捕的，3 年内杀了 41 个人的杀人狂，你的职业声望将从此一落千丈。"

"你现在就可以报警。"滑膛平静地说。

"这桩业务是不是涉及你的某些个人经历？"许雪萍问。

滑膛不得不佩服她的洞察力，他没有回答，默认了。

"因为那个女人？"

滑膛沉默着，对话已超出了合适的范围。

"好吧，"朱汉扬缓缓吐出一口白烟，"这桩业务很重要，我们在短时间内也找不到更合适的人，只能答应你的条件，告诉你原因，一个你做梦都想不到的原因。我们这些社会上最富有的人，却要杀掉社会上最贫穷、最弱势的人，这使我们现在在你的眼中成了不可理喻的变态恶魔，在说明原因之前，我们首先要纠正你的这个印象。"

"我对黑与白不感兴趣。"

"可事实已证明不是这样，好，跟我们来吧。"朱汉扬将只抽了一口的整根雪茄扔下，起身向外走去。

滑膛同社会财富液化委员会的全体常委一起走出酒店。

这时，天空中又出现了异常，大街上的人们都在紧张地抬头仰望。哥哥飞船正在低轨道上掠过，由于初升太阳的照射，它在晴朗的天空上显得格外清晰。飞船沿着运行的轨迹，撒下一颗颗银亮的星星，那些星星等距离排列，已在飞船后面形成了一条穿过整个天空的长线，而哥哥飞船本身的长度已经明显缩短了，它释放出星星的一头变得参差不齐，像折断的木棒。滑膛早就从新闻中得知，哥哥飞船是由上千艘子船形成的巨大组合体，现在，这个组合体显然正在分裂为子船船队。

"大家注意了！"朱汉扬挥手对常委们大声说，"你们都看到了，事态正在发展，时间可能不多了，我们工作的步伐要加快，各小组立刻分头到自己分管的液化区域，继续昨天的工作。"

说完，他和许雪萍上了一辆车，并招呼滑膛也上来。滑膛这才发现，酒店外面等着的，不是这些富豪平时乘坐的豪华车，而是一排五十铃客货车。"为了多拉些东西。"许雪萍看出了滑膛的疑惑，对他解释说。滑膛看看后面的车厢，里面整齐地装满了一模一样的黑色小手提箱，那些小箱子看上去相当精致，估计有上百个。

没有司机，朱汉扬亲自开车驶上了大街。车很快拐入了一条林荫道，然后放慢了速度，滑膛发现原来朱汉扬在跟着路边的一个行人慢行，那人是个流浪汉。这个时代流浪汉的衣着不一定褴褛，但还是一眼就能看出来，流浪汉的腰上挂着一个塑料袋，每走一步袋里的东西就叮哐响一下。

滑膛知道，昨天他看到的流浪者和拾荒者大量减少的谜底就要揭开了，但他不相信朱汉扬和许雪萍敢在这个地方杀人，他们多半是先将目标骗上车，然后带到什么地方除掉。按他们的身份，用不着亲自干这种事，也许只是为了向滑膛示范？滑膛不打算干涉他们，但也绝不会帮他们，他只管合同内的业务。

流浪汉显然没觉察到这辆车的慢行与自己有什么关系，直到许雪萍叫住了他。

"你好！"许雪萍摇下车窗说。流浪汉站住，转头看着她，脸上覆盖着这个阶层的人那种厚厚的麻木。"有地方住吗？"许雪萍微笑着问。

"夏天哪儿都能住。"流浪汉说。

"冬天呢？"

"暖气道，有的厕所也挺暖和。"

"你这么过了多长时间了？"

"我记不清了，反正征地费花完后就进了城，以后就这样了。"

"想不想在城里有套三室一厅的房子，有个家？"

流浪汉麻木地看着女富豪，没听懂她的话。

"认字吗？"许雪萍问，流浪汉点点头后，她向前一指，"看那边——"那里有一幅巨大的广告牌，在上面，青翠绿地上点缀着乳白色的楼群，像一处世外桃源，"那是一个商品房广告。"流浪汉扭头看看广告牌，又看看许雪萍，显然不知道那与自己有什么关系，"好，现在你从我车上拿一个箱子。"

流浪汉走到车厢处拎了一个小手提箱走过来，许雪萍指着箱子对他说："这里面是 100 万元人民币，用其中的 50 万元你就可以买一套那样的房子，剩下的留着过日子吧。当然，如果你花不了，也可以像我们这样把一部分送给更穷的人。"

流浪汉眼睛转转，捧着箱子仍面无表情，对于被愚弄，他很漠然。

"打开看看。"

流浪汉用黑乎乎的手笨拙地打开箱子，刚开一条缝就啪的一声合上了，他脸上那冰冻三尺的麻木终于被击碎，一脸震惊，像见了鬼。

"有身份证吗？"朱汉扬问。

流浪汉下意识地点点头，同时把箱子拎得尽量离自己远些，仿佛它是一颗炸弹。

"去银行存了，用起来方便一些。"

"你们……要我干啥？"流浪汉问。

"只要你答应一件事：外星人就要来了，如果他们问起你，你就说自己有这么多钱。就这一个要求，你能保证这样做吗？"

流浪汉点点头。

许雪萍走下车，冲流浪汉深深鞠躬："谢谢。"

"谢谢。"朱汉扬也在车里说。

最令滑膛震惊的是，他们表达谢意时看上去是真诚的。

车开了，将刚刚诞生的百万富翁丢在后面。前行不远，车在一个转弯处停下了，滑膛看到路边蹲着三个找活儿的外来装修工，他们每人的工具只是一把三角形的小铁铲，外加地上摆着的一个小硬纸板，上书"刮家"。那三个人看到停在面前的车，立刻起身跑过来，问："老板有活吗？"

朱汉扬摇摇头："没有，最近生意好吗？"

"哪有啥生意啊，现在都用喷上去的新涂料，就是一通电就能当暖气的那种，没有刮家的了。"

"你们从哪儿来？"

"河南。"

"一个村儿的？哦，村里穷吗？有多少户人家？"

"山里的，50多户。哪能不穷呢，天旱，老板你信不信啊，浇地是拎着壶朝苗根儿上一根根地浇呢。"

"那就别种地了……你们有银行账户吗？"

三人都摇摇头。

"那又是只好拿现金了，挺重，辛苦你们了……从车上拿十几个箱子下来。"

"十几个啊？"其中的一个问。对朱汉扬刚才的话，他们谁都没有去细想，更没在意，只是从车上拿了箱子，堆放到路边。

"10多个吧，无所谓，你们看着拿。"很快，15个箱子堆在地上，朱汉扬指着这堆箱子说，"每只箱子里面装着100万元，共1500万元，回家去，给全村分了吧。"

一名装修工对朱汉扬笑笑，好像是在赞赏他的幽默感，另一名蹲下去打开了一只箱子，同另外两人一起看了看里面，然后他们一起露出同刚才那名流浪汉一样的表情。

"东西挺重的，去雇辆车回河南，如果你们中有会开车的，买一辆更方便些。"许雪萍说。

三名装修工呆呆地看着面前这两个人，不知他们是天使还是魔鬼。很自然地，一名装修工问出了刚才流浪汉所问的问题："让我们干什么？"

回答也一样："只要你们答应一件事：外星人就要来了，如果他们问起你们，你们就说自己有这么多钱。就这一个要求，你们能保证做到吗？"

三个穷人点点头。

"谢谢。"

"谢谢。"

两位超级富豪又真诚地鞠躬致谢，然后上车走了，留下那三个人茫然地站在那堆箱子旁。

"你一定在想，他们会不会把钱独吞了。"朱汉扬扶着方向盘对滑膛说，"开始也许会，但他们很快就会把多余的钱分给穷人的，就像我们这样。"

滑膛沉默着，面对眼前的怪异和疯狂，他觉得沉默是最好的选择。现在，理智能告诉他的只有一点：世界将发生根本的变化。

"停车！"许雪萍喊道，然后对在一个垃圾桶旁搜寻易拉罐和可乐瓶的小脏孩儿喊，"孩子，过来！"

孩子跑了过来，同时把他拾到的半编织袋瓶罐也背过来，好像怕丢了似的。

"从车上拿一个箱子。"孩子拿了一个，"打开看看。"孩子打开了，看了，很吃惊，但没到刚才那四个成年人的那种程度。

"是什么？"许雪萍问。

"钱。"孩子抬起头看着她说。

"100万块钱，拿回去给你的爸爸妈妈吧。"

"这么说真有这事儿？"孩子扭头看看仍装着许多箱子的车厢，眨眨眼说。

"什么事？"

"送钱啊，说有人在到处送大钱，像扔废纸似的。"

"但你要答应一件事，这钱才是你的。外星人就要来了，如果他们问起你，你就说自己有这么多钱。你确实有这么多钱，不是吗？就这一个要求，你能保证做到吗？"

"能！"

"那就拿着钱回家吧，孩子，以后世界上不会有贫穷了。"朱汉扬说着，启动了汽车。

"也不会有富裕了。"许雪萍说，神色黯然。

"你应该振作起来，事情是很糟，但我们有责任阻止它变得更糟。"朱汉扬说。

"你真觉得这种游戏有意义吗？"

朱汉扬猛地刹住了刚开动的车，在方向盘上方挥着双手喊道："有意义！当然有意义！！！难道你想在后半生像那些人一样穷吗？你想挨饿和流浪吗？"

"我甚至连活下去的兴趣都没有了。"

"使命感会支撑你活下去，这些黑暗的日子里我就是这么过来的，我们的财富给了我们这种使命。"

"财富怎么了？我们没偷没抢，挣的每一分钱都是干净的！我们的财富推动了社会前进，社会应该感谢我们！"

"这话你对哥哥文明说吧。"朱汉扬说完走下车，对着长空长出了一口气。

"你现在看到了，我们不是杀穷人的变态凶手。"朱汉扬对跟着走下车的滑膛说，"相反，我们正在把自己的财富散发给最贫穷的人，就像刚才那样。在这座城市里，在许多其他的城市里，在国家一级贫困地区，我们公司的员工都在这样做。他们带着集团公司的全部资产：上千亿的支票、信用卡和存折，一卡车一卡车的现金，去消除贫困。"

这时，滑膛注意到了空中的景象：一条由一颗颗银色星星连成的银线横贯长空，哥哥飞船联合体完成了解体，1000多艘子飞船变成了地球的一条银色星环。

"地球被包围了。"朱汉扬说，"这每颗星星都有地球上的航空母舰那么大，一艘单独的子船上的武器，就足以毁灭整个地球。"

"昨天夜里，它们毁灭了澳大利亚。"许雪萍说。

"毁灭？怎么毁灭？"滑膛看着天空问。

"一种射线从太空扫描了整个澳大利亚，射线能够穿透建筑物和掩体，人和大型哺乳动物都在 1 小时内死去，昆虫和植物安然无恙，城市中，连橱窗里的瓷器都没有被打碎。"

滑膛看了许雪萍一眼，又继续看着天空，对于这种恐惧，他的承受力要强于一般人。

"一种力量的显示，之所以选中澳大利亚，是因为它是第一个明确表示拒绝保留地方案的国家。"朱汉扬说。

"什么方案？"滑膛问。

"从头说起吧。来到太阳系的哥哥文明其实是一群逃荒者，他们在第一地球无法生存下去，他们失去了自己的家园，这是他们的原话。具体原因他们没有说明。他们要占领我们的地球四号，作为自己新的生存空间。至于地球人类，将被全部迁移至人类保留地，这个保留地被确定为澳大利亚，地球上的其他领土都归哥哥文明所有……这一切在今天晚上的新闻中就要公布了。"

"澳大利亚？大洋中的一个大岛，地方倒挺合适，澳大利亚的内陆都是沙漠，50多亿人挤在那个地方很快就会被全部饿死的。"

"没那么糟，在澳大利亚保留地，人类的农业和工业将不再存在，他们不需要从事生产就能活下去。"

"靠什么活？"

"哥哥文明将养活我们，他们将赡养人类，人类所需要的一切生活资料都将由哥哥种族长期提供，所提供的生活资料将由他们平均分配，每个人得到的数量相等，所以，未来的人类社会将是一个绝对不存在贫富差别的社会。"

"可生活资料将按什么标准分配给每个人呢？"

"你一下子就抓住了问题的关键：按照保留地方案，哥哥文明将对地球人类进行全面的社会普查，调查的目的是确定目前人类社会最低的生活标准，哥哥文明将按这个标准配给每个人生活资料。"

滑膛低头沉思了一会儿，突然笑了起来："呵，我有些明白了，对所有的事，我都有些明白了。"

"你明白了人类文明面临的处境吧。"

"其实嘛，哥哥的方案对人类还是很公平的。"

"什么？你竟然说公平？！你这个……"许雪萍气急败坏地说。

"他是对的，是很公平。"朱汉扬平静地说，"如果人类社会不存在贫富差距，最低的生活水准与最高的相差不大，那保留地就是人类的乐园了。"

"可现在……"

"现在需要做的很简单，就是在哥哥文明的社会普查展开之前，迅速抹平社会财富的鸿沟！"

"这就是所谓的社会财富液化吧？"滑膛问。

"是的，现在的社会财富是固态的，固态就有起伏，像这大街旁的高楼，像那平原上的高山，但当这一切都液化后，一切都变成了大海，海面是平滑的。"

"但像你们刚才那种做法，只会造成一片混乱。"

"是的，我们只是做出一种姿态，显示财富占有者的诚意。真正的财富液化很快就要在全世界展开，它将在各国政府和联合国的统一领导下进行，大扶贫即将开始，那时，富国将把财富向第三世界倾倒，富人将把金钱向穷人抛撒，而这一切，都是完全真诚的。"

"事情可能没那么简单。"滑膛冷笑着说。

"你是什么意思？你个变态的……"许雪萍指着滑膛的鼻子咬牙切齿地说，朱汉扬立刻制止了她。

"他是个聪明人，他想到了。"朱汉扬朝滑膛偏了一下头说。

"是的，我想到了，有穷人不要你们的钱。"

许雪萍看了滑膛一眼，低头不语了。朱汉扬对滑膛点点头："是的，他们中有人不要钱。你能想象吗？在垃圾中寻找食物，却拒绝接受 100 万元……哦，你想到了。"

"但这种穷人，肯定是极少数。"滑膛说。

"是的，但他们只要占贫困人口十万分之一的比例，就足以形成一个社会阶层，在哥哥那先进的社会调查手段下，他们的生活水准，就会被当作人类最低的生活水准，进而成为哥哥进行保留地分配的标准……知道吗，只要十万分之一！"

"那么，现在你们知道的比例有多大？"

"大约千分之一。"

"这些下贱变态的千古罪人！"许雪萍对着天空大骂一声。

"你们委托我杀的就是这些人了。"这时，滑膛也不想再用术语了。

朱汉扬点点头。

滑膛用奇怪的目光看着朱汉扬，突然仰天大笑起来："哈哈哈……我居然在为人类造福？！"

"你是在为人类造福，你是在拯救人类文明。"

"其实，你们只需用死去威胁，他们还是会接受那些钱的。"

"这不保险！"许雪萍凑近滑膛低声说，"他们都是变态的狂人，是那种被阶级仇恨扭曲的变态，即使拿了钱，也会在哥哥面前声称自己一贫如洗，所以，必须尽快从地球上彻底清除这种人。"

"我明白了。"滑膛点点头说。

"那么你现在的打算是什么？我们已经满足了你的要求，说明了原因。当然，钱以后对谁意义都不大了，你对为人类造福肯定也没兴趣。"

"钱对我早就意义不大了，后面那件事从来没想过……不过，我将履行合同。今天零点前完工，请准备验收。"滑膛说完，起身离开。

"有一个问题。"朱汉扬在滑膛后面说，"也许不礼貌，你可以不回答。如果你是穷人，是不是也不会要我们的钱？"

"我不是穷人。"滑膛没有回头地说，但走了几步，他还是回过头来，用鹰一般的眼神看着两人，"如果我是，是的，我不会要。"说完，大步走去。

"你为什么不要他们的钱？"滑膛问一号目标，那个上次在广场上看到的流浪汉。现在，他们站在距广场不远处公园里的小树林中，有两种光透进树林：一种幽幽的蓝光来自太空中哥哥飞船构成的星环，这片蓝光在林中的地上投下斑驳的光影；另一种是城市的光，从树丛外斜照进来，在剧烈地颤动着，变幻着色彩，仿佛表达着对蓝光的恐惧。

流浪汉"嘿嘿"一笑："他们在求我，那么多的有钱人在求我，有个女的还流泪呢！我要是要了钱，他们就不会求我了，有钱人求我，很爽的。"

"是，很爽。"滑膛说着，扣动了大鼻子的扳机。

流浪汉是个惯偷，一眼就看出这个叫他到公园里来的人右手拿着的外套里面裹着东西，他一直很好奇那是什么，现在突然看到衣服上亮光一闪，像是里面的什么活物眨了下眼，接着便坠入了永恒的黑暗。

这是一次超速快冷加工，飞速滚动的子弹将工件眉毛以上的部分几乎全切去了，在衣服覆盖下枪声很闷，没人注意到。

垃圾场。滑膛发现，今天拾垃圾的只有她一人了，其他的拾荒者显然都拿到了钱。

在星环的蓝光下，滑膛踏着温软的垃圾向目标大步走去。这之前，他100次提醒自己，她不是果儿，现在不需要对自己重复了。他的血一直是冷的，不会因一点点少年时代记忆中的火苗就热起来。拾荒女甚至没有注意到来人，滑膛就开了枪。垃圾场上不需要消声，他的枪是露在外面开的，声音很响，枪口的火光像小小的雷电将周围的垃圾山照亮了一瞬间，由于距离远，在空气中翻滚的子弹来得及唱出它的歌，那呜呜的声音像万鬼哭号。

这也是一次超速快冷却，子弹像果汁机中飞旋的刀片，瞬间将目标的心脏切得粉碎，她在倒地之前已经死了。她倒下后，立刻与垃圾融为一体，本来能显示出她存在的鲜血也被垃圾吸收了。

在意识到背后有人的一瞬间，滑膛猛地转身，看到画家站在那里。他的长发在夜风中飘动，浸透了星环的光，像蓝色的火焰。

"他们让你杀了她？"画家问。

"履行合同而已，你认识她？"

"是的，她常来看我的画，她认字不多，但能看懂那些画，而且和你一样喜欢它们。"

"合同里也有你。"

画家平静地点点头，没有丝毫恐惧："我想到了。"

"只是好奇问问，为什么不要钱？"

"我的画都是描写贫穷与死亡的，如果一夜之间成了百万富翁，我的艺术就死了。"

滑膛点点头："你的艺术将活下去，我真的很喜欢你的画。"说着他抬起了枪。

"等等，你刚才说是在履行合同，那能和我签一个合同吗？"

滑膛点点头："当然可以。"

"我自己的死无所谓，为她复仇吧。"画家指指拾荒女倒下的地方。

"让我用我们这个行业的商业语言说明你的意思：你委托我加工一批工件，这些工件曾经委托我加工你们两个工件。"

画家再次点点头："是这样的。"

滑膛郑重地说："没有问题。"

"可我没有钱。"

滑膛笑笑："你卖给我的那幅画，价钱真的太低了，但它已足够支付这桩业务了。"

"那谢谢你了。"

"别客气，履行合同而已。"

死亡之火再次喷出枪口，子弹翻滚着，呜哇怪叫着穿过空气，穿透了画家的心脏，血从他的胸前和背后喷向空中，他倒下后两三秒钟，这些飞扬的鲜血才像温热的雨洒落下来。

"这没必要。"

声音来自滑膛背后。他猛地转身，看到垃圾场的中央站着一个人，一个男人，穿着几乎与滑膛一样的皮夹克，看上去还年轻，相貌平常，双眼映出星环的蓝光。

滑膛手中的枪下垂着，没有对准新来的人，他只是缓缓扣动扳机，大鼻子的击锤懒洋洋地抬到了最高处，处于一触即发的状态。

"是警察吗？"滑膛问，口气很轻松随便。

来人摇摇头。

"那就去报警吧。"

来人站着没动。

"我不会在你背后开枪的,我只加工合同中的工件。"

"我们现在不干涉人类的事。"来人平静地说。

这话像一道闪电击中了滑膛,他的手不由得一松,左轮的击锤落回到原位。他细看来人,在星环的光芒下,无论怎么看,他都是一个普通的人。

"你们,已经下来了?"滑膛问,他的语气中出现了少有的紧张。

"我们早就下来了。"

接着,在第四地球的垃圾场上,来自两个世界的两个人长时间地沉默着。这凝固的空气使滑膛窒息,他想说点什么,这些天的经历,使他下意识地提出了一个问题:

"你们那儿,也有穷人和富人吗?"

第一地球人微笑了一下说:"当然有,我就是穷人,"他又指了一下天空中的星环,"他们也是。"

"上面有多少人?"

"如果你是指现在能看到的这些,大约有50万人,但这只是先遣队,几年后到达的1万艘飞船将带来10亿人。"

"10亿?他们……不会都是穷人吧?"

"他们都是穷人。"

"第一地球上的世界到底有多少人呢?"

"10亿。"

"一个世界里怎么可能有那么多穷人?"

"一个世界里怎么不可能有那么多穷人?"

"我觉得,一个世界里的穷人比例不可能太高,否则这个世界就变得不稳定，那富人和中产阶级也过不好了。"

"以目前第四地球所处的阶段，很对。"

"还有不对的时候吗？"

第一地球人低头想了想，说："这样吧，我给你讲讲第一地球上穷人和富人的故事。"

"我很想听。"滑膛把枪插回怀里的枪套中。

"两个人类文明十分相似，你们走过的路我们都走过，我们也有过你们现在的时代：社会财富的分配虽然不均，但维持着某种平衡，穷人和富人都不是太多，人们普遍相信，随着社会的进步，贫富差距将进一步减小，他们憧憬着人人均富的大同时代。但人们很快发现事情要复杂得多，这种平衡很快就被打破了。"

"被什么东西打破的？"

"教育。你也知道，在你们目前的时代，教育是社会下层进入上层的唯一途径，如果社会是一个按温度和含盐度分成许多水层的海洋，教育就像一根连通管，将海底水层和海面水层连接起来，使各个水层之间不至于完全隔绝。"

"你接下来可能想说，穷人越来越上不起大学了。"

"是的，高等教育费用日益昂贵，渐渐成了精英子女的特权。但就传统教育而言，即使仅仅是为了市场的考虑，它的价格还是有一定限度的，所以那条连通管虽然已经细若游丝，但还是存在着。可有一天，教育突然发生了根本的变化，一个技术飞跃出现了。"

"是不是可以直接向大脑里灌知识了？"

"是的，但知识的直接注入只是其中的一部分。大脑中将被植入一台超级计算机，它的容量远大于人脑本身，它存储的知识可变为被植入者的清晰记忆。但这只是它的一个次要功能，它是一个智力放大器，一个思想放大器，可将人的思维提升到一个新的层次。这时，知识、智力、深刻的思想，甚至完美的心理和性格、艺术审美能力等，都成了商品，都可以买得到。"

"一定很贵。"

"是的，很贵，将你们目前的货币价值做个对比，一个人接受超等教育的费用，与在北京或上海的黄金地段买两到三套150平方米的商品房相当。"

"要是这样，还是有一部分人能支付得起的。"

"是的，但只是一小部分有产阶层，社会海洋中那条连通上下层的管道彻底中断了。完成超等教育的人的智力比普通人高出一个层次，他们与未接受超等教育的人之间的智力差异，就像后者与低等动物之间的差异一样大。同样的差异还表现在其他许多方面，比如艺术感受能力等。于是，这些超级知识阶层就形成了自己的文化，而其余的人对这种文化完全不理解，就像低等动物不理解交响乐一样。超级知识分子可能都精通上百种语言，在某种场合，对某个人，都要按礼节使用相应的语言。在这种情况下，在超级知识阶层看来，他们与普通民众的交流，就像我们与动物的交流一样简陋了……于是，一件事就自然而然地发生了，你是个聪明人，应该能想到。"

"富人和穷人已经不是同一个……同一个……"

"到那时候，甚至可能会说富人和穷人已经不是同一个物种了，就像穷人和动物不是同一个物种一样，穷人不再是人了。"

"哦，那事情可真的变了很多。"

"变了很多，首先，你开始提到的那个维持社会财富平衡、限制穷人数量的因素不存在了。即使动物的数量远多于人，它们也无力制造社会不稳定，只能制造一些需要费神去解决的麻烦。对穷人的同情，关键在于一个'同'字，当双方相同的物种基础不存在时，同情也就不存在了。这是人类的第二次进化，第一次与猿分开来，靠的是自然选择；这一次与穷人分开来，靠的是另一条同样神圣的法则：私有财产不可侵犯。"

"这法则在我们的世界也很神圣的。"

"在第一地球的世界里，这项法则由一个叫社会机器的系统维持。社会机器是一种强有力的执法系统，它的执法单元遍布世界的每一个角落，有的执法单元只有蚊子大小，但足以在瞬间同时击毙上百人。他们的法则不是你们那个阿西莫夫的三定律，而是第一地球的宪法基本原则：私有财产不可侵犯。他们带来的并不是专制，他们的执法是绝对公正的，并非倾向于有产阶层，如果穷人那点儿可怜的财产受到威胁，他们也会根据宪法去保护的。

"在社会机器强有力的保护下，第一地球的财富不断地向少数人集中。而技术发展导致了另一件事，有产阶层不再需要无产阶层了。在你们的世界，富人还是需要穷人的，工厂里总得有工人。但在第一地球，机器已经不需要人来操作了，高效率的机器人可以做一切事情，无产阶层连出卖劳动力的机会都没有了，他们真的一贫如洗。这种情况的出现，完全改变了第一地球的经济实质，大大加快了社会财富向少数人集中的速度。

"财富集中的过程十分复杂，我向你说不清楚，但其实质与你们世界的资本运作是相同的。在我曾祖父的时代，第一地球60%的财富掌握在1000万人手中；在我爷爷的时代，世界财富的80%掌握在1万人手中；在我爸爸的时代，财富的90%掌握在 42 人手中。

"在我出生时，第一地球的资本主义达到了顶峰上的顶峰，创造了令人难以置信的资本奇迹：99%的世界财富掌握在 1 个人的手中！这个人被称作终产者。

"这个世界的其余 20 亿人虽然也有贫富差距，但他们总体拥有的财富只是世界财富总量的 1%，也就是说，第一地球变成了由一个富人和 20 亿个穷人组成的世界，穷人是 20 亿，不是我刚才告诉你的 10 亿，而富人只有一个。这时，私有财产不可侵犯的宪法仍然有效，社会机器仍在忠实地履行着它的职责，保护着那一个富人的私有财产。

"想知道终产者拥有什么吗？他拥有整个第一地球！这个行星上所有的大陆和海洋都是他家的客厅和庭院，甚至第一地球的大气层都是他私人的财产。

"剩下的 20 亿穷人，他们的家庭都住在全封闭的住宅中，这些住宅本身就是一个自给自足的微型生态循环系统，他们用自己拥有的那可怜的一点点水、空气和土壤等资源在这全封闭的小世界中生活着，能从外界索取的，只有不属于终产者的太阳能了。

"我的家坐落在一条小河边，周围是绿色的草地，一直延伸到河岸，再延伸到河对岸翠绿的群山脚下，在家里就能听到群鸟鸣叫和鱼儿跃出水面的声音，能看到悠然的鹿群在河边饮水，特别是草地在和风中的波纹最让我陶醉。但这一切不属于我们，我们的家与外界严格隔绝，我们的窗是密封舷窗，永远都不能开的。要想外出，必须经过一个过渡舱，就像从飞船进入太空一样。事实上，我们的家就像一艘宇宙飞船，不同的是，恶劣的环境不是在外面而是在里面！我们只能呼吸家庭生态循环系统提供的污浊的空气，喝经千万次循环过滤的水，吃以我们的排泄物为原料合成再生的难以下咽的食物。而与我们仅一墙之隔，就是广阔而富饶的大自然，我们外出时，穿着像一名宇航员，食物和水要自带，甚至自带氧气瓶，因为外面的空气不属于我们，是终产者的财产。

"当然，有时也可以奢侈一下，比如在婚礼或节日什么的，这时我们走出自己全封闭的家，来到第一地球的大自然中，最令人陶醉的是，呼吸第一口大自然的空气时，那空气是微甜的，甜得让你流泪。但这是要花钱的，外出之前我们都得吞下一粒药丸大小的空气售货机，这种装置能够监测和统计我们吸入空气的量，我们每呼吸一次，银行账户上的钱就被扣除一点。对于穷人，这真的是一种奢侈，每年也只能有一两次。我们来到外面时，也不敢剧烈活动，甚至不动，只是坐着，以控制自己的呼吸量。回家前还要仔细地刮刮鞋底，因为外面的土壤也不属于我们。

"现在告诉你我母亲是怎么死的。为了节省开支，她那时已经有 3 年没有去过一次户外了，节日也舍不得出去。这天深夜，她竟在梦游中通过过渡门到了户外！她当时做的一定是一个置身于大自然中的梦。当执法单元发现她时，她已经离家有很远的距离了，执法单元也发现了她没有吞下空气售货机，就把她朝家里拖，同时用一只机械手卡住她的脖子。它并没想掐死她，只是不让她呼吸，以保护另一个公民不可侵犯的私有财产——空气。但到家时她已经被掐死了，执法单元放下她的尸体对我们说：她犯了盗窃罪。我们要被罚款，但我们已经没有钱了，于是母亲的遗体就被没收抵账。要知道，对一个穷人家庭来说，一个人的遗体是很宝贵的，占它重量 70% 的是水啊，还有其他有用的资源。但遗体的价值还不够交纳罚款，社会机器便从我们家抽走了相当数量的空气。

"我们家生态循环系统中的空气本来已经严重不足，一直没钱补充，在被抽走一部分后，已经威胁到了内部成员的生存。为了补充失去的空气，生态系统不得不电解一部分水，这个操作使得整个系统的状况急剧恶化。主控电脑发出了警报：如果我们不向系统中及时补充 15 升水的话，系统将在 30 小时后崩溃。警报灯的红色光芒弥漫每个房间。我们曾打算到外面的河里偷些水，但旋即放弃了，因为我们打到水后还来不及走回家，就会被无所不在的执法单元击毙。父亲沉思了一会儿，让我不要担心，先睡觉。虽然处于巨大的恐惧中，但在缺氧的状态下，我还是睡着了。不知过了多长时间，一个机器人推醒了我，它是从与我家对接的一辆资源转换车上进来的，它指着旁边一桶清澈晶莹的水说：'这就是你父亲。'资源转换车是一种将人体转换成家庭生态循环系统所用资源的流动装置，父亲就是在那里将自己体内的水全部提取出来的。而这时，就在离我家不到 100 米处，那条美丽的河在月光下哗哗地流着。资源转换车从他的身体中还提取了其他一些对生态循环系统有用的东西：一盒有机油脂、一瓶钙片，甚至还有硬币那么大的一小片铁。

"父亲的水拯救了我家的生态循环系统，我一个人活了下来，一天天长大。5 年过去了，在一个秋天的黄昏，我从舷窗望出去，突然发现河边有一个人在跑步，我惊奇是谁这么奢侈，竟舍得在户外这样呼吸？！仔细一看，天哪，竟是终产者！他慢下来，放松地散着步，然后坐在河边的一块石头上，将一只赤脚伸进清澈的河水里。他看上去是一个健壮的中年男人，但实际已经 2000

多岁了，基因工程技术还可以保证他再活这么长时间，甚至永远活下去。不过在我看来，他真的是一个很普通的人。

"又过了2年，我家的生态循环系统的运行状况再次恶化，这样小规模的生态系统，它的寿命肯定是有限的。终于，它完全崩溃了。空气中的含氧量在不断减少，在缺氧昏迷之前，我吞下了一枚空气售货机，走出了家门。像每一个家庭生态循环系统崩溃的人一样，我坦然地面对着自己的命运：用完我在银行那可怜的存款，然后被执法机器掐死或击毙。

"这时我发现外面的人很多，家庭生态循环系统开始大批量地崩溃了。一个巨大的执法机器悬浮在我们上空，播放着最后的警告：'公民们，你们闯入了别人的家里，你们犯了私闯民宅罪，请尽快离开！不然……'离开？我们能到哪里去？自己的家中已经没有可供呼吸的空气了。

"我与其他人一起，在河边碧绿的草地上尽情地奔跑，让清甜的春风吹过我们苍白的面庞，让生命疯狂地燃烧……

"不知过了多长时间，我们突然发现自己银行里的存款早就用完了，但执法单元们并没有采取行动。这时，从悬浮在空中的那个巨型执法单元中传出了终产者的声音：'各位好，欢迎光临寒舍！有这么多的客人我很高兴，也希望你们在我的院子里玩得愉快，但还是请大家体谅我，你们来的人实在是太多了。现在，全球已有近10亿人因生态循环系统崩溃而走出了自己的家，来到我家，另外那10亿可能也快来了，你们是擅自闯入，侵犯了我这个公民的居住权和隐私，社会机器采取行动终止你们的生命是完全合理合法的，如果不是我劝止了它们那么做，你们早就全部被激光蒸发了。但我确实劝止了他们，我是个受过多次超等教育的有教养的人，对家里的客人，哪怕是违法闯入者，都是讲礼貌的。但请你们设身处地地为我想想，家里来了20亿客人，毕竟是稍微多了些，我是个喜欢安静和独处的人，所以还是请你们离开寒舍。我当然知道大家在地球上无处可去，但我为你们，为20亿人准备了2万艘巨型宇宙飞船，每艘都有一座中等城市大小，能以光速的百分之一航行。上面虽没有完善的生态循环系统，但有足够容纳所有人的生命冷藏舱，足够支持5万年。我们的星系中只有地球这一颗行星，所以你们只好在恒星际寻找自己新的家园，但相信一定能找到的。宇宙之大，何必非要挤在我这间小小的陋室中呢？你们没有理由恨我，得到这幢住所，我是完全合理合法的。我从一个经营妇女卫生用品的小公司起家，一直做到今天的规模，完全是凭借自己的商业才能，没有做过任何违法的事，所以，社会机器在以前保护了我，以后也会继续保护我，保护我这个守法公民的私有财产。它不会容忍你们的违法行径，所以，还是请大家尽快动身吧。看在同一进化渊源的分儿上，我会记住你们的，也希望你们记住我，保重吧。'

"我们就是这样来到了第四地球，航程延续了3万年，在漫长的星际流浪中，损失了近一半的飞船，有的淹没于星际尘埃中，有的被黑洞吞食……但，总算有1万艘飞船、10亿人到达了这个世界。好了，这就是第一地球的故事，20亿个穷人和一个富人的故事。"

"如果没有你们的干涉，我们的世界也会重复这个故事吗？"听完了第一地球人的讲述，滑膛问道。

"不知道，也许会，也许不会，文明的进程像一个人的命运，变幻莫测的……好，我该走了，我只是一名普通的社会调查员，也在为生计奔忙。"

"我也有事要办。"滑膛说。

"保重，弟弟。"

"保重，哥哥。"

在星环的光芒下，两个世界的两个男人分别向两个方向走去。

滑膛走进了总统大厅，社会财富液化委员会的 13 个常委一起转向他。朱汉扬说：

"我们已经验收了，你干得很好，另一半款项已经汇入你的账户，尽管钱很快就没用了……还有一件事想必你已经知道：哥哥文明的社会调查员已降临地球，我们和你做的事都无意义，我们也没有进一步的业务给你了。"

"但我还是揽到了一项业务。"

滑膛说着，掏出手枪，另一只手向前伸着，啪啪啪啪啪啪啪，7 颗橙黄的子弹掉在桌面上，与手中大鼻子弹仓中的 6 颗加起来，正好 13 颗。

在 13 个富翁脸上，震惊和恐惧都只闪现了很短的时间，接下来的只有平静，这对他们来说，可能只意味着解脱。

外面，一群巨大的火流星划破长空，强光穿透厚厚的窗帘，使水晶吊灯黯然失色，大地剧烈震动起来。第一地球的飞船开始进入大气层。

"还没吃饭吧？"许雪萍问滑膛，然后指着桌上的一堆方便面说，"咱们吃了饭再说吧。"

他们把一个用于放置酒和冰块的大银盆用 3 个水晶烟灰缸支起来，在银盆里加上水。然后，他们在银盆下烧起火来，用的是百元钞票，大家轮流着将一张张钞票放进火里，出神地看着黄绿相间的火焰像一个活物般欢快地跳动着。

　　当烧到 135 万元时，水开了。

图书在版编目（CIP）数据

时间移民：汉英对照 / 刘慈欣著；（美）刘宇昆
（Ken Liu）等译. —北京：北京联合出版公司，2022.5
ISBN 978-7-5596-6070-1

Ⅰ.①时… Ⅱ.①刘… ②刘… Ⅲ.①幻想小说—小
说集—中国—当代—汉、英 Ⅳ.① I247.7

中国版本图书馆CIP数据核字（2022）第046746号

时间移民：汉英对照

作　　者：刘慈欣
译　　者：［美］刘宇昆（Ken Liu）等
出 品 人：赵红仕
责任编辑：龚　将

北京联合出版公司出版
（北京市西城区德外大街83号楼9层　100088）
北京世纪恒宇印刷有限公司印刷　新华书店经销
字数 303 千字　　880 毫米 × 1230 毫米　1/32　13.75 印张
2022 年 5 月第 1 版　　2022 年 5 月第 1 次印刷
ISBN 978-7-5596-6070-1
定价：59.80 元